THE TIGER
IN THE WELL

The TIGER in the WELL

PHILIP PULLMAN

ALFRED A. KNOPF
New York

This is a Borzoi Book published by
Alfred A. Knopf, Inc.

Copyright © 1990 by Philip Pullman
Jacket art copyright © 1990 by Linda Benson
All rights reserved under International and Pan-American Copyright Conventions. Published in the United States by Alfred A. Knopf, Inc., New York. Distributed by Random House, Inc., New York.

Manufactured in the United States of America
Book design by Mina Greenstein
2   4   6   8   10   9   7   5   3   1

Library of Congress Cataloging-in-Publication Data
Pullman, Philip, 1946–
The tiger in the well / by Philip Pullman.
p.   cm. Summary: In London in 1881, twenty-four-year-old Sally finds her young daughter and her possessions assailed by an unknown enemy, while a shadowy figure known as the Tzaddik involves her in his plot to defraud and exploit the hordes of Jewish immigrants pouring into the country.
ISBN 0-679-80214-2 (trade)   ISBN 0-679-90214-7 (lib. bdg.)
[1. London—Fiction.   2. Jews—England—Fiction.
3. Mystery and detective stories.]   I. Title.
PZ7.P968Ti   1990
[Fic]—dc20   90-4159   CIP   AC

For Jude

Contents

BOOK THREE

BOOK
ONE

1

The Process Server

ONE SUNNY MORNING IN THE AUTUMN OF 1881, SALLY
Lockhart stood in the garden and watched her little daughter
play, and thought that things were good.

She was wrong, but she wouldn't know how or why she
was wrong for twenty minutes yet. The man who would show
her was still finding his way to the house. For the moment
she was happy, which was delightful, and she knew she was,
which was rare; she was usually too busy to notice.

She was happy, for one thing, about her home. It was a
large place in Twickenham called Orchard House—a Regency
building, open and airy, with iron balconies and a glass-roofed
veranda facing the garden. The garden itself, enclosed by a
mellow brick wall, consisted of a wide sunny lawn with some
flower beds and a vine and a fig tree against the wall on one
side, and the group of old apple and plum trees at the bottom, which gave the house its name.

Against the wall on the side opposite the fig tree a curious
structure had been built: glass-roofed like the veranda, but
open all the way along, and containing what looked like a
track for a large model railway, supported on trestles about
three feet high. It had been built to shelter some experiments in the photography of motion, and there was more
work to do on it, but it would wait until her friends came
back.

Her friends: she was happy in her friends. Webster Garland,
sixty-five, a photographer and her partner in Garland and
Lockhart, the firm that joined their names, and Jim Taylor,

at twenty-one, three or four years younger than herself, were all she had for family, apart from her daughter. They shared the house, they'd shared adventures; they were bohemian, they were unrespectable, they were staunch and faithful, and at the moment they were in South America. Every few years, Webster Garland gave in to the urge to wander into some wild part of the world and photograph it. This time Jim had gone with him; so Sally was on her own.

But not really alone. There was the staff—and that was something else she was happy with: Ellie, the maid, and Mrs. Perkins, the cook-housekeeper, and Roberts, who looked after the garden and the horses. And there was the photography shop in the High Street, where she went once a week to look over the accounts. And there was her own business in the City: a financial consultancy which she'd built up successfully against the expectations of everyone who thought that women couldn't do that sort of thing, or shouldn't if they wanted to remain feminine, or wouldn't if there wasn't something wrong with them. She'd become so busy that she recently had to take on a partner: a dry, ironical young woman called Margaret Haddow, a university graduate and a feminist like herself. And, finally, the nurse she'd engaged to help her with the child: Sarah-Jane Russell, eighteen, competent, kindly, and in love (without his knowledge, or anyone else's) with Jim Taylor.

But the center of all this happiness was the child. Harriet was a year and nine months old: autocratic, willful, and so solidly sure of everyone's love and attention that she gave off happiness herself as the sun gives off light. Her father Frederick Garland, Webster's nephew, had never seen her, for he had died in a fire on the night she was conceived; and if he'd lived, Sally would be Mrs. Garland, and Harriet legitimate. Sally's love for Frederick had been hard won and given without stint. What she felt for Harriet was as deep as her blood, as deep as her life itself. She'd never loved anyone or anything as much, never known it was possible. At first, after Frederick's death, when their business lay in ruins, she felt she didn't want to live, but when she felt the stubborn life inside her she knew she did, and knew she must. And apart from the terrible gap that Frederick had left, life was good now—as good as it ever could be for an unmarried mother in Queen Victoria's time; better by far than for plenty of women trapped in unhappy marriages. She had money and independence and friends, and a home, and interesting work, and she had her precious Harriet.

She plucked two figs, newly ripened, and took them over to the orchard. Sarah-Jane was sitting on the tree seat Webster had built, sewing something, while Harriet was helping her toy bear, Bruin, climb a rope to get some imaginary honey. Sally joined Sarah-Jane on the seat.

"D'you like figs?" Sally said, handing one to Sarah-Jane.

"I love them," said the nurse. "Thank you."

Sally could see past the side of the house to where someone was consulting a paper at the front gate. He opened it and came through, moving out of sight as he made for the front door.

"Hattie-face, come and share the fig," she said.

Harriet, seeing food, dropped Bruin and came at once. She looked suspiciously at the soft red flesh packed with tiny seeds. Sally took another bite.

"Like this," she said. "If you don't try it, you won't know what it's like. Bruin will have some."

They fed Bruin, and then Harriet nibbled the fig, and then she wanted all the rest.

"She's growing so fast," said Sarah-Jane. "Look, I can't turn these petticoats down any more. They'll do this time but then she'll need new ones."

"We ought to measure her," said Sally. "Draw a line on the wall. Shall we do that, Hattie? See how tall you're getting?"

"Fig," said Harriet accusingly, holding out her hand for Sarah-Jane's. "Fig, please."

Sally laughed. "No, that's Sarah-Jane's. Look, here comes Ellie with a visitor."

Harriet, proprietorial, turned to see who had come to pay court to her this time. Ellie was making her way down the lawn, followed by the man Sally had seen at the front gate. He was slight and appeared to be middle-aged, and he wore a shabby brown suit and a bowler hat. He was holding a large white envelope.

"Miss Lockhart," said Ellie uncertainly. "This gentleman says he's got to see you in person, miss."

The man raised his hat. "Miss Lockhart?"

"Yes?" said Sally. "What can I do for you?"

"I am under instructions to give this into your hands, miss."

He held out the envelope. Sally saw a red legal seal on it. Automatically she took it from him. It's very hard not to take things people hand you; politeness is an easy thing to take advantage of.

The man doffed his hat again and turned to go. Sally stood up.

"Wait, please," she said. "Who are you? And what's this?"

"It's fully explained inside," he said. "As for me, I'm a process server, miss. I've done my duty, and now I must be on my way, else I shall miss my train. Beautiful weather for the time of year . . ."

With a nervous little smile he turned and set off back up the garden. Ellie, after a troubled glance at Sally, hastened after him.

Harriet, disappointed that the visitor hadn't come to see her, turned back to Bruin. Sally sat down. She was conscious that she might have made a mistake in accepting the envelope so tamely. Couldn't you refuse to accept a summons, or something? Didn't you by accepting it admit that there was a case to answer? Oh, it was bound to be nonsense anyway. Someone had made a mistake.

She tore open the thick paper and pulled out a long, carefully folded document. The royal arms were embossed at the top, and paragraph after paragraph of legal copperplate stretched out below. Sally sat down again and began to read.

It was headed IN THE PROBATE, DIVORCE, AND ADMI-RALTY DIVISION OF THE HIGH COURT, and it began:

> On the 3rd day of January, 1879, the petitioner, Arthur James Parrish, was lawfully married to Veronica Beatrice Lockhart (hereinafter called "the respondent") at St. Thomas's Church, Southam, in the County of Hampshire.

Sally gave a little gasp. This was ridiculous. Veronica Beatrice was her own name—one she'd never answered to since she, a strong-willed child like Harriet, had informed her father that she was Sally, and refused to answer to anything else. But . . . married? Someone was claiming to be married to her?

She read on:

> The petitioner and respondent last lived together at 24, Telegraph Road, Clapham.
> The petitioner is domiciled in England and Wales, and is by occupation a commission agent, and resides at 24, Telegraph Road, Clapham, and the respondent is by occupation a financial consultant and resides at Orchard House, Twickenham.
> There are no children of the family now living except Harriet Beatrice Rosa . . .

Sally put the paper down.

"Oh, this is stupid," she said. "Someone's playing a joke."

Sarah-Jane looked up. Sally saw the question in her face.

"I'm being sued for divorce," she said, and then laughed. But it was a short laugh, and Sarah-Jane didn't smile.

"It's an expensive joke for someone to play, going to all those lengths," she said. "You'd better read the rest of it."

Sally took up the paper again. Her hands were trembling. She read on with increasing disbelief, through several more paragraphs of legal language, and came to a long section headed PARTICULARS.

It was easy to follow, next to impossible to take in. It related the story of a marriage that had never existed; it told how Sally and this Mr. Parrish had married, settled in Clapham, had a child, Harriet (whose birthday, at least, was accurate); how Sally had persistently and willfully treated her "husband" with cruelty, his business associates with scorn, and their guests with contempt, until he found it impossible to bring anyone home and be sure she would receive them in a decent and civil manner; how she had taken to drink, and appeared drunk in public on more than one occasion (details provided, witnesses named); how she had mistreated the servants, forcing three separate maidservants to leave without notice (names and addresses provided); how she had misused the money her "husband" had settled on her, and insisted against his wishes on setting up in business on her own; how he had attempted to reason with her, and live with the situation, and treated her with every consideration; how, shortly after the birth of their child, she had deserted the family home, taking the child with her; how she was not a fit person to have custody of the child, because she was currently associating with persons of doubtful morality, sharing a household with two unmarried men (names provided); and there was more. There were five closely written pages, but she had to push it away after scanning only two of them.

"I don't believe it," she said, hardly in control of her voice. She thrust the paper at Sarah-Jane and stood up blindly. While Sarah-Jane looked at it Sally walked to the end of the orchard, plucked a twig off the apple tree, and shredded it to pieces. She felt as if someone had crept into her life and befouled everything in sight. That anyone could write such a pack of filthy lies about her—but it was impossible. She couldn't take it in.

There was worse to come. She heard Sarah-Jane gasp, and turned quickly.

Sarah-Jane was holding out the last section of the document. It was headed PRAYER.

Sally took it and sat down. She felt unable to stand. The page read:

The petitioner therefore prays:
That the said marriage be dissolved.
That the petitioner be granted the custody of the child Harriet Beatrice Rosa, with immediate effect.
That . . .

It was enough. Sally wanted to read no more. Someone, someone unknown, this Parrish, a liar, a madman, wanted to take her child away from her.

Only a few yards away Harriet sat on the grass, teasing out the end of a piece of old rope Webster had given her and seeing how it wanted to twist together again. Bruin lay forgotten beside her. She was utterly absorbed, concentrating fiercely on the extraordinariness of things like rope. Sally got to her feet and ran to her and caught her up in a hungry embrace, aware of her own strength and trying not to hurt her, but wanting her as close as she could get.

Harriet submitted to it patiently; embraces had to be put up with. Finally Sally let her go, kissed her, and put her gently down on the grass again. Harriet picked up the rope and carried on.

"I'm going to the City," she said to Sarah-Jane. "I've got to take this to my solicitor. It's nonsense, of course. The man's mad or something. But I must get this straightened out at once. The case is—"

"A fortnight," Sarah-Jane said. "In the Royal Courts of Justice. That's what it says."

Sally took up the document again. She didn't like touching it. She put it back in the envelope and kissed Harriet once, twice, three times and went to get ready for the train to London.

SALLY'S SOLICITOR Mr. Temple, an old friend of her father's who'd helped her set up in business, had died the year before. The leading partner in the firm was now a Mr. Adcock, whom she did not know very well. She didn't much like what she did know; but she couldn't afford to think of that. He was a smooth, youngish man, who was the sort of person so anxious for the approval of his elders that he aped their opinions, their manners, and their fashions. Mr. Temple had taken snuff; in him it had seemed natural. Mr. Adcock did, too, but in him it seemed affected. Sally, of course, hadn't seen him in his club, but if she had she'd have raised her eyebrows at the conservatism of the views he expressed— and at the fact that they became more loudly expressed, and more conservative, when any distinguished elderly member was nearby.

When Sally arrived at his office he was busy with another client, and she sat with the old clerk, Mr. Bywater, who'd served the firm for fifty years. He knew her business better than Mr. Adcock did, and she was so much on edge that she couldn't help telling him what she'd come about. He sat, ancient and impassive, while she told the whole story. She feared his sharp tongue, but she felt better when she'd finished.

"Dear, oh dear," he said. "Why didn't you tell Mr. Temple about the child?"

"Because . . . oh, Mr. Bywater, you can imagine, can't you? He was ill. And I was fond of him. I didn't want to lose his good opinion."

"His good opinion was based on your sense," he said, "not your sanctity. You should've told him. You made a will? Thought not. Who's that fellow's solicitors? Grant, Murray, and Gurney. Hmm. See what I can find out. I think Mr. Adcock's ready for you now."

He leaned toward the door, listening, and then knocked and announced her.

Mr. Adcock was all smooth affability. *This is a purely professional relationship*, she reminded herself; *he's a solicitor, he's trained in the law, never mind his manner.*

She went through the facts as clearly as she could, starting with Harriet. Mr. Adcock listened, his expression becoming graver by the minute. Occasionally he made a note.

"May I see the petition?" he said when she'd finished.

He read it through while she sat, composed, upright, trembling.

"These are very serious allegations," he said when he'd reached the end. "He alleges desertion, misuse of funds, drunkenness even. . . . Miss Lockhart, may I ask you if you drink?"

"Do I drink? I take a glass of sherry sometimes, but what on earth does that matter?"

"We have to be sure of our ground. These servants, for instance, whose dismissal is complained of—if we could establish precisely what happened, we could construct a sound defense."

Sally felt a shiver of dismay. "Mr. Adcock, there weren't any servants. There never was a household in what-is-it, Telegraph Road, Clapham. I never was married to this Mr. Parrish. The whole thing is a fabrication. He's made it all up. It's a huge lie."

He looked at her in a manner she recognized: quizzical, indulgent, knowledgeable. It was Mr. Temple's expression, but in that old gentleman it had been backed by real humor and deep knowledge.

"I think you must allow your professional adviser to judge what's relevant and what isn't," he said, smiling. "Of course the heart of your case will be that this marriage did not take place. But we have to cover all eventualities, do we not? It would be unfortunate if we left any part of the case vulnerable. We shall have to go through these particulars point by point and be able to satisfy the judge that there is a complete explanation for all of them. Now, in the first place . . ."

He took a sheet of paper out of a drawer and flipped up the lid of a silver inkwell. His desk was bare except for the blotter and an inkstand. Sally liked desks covered in books and papers and pencils and sealing wax and all the impedimenta of a job being done, as hers was; *No,* she told herself, *stop comparing.*

Mr. Adcock dipped the pen in the ink and fastidiously dabbed it on the edge of the pot to avoid taking up too much.

"Now, then," he said. "When did you first meet Mr. Parrish?"

Sally took a deep breath. "I have never met Mr. Parrish. Until this morning I'd never heard of him. Mr. Adcock, with the greatest respect, I think that all those absurd allegations aren't worth wasting time on. The only important thing is whether or not I'm married to him, and I'm not."

"Of course, of course," said Mr. Adcock. "That is the central point in your defense. Make no mistake about that. He will have to prove that a marriage took place, and if as you say it didn't, there will be no marriage certificate, no entry in the register of . . . St. Thomas's Church at Southam in Hampshire. But you see the tendency of these allegations is to demonstrate that you are not a fit person to have charge of the child, and you wouldn't wish that implication to rest unchallenged, would you?"

"I suppose not. But I'd reject his right to suggest it."

"It *has* been suggested. That is precisely why we must counter it as fully as possible. You must conceal nothing, Miss Lockhart."

"There's nothing to conceal!"

"You concealed the birth of your child," he said, his big eyes reproachful.

She didn't answer. Then she sighed heavily.

"Very well," she said, and, with an effort, made herself sit perfectly upright. "As you say, Mr. Adcock. Where shall we start?"

AN HOUR and a half later, Sally wearily left him tidying the papers he'd covered with his delicate writing and went to say good-bye to the clerk.

"Mr. Bywater, what does a commission agent do?" she said.

"Is that what Parrish claims he is?" said Mr. Bywater. "Say there's a feller in the Indian civil service. Calcutta. He wants to send some luggage home, make sure it gets to his old ma in Littlehampton. Complicated job. Lots of parcels. Commission agent looks after it. Or someone's going out east for the first time. Business. Needs to make sure his samples, his left-handed screw-flange triple-expansion steam-powered soda water bottle opener that weighs a ton and a half gets to Shanghai so's he can show the local panjandrum how it works. Commission agent sees to it. Fixes up shipping, insurance, storage, packing, the lot. Gets a commission. Hence the name. Marriage brokers, some of 'em. Round up a bunch of unclaimed lovelies, pack 'em in a boat, herd 'em ashore at Bombay. Take a cut from the husbands later, probably. Slice of wedding cake. Negotiate contracts, buy for you, sell for you, exchange your money, get you a passport, arrange your train tickets to Siberia with a box at the Vladivostok Music Hall thrown in, fix an introduction to the Dalai Lama, cut you in on a Mississippi riverboat poker game, do anything at all. Nice life. Variety. Your man's got an office in Blackmoor Street, by the way. Just off Drury Lane."

"Has he?" said Sally. "Perhaps I'll go there now. He won't be expecting that."

"Mr. Adcock would find himself defending a murder case," said the old clerk. "Keep away, I should. Have nothing to do with him. The best line is, you're not married to him, you never heard of him, you don't know what he's talking about. Don't be provoked. He'll be anxious, you know."

"Will he?"

"Course he will. He's telling a barefaced lie. Whether the court believes it or not depends on how we react to it. Who's Mr. Adcock engaging?"

"What, to appear in court? A Mr. Coleman. Apparently he's very good."

"Well, they all are, silks. Have to be, otherwise the whole edifice of the law would come crashing down around our ears, wouldn't it? Couldn't have that."

A silk was a Queen's Counsel: an eminent barrister. Mr. Adcock, as a solicitor, couldn't appear himself in the High Court, so he had to brief this Mr. Coleman to argue Sally's case. She trusted he'd do it well; she had to.

WITH JIM TAYLOR away in South America (his last letter had been dated from Manáos, and they'd been about to leave with a guide for the jungle), Sally had no means of inquiring into this Mr. Parrish's affairs without calling in a professional agent. Parrish was clearly very familiar indeed with her life, and it chilled her to think of how long and how closely some-one must have been burrowing into her past. They'd got everything right: they'd chosen to strike when she was alone, with her friends away so that they couldn't testify on her behalf; they'd picked a time for this fake marriage when Sally had been almost entirely occupied with a dangerous adven-ture involving an arms manufacturer, and when she'd left few traces—nothing to prove she hadn't been at that church on that date. And they'd got the address of her business right, and Harriet's birthday, and they knew how much money she had invested in which stocks.

The biggest question was one she hadn't confronted yet. But as she walked away from her lawyer's office and headed up the Strand toward Drury Lane, it began to ask itself more and more insistently: *Why? Why's he doing it? Why?*

The brass plate beside the door in Blackmoor Street didn't tell her anything, except that Arthur Parrish, Commission Agent, shared the building with G. Simonides, Ltd., the An-glo-Levantine Trading Company, and T. and S. Williamson, Spice Importers. Better not to linger: Parrish was bound to know what she looked like, and—

Well, what if he did see her? She was thinking like a crim-inal. She had no need to skulk about, feeling guilty. This craziness was infecting her already.

She left and went back down to the Strand. At number 223 there was a gunsmith's.

"I want to buy a pistol," she said to the lugubriously mustached assistant.

"Target pistol, miss?"

"A revolver."

Target pistols were light, single-shot weapons which were often used indoors; their effective range was about ten yards. Sally had two of those already, but she had something more substantial in mind now. She looked at a Webley Pryse, a Tranter, and hesitated over a Colt, but she settled in the end for a British Bulldog: a nickel-plated five-shot pistol which was not only powerful but also small enough to fit in a pocket.

"It's got a strong recoil, that one, miss," said the assistant. "Painful to shoot if you're not used to it. Aim a good way below the target, else you'll miss it entirely."

"I'd like the Colt," she told him, "but it's too big. This is just right. I'll get used to it; I've done a lot of shooting. And a box of fifty cartridges, please."

It cost her a little under four pounds. She had the gun and the cartridges wrapped and then took them with her, rather to the assistant's surprise; ladies and gentlemen out shopping almost invariably had their purchases delivered rather than walk through the streets carrying a package. Sally felt a little beyond gentility by now and carried the parcel without a qualm.

She had, as she'd said, done a good deal of shooting. Her father had taught her, and given her a light Belgian pistol for her fourteenth birthday. She naturally didn't tell the shop assistant, but she'd twice shot to kill. The first time was when she was sixteen and in deadly danger from Ah Ling, the leader of a Chinese secret society, who was the man who'd killed her father. He was half Dutch, and under the name of Hendrik Van Eeden he had been smuggling opium in Mr. Lockhart's ships without Sally's father's knowledge. Sally had shot him in a cab near the East India Docks, to save herself from death at his hands. Whether she'd killed him or not she didn't know, for she had fled in horror at what she'd done, and no body was ever found. She supposed he'd escaped and gone back to the East.

The second time had been revenge for the death of Frederick Garland. She'd fired a bullet into the mechanism of the Steam Gun, the appalling weapon invented by the arms manufacturer Axel Bellmann, intending to kill him and to die herself. She, plainly, was still alive, and profoundly glad of it now. Axel Bellmann was not. She wasn't comfortable with the side of herself that carried guns and shot to kill; after the destruction of the Steam Gun she'd tried her best to become gentle, motherly, pacific.

Well, it hadn't worked. She would have a lot of traveling, a lot of digging, a lot of finding out to do before this case came to court; she didn't want to be unprepared if there was to be fighting as well.

But again: *Why? What's he after? What have I done to him? Why? And who is he?*

2

The Journalist

MUCH FARTHER DOWN THE RIVER THAN TWICKENHAM LAY the London Docks, where at about the same time that Sally was going to bed, a steamer called the *Haarlem* was tying up. She was carrying passengers from Rotterdam. A customs officer had come aboard at Gravesend, as was the rule, but these passengers had little to declare. It had been a rough crossing. All of them were poor, and many of them were hungry, and a few were ill.

The gangway was lowered, and those huddled on the deck began to gather their possessions and stumble down onto the wet stones of the dockside. Women with scarves around their heads, bearded men with peaked caps or—one or two—shabby hats of fur, patched trousers, worn-out boots; and their belongings—a cardboard box tied up with string, a rolled-up mattress, a shapeless bundle in a blanket, a basket full of clothes, a saucepan, a kettle. . . . As one by one they left the ship and moved uncertainly along the dark dockside toward the gaslight flaring over the gate, a dockworker turned to his mate and said, "What's that lingo, Bert?"

"What they're talking? Yiddish, Sam."

"Yiddish? Where'd they speak that?"

"In Cable Street, for a start. They're Jews, mate. They just come from Russia or somewhere. Don't you know nothing?"

The first man turned back and looked at the stream of refugees. They were still coming off the ship—how many had they got packed in there?—a hundred or more of them, and they were still coming. There was a child of about five struggling along with a heavy basket in one hand, tugging at the hand of a sleepy toddler with the other, while their shawled mother clutched a baby to her and dragged along a bundle of possessions clumsily wrapped in canvas. There was an old man with a swollen leg, hobbling along painfully on a crutch. There was an old woman, too ill even to move, carried by two middle-aged men who might have been her sons. Individual faces stood out: a young woman of startling dark-eyed beauty; a thin man with an expression of surpassing craftiness; a child hollow-eyed with illness; a stout woman so cheerful she was infecting all those near her with laughter; a young man, red-bearded, blazing-eyed, with the marks of consumption in his cheeks; an old man in a torn coat and a greasy fur hat, with a long white beard and white corkscrew ringlets framing the face of a learned, gentle saint; a sharp-eyed opportunist, more or less clean-shaven, with a black cap and a fur-collared coat.

The workmen watched them shuffle along to the gate, where a uniformed official stood in the gaslight, barring the way. He was trying to explain something to those in front.

"Addresses? You—got—addresses to go to? You got to have an address. Piece—of—paper. Name—and—address. Somewhere to go to. Savvy?"

A gaunt man in a tattered overcoat, whose pale wife was clutching one small child and trying to control another, eventually found a scrap of paper.

"Fashion Street," the officer read. "All right. Straight on up Dock Street under the railway bridge and carry on going, then it's about half a mile up on the right. Next!"

After a quick glance at the addresses they showed, he let them through and out into the city. A dozen or so people—relatives or friends—were waiting outside the gate, peering eagerly or anxiously in at the arrivals. Those who hadn't got a piece of paper with a recognizable address on it were directed to the Jewish Shelter in Leman Street, not far away.

Among the passengers were two girls traveling alone, and

their nervousness attracted the attention of a middle-aged woman in a fur coat. As they walked uncertainly through the gate, watched by the young man with the red beard, she beckoned them, laid a friendly hand on their sleeves, and spoke to them in Yiddish. Little by little the line of immigrants filtered through the dock gate and trickled into the vast pool of humanity in the East End.

SCENES LIKE that were still new in the Port of London, which was why the workman didn't know where the passengers had come from. The immigrants had been driven abroad by the first pogroms, the vicious attacks on the Jews in Russia which had begun that winter after the assassination of the czar.

The first family in the line had come from Kiev. The husband was a tobacco merchant whose shop had been smashed and whose goods stolen and thrown out to a screaming mob while Russian soldiers looked on. The old man with the swollen leg was a tailor, also from Kiev; he'd been forced to hobble through the streets in front of a jeering mob while his house was looted and his wife knocked into the gutter. The old man with the ringlets was a scholar from Berdichev. All his books had been torn up and burned in front of him, and when he tried to save them, a Cossack with a drawn sword had forced him back.

One by one, family by family, they drifted westward with their bundles of possessions, and the letter from a cousin in London, or a brother in America, or a sister in Hull, as a guarantee that there would be shelter for them when they arrived; or with nothing more than hope. Many of them were driven on by the knowledge that someone else—a friend or a neighbor, a friend of a friend—had had such a letter, perhaps enclosing a bit of money, and they refused to be put off by the warning of the British consulate that England was full of unemployed men already, and they'd be better off hungry in Russia than starving in London.

So they came to the railway stations in Moscow or St.

Petersburg and boarded the trains that led through Poland or
through Austria-Hungary, and reached Hamburg or Rotterdam
or Libau, where they spent their last bit of money on a steamer
ticket. Some parties had made arrangements for the sea journey back in St. Petersburg, and paid for a courier to see
them to the port and through customs, and to escort them to
the Jewish Shelter at the end of their journey. For some,
London was not the end of it, and the courier would take
them on by train to Liverpool, where they would board another ship to New York.

And when they arrived, with no English and no money,
there was nothing to look forward to but poverty and sweated
labor.

Thousands upon thousands would come in the years that
followed, and each of them had a story to tell; but we're
concerned with the story of Sally Lockhart, so the individual
we'll follow now is the red-bearded young man with consumption.

He was not Russian but German, and his name was Jacob
Liebermann. He was a journalist by profession, a socialist by
conviction, and he had left Berlin one step ahead of the police—as he thought. In fact, they were well aware of it and
glad to see him go. In Bismarck's Berlin, Jews were tolerated
as long as they kept to themselves and made money which
the state could tax. Socialists were not tolerated at all. Liebermann had written a score of articles in the socialist papers
of the other German cities and had begun to try his hand at
public speaking, though he was badly troubled by nervousness. He'd gone too far when he'd written an article revealing the part played by Bismarck's private banker in various
antiliberal measures taken by the German parliament, and
he'd been given a hint that it would be better for him to
leave the country.

So he did, and in the course of his travels he'd been given
a task to do by the man he was going to see now; which was
why he slung a rucksack over his shoulder, turned up his
collar and pulled down his cap, and, with frequent stops un-

der streetlights to consult a ragged map, began to make his way toward Soho.

A BASEMENT ROOM; warm and dry and well lit, furnished with a collection of rough benches and chairs, and lined with bookshelves. At one end, a rudimentary platform with a table and two chairs. A row of windows high along one wall, which would have shown the feet of passers-by if there'd been any light in the street to see them by, and if the glass hadn't been filthy on the outside and streaming with condensation within.

At the moment, the room was resounding with an argument in four languages—English, Polish, German, and Yiddish. The speaker on the platform, an excitable man in a frock coat, was hammering his fist on the table and bellowing in Yiddish; the other languages came from the floor, where thirty or so other men were listening, heckling, shouting, arguing, smoking, nodding, or even (in the case of two of them) playing chess.

From the level of passion involved, anyone might have thought it was a meeting of anarchists, differing only over the amount of dynamite to put in their latest bomb. In fact, they were of quite another persuasion, and they abominated anarchists. This was a meeting of the League of Democratic Socialist Associations, and they were discussing the question of whether the new journal they were about to launch should be published in Yiddish, or in German, or in Polish, or in Russian. There were enough exiles, it was reckoned, to support a journal in any one of those languages, not to mention the new floods that were coming in every week. There were arguments in favor of each language, and they were all put forward several times, both well and badly; but none was prevailing. Would it end in stalemate?

Finally a whisper could be heard: "Ask Goldberg. See what he says. Why don't we ask Goldberg? Goldberg's always worth listening to. We should have asked him before. See what Goldberg says. . . ."

And before long that notion had seized the whole gathering, and they turned to the back of the room, where the man called Goldberg was sitting.

He was a striking-looking man in his late twenties: thick black hair, a powerful nose, fierce black eyes. He was thickset, with a stevedore's shoulders and the fists of a prize fighter, and he was sitting at a table with a scatter of papers in front of him, writing furiously, jabbing his pen into the inkwell with a savage energy, disregarding the splashes that resulted on the table, the paper, his hands. A cigar of terrifying pungency was clamped between his teeth.

He looked up, aware that the debate had halted, and one of the men at the back of the room said in Yiddish, "Comrade Goldberg, we can't decide. The arguments for Polish sound irrefutable until I hear the arguments for German, and then the arguments for Russian knock *them* into a cocked hat, while I know all the time that the journal ought to be in Yiddish. But—"

Five voices rose at once to denounce him, but he simply raised his over the hubbub, and went on: "But we haven't heard from you! Give us the benefit of your judgment: which language should our journal be published in?"

Goldberg took the cigar out of his mouth, eased off the ash, and said simply, "English."

The hubbub redoubled. Goldberg seemed to have expected that, because he continued scribbling from where he'd stopped with hardly a second's pause. A man sitting nearby leaned over and jabbed vigorously with his forefinger, making a point so passionately that he nearly upset the ink. Goldberg inclined his head to listen, moving the ink out of range with his left hand while continuing to scribble with the right. Then he said a word or two in response; his hand never ceased to scrawl until he reached the bottom of a page, when he flung the paper aside and began his assault on the next.

The argument continued until finally the chairman had had enough. He banged on the table with a cobbler's hammer, calling for silence.

"Comrades! Comrades! Argument and debate are the very lifeblood of democratic socialism, but we should allow each other to listen as well as speak! Comrade Goldberg, could you explain your preference for English?"

He had been speaking in Yiddish, and Goldberg answered in the same language. His voice, when he raised it to speak, was harsh and powerful.

"There are three reasons," he said. Everyone had turned to hear, and sat twisted in their chairs, arms thrown over the back. "First, we are in England. There are some of us who want to go back to where we came from, others who want to live in Palestine, others who want to go to America, but shall I tell you where most of you will die and be buried? In England, comrades. Your children will have children who were born here and will consider themselves English, and will know no Polish, no German, no Russian. A journal in Polish, for example, would have a declining circulation by its very nature. As for Yiddish, the same argument applies, with the added disadvantage that it will limit the circulation to Jews. Is this a Jewish movement exclusively? Was socialism invented to benefit Jews and to exclude Gentiles? That's not my understanding, comrades. But I look around the room tonight, and if I looked at a score of similar meetings I'd find the same—and what do I see? Every one of us is Jewish. Why do you exclude Gentiles? Oh, you don't have a policy of exclusion, no, no—you just happen to print your notices in Yiddish. Comrades, if this is socialism, I don't like it. You should welcome men of talent and good will from the community you live in, and the way to do that is to publish in English. You should welcome men of talent and good will even if they're women. In fact—"

The rest of that sentence was lost in an uproar of protest and counterprotest, but Goldberg had been expecting it and grinned, waiting for the noise to subside. He carried on: "Yes, we should make no distinctions. That's the first reason. The second is simpler; I can see that whatever it's called, this journal, I shall be writing most of it, and I'm going to write in English, and you haven't got enough money to pay for a translator. Besides, writing in English is the only way to improve it."

"But your English is very good, Comrade Goldberg," said a timid voice.

"Oh, my English is impeccable," said Goldberg cheerfully. "It's my English readers' English I want to improve."

Laughter.

"And what about the third reason?" called someone.

"Oh, the third reason is the most convincing of all. In fact, it's so powerful that once you've heard it you won't entertain any other consideration for a moment. It convinced me, I can tell you that. Unfortunately, I've forgotten what it was."

Grins, more laughter; Goldberg knew exactly how to control an audience, and he had them on his side now. They'd grumble and argue, but he knew he'd won.

"I move," said an elderly man in a battered cap, "that Comrade Goldberg's suggestion be adopted, bitterly though it pains me, who will have to spell out every word letter by letter."

"But we haven't debated the proposition!" came another voice. "If Comrade Goldberg wants to pitch all our traditions out the window and make us all into Englishmen, it seems to me that we need to discuss it more fully. To begin with . . ."

As the Democratic Socialists settled back to enjoy the business of debating what they all knew would be the result, Goldberg struck a match and relit his cigar before stabbing the pen at the ink and taking up his sentence from where he'd left off.

The room was so crowded and noisy that no one noticed the door open and a slender figure edge through. The red-bearded young man from the ship, rucksack in his arms, gazed around, blinking with smarting eyes through the reek of smoke. He asked a question of the man nearest to him and looked where he pointed, and then made his way through the crowded chairs to the table where Goldberg was sitting. Goldberg, still furiously scribbling, took no notice.

Finally the young man coughed and said, "Comrade Goldberg?"

"Yes?" said Goldberg, without looking up.

"My name is Jacob Liebermann, comrade. I arrived in London only today. I—"

"Liebermann! Ah, man, it's good to meet you! That article in the *Arbeiter Freind* . . . a delightful piece of writing! Come and sit down."

He shook hands and pulled out a chair. Liebermann sat down, trying to conceal the emotion in his face. To have been read and praised by the great Daniel Goldberg! But Goldberg was looking at him more closely now, and he put the cigar aside.

"You're not well," he said quietly. "What is it? Consumption?"

Liebermann nodded. He was nearly at the end of his strength.

"All right, let's get out of this smoky place. These people will be arguing till midnight," said Goldberg. "Come with me. I've got a room upstairs. Give me your rucksack."

He gathered up all his papers, slung the rucksack over his shoulder, capped the ink and put it in his pocket, and shoved his way briskly through the crowd. Liebermann followed, sagging with weariness.

"That job I was doing . . ." Liebermann said as they made their way upstairs. "Larousse gave me your message. . . . After I left Berlin, I went to Latvia. . . . I've got some news. . . ."

"I remember. Good. Tell me, then."

"Comrade Goldberg, there's a conspiracy against the Jews. There are hundreds of Jews, maybe thousands, gathered at the frontiers, with no money, no papers. . . . Those who do have tickets crowd into the railway station and the seaports—"

"Yes. I know all that. What's the news?"

"I was coming to that."

"Well, come to it sooner. That was the one trouble with your banking piece, if you'll let me say so; you didn't begin it quickly enough. Give the whole story in the first sentence. Argument is different, essays are different, travel sketches and that kind of thing are different, but to tell a news story you give it in the first sentence. The rest is enlargement, background, explanation, development—you can throw it away if you want. I know all that stuff about frontiers and passports and no money. Give me the story now in one sentence."

"The man behind it is known as the Tzaddik, and he is on his way to London."

"That's better. We'll make a journalist of you yet."

They had arrived outside a door on a tiny second-floor landing. Goldberg opened it and let Liebermann through, and then struck a match to light an oil lamp. Liebermann sank into the nearest chair and coughed. Goldberg looked at him; the feverish cheeks, the bright eyes were alarming. He put down the rucksack, cleared a space among the reference books and government reports for the papers he was carrying, and poured Liebermann a glass of brandy.

"So, what do you know of this man, the Tzaddik?"

Liebermann took the glass with two hands and sipped, closing his eyes as the liquid warmed his mouth and throat. Goldberg sat at the table.

"I first heard of him in Riga," Liebermann began. "I was with a comrade who was showing me the office of something called the Aliens' Registry Bureau of the British consulate."

"No such thing," said Goldberg. "It's a fake." Out came the bottle of ink from his overcoat pocket; out came the pen. He put the papers he'd brought up under a fist-sized stone on the floor, uncapped the ink, and began to write as Liebermann spoke.

"So I found out. I pretended to be a Russian Jew, wanting to come to England. The man there—British—asked me a number of questions, looked at my papers, then made me pay a fee and wrote my name in a book. It would guarantee me residence in London for three months, he said. There were dozens of people there; some of them couldn't pay, they had no money left. They'd had to face this kind of thing all the way from Kiev. A transit fee in Moscow, a registration pass somewhere else, a particular stamp in their passport at the frontier—it went on and on; every time they moved, they had to pay someone a fee."

"The Tzaddik," prompted Goldberg.

"Ah, yes. The comrade I was with told me about him. It seems that the people—the Jews—are all afraid of some mysterious figure they call the Tzaddik; as if their misfortunes—all these obstructions in their way, all the fraud and the persecution—were all the work of this one man. But, you see, they're superstitious, they think he's . . . not human. From the villages out in the *shtetl* to the slums of Warsaw and Bucharest and Vienna, they all talk of the Tzaddik as if he were a demon, something supernatural. They say he has a *dybbuk* for a servant: a little imp from hell that waits on him. They call him Tzaddik—righteous one, saint, holy man—as a way of keeping the evil at bay, like a kind of desperate joke. When I first heard that sort of talk I threw up my hands: what can you do with rank superstition? But now . . . well, I've seen him, Goldberg. I think they're right.

"It happened like this: My comrade in Riga took me to a warehouse in the docks that overlooked the gangplank of a steamship. This was late at night; the docks had been closed earlier in the evening, and if we'd been caught, we'd have gone to prison. We were going to see the Tzaddik boarding the steamer. It was very secret; no one usually sees him, because he always travels at night. We waited there till past midnight, and then a carriage rolled up beside the gangplank.

"It was a big, luxurious carriage, strongly made, heavily built. We couldn't see them unloading him from where we were, but—"

"Unloading him?" said Goldberg.

"You'll see. When the carriage moved away, there he was on the gangplank, being hauled up by two sailors and pushed up by two footmen. He's in a wheelchair. Immensely fat. A servant closeby, holding a rug or something. And—I don't care if you don't believe this—I saw the *dybbuk*."

Goldberg looked up. Liebermann's face was tense, and he'd nearly finished the brandy. Goldberg poured some more, and Liebermann went on. "A little shadow like a cat—the size of a cat—but human. A homunculus, like the medieval magicians used to make in those old stories. Skipping and running up the gangplank after him. . . ."

He closed his eyes and sighed, trembling.

"Anyway, they took the man on board and then lifted up the carriage, too, with a crane. And I left, with my comrade, and came on overland to Rotterdam. That was where I next heard of the Tzaddik. It was on board the ship, the night we sailed. I was on the deck—the air below was filthy and full of smoke—and I was trying to get warm behind some kind of lifeboat. And I heard two men talking. The ship's engine was turning over; I could feel the throbbing in the bulkhead behind me—is that the word? It was near the chimney—funnel—and I could see the lights of the city behind the customs shed. I was huddled down there under my raincoat, and I saw the men's outline against the sky, leaning on the rail. They were speaking in English.

"One of them said, 'Fifty-six passengers at five guilders each. Two hundred and eighty guilders. You owe me ten percent—twenty-eight.' I recognized his voice: he was the official who'd stamped the papers for the passengers to come on board.

"The other man said, 'You never said ten percent. We agreed on five.'

"The official said, 'The price has gone up. This is the last run we can do from Rotterdam like this; the authorities are beginning to want their cut. I must have my profit. Ten percent, or I go to the Tzaddik.'

"The other man grumbled, but paid over some coins. Then

he said, 'The Tzaddik's in Russia, the last I heard. Are you going back there, then?'

" 'He's coming this way,' said the official. 'He's on his way to London. The network's almost all in place.'

"The second man said, 'If we can't use this dodge again, what are we going to do next time?'

"The first man said, 'Go and see a man in Blackmoor Street when you get to London. A Mr. Parrish. He'll tell you.'

"I didn't hear what the second man said, because the ship's whistle blew. I saw them shake hands, and then the official left. The other man stayed there until the boat had drawn away from the dockside and we were passing out of the harbor, and then he went below. As for me, that was when I began to feel seasick."

He stopped and sank back in the chair. Goldberg was tapping the pen against his teeth, his eyes intense with speculation.

"Did you say Parrish?" he said. "Of Blackmoor Street?"

"That's what I heard. But no more than that. I'm sorry, Goldberg, but I couldn't follow him when we left the boat. I was nearly finished. So I don't know any more about this Parrish. Does it mean anything to you?"

"Oh, yes," said Goldberg. "I've heard of Mr. Parrish. But I didn't know he was mixed up in this. . . . Liebermann, this is extraordinarily interesting. I'm very much obliged to you."

Liebermann's eyes were closed. There was no fire in the room, and it was chilly. Goldberg pulled the blankets off the bed and wrapped them around the other man. He looked longingly at his cigars, but contented himself with putting one between his teeth unlit; and then he turned his overcoat collar up, wrapped the muffler around his neck, and began to write.

3

The Marriage Register

NEXT MORNING, HAVING TOLD SARAH-JANE NOT TO LET Harriet out of her sight and Ellie not to admit any strangers, Sally set off for her office in the City.

It stood up three narrow flights of stairs at the top of an old building in Bengal Court, not far from St. Paul's. She shared the building with an insurance agent, a spectacle maker, a tobacco importer, an agent for an American typewriter manufacturer, and the office of the *Tricycling Gazette*. It was a busy place, and the other occupants were friendly, though Sally was struck by the thought that any of them might have been spying on her. How could Parrish know so much if he didn't have spies?

Margaret Haddow was already in when Sally arrived. She was a year or two younger than Sally, but because of her dark, rather austere looks and her dry manner she seemed older. Sally trusted her implicitly. Their clerk, Cicely Corrigan, came in from Bromley, having had to settle her crippled mother for the day, so she usually arrived a little later.

"Are we busy today?" said Sally, hanging up her cloak and hat.

"Not very," Margaret told her. "We've got to look at those South American mining shares before tomorrow, and I'd like to go over Mr. Thompson's file with you. Then I was going to see a Mrs. Wilson, but not till three o'clock. I thought we might look at the Australian gold fields—I've got an idea they're going to move up."

"Can you leave that for now and do something for me?"

"Yes, I expect so. What is it?"

Sally told her everything. The story sounded no more credible now that it was so familiar. Margaret knew about Harriet and had visited Orchard House a number of times, and her reaction was a good deal more sympathetic than that of the lawyer and the clerk.

"This is monstrous!" she said. "What can I do? Would you like me to testify in court or something? Just tell me."

"I hope it won't come to court," said Sally. "I hope I can find out why he's doing it before that. If I know what it's all about, then I'll know how to fight it. I'm going to go and look at the register in this church today—there's a train in forty minutes—but I must find out about Parrish. Could you go to his office for me?"

"Of course! What d'you want me to do there? Shoot him?"

Sally smiled. "Not yet. But if you could make up some plausible story—some commission for him—and see what you can find out about his business. . . . Anything at all. I don't know what to look for, because I don't know anything about him. Whatever you find out will help."

SALLY'S TRAIN took her to Portsmouth by midday, and a hansom cab took her to the rectory of St. Thomas's in the parish of Southam. The area was an undistinguished suburb of Portsmouth: dull terraces of small brick houses, a row of dingy shops, an area of scrubland by the railway line awaiting development. The church was no more than fifty years old: old enough to be dirty, not old enough to be interesting. The rectory looked the same.

The rector, a Mr. Murray, was having luncheon, so the maidservant told her. Would she care to come back in half an hour? Sally agreed and wandered into the church to pass the time. It was a conventional Gothic revival building of no beauty at all, and the only point of interest was the list of incumbents on the wall. There had been five previous rectors of Southam. The current one, the Reverend Mr. Murray, had only been in office since the year before; he hadn't been here when the supposed marriage took place. The rector then had been called Beech.

When she judged that Mr. Murray had finished his luncheon, she went back to the rectory. The maid showed her into a study, and Mr. Murray rose to shake her hand. He was tall, thin, middle-aged, and severe.

"I wonder if I might look at your parish records?" she said.

"You're aware we only go back to eighteen thirty-two?" said Mr. Murray. "If you're hunting ancestors, there will not be many here."

"The register of marriages is all I want," said Sally. "For eighteen seventy-nine. Mr. Murray, what sort of parish is this? Is it a settled kind of place?"

"Very mixed. There is a small congregation—too small. There's a lot of movement in and out. People are restless these days; they don't stay in the place where they were born. In my last parish—in the country—I could walk through the village and name everyone I saw, and all their family, and tell you everything there was to know about them. I can walk the streets of this parish all day and hardly see a face I know."

"Your predecessor, Mr. Beech—did he retire?"

There was a silence. "Why do you ask?" he said.

"I wanted to ask about a marriage that took place here in eighteen seventy-nine. If it's in the register, I wanted to ask him if he remembered it."

"I see. Well, yes, he is retired now. I'm afraid I can't give you his address."

"Can't?"

"I don't know it," he said shortly. "If you wish to see the register, you'd better come into the church."

He stood up and opened the door. She followed him out of the rectory and through a rank, dusty garden to the side door of the church.

In the gray afternoon light of the vestry, he took a pile of books out of a musty-smelling cupboard and put them on a table for her.

"Here is the book you want," he said, showing her a wide green volume. "This has been in use here since eighteen thirty-two. Every marriage solemnized in this parish is recorded in here. What was the date you wanted?"

"Eighteen seventy-nine," she said. "January. Are there many marriages taking place here, Mr. Murray?"

"Two or three a quarter. Not many, I suppose. Here we are."

He handed her the open book. There were two printed forms on a page, with space to fill in the details of each marriage. For the first one on that page, she saw, the groom had not been able to write, and had signed with a shaky X. His wife's penmanship was not much firmer.

She looked at the second: and there was her name.

On 3 January 1879, Arthur James Parrish had married Veronica Beatrice Lockhart. She caught her breath involuntarily and then controlled herself and read on. The ages of Parrish and herself were simply recorded as *full*, but that was standard practice, she saw from the other entries. His rank or profession was given as commission agent, and they both apparently resided in the parish of Southam. Under the column for father's name and surname, hers was blank apart from a line drawn across it, as was the entry for her father's rank or profession. His father, apparently, was called James John Parrish, and he was a clerk.

"Is there no record of anyone's address?" she asked. "Not even the witnesses?"

"None at all. That isn't recorded."

"So these witnesses could come from anywhere? Do you recognize their names?"

The witnesses' names were given as Edward William Sims and Emily Franklin. Mr. Murray looked briefly and shook his head.

But there was no doubt of her handwriting. That was her signature, or an extraordinarily good imitation. They must have gotten hold of a legal document from somewhere, since she normally signed herself Sally; but it was her *V*, her *B*, her swift untidy *Lockhart*. The rest of the writing, apart from Parrish's, was in the hand of the Reverend Mr. Beech.

"Is there any way in which an entry like this could be tampered with?" she said.

"Tampered with?"

"Well, forged. I mean, could someone put in a fake entry for some period in the past?"

"Impossible, I should say. They're consecutive, after all. Entries have to be made at the time of marriage—and you'll see they're all numbered. This one is marriage number two hundred and three, for instance. Number two hundred and four took place in—let me see—the following March. No, they couldn't be put in out of sequence, if that's what you mean. If you wanted to put in a fake record for eighteen seventy-nine, say, it would have to be done at that time."

"Are there any other records?"

"I have to inform the local registrar every quarter about the marriages which have taken place. I send off a form like this"—he showed her a slip of paper—"with all the details from the register. From there—well, I don't know what happens, to be frank. Occasionally they query one if there's been a mistake, a word left out or an inconsistent spelling, so someone must be checking them. Presumably they send them on to Somerset House."

Somerset House in London was where the General Register of Births, Deaths, and Marriages was kept. She was going to go there next, but she knew what she'd find.

"I see," she said. "Well, thank you, Mr. Murray. I'll just make a copy of this one, if you don't mind."

She copied the form in full; it didn't take long. He waited nearby and anxiously put away the books when she'd finished.

"The previous incumbent, Mr. Beech," she said. "Is there anyone in the parish who might know where he's gone? Your servants, for instance?"

He looked uncomfortable, and more austere than ever.

"The rectory staff are all, how shall I say, all new," he

said. "The previous cook-housekeeper left before I arrived, and Mr. Beech did not keep a carriage, so there was no groom. There was a female servant who left shortly after I came. I had to give her notice. I don't know where she went."

"What about the churchwardens? Isn't there anyone who could tell me where he is now? Would the bishop know?"

"I . . . to be frank, Miss Lockhart, the affairs of the parish were not in good order when I came here. Mr. Beech had not been well for some time. I think that whatever your inquiry may concern, Mr. Beech—wherever he may be—is not likely to be able to help."

"I don't understand," she said. "Do you mean he's still unwell? Mr. Murray, my reason for asking is desperately serious. The last thing I want to do is persecute Mr. Beech, but if I could speak to him—"

"Miss Lockhart, I don't know where he is, and I very much doubt whether anyone else in the parish does either. As for the bishop"—he shrugged. "Inquire, by all means. Are you"—he looked at the cupboard where he'd put the registers—"are you implying that these records are not accurate? Your question about tampering with them—that's a serious matter."

"I agree," she said. Could she tell him? He might know more than he was willing to tell without knowing her reasons. On the other hand, could she trust anyone? "It's very serious. I can't say any more at the moment, but if I could find Mr. Beech he might be able to help me enormously."

He looked at her steadily, his eyes dark in his cadaverous face, his expression ungiving. Then he turned away and held open the door.

She stood up to go. He locked the vestry behind her, and they shook hands and parted in silence.

BEFORE THE train left for London, Sally had time to try something else. She made her way to the main post office and asked for the chief clerk.

He came to the counter; Sally would have preferred a private interview, but the clerk looked impatient. She stood between a man handing over a large parcel and an elderly lady buying some penny stamps and said, "I'm trying to trace someone who lived in Portsmouth three years ago. Is there any chance he might have left a forwarding address, do you think? His name is Beech. The Reverend Mr. Beech, of Southam Rectory."

The clerk sighed. "Doubt it, miss. D'you want me to look?"

"Yes, I do. That's why I asked."

He gave her a sour look and vanished into a room at the back. The lady buying stamps moved away, and a man took her place and bought a postal order. When that transaction had finished, the clerk came back.

"No record of any Beech," he said. There was a glint of watery triumph in his eye at being able to disappoint her so easily.

"Thank you," she said, smiling sweetly to disconcert him, and turned away.

As she left the post office, she felt a hand on her sleeve.

"Oh, miss, excuse me, but—"

It was the old lady who'd been buying stamps.

"Yes?" said Sally.

"I couldn't help overhearing, and perhaps I shouldn't interfere, but I was a parishioner of Mr. Beech's, and if you're looking for him . . . ."

"I am! Oh, I'm glad you overheard. Do you know where he is?"

The old lady looked around and then leaned a little closer. Sally smelled the lavender water on her and the mothballs on her fur stole.

"I believe he's in prison," she whispered.

"Really? But why?"

"I can't tell you exactly, because I don't know. And heaven knows I would hate to malign a poor gentleman who had fallen into temptation, but the truth will out. I left the congregation of St. Thomas's a year or two before he was . . . removed, but you know one hears things. . . . He always

struck me as a nervous gentleman. No family—a bachelor—
and one doesn't like that in a clergyman somehow. He didn't
seem at all a well man during the last year I attended his
church, and, you know, when the hand that gives you the
Communion wafer shakes *quite* so much, it disturbs one's
thoughts, d'you see. . . ."

"And you think he's in prison?" Sally prompted.

"Well, one hears things. Of course, one wouldn't want to
credit *everything* one was told, but he did leave *so* suddenly,
and one heard that the church authorities had kept it out of
the newspapers, but my good friend Miss Hyne has a second
cousin in the Home Office, and though he didn't of course
say what he knows, he did leave her with *little doubt* that Mr.
Beech is now in prison."

"How extraordinary," said Sally. "But what was he accused of?"

"Ah, as to that, one could not say. But there's no doubt
that the church silver—and, of course, some of it was the
gift of the Crosse family, magnificent vessels—had been sadly
depleted. One looked for the appearance of that beautiful
chalice in vain, and one could not help drawing certain con-
clusions."

"I see," said Sally. "Well, thank you very much,
Mrs. . . ."

"Miss Hall. Are you a stranger in Portsmouth?"

Sally got away from the old lady as politely as she could.
She was inquiring on behalf of a missionary society, she said;
Mr. Beech had once expressed an interest in their activities,
and as she had happened to be in the vicinity. . . . No, it
was very kind, but she wouldn't take tea with Miss Hall, as
she had a train to catch. Thank you, thank you, good-bye.

So, she thought, as the train steamed through the
Hampshire countryside under the pale autumn sunshine: a
vanishing clergyman, who might or might not be in prison,
and an incontrovertible entry in a register of marriages.
Someone must have planned this a long time ago: before
Harriet was even born, in fact. Someone had woven a net

around her so carefully that she'd never suspected it, and then waited for the best possible moment before tugging it swiftly tight.

Her hand felt for the squat shape of the pistol in her bag, and then she thrust it away. Not yet. *Get someone in my sights first*, she thought; *I don't even know what Parrish looks like.*

But how chilling it was to find that invisible net around you, and how easy it would be, faced with evidence like that marriage register, to slip little by little into believing that it was true: that she really was married, and had lost her memory. . . .

MARGARET HADDOW rehearsed her story as she climbed the stairs to Arthur Parrish's first-floor office. Sally's situation was scarcely credible, but Sally was a vastly less conventional young lady than Sally herself thought, and Margaret, in her brisk, dry way, was extremely fond of her.

She knocked, was admitted, and shortly afterward sat down in a tidy little office across a desk from Mr. Parrish himself.

He was a neat man, with neat black hair and a neat little mustache. Dapper was the word for him, thought Margaret, except that there was a disconcerting stillness in his eyes and a greediness about the mouth. Not a hint of vanity, though he was conventionally handsome enough. His suit was dark, his collar starched, his cravat sober, and the three rings that sparkled on his fingers were no more than many men wore.

Margaret took it all in, trying not to stare. "Mr. Parrish, do you take commissions in America?" she began.

"Anywhere in the world," he said. "What did you have in mind?"

"I've got a cousin in Buffalo. In New York State. He wants to set up in business as an importer of fine china, and he's asked me to see about getting him some samples from the best manufacturers and sending them across to him."

Mr. Parrish jotted down some notes with a silver pencil.

"Most of these firms have their own agents," he said. "Your

cousin will be competing with established networks of salesmen, you know that, don't you?"

"He was hoping to specialize in the finer items, I think, from the more artistic manufacturers. But I know nothing about china, Mr. Parrish, and nothing about business. What would be the best way to proceed?"

He put down the pencil and explained that her cousin's best bet would be to write to the companies he was interested in and introduce himself, offering his services. He, Mr. Parrish, could certainly supply a list of names and addresses, and if desired buy and dispatch a sample from each firm for her cousin's inspection.

She was impressed. He was brisk and businesslike, and the advice he gave was sound. There was nothing to indicate that as a businessman he was anything but honest.

She thanked him, asked a couple of further questions to reinforce her story, and then said she'd write to her cousin and see what he said.

Then, as she stood up to leave, he startled her.

"By the way, Miss Haddow," he said. "Please assure my wife that she won't get anywhere by sending you to spy on me. All right? You understand? Of course, if you really have got a cousin in Buffalo who wants to deal in china, I can help you, by all means. Would you like me to proceed in the way I described? No? I thought not. Well, remember what I said."

She found herself speechless. Her face flaming, she looked down into his hard eyes for a moment more, and then turned on her heel and left.

"I DIDN'T SEE anything useful at all," she told Sally later on, over the tea table at Orchard House. "I feel such a fool. He knew who I was from the start; and I thought I was being so clever. . . ."

Harriet was upstairs in the bath, and soon, when Sarah-Jane had put her to bed, Sally would go up and spend a little time with her, making up stories or singing nursery rhymes. For the moment she and Margaret were alone, and the kettle hissing on the hearth and the occasional clop of hooves on the road outside the front gate were the only sounds. Sally usually liked to watch the light fading from the garden, but she'd drawn the curtains early tonight; it looked less like light fading than like darkness gathering, and she wanted to keep it out.

There was a knock, and Ellie came in to remove the tea things. She was a steady, pleasant girl who'd worked for the Garlands when they lived in Bloomsbury, before the fire in which Frederick had died. She'd recently become engaged to the local doctor's groom, so she'd be leaving. Sally was pleased for her, but sorry to be losing her.

A thought occurred to Sally as she handed Ellie her cup and saucer.

"Ellie," she said, "how many people knew that Mr. Webster and Mr. Jim were going to be away?"

"What, people in the town, miss? I should think most people that knows 'em. It wasn't a secret, as you might say."

"Have you told anyone where they were going?"

"Only Sidney, miss. My intended. Have I done wrong, miss?"

"No, not at all. But is there anyone who knows, for instance, that they're way off in the jungle now? Have you talked about Jim's latest letter, for instance?"

"Well, only Cook, I should think, miss. I can't remember really. Oh, now wait a minute. That letter with the ink that'd run—that last one—you remember, miss, you said it must have fallen in the Amazon. You read me what he'd writ, all about shrunken heads and that, and how he said him and Mr. Webster would either come home in a ship or in a cardboard box. That made Cook laugh, that did. She said if they sent his shrunken head home she'd hang it up over the stove to keep the flies off the meat. Anyway, miss, we was talking about this in the kitchen, and the knife man was there. He joined in as well; we had a right old laugh. I know you shouldn't laugh at that really, but Mr. Jim would laugh more than anyone."

"Of course he would. Who's the knife man?"

"I forget his name. Cook might know. The old knife cleaner, when he gave up last year, this feller came along instead. He comes once a month to sharpen the knives and scissors and all that, miss. But it's a funny thing . . ."

"What's funny, Ellie?"

"Well, he don't go to Dr. Talbot's. Sidney says old Mr. Pratt—the old knife cleaner—he still calls there. But he doesn't come here anymore; this new man does. Very friendly, ever so interested in everything, and he does a good job too. I mean, old Mr. Pratt, he was ever so slow. I don't think Cook would've told Mr. Pratt not to come anymore, she wouldn't do that, but it was just that this new man knocked one day and said Mr. Pratt had had to give up, and did we want his trade. Have I done anything wrong, miss?"

"Of course not, Ellie. When's he due to come again, do you know?"

"He came last week, so he won't be back for a while now. He doesn't come regular, he just calls every month or thereabouts."

"Next time he comes, could you let me know without telling him? Just come and find me and tell me he's in the kitchen."

"Right you are, Miss Lockhart. I'll remember."

She gathered up the teacups and plates, and left.

Margaret said, "A spy, then."

"It sounds like it, doesn't it?"

"D'you think you ought to go to the police?"

"They'd laugh, Margaret. Where's the crime? Don't forget, this man's married to me, or so they'd think. He's probably got every right to spy on his wife."

"Well, your lawyer, then. Tell him."

"Yes, I'll do that," said Sally. "I suppose that might help."

Shortly afterward, Margaret left for the station, and Sally went up to Harriet. They had an extra long time together;

Sally held her close and sang her all the nursery rhymes they could remember, and then offered to play a special game Harriet played with Bruin, but only Jim could play that properly; so Sally blew out the candle and lay on the bed in the dark while Harriet snuggled down beside her, and made up a story about Jim and Uncle Webster in the jungle. It was a poor, thin thing; she knew she hadn't a tenth of Jim's imagination. But it seemed to make Harriet happy as they lay in the dark together.

4

The Tax Collectors

BEFORE SHE WENT, MARGARET HAD SAID TO SALLY, "THERE was one thing. It's probably meaningless. But there are two offices at Parrish's, an inner one where he works and an outer one you go through to get to him. There were two clerks in the outer one and a lot of files and reference books and all the sort of clutter you might expect—except that it wasn't clutter, you know, it was almost crazily tidy. Well, as I came out there was a third man in there with the two clerks—he looked like a rent collector; he had a little leather bag. I was so furious with myself that I didn't really take in what they said, and they stopped talking when I went through, anyway, but I thought I heard the rent collector man say 'That'll do for the bleeding Jews, then, eh?' or else 'That'll bleed the Jews, then, eh?' That's all I heard. I've only just remembered."

It meant nothing to Sally. The men could have been discussing anything from a win in a horse race that would cost Jewish bookmakers a lot of money to something far more sinister, and in all probability it had nothing to do with her trouble. But she came back to it when Harriet was asleep. Searching around for something to take her mind off the problem, she picked up a copy of the *Illustrated London News* and flicked through it.

The word *Jews* in a headline caught her eye, and she looked at the article with it. There was an illustration of a riot in Kiev, and the article told vividly of how the Russian Jews, particularly those in Kiev, had been persecuted by mobs of townspeople, their shops ransacked and their houses looted. It didn't seem to be a case of random attacks or mindless violence, because there was some controlling organization behind it; signals were given by whistle, she read, and the rioters stopped their looting and beating when the whistle was blown, and vanished instantly into the crowd. The soldiers in the local garrison did nothing to protect the Jews. Some of them had stood and watched as an elderly Jew was taunted and beaten in the street.

Sally had read elsewhere that the Russian government had adopted a policy of anti-Semitism since the new czar had come to the throne. The old czar had been assassinated earlier that year, and obviously the government was trying to blame the Jews in some way, but she hadn't realized things had gone this far. Could this have been what the men in Parrish's office had been talking about? There was no way of knowing.

Elsewhere in the same journal there was an article on political economy, and she delved into that to try and distract her mind. But it merely irritated her. Someone was trying to revive an international workingmen's association, which had split into a socialist half and an anarchist half, and a man called Goldberg was calling for a common front against capitalism.

Since Sally considered herself a capitalist, this wasn't likely to appeal to her. She knew very little about socialism and cared less. Plainly, the economic relations between people weren't perfect, but there was little that agitation and propaganda and cheap journalism—she gathered that this Goldberg was some kind of journalist—could do to make them better.

She threw the magazine to the floor.

Oh, this helplessness. . . . A spy in the kitchen, a faked marriage register—what was going on? Why? The end of it all was that chilling line in the petition: someone wanted Harriet. They wanted to take her child away from her.

She went upstairs and took a lamp into Harriet's bedroom.

The child lay asleep, her stiff fair hair brushed and shining, one bare arm encircling her intent, contained, innocent face. Her Bruin lay on the pillow beside her, about to fall off onto the floor. Sally adjusted him, and then bent and kissed her. No one would take Harriet from her, ever.

She tucked her in and went downstairs again. She could write to Rosa; why hadn't she thought of it before? Frederick's sister was her oldest woman friend—and she was married to a clergyman, what was more, and he might well have some idea how to find the missing Mr. Beech from Portsmouth.

Good; something positive to do. She turned up the lamp, sat at the table, and began to write.

MR. PARRISH was attracting other attention than Sally's that night. In the pub at the corner of Blackmoor Street, sitting near the door so that they could keep an eye on things across the street, two boys in their teens had been waiting for some time. Most of the lights in the offices around had been put out as the buildings emptied and the clerks and the merchants who did business there left for their homes in Holloway, in Islington, in Camberwell, Acton, or Brixton. Mr. Parrish's office was still lit, but the boys in the pub knew why that was, and knew it was time for them to move.

They were both lean and hard-looking. They wore caps low over their eyes; one wore a white muffler, the other a blue and white spotted handkerchief around his neck, and both were wearing highly polished belts studded with brass nails, in the style that was fashionable south of the river in Lambeth. One was dark, the other red-haired. The dark one answered to the name of Bill. He wasn't above average height, and he was soft-spoken, but men twice his size thought hard before crossing him. There was a cold fearlessness in his eyes that gave them pause; and his knuckles were formidably scarred. His companion was called Liam, and he was even more chilling to look at, if possible. They didn't appear to have much to say to each other.

Leaving his pint of mild-and-bitter half drunk, Bill settled

the cap over his eyes and slipped out into the street. Liam
followed him without a word. In ten minutes or so, if things
went as they'd gone for the past three weeks, a man would
turn into Blackmoor Street and go into the office of Mr.
Parrish. Between Drury Lane, where the man came from,
and the door of the office building, there was a narrow entry
into a place called Clare Court, and there Bill and Liam turned
in, slipping into it as innocently as if they lived there.

Bill's Lambeth-sharpened senses told him that a policeman was coming along Blackmoor Street behind him. He
motioned to Liam, and they flattened themselves inside a
doorway and waited till the steady steps had gone past. Then
they turned their attention to the main inconvenience of Clare
Court—namely, the gaslight on a bracket eight feet up. Bill
had reconnoitered it earlier and worked out how to deal with
it.

"Here," he said quietly to Liam. "I'll give yer a hand up.
Take these and pull that pipe out of the fitting."

He handed Liam a pair of stout pliers, made a step for
him with his hands, and lifted him up. A quick wrench, and
the lamp went out at once. That left a stream of gas escaping
into the night; let it, thought Bill. They weren't going to be
there for long.

He took out a sliver of mirror, its edges bound with tape
in order not to cut his pocket, and held it at the edge of the
wall so that he could see when his man was coming. The
street was quiet now; even the pub was emptying, as the
men inside finished their drinks and went home to their
Carries, their Adelines, their Emilies. One or two late figures
appeared in Bill's mirror, giving him plenty of warning to
stand quietly in the shadows till they'd gone past.

Then came the man they'd been waiting for, only a minute or two late: a bulky fellow in a shabby tweed coat and a
bowler hat, with a leather bag slung over his shoulder.

"Here he comes," he whispered.

Liam moved forward, keeping in the shadow. Bill waited

till the man was going past the entrance to the court, and then said conversationally, " 'Scuse me, mate?"

The man stopped, hesitating, peering into the darkness. "What?" he said.

"Got a match?" Bill said.

The man fumbled in a pocket. It was all Bill needed. He reached forward, seized the lapel of the overcoat, and yanked as hard as he could. The man didn't have time to yell; Liam's fist met his jaw, and he slumped to the ground, dazed. The two boys dragged him swiftly into the darkness.

Off came the leather bag, which was heavy, and jingled. Bill slung it over his own shoulder and then saw, in the dim light from the street, a glint of silver by the man's lips.

"Watch it!" he said quietly, and Liam knocked the man's hand away. The police whistle rolled toward the gutter. Bill gripped the man's collar and twisted it tight.

"Listen," he whispered. "Don't bother to struggle. We could've stuck a shiv in yer ribs by now if we'd wanted. Still could, come to that. I want what you've got in yer pockets— come on. Hand it over. And you make one noise and you won't have time to feel sorry."

Trembling, the man knelt up and emptied his pockets. A horn comb, a handful of change, some keys—

"Everything," said Bill harshly.

A box of matches. A handkerchief. A pipe. A tobacco pouch.

Bill lost patience, ripped the man's jacket open, and reached inside. In the waistcoat pocket he found what he'd been looking for: a greasy, much-used little notebook.

"Right," said Bill. "Now I'm going to hit you in a minute, because I don't like your business."

The man flinched and said, "No—wait—don't—"

"Oh, it's all right, it's not coming quite yet. I'm telling you about it now, so's you can't complain I didn't warn you. But before I do, just tell me: How many other blokes are there working for your master?"

"None, I swear it—"

"You the only one?"

"Only one in this line, yes, honest!"

"He hasn't got another little sideline you don't want to talk about?"

"No! Please, mate, let me go! I'm only a poor man trying to earn a living—"

Bill hit him and pocketed the notebook. Then he stood up, and as the man lay groaning in the gutter, he said, "Oh, by the way, I wouldn't light me pipe if I was you. There's a leaking gas pipe on the wall. Could go up with ever such a bang. Like another smack? No?"

He kicked him instead. Then settling their caps firmly over their brows again, the boys made off down Clare Court and around the corner. As soon as they were clear, Liam said, "All right, let's have me cut, and I'll be off."

Bill reached into the leather bag and counted out a handful of coins.

"Here," he said. "Twenty. That's what we said."

"There's more than that in there, and no error."

"We said twenty," said Bill. "That's what yer got. If yer don't like it, I'll work with Bridie next time."

"Keep yer hands off Bridie," said Liam. "Leave her out of it."

A cold exchange of glances, and then they parted, Liam turning left and making south, for the river and Lambeth. Bill turned his steps toward Soho.

MARGARET HADDOW would have recognized Bill's unfortunate victim: it was the man she'd seen that morning in Mr. Parrish's office, the man who'd said something about Jews. His name was Tubb.

Twenty minutes after Bill had left him, he was climbing Mr. Parrish's stairs again, with considerably more reluctance than he'd felt that morning.

"You're late," said Mr. Parrish as he entered the inner office.

"Mr. Parrish, look, I'm sorry, I was robbed—"

Mr. Parrish's eyes widened as they took in the state of his employee. The bloody nose, the blackened, closing eye were distressing, but only aesthetically. The missing leather bag was another matter.

"Where's the bag?" he said.

"That's it. You see, sir, it's gone."

Mr. Parrish stood up.

"The book?"

Mr. Tubb gulped. "That as well. They took everything," he said. "They cleaned me out."

Mr. Parrish's jaw was clenched, his eyes ferocious.

"When?" he said.

"Just a minute ago. I came straight up here, sir—"

"Where?"

"That little alley off to the left out there. They hit me and dragged me in there, sir. I didn't have a chance—"

Mr. Parrish snarled and ran out. Mr. Tubb sank back self-pityingly and mopped his nose with his shirt cuff. After a minute Mr. Parrish came back, a little flushed from racing down the stairs and around the corner into Clare Court, casting about like a bloodhound, and then running back up the stairs again.

He flung the police whistle at Mr. Tubb's head.

"What'd I give you that for?" he shouted.

"I tried, Mr. Parrish—"

"I found it in the gutter, you poor cringing wreck!"

"They kicked it out me hand, sir—"

Mr. Parrish's anger exploded in a volley of blows that landed on Mr. Tubb's head and shoulders. They were less scientific than Bill's, but just as painful; and then Mr. Parrish drew back, with a sigh, and sat down calmly.

"Inventory," he said. "Come on, let's make a list. We're going to have to make this up again, you and me, Tubb. We might as well know what we've lost. I can't see Mr. Lee letting us get away with less than that, can you?"

Mr. Tubb snivelingly agreed. Mr. Parrish took his silver pencil and a sheet of paper.

"Right," he said. "How much was there in the bag?"

"Three hundred and thirty pounds," said Mr. Tubb miserably.

"Hmm. That's down a bit on last week," said Mr. Parrish. "You sure you got that right? What about the figures for each house? Oh, I know they were in the book, Tubb, but you've got a memory, haven't you? You know what your memory's for? It's for getting things to look right when you make them up. Off you go, then. Use your memory. How much did you take from twelve Greville Street?"

"Sixty-four pounds, Mr. Parrish."

"Good. You're getting the idea. Number fifty-two Dorset Place?"

Mr. Tubb made up another figure. Then he said, "Er—Mr. Parrish?"

"Yes?"

"What are we doing this for?"

"So you can go to twelve Greville Street tomorrow and get sixty-four pounds off 'em. And the same with Dorset Place and Tackley Street and all the rest. Mr. Lee would go short otherwise, and then we'd be in trouble, wouldn't we? You don't *have* to go tomorrow. You can go tonight if you like. Now then, how much did you collect from Endell Street?"

SOHO AT that time was one of the most crowded districts of London; it was dingy, noisy, smelly, and decidedly ungenteel. It was also lively, cosmopolitan, and fascinating.

Bill, the leather bag over his shoulder and the notebook in his pocket, slipped at an inconspicuous lope through the crowded, narrow streets, savoring the smells of soup, of garlic, of cheese, of grilled meat, of fried fish that filled the air. Soho was the best part of London to eat in, if you liked your food. You could get a three-shilling dinner in Soho that would leave you gasping; and Bill was hungry. He did stop once, to gaze into the window of a Jewish baker's and turn over the money in his pockets. It was enough. He had a penny or two left, and he went inside and bought a bagel.

He'd finished it by the time he got to Dean Street. There was a music hall bill on at the New Royalty Theatre, a tiny place on the left, but Bill ignored it. He ignored, too, the premises of the Society of Benevolence and Concord, where, according to a placard, Mrs. Letitia Mills was giving a lecture on the benefits of temperance, with lantern slides.

Next door to that emporium of plain living and high thinking stood a shabby boardinghouse, its front door open and spilling light and noise onto the street. Bill slipped inside, edging his way past the crowd in the corridor who couldn't get into a socialist meeting in the dining room and had to heckle through the doorway, and climbed the stairs to the third floor. Though it was technically a boardinghouse, the place seemed to be more like a club; one room was filled with books and newspapers, with three or four people reading or writing silently; in another, three games of chess were going on, with spectators arguing in whispers; in another, a vastly bearded man was explaining the advantages of anarchism to a small group of students, none of whom seemed to be inclined to take his word for it.

Bill knocked at a door showing a line of light under it, and a voice shouted, *"Ja? Immer herein!"*

Bill went in. The room was hot and smoky, and the lamp on the table shone on a clutter of books, papers, and journals that spread from the table to the floor and stood in piles around the tattered carpet.

Behind the table sat the man he'd come to see, and in front of it sat a man called Kid Mendel. Bill stood still, his eyes wide, and automatically took off his cap, for Kid Mendel was the acknowledged leader of the Jewish gangs in Soho. The Jews and the Irish and the Italians between them held a rough balance of power, and Kid Mendel was a statesman, a king among them. He was a man in his thirties, tall, beautifully dressed, with humorous eyes and a slightly balding forehead. He was known to have killed two men with his own hands and to have organized the Wellington Street bank robbery; even the police knew it. But he was too clever for the police. He'd made it known that he intended to retire to Brighton in time for the new century, wealthy and respected by everyone, and then look for a seat in Parliament, and as he said that with a straight face, and as he was Kid Mendel, no one expressed any disbelief.

And if this great man was visiting Mr. Goldberg, the man Bill had come to see, it sent that gentleman up in Bill's estimation too.

Mr. Goldberg waved his cigar.

"My friend Bill Goodwin," he said. "We've nearly finished, Bill."

"How do you do?" said Kid Mendel, and Bill came awkwardly forward to shake his hand. "Where do you come from, Bill?"

"Lambeth, Mr. Mendel," Bill said hoarsely.

"Dan tells me you're a useful fellow. Perhaps we can have a chat sometime. Well, I must be going, my dear chap," he said to Mr. Goldberg, getting up. "Very interesting talk. Something promising there, if I'm not mistaken. Good-bye, Bill."

Bill watched him go, awestruck.

Goldberg laughed, and Bill turned back. The man behind the table was younger than Kid Mendel, but that was all Bill knew about him. He was mysterious; he was a little devilish. Bill wouldn't have been surprised to see horns and cloven hoofs, and hear the swish of a snaky tail; certainly the fumes of his cigar were sulfurous enough. He'd turned up one day in the police court at Lambeth, where Bill was starring in a program that also featured a blackjack, a broken window, and a quantity of stolen silver. Bill had never seen him before, but he'd found himself so convinced by Mr. Goldberg's evidence that he began to remember quite vividly being with him on the day in question, helping at a Jewish orphans' outing to Hampstead Heath.

"I got it, Mr. Goldberg," he said, and laid the leather bag on the table. "And this."

He dropped the greasy notebook beside it.

"Good," said Mr. Goldberg. "Sit down. Have you counted it?"

"Course not." Bill seemed affronted at the very idea. "I ain't touched it. Apart from giving Liam his cut."

Goldberg cleared a space by sweeping the immediate clutter aside with an arm, and tipped the bag out. A cascade of golden sovereigns, silver, and bundled notes fell out. Goldberg counted it swiftly.

"Three hundred and thirty. Here's twenty for you, and ten to me for expenses, and that leaves three hundred. Now listen. You know the Jewish Shelter in Leman Street?"

"Leman Street—what, down by the docks?"

"That's the one. I want you to take this money there and hand it to the superintendent. Tell him it's from a donor who wants to remain anonymous. If he starts making a fuss, just ask him if he wants it or not."

"Right, Mr. Goldberg. What's the notebook for? I tried to read it, but I couldn't make anything out. Must be his handwriting."

"Must be, Bill. Now look—the *melamed*'s here. Mr. Kipnis. He's waiting for you next door. Take your book—there you are—on the chair by the window."

Bill took the little cloth book Goldberg pointed out, thanked him, and left the room. Goldberg relit the cigar and settled back, feet on the table, to study the notebook.

A *melamed* was a teacher of Hebrew: not a learned man like a rabbi, but a poor drudge who spent his days drilling the elements of the language into the heads of naughty boys. In the case of Bill, it wasn't Hebrew he was teaching but the art of reading English, for Bill was illiterate, and as a Jew he felt that to be shameful.

He hadn't always known he was a Jew. He wasn't entirely sure who he was, or where he came from. He'd grown up among the Irish families in Lambeth and had avoided the Board Schools, running wild and learning nothing but violence and cunning. At thirteen his life had lurched in another direction: he had taken to helping out in the household of Reuben Levy, a poor tailor in Walnut Tree Walk, and had fallen in love with Rebecca, the tailor's daughter—or not so much with her as with the richness and warmth and beauty of her family life, with its networks of ritual and remembrance. It was glamour. He wanted it. He wanted to belong.

There was no reason to suppose he wasn't Jewish. He certainly looked more Jewish than Irish. He'd heard there was a ceremony of some sort you had to go through to be a full Jew; but before it came to that, he must learn to read and write. One thing that he'd noticed about all the Jews he knew was that they were learned. Old Reuben Levy—at the drop of a hat he'd put down his work and start arguing and giving learned opinions about politics, about religion, about literature, about the law, about anything else at all; and his fellow Jews would join in—ordinary, poor workingmen talking like Solomon. A man like Kid Mendel, thought Bill, was bound to study deeply; bound to be able to read. That's what made him the man he was.

He kept this desire to himself until he met Mr. Goldberg. Mr. Goldberg had found the broken-down old *melamed*, Mr. Kipnis, whose nerves had gone for teaching small boys, and brought the two of them together; and now Bill toiled obsessively, learning *A* and *B* and *C* and scratching them on a slate while Mr. Kipnis refreshed himself with furtive sips from a flask.

And in the room next-door Dan Goldberg dropped the greasy notebook into a drawer, poured himself a glass of brandy, and took out his notes on this other extraordinary affair of Mr. Parrish's: this lawsuit involving a woman called Lockhart.

5

Target Practice

NEXT MORNING SALLY HAD THREE CLIENTS TO SEE AND A
number of letters to write, and it wasn't until the afternoon
that she managed to find time to visit the lawyer.

He seemed surprised to see her.

"There is very little new to report," he said. "The case is
due to come to court, as you know, on the fourteenth of next
month—surprisingly soon, but that might be, perhaps, a good
thing?"

"How can it be good, Mr. Adcock? It hardly gives us time
to do anything!"

"What is there to do?"

He spread his hands. She could hardly contain her impatience.

"You don't mean to tell me there's nothing to be done?
For goodness' sake, what on earth—"

"We claim that he is mistaken on the marriage point,"
said Mr. Adcock. "That is what we do. I have been drafting
replies to all the particulars, and if you wish we can discuss
them again, point by point, though I must say that I have
another client to see at three—"

"Mr. Adcock, I've been to look at the marriage register in
Portsmouth, and it's been forged."

"I beg your pardon?"

He listened attentively as she told him what she'd found
out. Then he frowned, pursing his lips, and tapped the table
thoughtfully.

"The register was intact? It had not been tampered with—
a page inserted or replaced—anything of that sort?"

"That was particularly what I was looking for. No, there
was nothing like that. It was intact. It says that I married
that man on January third, eighteen seventy-nine—but I
didn't, I swear I didn't. And we've got to find Mr. Beech,
the rector who filled it in, d'you see? If we can find him,
and he can confirm that it never happened, then the case is
over. We've won."

He smiled indulgently.

"I regret to remind you," he said, "but it really isn't that
simple. By all means look for this Reverend Mr. Beech, if
you think it worthwhile. I shall engage an inquiry agent if
you wish, though that will of course be an extra expense.
But he may confirm the other side's story and not yours. And
I must remind you that that is only one element in the petition. There remain all the other charges: desertion, being
incapable through drink, mistreating servants, the misappro-
priation of funds, the unfitness to have charge of a child, the
living in close association with persons of doubtful morality. . . ."

He spread his hands. As he listed the charges in his precise, melodious voice, they felt like blows to her heart: she
hadn't looked at the document for a day or so, and she'd
forgotten the effect it had. Someone must hate her, to attack
her like that. The sensation of being hated by someone you
know for a reason you can understand is bad enough; the
knowledge that you're hated by someone you don't know for
a reason you can't imagine is far worse. It came to Sally again
in a rush and weakened her, so that she couldn't argue with
the lawyer. Instead she nodded unhappily, her eyes on the
floor.

"Yes," she said finally. "I see. Well, I'd like you to engage that inquiry agent to try and find Mr. Beech. The only
clue is that he left under some kind of a cloud, that he might
have stolen some of the church's silver, and that he might
be in prison. But, of course, that's just rumor."

He looked alarmed.

"My dear Miss Lockhart, may I counsel you—may I *beg* you not to repeat those things? The law of slander, I need hardly remind you, exists precisely to prevent statements of that kind, and the last thing I want is for you to fall foul of that as well."

"Yes. Very well. But you will tell the inquiry agent?"

"I shall give him every possible clue. We might also sanction some inquiry into Mr. Parrish himself, if you are agreeable. His affairs, his background, hmm? It might be useful."

Sally, encouraged to hear him actually suggesting something positive, agreed. Then she said, "Mr. Adcock, if worst came to worst, what would happen?"

"Oh, I don't think you need think of that. Let's cross one bridge at a time."

"But I want to know. Can they take Harriet—my child—can they take her away from me?"

"*If* the court's decision was for the petitioner, then you would be ordered to give up the child to the custody of her fa—of Mr. Parrish. But let's not—"

"And if I refused?"

"Well, you'd be in contempt of court and liable to arrest and imprisonment."

"And would they take Harriet away from me by force?"

"Miss Lockhart, it really isn't profitable to pursue this line of thinking—"

"Would they? By force?"

"Well, in the end, if all else failed, yes, that would be the outcome. But there is no point in looking to extremes. The law is for man, not man for the law. There is the spirit of compromise. With discussion and reason, all things can be resolved. . . ."

"How can I compromise when someone I've never heard of wants to take my child away? How can you talk of compromise? What is there to compromise about? I don't understand, Mr. Adcock." She held up her hand to stop him, and then stood up to leave. "All right. I'm sorry, you were only answering my question. I'll go now. Hire this inquiry agent, by all means; it's a very good idea. Shall I come again soon?"

"We have just over a fortnight. Yes, we ought to meet again before the case comes up. . . . In about a week?"

Sally felt that they ought to meet every day, that he ought to spend his time on nothing else, but she nodded.

"And the barrister, Mr. Coleman? When will I meet him?"

"Oh, he's a very busy man. I'm not sure that he'd want to take up time like that."

Sally, amazed, sat down again. "Do you mean that he'd come to the court to defend me without even listening to what I had to say?"

"I am your solicitor, Miss Lockhart. I listen to what you say, and I instruct him. He will have all the papers, believe me. I can ask for a meeting if you wish, but I can assure you that Mr. Coleman, Q.C., is a most eminent and able counsel. You could not be in better hands."

"I'm glad of that. But I would certainly like to meet him, papers or no papers. Could you arrange that?"

"I shall do my best. Though, as I say, he is extremely busy."

Sally left the office, heavy-hearted. She stopped to say good-bye to Mr. Bywater, the old clerk, and he beckoned her close.

"Got something for you," he said.

He took a slip of paper from his waistcoat pocket.

"I had a word with a feller I know, used to be clerk to these solicitors your man's with. Asked my pal to sniff around. Well, of course, he can't be privy to the day-to-day business of the firm anymore, out of the question, but he did recall the name of Parrish. Seems that three or four years ago, there was a case brought against a man in Blackmoor Street—"

"That's where Parrish's office is!"

"Wait," he said severely. "I'm coming to that. The defendant, Belcovitch, was accused of some kind of malpractice, some complicated commercial business—look it up if you like, it's all there somewhere. Point is, he lost, and lost again on appeal. That's the surface point. The real point is, he hadn't done it, but that didn't come out till much later, and then only in the course of another case altogether. Too late then. Belcovitch had drowned himself. Now then, the plaintiff— man who brought the case against him—was called Lee. Some time later, when the business was on the market, Lee bought it, and set up your man Parrish as manager. Changed the name. All perfectly legal, no hanky-panky. Point of *this* is, Parrish isn't the boss. Lee is. Don't know anything about Lee. All my pal recalls is that an address in Spitalfields came into it somewhere. Kind of a French name, he thought, but he couldn't recall it exactly. *F*-something square. Here you are."

He handed Sally the slip of paper with the address written on it in precise copperplate.

"No number," he added.

"Is this Mr. Lee's address? Or wasn't your friend sure?"

"That's what he can't recall. Something to do with the case of *Lee v. Belcovitch*, that's all he remembered."

"Belcovitch . . . Was he Jewish, this man who lost the case?"

"Don't know. I daresay, but I don't suppose we'll know for certain. Is that important?"

"No. Probably not. It's just something that crossed my mind. Thank you very much, Mr. Bywater. Thank your friend for me. Will you tell Mr. Adcock about this?"

"If you'd like me to, miss. Can't do any harm."

His tone said clearly that he didn't think it would do much good, either. She thanked him, said good-bye, and left.

A COUPLE of words on a slip of paper, and only the most distant connection to her case; it didn't seem worth going there now. The afternoon was drawing in, and she didn't want to be late home. As she wandered up Middle Temple Lane toward Fleet Street she felt herself yawning again and again, a huge weariness settling over her. All she wanted to do was sleep, but she couldn't, because all around her some- one was setting traps, laying nets, putting down poison. She

must be vigilant and energetic; she must throw off this ridiculous business like someone brushing away cobwebs. It was
no more substantial, after all. The man must be mad.

She drew herself upright and held her head high, opening
her eyes wide, trying to dispel this tempting sleepiness. She
hadn't realized how tired you get when you are worried.

As she turned into Fleet Street she stopped at a newsstand
and bought the latest *Illustrated London News*, and a *Jewish
Chronicle*. She was curious, now she thought about it, to read
more about the Russian persecutions. The arms manufacturer Axel Bellmann, who'd been responsible for Frederick's
death, had been backed by Russian money, and she'd taken
an interest in that country's affairs ever since.

Frederick . . .

Sometimes, when she least expected it, she had the over-
powering sensation that he was beside her, and all she had
to do was turn her head and she'd see him. It was a sense of
utter conviction. She was not imagining it or daydreaming;
he was there.

She had that sense now, as she moved away from the
newsstand, and it was so vivid that she gasped and turned
half-around with eager happiness, and her lips had formed
the start of "Fred—"

Nothing there. A dim, gray afternoon, a curious passer-by
in a black coat, the crowded traffic of Fleet Street. No
Frederick.

But the sense of his presence didn't vanish at once. That
instant flash of total happiness and certainty still illuminated
things, as one of Webster's magnesium flares left a drifting
image of itself in your eyes for a long time after it had burned
up and died.

She tucked the papers under her arm and set off for the
station and home.

THAT EVENING, Sarah-Jane Russell went to visit her married
sister in Twickenham. Sally was alone, and for no reason she
could name, she set about tidying up the breakfast room.

It was the center of the home, the place where they sat in the evening and worked and read and talked, and where they ate except on the (very few) formal occasions when they used the dining room. It was the biggest room in the house, and it opened through French windows onto the veranda over-looking the lawn. It was part studio, part sitting room, part library. The one thing it wasn't was a laboratory. Webster Garland was fond of conducting chemical experiments, and the old kitchen at Burton Street in Bloomsbury, which had served as their sitting room when they lived there, was often pungent with fumes or smoke; but Sally had banished activities like that from the breakfast room at Orchard House.

She turned the gas lamps up and cleared the great table first, putting away the atlas in which she'd been following their South American trip, and tidying all her work papers into the little walnut bureau by the window. There was a vase of flowers on the table, too, which Margaret had brought her; she put it on the mantelpiece, next to the wooden clock they'd brought from Switzerland the year before. Then the books, two neat piles of them. There were books every-where in the room, but she'd kept these two piles as Webster and Jim had left them: in one a textbook of physics, an ac-count of someone or other's travels to Bolivia, in German, and a German dictionary, with a feather in one, a scrap of litmus paper in the other to serve as bookmarks. She put them on the little revolving bookcase by Webster's chair. Jim's books were penny dreadfuls for the most part, lurid shockers with titles like *Skeleton Gulch* or *Wildfire Ned*. She smiled as she picked them up, thinking of his pride when one of his stories was published for the first time. There was a copy of *Great Expectations*, too, and *Redgauntlet*. She put them all on the bookshelf that ran the length of the wall, and then took up the painting on the easel by the door.

Webster had bought it not long before he left, and hadn't yet had it framed. It was a little oil sketch by Camille Pissarro, one of the Impressionists: sunlight on a suburban road on a spring morning, and such freshness and vigor in the light that you could almost feel the breeze on your face that was making those little dabs of flake white scud along the blue. Webster had bought the Impressionists from the time of their first exhibition five or six years before, recognizing in their experiments with light some of his own concerns with recording the passage of time through photography.

Well, this Pissarro would have to wait until Webster's return before it was framed. Sally had said she'd arrange it, but this wasn't the time. She took the little picture upstairs to his study, and then folded the easel and put it away.

The stereoscope on its little mahogany stand on the sideboard, and the box of pictures . . .

That had been the start of Garland and Lockhart. She had persuaded Frederick to take a series of comic pictures to view through stereoscopes, those parlor optical toys which gave a magical impression of three dimensions, and they'd sold so well that they were able to go on and produce many more series and start their business properly. And here they all were: the scenes from Shakespeare, the castles of Great Britain, the corners of Old London. . . . And the very first ones: Jim as the boy David, with a monstrous papier-mâché head of Goliath; Sally herself as a kitchen maid discovering a swarm of goose-sized black beetles in the cupboard; the little girl Adelaide, whom they'd rescued from a dismal lodging house in Wapping, sitting on the knee of Frederick's assistant Trembler Molloy to illustrate a sentimental song. . . . Adelaide had vanished. She must be somewhere in London now, but they'd never found her. The city had swallowed her up in a moment.

These stereographs brought back that time so sharply that she found herself blinking back tears. She returned the pictures to their box, shut the lid, and put them and the stereoscope away in the cupboard.

Harriet's toys . . . There was bound to be something behind a cushion or under a chair. Sally cast about and found one of her blocks down the back of the sofa. She'd take it upstairs later on.

And she'd take up Frederick's portrait, too. It stood in a silver frame on the piano: a full-length photograph showing him not dressed up stiffly as for a formal portrait, but in his everyday wear, as she remembered him, his hair disordered, his eyes laughing. It was the only picture of him she had. It had been taken by Charles Bertram, Webster's partner in his photographic experiments, who was now in South America with them. Charles was a good man; he was kindly and gentle, and the year before he'd asked her to marry him, and she'd been anxious not to hurt him as she said no.

A thought came to her. Suppose she'd agreed to marry Charles: would Parrish have sprung the trap then? He'd laid it long before, after all. And would he have challenged the wedding before it took place or waited till afterward, so that she'd seem to be committing bigamy?

It would have been hideous, but Charles would have trusted her. And Mr. Temple had still been alive then. Even if Parrish had claimed at that time that Harriet was his child, she'd have had a far better chance of fighting him off.

Well, she'd refused Charles's offer, and she mustn't start wishing she hadn't. Things were as they were.

She took the photograph, and Harriet's block, and one or two other bits and pieces, and put them in her bedroom. Then she took a leather case from her wardrobe and brought it downstairs, and looked into the kitchen, where Mrs. Perkins, the cook, was reading her newspaper, the cat in her lap.

"Hello, miss," said the cook. "Ellie tells me you were asking about the knife man."

"Yes. I don't think he's what he seems to be. I don't suppose he'll come again, but if he does I'd like to catch him—just come in without him expecting it. Mrs. Perkins, I just looked in to say I'm going to do some shooting, so don't be startled."

"Very well, miss. Thanks for letting me know."

In the breakfast room, now cleared and tidy and looking almost austere, she unfolded a large, heavy screen covered

with a light green Morris-printed cloth and stood it against
the far wall.

She took off the cloth and laid it on the table. Underneath
it, the screen was plain soft wood, pitted with holes. She
pinned a paper target on it, adjusted the light to shine on it
more clearly, and then opened the box she'd brought from
her bedroom.

It contained her target pistol: a single-shot French model
made by Flaubert, a beautifully balanced gun with which
she'd often shot against Jim or Charles. She was better than
they were, but she could never match Webster, even though
he'd never shot before she'd shown him how to. His hand
was as steady as his eye. There was a vogue for this kind of
shooting; the light guns were called saloon pistols, after the
sort of rooms they were often used in. A good pistol like her
Flaubert was utterly accurate up to ten yards or so, which
was all you needed, and it didn't make much noise.

She pushed an armchair aside, loaded the pistol and fired
a shot. Not good, too far to the left. Never mind. Here was
something she knew how to do, and a job for which she had
the tools.

She practiced for half an hour or so, firing off a box of fifty
cartridges, taking her time, pausing to clean the gun and put
up a fresh target, and she felt much better when she'd finished. Her shots were bunching closely around the center of
the target, and she'd found that calm, detached rhythm that
made for concentration.

Before she put away the target and covered the screen again,
she decided to try the new pistol, the British Bulldog.

It was an ugly thing, not at all like the long, elegant
Flaubert. She put a cartridge in the chamber, held the pistol
firmly, bracing herself for the recoil, and aimed low, as the
gun shop assistant had advised her.

When she pulled the trigger, the noise filled the room and
shook the windows. Her wrist felt as if a horse had kicked
it: so much for her boast that she was used to it. And as for
the heavy screen, which had absorbed fifty shots from the

saloon pistol without moving, it had been slammed back against the wall and was split from top to bottom.

Blinking through the fumes which now filled the room, she put down the revolver and went across to the screen, shaking her wrist. The bullet had gone right through and buried itself in the wall behind. At least she'd put it close to the center of the target, she thought. She stood the screen up and put the revolver away. She knew for certain that if she fired it, she'd do some damage; but if she didn't fire it two-handed, she'd damage herself. If you weren't careful, you could break your wrist.

She tidied up, opening the windows to the chill autumn night to clear the room of fumes, and throwing the cloth over the screen. Then, as she occasionally did, she took one of Jim's cigarettes from the box on the sideboard and sat down to smoke it. Empty the room of one kind of smoke, fill it with another, she thought.

She looked idly through the papers she'd bought. There was nothing about the Russian business in the *Illustrated London News*, but in the *Jewish Chronicle*, to her surprise, she found an article by Daniel Goldberg. She was surprised because she hadn't thought that the *Jewish Chronicle* was especially sympathetic to socialism, and because she'd had the impression that Goldberg was some kind of agitator or demagogue. But this article was calm and closely reasoned. He was putting the case for considering the problem of Jewish immigrants as part of a wider social question, involving the relations of all men and women to one another and to the means of production and exchange.

He wrote well. His tone was light and persuasive and clear, and she found herself grudgingly admitting the force of his case.

The last paragraph read:

There is, however, one burden which Jews have to carry merely because they are Jews, and which their fellow workers are spared. I refer to the attentions of Mr. Arnold Fox. This gentleman, in the fervor of his anti-Semitic zeal, is now collecting what he fondly takes to be information regarding the influx of large numbers of Jews from Russia. He will certainly use whatever facts his imagination can find to discredit all Jews in the eyes of English people; and we should certainly avoid giving him any ammunition. I write this in the perfect confidence that all the Jewish sweatshop owners who read the *Chronicle* will instantly treble the wages and halve the hours of their workers in order to spite Mr. Fox. Such is the power of the press.

Sally smiled and put down the paper. She knew very little about the sweating system, the practice of employing poor people at starvation wages in unhealthy surroundings. Was it tailoring? Cabinetmaking? Shoemaking? It was clearly a loathsome business, but there was bound to be more to it than simply the malice and greed of the owners, as Goldberg was implying.

She looked at the Swiss clock on the mantelpiece. Half past ten; she wasn't tired, but she'd go to bed. Read a penny dreadful.

She got up to open one of the top windows a fraction, to let out some of the fumes of cordite which were still lingering.

As she parted the curtains, she heard the crash of glass.

It was somewhere off to the left—where Webster's tracking-camera shed, roofed with glass, stood against the wall.

She could see nothing in the window but the reflection of the room behind her, and quickly pulled the curtain across again so that she was standing between it and the window. There was another crash, and as her eyes accustomed themselves to the dim light from the cloudy sky, she saw a figure—a boy or a youth—crouching on the wall above the camera shed and raising an arm as if to fling down a stone.

Then he threw it, and she heard the shards of glass shower to the wooden floor, and heard a high-pitched laugh. The boy raised his face to the sky and sidled along the wall, above the next pane of glass.

Sally ran to seize the lamp and flung open the French window, calling "Stop that! Stop that at once!"

A shrill laugh, and the figure hurled down another stone, and then took a stick and beat down furiously with it, laying about him like a maniac, with glass showering and crashing to the ground and high into the air.

Sally ran out onto the veranda and then down the steps onto the damp lawn, holding the lamp high.

"Stop it!" she shouted. "Stop it and get down!"

The boy stood up straight, still shrieking with laughter, and danced along the wall, and she began to feel uncertain: there was something hideous about his uncontrolled laughter. It was as if he wasn't sane, or as if he were a demon or an elemental spirit. No, she thought angrily, don't be stupid—but there was such a gust of malignity coming from the prancing faceless figure that she quailed a little.

The pistol.

She could run in and load it and—

She had hardly begun to turn when she heard a scream from the house behind her.

Sarah-Jane's voice—

She whirled around, and then there came another scream, Ellie this time, and the sound of a door banging somewhere.

The figure on the wall forgotten, Sally ran in through the French window and flung open the door to the hall.

Ellie was crouching by the stairs, sobbing. The rug on the floor was rucked up, and something—a china cup or a plate—lay shattered on the floor.

"Ellie, what is it?"

Sally crouched down, putting the lamp she still carried on the hall stand.

"Up there, miss," Ellie stammered, looking up the stairs.

Sally, remembering Sarah-Jane's scream, left Ellie and ran up the stairs to the landing. There she stopped. It was dark, but in the light from below she could see that all the doors were shut.

"Sarah-Jane?" she said, her voice shaking. "Sarah-Jane?"

Silence, and a slow drench of fear from her head to her toes.

Then quietly, Harriet's door at the end of the corridor opened, and Sarah-Jane came out.

They ran to each other.

"What is it? Is she all right? What happened?"

"Yes, yes, she's safe—she's asleep. There's nothing wrong at all. Oh, I was so frightened—"

Sarah-Jane still had her cloak and bonnet on. Her hands were cold.

"But what happened?" said Sally.

They were speaking in urgent whispers.

"I'd just come in through the gate, and I looked up at Harriet's window, I don't know why, and—oh, it was horrible, I saw a face there, a man's face. That was when I screamed—and I rushed in, and Ellie was just coming from the kitchen, and I ran up the stairs—and there he was at the top. He just ran straight past, and I think I screamed again, and then there was a crash from below—he ran into Ellie— and I went in to Harriet. . . ."

"He'd been in there?" Sally was horrified.

Ellie was coming upstairs shakily with the lamp.

"Is she all right, miss?" she said from the end of the landing. "He ran into me, miss, and I fell over, and then he went out the door and . . ."

Sally went in to Harriet. Ellie held the lamp in the doorway while Sally bent over the bed. Harriet was sleeping as soundly and peacefully as if nothing had happened. They could hear her quiet breathing; everything was silent now. The crashing of glass had stopped.

Sarah-Jane was looking out the window.

"He's gone," she whispered.

Sally knelt by the bed and stroked Harriet's face, tucking one bare arm gently back beneath the blankets.

"She seems to be all right," she whispered. "Ellie, could you lock all the doors and the French windows, and make sure the windows are fastened? Did he hurt you when he knocked you down?"

"No, miss. Only a shock. I'll do the doors now, miss. Then I better see if Cook's all right. She probably never heard nothing. . . ."

She went down, leaving the lamp with Sarah-Jane.

"Should we go to the police?"

"Yes. But in the morning. I'm not going to walk up there in the dark tonight, nor is anyone else. We'll lock up everything; they won't come in again."

She took the lamp from Sarah-Jane and thought that the first thing she'd do was load the revolver, and never mind the recoil. Sarah-Jane was looking on the floor, and then she lifted the counterpane and looked under the bed.

"What is it?" asked Sally.

"I can't find Bruin. You know how she fusses if he's not there."

"He's probably down in the bed somewhere," Sally said, waiting for her to come out. "We'll find him in the morning."

6

Middle Temple Lane

BUT THEY DIDN'T. HARRIET MISSED HIM WHEN SHE WOKE up at seven o'clock, and ransacked her room looking for him, pulling back the covers from her bed and lifting the edges of the carpet as well as tipping all the blocks out of the block box and waking Sally up. Sally unenthusiastically joined in the search, but they still hadn't found him by breakfast time, and Sally told Harriet that he'd probably gone off to hibernate. Harriet liked the sound of that word, but didn't think much of Bruin for not telling her he was going.

Sally didn't know what to make of it. Why should they want to take a child's woolly bear? *They* meant Parrish, of course. Had these men intended to snatch Harriet herself, but been frustrated? But why should they bother to do that, when he had a court action pending which would make his claim legal?

It didn't make any sense, and it was one more tangle of anxiety. As soon as breakfast was over Sally went up to the glazier's in the High Street to see about repairing the broken glass, and then to the locksmith's to order new locks for all the doors, and safety closures for the windows.

The police took notes, and a sergeant promised to come along to Orchard House with a constable as soon as possible and look around. His manner changed as soon as he realized that Sally, an unmarried woman, was talking about her own child. He didn't actually say that she'd brought the problem on herself, but he implied it as clearly as he could. She left discouraged.

And there was work to be done. Part of her wanted to stay close to Harriet all day long, but she had clients to see, appointments to keep, and she couldn't keep passing it all on to Margaret. Besides, the legal business was going to cost a good deal, and repairing the glass and making the house more secure wouldn't come cheaply either. If she didn't earn some money, their comfortable life would soon break up.

So she hurried off to the City, intending to get through what had to be done as quickly as possible, and then take an hour or so to look at the house in Clapham where Parrish claimed that she had lived with him when they were first married.

TELEGRAPH ROAD was one of a number of identical streets of terraced houses not far from the common. Roads like this were springing up all over the suburbs, and edging the country aside as the city spread outward. Clerks, small businessmen, shopkeepers, those were the kind of people who lived in them. She'd have expected a commission agent to live with a little more style, but perhaps if he was starting out. . . . There didn't seem to be anyone at home, and she toyed with the idea of ringing the bell, just to see.

She hesitated. Well, what else had she come for?

She walked in through the narrow little brick gateway, only a step or two from the front door, and pulled the bell. It jangled loudly in the tiny hall. No response, and she rang it again, relieved; but just as she was about to turn away, she heard footsteps.

A middle-aged woman in an apron and a cap opened the door.

"Is Mr. Parrish at home?" Sally asked.

"No. Would you be Mrs. Parrish?"

Her tone was unfriendly, and so was her face.

"Certainly not," said Sally. "When is he expected home?"

"I couldn't say."

"Is he at work at the moment?"

"Probably."

"How long have you worked for him, can I ask?"

"Long enough to know what's going on. I shall tell Mr. Parrish about this, don't you worry."

She made as if to close the door.

"No—wait—please, what's your name?" Sally said, putting out a hand.

The only reply was a glare of disdain, and then the door was slammed in her face.

Sally sighed.

She left the tiny garden and, without stopping in case she decided not to, went next-door and knocked. The door was opened almost at once; she hadn't imagined that flutter of the lace curtains, then.

"Yes?" said the maid.

"Is the lady of the house in?"

"I'll see, ma'am. Who shall I say, ma'am?"

"My name is Lockhart."

Less than fifteen seconds later a woman of forty or so, alive with curiosity, came to the door.

"I'm sorry to take up your time," Sally said, "but your neighbor, Mr. Parrish—do you know him?"

"Mr. Parrish—well, yes. Why? Who are you?"

"I'm trying to find him. It's in connection with . . . a family matter," she said, improvising; she should have thought to have a story ready.

Instantly the woman's face closed up.

"You're his wife, aren't you?" she said. "I know all about you. I think it's disgraceful, if you want my opinion. I think you should be ashamed of yourself. He's a good man, your husband. But you—I haven't got a good word to say for you."

And for the second time in five minutes, a door was slammed in Sally's face.

It was hard not to feel it personally. It was hard to shrug and walk away lightly. There were people—perhaps many people—who believed this lie, who looked at her and saw a deserting wife, the wrecker of a home.

She wondered, as she walked blindly along the street, how long she could keep believing in herself. At some point the pressure would be too great, perhaps, and she'd realize that she'd been wrong all this time. Of course she was married to him—she couldn't think why she'd denied it—she was so ashamed—and all that would be left would be the fight to keep Harriet. . . .

No! She wouldn't do that, would she? *You* know *what's happened to you, don't you?*

But there was that entry in the registry, and . . .

She found herself outside a church similar in age and style to St. Thomas's in Portsmouth: a dull building put up to serve a dull area, and built where it was for no better reason than that the developer had an awkward space to fill. Without actually deciding to, she made her way inside and found the place occupied by three ladies arranging flowers and one somber-suited, shrewd-looking elderly man tidying prayer books.

She went up to him and said quietly, "Excuse me, who is the rector of this parish?"

"It's a vicar here, miss, not a rector," said the man. "Mr. Harding's away at the moment. He'll be back on Saturday. Can I help you? I'm the verger. The name's Watkins."

"I'm just trying to find someone who knows a Mr. Parrish," she said.

His expression tightened. "Would that be Mr. Arthur Parrish? The churchwarden?"

"Is he a churchwarden here? I didn't know. But that's his name, yes."

"Well . . . he's known here, of course, miss. Did you want his address?"

"No. It's not that, exactly. . . ."

She must have looked distressed, and she certainly felt light-headed, because he said, "Would you like to step into the vestry, miss? I'll fetch you a glass of water."

She followed him. The dim little room, hung about with the choristers' surplices, had the same dry, musty smell as the one in Portsmouth, and made her think again that she'd forgotten things—that the past was replaying itself like a sequence of photographs, but differently.

Presently Mr. Watkins came back with a glass of water. He shut the door carefully, having looked around outside.

"What was it you wanted to know, miss?" he said, handing her the water.

"Thank you. It's hard to explain. I'm trying to find out about Mr. Parrish. Is he . . . is he well respected in the neighborhood?"

"Yes, I suppose you could say that," said Mr. Watkins. "Performs his duties as a churchwarden conscientiously. Regular attender. Generous contributor. Supplied a crate of oranges for the choir's annual treat. Well-spoken gentleman. Not much more I can say, miss."

"Has he a family?"

He was silent, seeming to assess her before answering. She waited without prompting him.

"I have heard there is a Mrs. Parrish," he said finally.

"Have you seen her?"

"No. May I ask why you're inquiring, miss? I don't know whether I'm doing right, you see. It would help me to judge if I knew what your interest was."

"Yes. It's quite simple. Mr. Parrish is claiming that he is married to me, and I know he is not. I know nothing about him. His neighbors won't talk to me, and I thought . . . I thought I might learn something here."

He nodded.

"I see. Well, that's an unusual situation, as you might say. I don't know if the vicar would be able to help you. . . . He's on very good terms with Mr. Parrish. Makes a joke about it sometimes, the vicar does. 'Mr. Parrish is my parish,' he says. Or 'Where would my parish be without Parrish?' Last week he said, 'My parish would perish without Parrish.' Oh, and the oranges he bought for the annual treat, the vicar called 'em 'Parrishable goods.' They laughed for hours over that one. Enjoys his joke, the vicar. He's very thick with Mr. Parrish."

"Then he would *not* be able to help me," Sally said. "I've learned that much by now. How long has Mr. Parrish been churchwarden here?"

"Let me see. He came here two years ago, from somewhere on the south coast, if I remember right—"

"Portsmouth."

"That's it. He introduced himself to the vicar very early on. He's not shy, not backward in coming forward, as you might say. I think he even had a letter of introduction, so the vicar said to me. Enjoys passing things on, the vicar. I wonder . . ."

He eyed the shabby bureau in the corner. Then he seemed to make up his mind.

"Look, I'm going to do something I shouldn't do," he said. "The only reason is that I don't like Mr. Parrish. I shouldn't say that. I know it's my Christian duty to have a respect for everyone, but I can't help it. I don't trust the man."

He pulled out a key ring on a chain and unlocked the bureau. He looked through an untidy pile of papers and handed Sally a letter.

"Mess this place is in," he said. "He's a fine man, the vicar, good-hearted, jolly as you please, but he's too trusting. And he could do with someone to keep order in here. It's not my place to tell him, mind you."

Sally read the signature and sat up. It was a letter from the Reverend Mr. Beech. It said:

Dear Mr. Harding,

I have the pleasure of writing to recommend and introduce Mr. Arthur Parrish to you.

He has been a member of my congregation for five years, during which time he has distinguished himself not only by his regular and reverent attendance at Christian worship but also by his many personal qualities.

I understand that he is moving to a house in your parish, and I would like to assure you that in him you will find a devoted Christian and a hardworking friend.

> Believe me to be,
> Yours very truly,
> Gervase Davidson Beech.

It was dated 14 July 1879—six months after the entry in the register, and after the new rector had taken over in the Portsmouth church. The address it came from was printed smudgily on the cheap paper. It was St. Anselm's, Taverham Walk, Norwich.

Her heart leaped up.

"Thank you very much," she said. "I can't tell you how useful this is. Is it—I don't know about these things—is it usual for clergymen to write letters like this?"

"Being only a verger, I wouldn't know, miss," he said. "Except that Mr. Harding's very open and free, as I said. And I've never known it. He made a point of telling me about it and showing me the letter. So I suppose it isn't very usual, no."

She read the letter again. The handwriting was cramped and scholarly, and oddly shaky in parts, as if Mr. Beech was old and infirm. Well, be that as it may, she had an address now, and that was worth the journey.

"Thank you, Mr. Watkins," she said, standing up. "You've been very helpful. This man Mr. Beech was the clergyman who signed the register for the marriage Mr. Parrish claims he went through with me, and I've been trying to trace him."

The old verger looked out the vestry door and shut it again. "Let me have your address, miss," he said. "Just in case I hear anything, you know. I don't suppose I will. Mr. Parrish is very popular here, no doubt about that, oranges and all, a cheery word for everyone, generous with the collection. But you know how it is; there's some folk you trust, and there's some you don't."

She wondered if she should tip him, but decided on a donation to the poor box instead; and with Mr. Beech's address in her bag, she set off home for Twickenham.

AND FOUND a visitor.

"Rosa! How wonderful to see you! But you've come so quickly!"

"As if I'd skulk at home. What d'you take me for?"

Rosa was the oldest friend she had, apart from Jim Taylor. She was Frederick's sister. When Sally met them both, Rosa was earning her living as an actress, to the scandal of her parents. Both she and Frederick had been a severe disappointment to their father; he was a bishop, and though he was Webster Garland's brother, there was nothing of genius, nothing of humor, nothing of generosity in him. With many tears and prayers and supplications, he'd cut off his children from all contact with himself and their mother. Only when Rosa married a clergyman herself and abandoned the stage did he deign to acknowledge her again. Frederick's death had been keenly felt, no doubt, but noted in silence. The fact that Frederick had fathered a child would never be mentioned, Sally knew; though she thought Rosa had hinted the fact to her mother.

Rosa's husband, the Reverend Nicholas Bedwell, was a different kind of man altogether. He'd had a share in Sally's first adventure, which was how he'd met Rosa. He'd been a boxer in his youth; he was fearless and friendly, and though as a priest he regretted the fact that Sally had borne a child out of wedlock, as a man he understood, and both he and Rosa loved Harriet without measure. As a matter of discretion, Sally was known as Mrs. Lockhart when she stayed with them. In a real sense she *was* a widow, and the deception, impatient though both Sally and Rosa were with it, made it possible to keep their friendship open.

Nicholas Bedwell had a living in a busy parish in Oxfordshire and couldn't get away; but Rosa had come at once, leaving her own two children for a day or so with their nurse. She and Sally sat down in the breakfast room (newly secured by the locksmith) and drank tea, and Sally told her everything, from the moment the divorce petition came to her discovery of Mr. Beech's address.

"That's the most preposterous tale I've ever heard," said Rosa. "He can't get away with that. What does your lawyer say? I mean, they'll laugh it out of court, won't they?"

"I wish he'd be a little more optimistic," Sally told her. "He wants to concentrate on defending all this nonsense." She flicked the petition, which lay on the tea table between them. "All the rubbish about being a drunkard and so on. I don't think that matters. I think he ought to concentrate on the marriage thing and hammer that for all he's worth till it falls apart. But he's equivocating. . . . I don't know."

"Change him. Go to someone else. For goodness' sake, go to someone competent!"

"I'm sure he is competent. He obviously knows the law. And he did make some sensible suggestions when I last saw him. . . ."

But it was I who went to Clapham and found Mr. Beech's address, she thought, *and it was I who discovered the register in Portsmouth. Has this expensive inquiry agent done anything yet?*

Rosa's red hair shone in the firelight. She was frowning.

"I wonder if we ought to have Harriet in Cowley?" she said, meaning her home in Oxford. "That's at the heart of it, isn't it? This man wants Harriet. He doesn't care twopence about you; all this divorce business is only to get hold of her."

"And give him the right to have her. The point is that if the child's illegitimate, the mother has the right of custody. But if the parents are married, then the father has the right. The lawyer explained that. So, yes, it's all about her. But I have to fight it legally, Rosa. I have to go through this farce, I have to fight it in the courts, because if I don't they'll just find for him automatically and I'll lose her."

Suddenly, and quite to her own surprise, she burst into tears. They were alone in the room, since Harriet was being bathed by Sarah-Jane, and Rosa got up at once and put her arms around her, and Sally clung as she'd clung to no one since Frederick had died.

"I just don't know *why!*" she said, when the crying had ebbed. They were sitting side by side on the old sofa. "If I knew that, I could . . . I don't know . . . offer something else, buy him off, fight him differently. But it's this not knowing that makes me so frightened. . . . It's like fighting a ghost or a madman or something. And to find that he was laying the plans for this all that time ago, before there was any Harriet, that someone's been watching me all this time. . . ."

"Have you checked everything?"

"Everything? I think so, I think so. . . . What else can I look at?"

"Somerset House. You know, the Registry of Births, Deaths, and Marriages. There'll be a record of Harriet's birth, won't there?"

Sally sat up. "Yes! Of course! Why didn't I think—" But then her expression darkened again, and she sank back in a way that was new to Rosa, a hunted, hopeless way. "He'll have altered it," she said. "I know he will. I'll go and look, but I know what I'll find."

"No," said Rosa. "*I'll* go and look. I'll go tomorrow. You know, if they set this all up before Harriet was even born, they can't want her for herself. They only want her because it's the best way of hurting you."

Sally thought about it. It was true, but that didn't make it any easier to understand. She glanced involuntarily at the wall. Rosa followed her eyes, and saw the bullet mark from the night before. She raised her eyebrows.

"Yes," Sally said. "I've got another pistol. I thought . . ."

"And I thought you'd had enough of pistols," said Rosa gently. "After the first time."

The first time was when Sally had shot Ah Ling, the

Chinese-Dutch pirate. Rosa had been nearby and had arrived just too late to prevent it. Sally had thrown the gun away then, hoping never to touch one again.

"But it's . . . I feel safer . . . No, that's not true either. I feel *angry*, Rosa. With a gun I can . . . Oh, I don't know. It's wrong, yes, I know. But if the only way to save Harriet was to kill that man, I wouldn't think twice about it. I'd pull the trigger cheerfully. And at the moment the only thing that stops me giving in to despair is the thought that I *could* do that. Does that make me an animal or something? Immoral? Inhuman? Unwomanly? I don't care. I'm *not* going to give in. I'm not going to sit around weakly and let it happen. I'll fight it legally all the way, and then if need be . . ."

She sat there, her hands clenched on her knees. Rosa watched her, and then put her hand over Sally's.

"But I've made some progress," Sally said. "I've found out Mr. Beech's address."

"And I'm going to find the birth certificate," said Rosa.

"And there's this person Mr. Lee of somewhere in Spitalfields. He comes into it somewhere. Let's go and put Harriet to bed, and then you can help me write to Mr. Beech. D'you think Nick would know how to trace mysterious clergymen?"

THE NEXT DAY Rosa went to Somerset House and came back baffled, having paid a penny for a copy of the birth certificate of a Harriet Beatrice Rosa Parrish, who it said had been born on 30 September 1879 at Telegraph Road, Clapham. Her father's name was Arthur James Parrish; her mother was Veronica Beatrice Parrish, formerly Lockhart. Of Harriet Beatrice Rosa Lockhart, born on the same day at Orchard House, Twickenham, there was no record at all.

"I'm beginning to see what you mean," she said. "It's a lie and a fake, but the *lengths* they must have gone to. . . . We'll get them. We'll beat them somehow."

She didn't say, though Sally didn't need reminding, that it was a pity Sally hadn't had Harriet baptized, because then there'd have been a certificate to show that and support Sally's side of the case. Well, it was too late for that now.

Rosa stayed two days at Orchard House. It was a strange time; there was a storm over Sally's head somewhere, and she knew it was going to break, but Rosa's energy and common sense made it impossible to believe that it would hurt her. And yet she knew it would. Sally felt as if she were half out of one world and half into another, and didn't know where she belonged.

The day Rosa left, another legal document arrived. As soon as she opened it, she hastened to Middle Temple Lane.

"It's an injunction," the lawyer said. "Oh, dear. How very unfortunate. What have you been doing, Miss Lockhart?"

"An injunction—what's that?"

"It's an order of the court requiring you to refrain from— oh, dear, dear, dear—have you been to Mr. Parrish's house?"

"Yes."

"And have you been disturbing—at any rate, you have upset a neighbor, it seems."

"*What?* I spoke to her for less than a minute. She was the one who upset me, if anything. What on earth is this injunction for? Does he mean I'm not allowed to go and ask people questions, for heaven's sake?"

"Precisely that. It was most unwise, Miss Lockhart. It puts us in a difficult position as regards—"

"Has your inquiry agent started asking questions yet?"

"No, he has not."

"Well, for goodness' sake, why not? There's hardly any time left!"

"Miss Lockhart, I must ask you not to raise your voice to me in that fashion. I am quite aware that the feminine nature is more excitable than the masculine, but I had given you credit for some self-control. I have not yet appointed an inquiry agent."

Sally pressed her fists together to try and stay calm.

"But, Mr. Adcock, we spoke about this three days ago. *Please*—why haven't you appointed an agent yet?"

"For the best of all reasons. I want to make perfectly sure that we appoint only the best. I have been pursuing references—would you like to see the testimonials I have been looking through? Miss Lockhart, you must not lose faith in your solicitor. I fully understand the anxiety you must feel, but it does not help to let it become agitation. And it certainly does not help to take steps of the sort you have done and initiate inquiries on your own account. Have you considered how difficult you have made it for the agent we appoint? He will have to counter the bad impression left by you before he can even begin. And, in fact, now that I look again at this injunction it is a moot point whether we shall be able to make this sort of inquiry at all. Only in the most delicate and tangential way. . . . And then with so many safeguards that . . . Miss Lockhart, I fear that you have damaged your interests to some extent. The other side is bound to argue that—"

Sally stood up.

"I'm trying to understand," she said. "Believe me, Mr. Adcock, I'm trying to understand how it is that an innocent woman can have her own child taken away by a total stranger, and how when she asks questions about it she's threatened with legal action—what sort of law is this that makes it worse for you if you just try to find out why you're being persecuted in the first place? Do you know what this *feels* like?"

He spread out his hands. He intended to look wise and tolerant and understanding; in fact, he looked weak and foolish. Sally looked away and moved to the door.

"If I don't visit his house again, will I be safe from legal action?" she said, one hand on the handle.

"It's worded quite widely. . . . As far as I can tell, yes, his house, and those neighbors whom you, ah, visited, and any other premises where annoyance was likely to be caused. One could argue that this was too wide. I think it would be reasonable to argue that. If you wish, I can—"

"No. Don't waste the time. Have you arranged a meeting with Mr. Coleman yet? The barrister?"

"Ah. There we have been fortunate. Mr. Coleman is agreeable to a meeting at half past five on the afternoon of the seventeenth."

"The day before . . ."

"As you say, the day before the court case. I had to put your point of view quite strongly to Mr. Coleman, Q.C. He is not of the opinion that it will help, but he has generously agreed to meet your wishes."

Well, that's something, anyway, Sally thought. She was becoming obsessed now. The case had inflamed her mind to the point where she could not concentrate on anything else for more than a couple of minutes at a time. She dwelt endlessly on Mr. Adcock's words, trying to sift something hopeful out of them like a miner panning for gold, trying to be fair, trying not to brood over how slow he was being, trying to see it as sensitivity to the law and judicious shrewdness.

But she couldn't keep it up for long. Privately she raged. How could the law be used so viciously, in such an unprincipled way? Didn't the lawyers who drew up petitions and injunctions and prepared cases ever think of the meaning of what they were doing? Was the whole majesty and splendor of the English legal system so easily bent to do something so obviously wrong?

She didn't dare think it was. She was still incredulous, still hopeful that the court would throw the case out, still unable, with part of her mind, to feel it was anything more than a bad dream. It was the perfect state to have your victim in, if you were the predator.

MR. PARRISH, by contrast, had just been having a highly satisfactory meeting with his lawyer.

"They've engaged Coleman," Mr. Gurney told him.

"Is he good?"

"The best."

"Well, who've we got? Haven't we got the best? If not, why not?"

"We don't need the best. We've got Sanderson. Second

best is good enough with a cast-iron case like this. Coleman
wouldn't have a hope if he was Demosthenes and Cicero
rolled into one."

Mr. Parrish had heard of those gentlemen, but not recently. He grunted.

"I suppose you know what you're doing," he said.

"Coleman knows it too. He'll do a damn fine job. I look
forward to hearing his arguments. But he won't win, and he
knows it. And I know he knows it, because I know his clerk."

"Good," said Parrish. "What about the other business? The
financial side?"

"That's contingent upon the decision going the right way,
as you know. Which it will. Your wife's property is, legally
speaking, your property; there's no need for a separate rul-
ing. The law's quite clear."

"So all her property's mine?"

"I wouldn't put it quite like that," said Mr. Gurney, whose
conscience, though it had largely drained away, had left the
odd puddle of fastidiousness behind. "I'd prefer to say that
your property, which your wife has misappropriated against
your wishes, will naturally and properly revert to your control."

"Say what you like," said Mr. Parrish. "A nod's as good
as a wink. What it boils down to is that as soon as the court's
found for me, not only the child, bless her heart, but the
money and property my wife controls come to me. That
right?"

"Precisely so," said the lawyer.

"No snags? No last-minute hitches? You sent that injunction?"

"The injunction will have been served this morning."

"Capital," said Mr. Parrish. "You know, Mr. Gurney, even
more than getting my money back, you know what I'm looking forward to?"

Mr. Gurney made an indeterminate noise expressive of
polite inquiry.

"My little baby girl," said Mr. Parrish. "I'd leave her mother all the money, I would really, for the sake of her little golden head on my shoulder again. You got any kiddies, Mr. Gurney?"

The lawyer had two sons at Eton, both stupid, both idle, both hideously expensive to support. The idea of their little golden heads on his shoulder filled him with nausea. He emitted another indeterminate noise.

"Still," said Mr. Parrish, getting up, "in justice to myself, I can't overlook the financial aspects. I'm reassured to think that my little girly won't go short."

And with these words, he left. Mr. Gurney would have wondered at his client, if he'd had anything left to wonder with; but what imagination and sympathy and human concern he'd been born with had trickled away with his conscience years before. He put Mr. Parrish's papers away and turned back to the straightforward, cleanly matter of evicting a widow from her tenement.

SALLY REALIZED as she came away from Middle Temple Lane that she hadn't told Mr. Adcock about the break-in, and the man in Harriet's room, and the missing toy bear.

She stopped in the gatehouse where the lane turned into Fleet Street. Should she go back and tell him? The thought of his probable reaction decided her not to. There'd be a law against objecting to people stealing from you; she was very unwise to have gone to the police, since that would brand her as an agitator and a troublemaker and prejudice the courts against her; she must be prepared for further injunctions restraining her from even mentioning the matter; she must remove all the new locks and put back the old ones, so as to avoid making difficulties for burglars. . . .

She couldn't even laugh at her own imagination. She hadn't laughed for days; she'd hardly smiled. She didn't know, and Rosa hadn't wanted to tell her, but she was paler than she'd ever been, and there were dark shadows under her eyes. She knew she wasn't eating; she just didn't feel like it. She'd been sleeping badly, waking at the slightest noise and then not being able to sleep again, and when she did drift off, her sleep was filled with disturbing dreams. She'd dreamed the night before that she'd left Harriet waiting on a bench in the park while she went to consult the lawyer, and forgotten about her, and only remembered when she got home; so she had to rush back there in a panic, and of course the bench was empty. She woke sobbing with guilt, and went in to the sleeping child, and lay on the bed beside her and held her tight, whispering that she'd never abandon her, never leave her alone, while the cold, gray light of the dawn filtered in and reminded her that they were one day closer to the court case.

It felt like waiting for an execution.

So she was not in a mood to react favorably when a hand tugged at her sleeve as she turned into Fleet Street.

She looked around, expecting a beggar, and automatically reached for her purse to find a coin and get rid of him quickly. But the figure she saw was clearly not a beggar.

It was a young man with a cap low over his eyes, a blue spotted handkerchief about his neck, and a wide brass-studded belt holding up his corduroy trousers. What she could see of his face was not encouraging: for Bill's experiences of life had left his habitual expression one of sullen threat.

She took it in, surprised, and then looked down at the rough-knuckled hand resting on her sleeve.

"Miss Lockhart?" he said, astonishing her further. "Listen. I know who you are. There's a bloke as wants—"

His low, hoarse mutter, the air of menace he wore, were too much for her. She shook her arm free, seized his arm instead, and to his amazement dragged him suddenly into the angle of the gatehouse and pushed him against the wall. Anger lent her strength, and the movement was so unexpected that Bill didn't resist, and in any case he was off balance. But before he knew what had happened, something hard and painful was thrust against his ribs. He looked down and saw the dull nickel-plated shine of a revolver.

She was standing so that her body shielded it from the view of passers-by. She knew what she was doing; he felt the skin crawl on his scalp as he noticed that the hammer was pulled back. A touch of the trigger, and he'd be dead. Her hand was rock-steady, and to judge by her expression, she'd be glad to do it.

"Tell him," she said, "that if he gives me the slightest excuse, I'll put a bullet through him. And that goes for his messenger boys, too. *And* for anyone who breaks into my house again. Stay away, you hear? Leave me alone!"

Her voice was low and intense, and the furious hatred in her eyes—fine dark eyes they were, not at all what you'd expected in one so blond—kept him silent. Ladies didn't behave like this. They didn't carry guns; they didn't display passion. So he stood still and silent against the wall of the gatehouse as the revolver slipped out of sight, as she stepped away, as the busy crowd swallowed her and she disappeared.

"She was like a tiger, Mr. Goldberg," said Bill. "She wouldn't listen. She'd've shot me soon as blinking."

It was late the same evening, and they were in an unsavory public house near Covent Garden. Goldberg, in a wide-brimmed slouch hat and a black cloak, was smoking a cigar which earned a look of respect even from the hardened laborers at the next table.

"No go, then," he said. "What was that about breaking in?"

Bill repeated what he remembered.

"Someone breaks into her house, and she thinks it's Parrish," said Goldberg. "You stop her in the street, and she thinks it's Parrish. Understandable, I suppose. Pity, though. We'll have to catch the right moment."

"D'you know where she lives, Mr. G.? We could keep a watch on her house, like."

"No, damn it, I don't. I made an excuse to go and see Parrish's lawyer a while back and picked up some papers off a desk while his clerk's back was turned, and that's how I came across her case. I don't know, Bill; it smells wrong. It's mischief. The more I see of Parrish, the more repellent he becomes. Well, we've failed today. Have to try something else next time."

7

The House by the Canal

THAT WEEKEND GOLDBERG TOOK BILL TO AMSTERDAM.
He was due to speak at a congress of the socialist parties
of Holland and Belgium, and his speech was expected to
make a stir. Bill had never been out of London in his life,
and he stuck close to Goldberg, though he tried to look as
tough and cool about it as he could. Nor, of course, could he
speak German, which was what Goldberg was speaking most
of the time. Goldberg introduced him as his bodyguard, a
comrade from London, and he shook hands politely, accepted large glasses of the light Dutch beer, and watched.
He was impressed by the respect all these people held
Goldberg in. Wherever they went, from private house to café
to meeting hall, Goldberg would be recognized and hailed
and surrounded by admirers of all kinds: elderly, academic-
looking gentlemen, vast and threateningly bearded Russians,
stolid workers and trade unionists, and, not least, young
women. Goldberg moved among them like a king come back
from exile; they hung on his words, they bought him drinks,
they gave him cigars, they stood up and applauded when he
entered a room, they gazed wide-eyed as he spoke in that
clear, harsh, laughing voice. Bill's estimation of him couldn't
help but move up, to see his friend and protector treated as
a man of such consequence.

He didn't know, because he couldn't read, that Goldberg's
articles had been syndicated throughout the radical press of
western Europe for some time; and he couldn't tell, because
he didn't understand politics, that Goldberg represented for

people a real possibility of advancing the socialist point of view into the mainstream of argument and out of the divided, shallow backwater that the failure of the First International had left it in.

There were delegates at the congress from Germany, from France, from Britain, from Russia, and from Denmark, as well as from Holland and Belgium. Bill was content at first to watch them all, to try and make out what language people were speaking even if he couldn't understand a word of what they said. He followed Goldberg everywhere, as close and faithful as a dog, and just as far from understanding what his master was saying or doing. On the second day, however, he heard someone speaking in Yiddish, and—again like a dog—pricked his ears and looked sharply around.

They were in a crowded café near the docks: a place thick with smoke and salty with the pickled reek of herrings. Goldberg was discussing some point of doctrine with a group from Berlin, and Bill had been watching them automatically, watching in particular how one young woman kept interrupting scornfully and how Goldberg dealt with her interruptions. He spoke to her with the same brusque humor that he used with the men, and no less cuttingly, though she blushed with anger more than once. She was dark-haired and stocky and proud-looking, with fine, large angry eyes. Bill thought she might be Jewish. He was wondering what it would be like to have such a girl gaze at him with the intensity with which she was staring at Goldberg, when he heard the Yiddish speaker behind him.

He turned around, and found himself looking into the man's eyes. He was in his early twenties, sitting at a table with two others, drinking schnapps: a bony, grim-looking face with a mop of black hair and a thin black beard. Evidently he was aware of Bill's connection with Goldberg, because he gave a nod of half-recognition and raised his glass in invitation. Bill looked at Goldberg, but he was busy, so he stood up and hesitantly went to the young man's table.

"Avram Cohn," said the young man, holding out his hand.

"Bill Goodwin," said Bill, shaking it.

Cohn said something in Yiddish. Bill felt embarrassed.

"Only English," he said. "I don't speak hardly any Yiddish."

"All right, we speak English," said Cohn. "Sit down, come on, drink some schnapps."

Flattered by the attention, Bill sat down. Cohn introduced the other two: a red-haired young man called Meyer, and a fanatical-looking man called Giuliani, who was perpetually gnawing: his nails, his lips, his beard.

"So you're from England," said Cohn.

"London, yeah," said Bill, taking the little glass of ice-cold spirits that Cohn poured for him. He watched Meyer, and then threw the glass back in one movement as Meyer had done. Then he had to catch his breath and blink back the tears in his eyes.

"You're an associate of the great Goldberg?" said Cohn, refilling the glass.

"Well . . . I sort of work for him, off and on."

"What kind of work?"

Bill wondered if he could tell them about Mr. Tubb. If they were socialists, then they were probably all right. And they were Jewish, so they'd approve of giving all that money to the Jewish Shelter. He drank the second glass (less of a shock this time, though he still didn't much like the taste) and then looked around. Goldberg was arguing loudly with the girl; no one else was close enough to hear.

"The last job I done," he said, "was tax collecting. There's a man in London called Parrish. He's making money out of the Jews, out of the sweatshops, yer see, and he's got half a dozen houses beside—places for gambling, places for girls, places where these nobby Johnnies go—rich fellers. So we thinks we'll take some of his profits away. The people's tax, Mr. Goldberg called it. He's going to write about him sooner or later, expose him, like, but I took three hundred quid off him the other day. Just . . . mugged him."

"Mugged him?" said Cohn. The three of them were listening closely, impressed, thought Bill.

"Just . . . attacked him. Took the money. We gave it to the Jewish Shelter."

"Ahh . . ." said Cohn. Their expressions were deeply interested, deeply respectful.

The man called Meyer said, "You don't mind violence, no? That's good. That's powerful."

"In the right cause," said Bill.

"Of course," said Meyer. "Of course. That's what I meant. Tell me, are the other comrades in London of the same mind as you?"

"Well, some," said Bill. "Yeah. The Fenians. The Irish boys. I know some of them. In Lambeth, where I come from."

"Fenians?" said Giuliani.

Cohn spoke rapidly in Yiddish. Giuliani, watching Bill, nodded. Then Cohn said, "You know some of the Fenians?"

"I got friends, yeah. They know I won't give 'em away. I know lots of Irish people, always have done."

"And what does Mr. Goldberg think of your Fenian friends?"

"Well . . . I don't really talk about them with him. He's got his own point of view, see. I mean, I respect him."

"Of course," said Cohn. "We all do. But he doesn't have to know everything, hmm? That's interesting, what you say about the Irish. I would like to meet some of them."

"I could introduce you," said Bill.

"You could? Ah, that's good. And another thing . . ."

He refilled Bill's glass. Bill watched, half wanting to say no, but feeling ashamed to. He put his elbow on the table, leaning in close, straining to hear as Cohn began to talk quietly, one comrade to another, about the political meaning of violence. Meyer genially put in a word here and there; Giuliani gnawed his fingernails. Casually, as if he was used to it, Bill drank the schnapps. Cohn's voice continued. It was like a world opening for Bill; it was like being initiated into a whole new language, suddenly, without the pain of learning it. The theory of . . . That there was a meaning behind . . . That violence could be pure and noble. . . . And he learned a new word: terrorism. Terrorist. It made him shiver with something that he could hardly tell from pleasure. Cohn talked on, about nationalism, about freedom, about communism, about anarchism, about dynamite.

WHEN THEY came away from the café, Bill found himself alone with Goldberg. He wasn't sure how it happened, and he wasn't sure where they were, except that suddenly there he was, alone and profoundly uncomfortable, and the source of his discomfort was Goldberg.

"What did you say to those lice in the café?" Goldberg said harshly.

"Eh?"

Bill blinked. It was like being hit, being spoken to like that. He tried to clear his head.

"They was telling me . . . they was asking . . . about the Irish and all. The Fenians. Dynamite and so on."

Goldberg's eyes were ferocious. Bill, frightened of nothing, found himself trembling with fear.

"And?" said Goldberg.

"They said . . . they was talking about summing, I dunno, terrorism—"

Without any warning he found himself pinned up against the wall with his feet off the floor. Goldberg was holding him there with one hand, and the other was gathered in a huge fist under his jaw. He'd known the man was strong, shoulders like a laborer, but the speed and violence of this—he had no breath to struggle with, even.

"That sort of talk is poison," Goldberg said. "That sort of man is poison. They're hangers-on, parasites, tapeworms. They've got nothing to do with us, nothing to do with progress, nothing to do with socialism. You know what bombs do? You seen a bomb go off? You seen innocent children

torn apart? I have. Fight? Of course we fight if we have to.
But we fight evil, not innocence. And we can tell the difference. All *they* want to do is kill, kill anyone, kill for the sake
of killing, spread panic, spill blood, destroy. How the hell's
that going to make things better in the world? Use your voice.
Use your mind. Use words. Tell people. Argue. Organize.
That's what works. That's what progress means. That's where
sense and courage and decency lie. If I see you with those
filthy cowards again, by God, that's the end for you. Use
your wits. Use your eyes. Compare. Listen. *Think*. Who are
the good people? Who are the bad? Use your *mind!*"

No one had ever spoken to Bill like that before. He felt
frightened, not so much of Goldberg's physical strength as
of the challenge. But it wasn't a deadening, sickening kind
of fear; there was excitement in it. And pride, too. Goldberg
thought he was worth something.

He wasn't entirely sure how he accompanied Goldberg to
the hall where he was to speak that afternoon. He remembered eating pickled herrings somewhere, he remembered
swallowing cup after cup of hot, strong coffee, he remembered walking along narrow streets and little quays and over
bridges and past barges tied up where dogs barked and pipe-
smoking men unloaded coal, bales of tobacco, salt. He remembered the hot, smoky hall, the crowded seats, the air of
excitement, the tense silence as Goldberg began to speak.
Bill was wedged into a corner at the back of the hall; he
couldn't even sit down, and much as he was longing to close
his eyes, he kept nodding and jerking awake again.

Goldberg was speaking in German. That clear, slightly
harsh, but expressive voice; those dramatic eyes, the humorous curl of the lip; the disordered notes, the way he little by
little moved away from the lectern until he was standing in
front of the audience with nothing between him and them,
the notes forgotten, the words coming from the heart now,
singing them almost, and Bill found himself held, enthralled
by the voice and the man's personality even if the words
were mysterious to him. There was passion and humor and

courage and vision; there was scorn and mockery and anger. There was intellectual force. There was hope. Bill was caught up completely. He stamped and cheered and shouted with all the rest of them, and Avram Cohn and Meyer and Giuliani and the Fenians and terrorism were forgotten.

HE FELT someone shaking his shoulder and woke. His head was aching horribly, and there was a vile taste in his mouth, and he thought he might be sick. Were they at sea already?

But Goldberg was speaking. Bill dragged himself up and listened.

"The Tzaddik—he's here. In Amsterdam. Come on, my boy, we're going spying. Headache? Serves you right. Stick to beer. Put your coat on—it's damn cold outside."

Bill wasn't at all sure where they were. An oil lamp showed him a narrow, cramped little room with an iron stove and round windows. Then it came back to him: they were on a barge. One of the boatmen was going to take them somewhere—to the docks? He'd forgotten. Never mind. Goldberg wanted him, and they'd found the Tzaddik.

He struggled up and forced his arms into the sleeves of his coat.

"What are we going to . . . ? The Tzaddik . . . d'you want to get him? What are we going to do?"

Goldberg was peering intently out the small round window. Bill could see little: it was dark outside, and he had no sensation of movement, but then the lighted window of a house moved past through the mist, and he felt suddenly giddy. He sat down on the bunk.

"We're going to spy, as I said," said Goldberg. "See if we can find out who he is, what he's doing. Just have a look at him."

Bill turned up his coat collar and tied the blue and white handkerchief around his neck. Then he became aware of another man in the cabin. He was lying on an upper bunk, hand behind his head, supported on his elbow.

"His carriage was unloaded earlier today from one of the

Rhine barges," said this man quietly. "They think he came up from Cologne. We're going up the Herengracht now to see if he's at the house we think is his."

"What you going to do then?" said Bill. "D'you want to smash him, or what?"

Goldberg looked around. "We want to find things out, Bill. That's all."

"You know what a *dybbuk* is?" said the other man.

"A *dybbuk?* What's that?" said Bill.

"It's an evil spirit. A demon. Well, this man has got a *dybbuk* as his personal servant. They usually take possession of people—enter their bodies. This one lives outside. People have seen it. You might see it yourself soon, if you keep your eyes open."

Bill didn't know whether to scoff. Goldberg turned back to the window, and the man in the bunk was watching him impassively.

The boat bumped gently against the side of the canal. Bill heard a voice outside making soothing noises to a horse and heard the soft whiffle of breath as it shook its head.

"Come on," said Goldberg. He reached up to shake hands with the man in the bunk and said something in German, and Bill nodded to him before following Goldberg up the little ladder to the deck.

The mist struck chill into him at once. It was completely dark. Everything was half air and half water; the few points of light that he could see—a few yellow windows, a dim gleam at the bow of the barge—were haloed with suffocating moisture. He stepped across the gap between the tarry deck and the stones of the bank, heard Goldberg say a word or two to the man with the horse, and tugged the coat tighter around him as the cold bit into his lungs.

The boatman clicked his tongue, and the horse took up the strain on the rope again. The barge moved forward heavily. Goldberg tapped his arm and beckoned, and Bill followed him down a dark alley between two big buildings that looked in the misty gloom like something between warehouses and mansions. Lights were gleaming on the second floor of one, but the other was dark.

On the other side they came out into a narrow street bordering another canal. The waterfront was lined with trees, and more of those tall, elegant brick houses stood on the other side of the narrow road, facing it. The whole world was silent, except for the eternal drip of water.

"What's the time?" whispered Bill.

"Past midnight. You slept off the schnapps yet? By God, listen. Can that be him, I wonder?"

Bill strained to hear, and then came the sound of hooves and iron wheels. Goldberg melted into the darkness behind the nearest tree trunk, and Bill slipped back into the alley. He stood pressed against the damp bricks as the hooves came closer and the carriage rolled to a halt.

Bill couldn't see Goldberg at all, though he knew he was only a few yards away. He reached into his pocket and brought out his slip of mirror.

In the glass, spectral in the light that was now streaming out of the house, was the reflection of a large black carriage with a driver on the box and two servants in livery busying themselves with some apparatus by the carriage door. They had swung out an iron platform from underneath the body of the vehicle, and they were adjusting the height of it. Once they'd done that, one of them laid a wooden ramp over the steps leading up to the house, and the other unfastened the carriage door. It was unlike a normal door: it looked as if the whole side of the carriage slid aside.

The servants entered the carriage, and a few moments later a vast chair on wheels began to emerge. The servants manipulated it with enormous care onto the iron platform, and then while one of them held it steady, the other turned a handle at the side, lowering the chair to the level of the pavement.

In the chair was seated, immobile, a huge man swathed in darkness. All Bill could see was the silhouetted bulk of him surmounted grotesquely by a top hat. At one point he saw a large gloved hand swing down limply, and heard a command in a soft, deep, cracked voice. The nearest servant gently picked up the hand and laid it with the other in the man's lap.

When the platform was finally lowered, both servants went behind the chair to push it up the ramp; and then Bill saw something that nearly made him faint.

Something climbed out of the man's head—a dark, lithe shape the size of a cat, that jumped lightly down onto his knees and crouched there chittering softly.

The *dybbuk*, thought Bill, and a cold thrill of fear suffused him, body and soul.

The shape was half human, half devil; it had hands, it had a tail, it radiated malevolence. It was the sort of shape that would spring and prance through hell, mocking the damned. Bill watched it for the few moments it took the servants to push the chair up the ramp and into the house, and then he realized that he hadn't been able to breathe for fear.

He let his breath out in a silent shuddering sigh.

Oh, ridiculous. It was the schnapps. It was the mist; he wasn't seeing properly. Certainly the surface of the little mirror kept fogging over with moisture. But the evil in that little dark shape, and the way it had crawled out of his head—or had it been sitting on his shoulder?

Then the dripping silence was broken. There was a moan from the carriage. A girl's voice, he thought—and in pain—

His hand trembling, he put up the mirror again. The driver still sat on the box with his back to Bill's alley, the horses were standing motionless at the other end, the steam from their flanks blending with the mist. The door of the carriage lay open.

And then that little fiend thing shot out of the house and sprang in a single leap off the pavement and into the carriage, and the girl screamed.

Before Bill could think, Goldberg had covered half the distance between his tree and the carriage. But before he got any farther, the girl herself appeared on the iron platform—

a dark cloak, a cascade of dark hair, mouth and eyes wide with panic—and then she fell full-length on the pavement.

She was up in a moment. She was seeing nothing: she was in some realm beyond fear, beyond thought. As if Goldberg wasn't there, she sped around him, her face fixed, and made straight for the bank and plunged into the water. She sank in a moment.

Bill leaped out of the alley and joined Goldberg on the edge. The water was black, and the mist was so thick over it that they couldn't see halfway across; they couldn't even see where the surface was. There were ripples spreading, but no sign of the girl.

A voice behind them, and Goldberg turned and replied in the same language. It was the driver. He looked back anxiously at the house, where light from the golden doorway soaked out into the mist. A servant appeared, and the driver beckoned.

"We're just passing by," Goldberg whispered to Bill.

Then he said something in Dutch to the driver—something about police, Bill thought. The servant heard, and nodded, and ran back to the house. Bill crouched down low over the edge, but he could see nothing. She'd vanished.

During the next few minutes three more servants came out of the house with lanterns, and one ran off over the little bridge nearby; and then two policemen arrived, with a net and a boat hook; and shortly after that a steam launch with electric lights came chugging under the bridge and tied up to the bank.

The policemen looked competent and unruffled. Bill supposed there was a routine procedure for finding and hauling out bodies. In normal circumstances the presence of policemen was uncomfortable for Bill, but after what he'd seen earlier, he could hardly get close enough to them. They were real, they were human, they weren't made of nightmares.

After a few more minutes, when they'd launched a dinghy and begun to trail their boat hooks through the water, Goldberg nudged Bill and spoke quietly.

"We're getting some funny looks from the servants. I think it's time we slipped away. They're not going to find her now, and I've seen enough."

He said something vague and general to the men on the bank, wished them good night or good luck, and began to trudge away. Bill followed. He cast a last glance back at the house, but there was no sign of the man in the chair or of his *dybbuk*.

8

The Knife Man

THE DAY AFTER HER ENCOUNTER WITH BILL, SALLY RE-
ceived a letter with a Norwich postmark. She tore it open at
once.

Dear Miss Lockhart,
    I regret to inform you that the Reverend Mr. Beech is no
longer resident at this address, and that his present whereabouts
are unknown to me.
    I am therefore returning your letter, and I hope that you will
excuse my opening it in order to ascertain your address.
                                I am,
                                Yours very sincerely,
                                T. D. Gunston, M.B., F.R.C.P.,
                                Director, St. Anselm's.

Her letter was enclosed. At first she didn't know what to
think: a wave of disappointment passed over her. She'd
thought, naturally, that St. Anselm's was a parish; but if it
was something that had a director, and if that director was a
medical man, the whole thing was confused again. A nursing
home? A mission?
    She left the breakfast table, took her cup of tea to the
bureau, and wrote to Dr. Gunston at once.

Dear Dr. Gunston,
    Thank you for returning my letter to Mr. Beech.
    I am most anxious to speak to him on a matter of the most

extreme importance. Time is short, and the only clue I had to
his whereabouts was the name of St. Anselm's, which I took to
be a parish of which he was the priest. You say he is no longer
resident there; may I ask what St. Anselm's is, and how long he
stayed with you?

Anything you can tell me will help me.

She signed it, stamped it, and put it in the post on her
way to the City.

She had taken to sitting for minutes on end at her desk,
saying nothing, toying at first with a pen, but then falling
completely still. It was like sleep—like real sleep, unlike the
broken state of wakefulness she suffered in bed. It was a
time when responsibility receded, and when she existed as
little as possible.

It worried Margaret Haddow, and it worried Cicely Corrigan,
their clerk. Cicely would bring Sally letters to sign or ask
irrelevant questions just in order to wake her out of this
unhappy trance, and on the day she wrote back to St. Anselm's, Margaret decided to take her out to lunch and talk
to her.

They went to a chophouse in Watling Street where they
had gone before. Women were so rarely seen in the City,
where you could stand at a busy junction at the busiest part
of the day and see nothing but men for ten minutes at a
time, that Sally and Margaret still felt a little like strangers;
and there were some eating places where, having been once,
they never went again. But this little place was friendly, the
booths they sat in were comfortable, and the food was good.

Margaret ordered for both of them: grilled lamb chops and
vegetables, and when the food came she made Sally eat it.

"What's the matter with you?" Margaret said. "I know what
you're worried about, but there's nothing the matter with
you, is there? You're healthy and clever and you've got a bit
of money and an extremely talented partner and all things
considered you're not badly off at all. Eat that chop. And
this cauliflower is excellent. Everyone cooks cauliflower for

far too long; they know when to take it out of the water in this place. Gravy?"

Sally smiled.

"I'm sorry," she said. "I've let it depress me too much. I find it hard to think of anything else. . . ."

"Well, think of this, then. We've got that fusspot Mrs. Carpenter coming this afternoon. She's going to say that her dear husband would have insisted on gold, gold never fails, put all your money in gold mines, my dear. She's got about six thousand pounds, and she wants some life insurance too. . . . What shall we tell her to invest in?"

Sally sipped some water.

"I like the look of those Bolivian railway shares," she said. "Hickson's promoting them, and he's done very well."

"Now I read something about Hickson recently—or did I hear it from Mr. Battle?" Mr. Battle was their downstairs neighbor in the office building—a journalist of sorts. Margaret tapped the table, trying to remember. "Oh, yes. Mr. Battle showed me an article in some paper, I can't remember what, attacking Hickson violently. It was only just this side of libel, said Mr. Battle, and he should know. It implied that Hickson owned a number of sweatshops under different names. I don't know how true it was; it felt like an attempt to discredit him without actually having any evidence. I'll have to ask Mr. Battle if he's still got it."

"Why did he show it to you?"

"We were talking about socialism. It was a socialist paper."

"Oh," said Sally. "What do you feel about Hickson, then?"

Margaret made a face. "Difficult," she said. "I know one ought to disregard that sort of thing, but . . ."

"You think there's something in it? Well, perhaps Hickson's not right for Mrs. Carpenter. What about chemicals? The Germans are doing extraordinary things. . . ."

They discussed Mrs. Carpenter's investments, and then the state of the market in general, and the effect the government's economic measures were having. It was the sort of talk that Sally usually enjoyed, and little by little her eyes became more animated and the color returned to her cheeks.

Margaret's treatment worked so well that Sally had some bread-and-butter pudding to follow the chop, and then they looked at the time and hurried back to Bengal Court for fear of missing Mrs. Carpenter.

THAT WEEKEND Sally decided to go to Oxford. Rosa had left an open invitation, and Sally felt sure it would do both her and Harriet good. Surely the child must be feeling something of Sally's anxiety? It didn't show, Harriet's nature being sturdy and cheerful and not especially reflective; but she too had begun to wake in the night, and had wet her bed twice in the past week, something they'd thought she'd grown out of.

So on Saturday morning they packed their bags and went with Sarah-Jane to Paddington Station to catch the train to Oxford. It was a brisk autumn day, and Sally thought back to the day nine years before when she and Frederick had come to Oxford to bring news of his brother to the same man she was going to see now. That business had ended in Matthew Bedwell's death at the hands of the man Sally had later shot; something as densely clustered with lawyers as her present situation couldn't involve that kind of violence, surely, and yet here she was, rolling along the beautiful High Street as the autumn sun touched the golden buildings, and she had a revolver in her bag with five bullets in it. . . .

They reached the rectory in time for lunch, and Harriet's cousins May and Matthew, six and four respectively, greeted her with glee. Rosa was deep in preparations for a village pageant; it was the closest she could come to the theater these days, except as a member of the audience.

Reverend Nicholas Bedwell, a powerfully built man whose cheerful face still bore a scar or two around the eyes from his boxing days, greeted her warmly.

"What a lot of nonsense," he said. "Rosa's told me all

about it. The fellow's clearly a scoundrel. Come and have some lunch, and we'll go for a walk in the afternoon. See if we can find some chestnuts."

The dining table was crowded, and the children were noisy, but they were indulged for once, since their father could see how happy it was making Sally.

In the woods that afternoon, as the Bedwells' spaniel frisked through the leaves and the children raced here and there hunting for chestnuts, Sally told Rosa and her husband about the injunction and the letter from St. Anselm's.

"I've heard of the place," Nicholas Bedwell said. "I don't know why it didn't come to mind earlier. It's a nursing home of some kind; it's run by one of those charities that look after clergymen in reduced circumstances—you know the kind of thing—usually they specify *aged and infirm* or something like that. You've written to the director?"

"Yes, at once. But I don't suppose he'll be able to tell me anything; he was quite clear about not knowing where Mr. Beech was now."

"I looked Beech up in Crockford's. The clerical directory. He's in his fifties, apparently—not aged yet, though he might be infirm, of course. Worked abroad as a missionary; perhaps he caught malaria or something of the sort."

"Where did he work?"

"China. But he was much younger. I suppose there are recurring diseases that catch up with you. . . . His last address is given as that place in Portsmouth, but my Crockford's is out of date. They running out of chestnuts? I'd better scatter some more."

Knowing that there wouldn't be many chestnuts, he'd brought along a pocketful of them to drop quietly in places where the children were about to look. Harriet had found three, to her great satisfaction.

They walked on, talking about autumn, and how the children were all growing, and where May and Matthew would go to school, and about Rosa's pageant; and when the chil-

dren were beginning to tire, they turned back to the rectory.
Mist was gathering, and someone somewhere was burning
leaves.

They roasted the chestnuts on the nursery fire, and then
Nicholas told them all a story. Harriet sat on Sally's lap,
leaning in close, her thumb in her mouth; the other two sat
beside Rosa on the sofa, each wide-eyed and intent on the
story, each becoming the princess and the poor woodcutter's
son, and each learning what it was to be brave, and fearful,
and loved, and triumphant, and responsible. Nicholas was as
good a storyteller as Jim, though his stories were very different.

Harriet didn't hear the story. She was tired, and the com-
forting voice and Mama's lap and breast and warm arms were
enough to make her content. When it was time for bed, Sally
carried her up and undressed her very gently.

"We won't wake her up just to wash her," she whispered
to Sarah-Jane. "I'd sooner she slept. Morning'll do."

She kissed Harriet's cheek, brushed the strong fair curls
away from her forehead, and laid her on the little bed next
to Sally's own.

Next morning they went to church. Sally wasn't sure what
she felt about that, though she always went when she stayed
with the Bedwells, out of politeness. It would be good to
believe in something like that, but it was too easy; the world
wasn't that simple. She looked around the old church, following the lines of the pulpit, reading the inscriptions on the
wall, trying to make out what the figures in the stained glass
were doing, and listening to Nicholas preach. More stories;
no one went to sleep when Nicholas preached, but the trouble was that he couldn't repeat his sermons from year to year.
People forget a plain, straightforward argument, but they don't
forget stories, and they'd soon remind him if they'd heard
one before.

Then lunch, and then all the good-byes. And the heaviness began to gather around Sally's heart, and she realized
why she'd come. It was the same impulse that had led her

to tidy the breakfast room and put all her old things away: the old way of things was coming to an end.

She and Rosa embraced tightly at the station.

"You can always send her here," Rosa whispered. "You could stay yourself, if you liked."

Sally shook her head.

"It's too late for that," she said. "I can't hide from it. It's going to happen, and we've got to be there. I'm going to see the Q.C. on Wednesday. If he's as good as the solicitor says, we'll win the case anyway."

"I mean it," Rosa said. "We'll make her a ward of court. Adopt her. Anything to put a spoke in his wheel."

Sally smiled. "I'd better get in," she said. "The guard's looking impatient. If Nick can find out anything about Mr. Beech—"

"He's writing letters now. We'll find him. Go on, quick, get in."

Sally joined Sarah-Jane and Harriet, the guard blew the whistle, the train began to move. Sally waved to Rosa for a long time as they steamed away into the autumn sunshine.

LATE ON Monday, after Sally had spent a difficult afternoon with two demanding clients, and then visited a house in Islington, she arrived home to find Ellie alight with impatience.

"Miss—miss," she whispered, as Sally came in through the door. "He's here, miss! The knife man!"

"The knife man . . ." Sally, tired, couldn't remember for a second. Then it came to her, and her eyes lit up. "Good," she said. "Where is he?"

"In the kitchen, miss—but he's nearly finished. He's just packing up. I'll go and see if I can keep him—"

"It's all right. I'm coming now."

She threw off her cloak and bonnet and strode quickly to the door at the back of the hall, in the darkness under the stairs, which led to the kitchen. She stopped, her hand on the handle, listening. She heard a man's voice indistinctly, and whispered to Ellie, "Go straight in and stand by the back door. Is there a key in it?"

Ellie nodded. Her eyes shone wide in the gloom.

"Lock it, then."

She turned the handle and stepped in. Ellie followed at once and darted to the back door. Mrs. Perkins looked up from the pastry she was making, surprised, and Sally stood blocking the other way out.

The man was standing, case in hand, beside the kitchen table. A row of neatly cleaned and sharpened knives lay in front of him. He stopped in midsentence, startled, and then removed his cap.

"Evening, ma'am," he said.

He was mustached, dark-haired, slightly stout. His expression was amiable.

"What's your name?" Sally said.

"Cave, ma'am. George Cave. Anything wrong, ma'am?"

She hesitated. "Would you come with me, please?" she said, standing aside. "I want to ask you some questions."

"If you like, ma'am, certainly," he said.

He put down the case he was holding and went ahead of her out into the hall. Mrs. Perkins and Ellie didn't move.

"In here," said Sally, indicating the breakfast room.

She sat down by the dining table while he stood peaceably by the door.

"Who sent you here?" she said.

"No one, ma'am. I'm in business for meself. I do a number of houses in the town—shops, too. I've taken over a lot of old Mr. Pratt's business. He couldn't manage it so well, being shaky on his legs, like."

"You don't go to Dr. Talbot's."

"Where's that, ma'am?"

"In Hartford Street."

"That's Mr. Pratt's patch. He still does Hartford Street and Nelson Square. Only a step away from where he lives, you see, ma'am, it's no trouble to him. And I don't mind,

I'm sure. There's plenty enough business to keep me going. The town's growing, you see. There's the new hotel, and—"

"Do you know a man called Mr. Parrish?"

He considered.

"Would he live in Twickenham, ma'am? Because I can't recall the name."

"No."

She looked at him fixedly and found her heart beating fast. He looked honestly puzzled.

"Do you ask my servants about my affairs?" she said.

"Certainly not, ma'am. Have I been accused of—"

"I know you discuss matters affecting this household. My maidservant has told me."

"Then you'd better speak to her about it, ma'am. I'm sure I'm not so interested in other folks' affairs that I'd want to go prying, like you seem to be saying. I'm an honest man, ma'am, always have been. There's plenty of people in town as'd speak for me. Nor I don't have to come here, neither. I got more'n enough business to keep me going. If you got a complaint, let's have it out in the open. Otherwise, I'll be off, and if your cook wants her knives looking after, she'll have to get someone else."

Sally was blushing hotly. She stood up.

"I'm sorry, Mr. Cave. I apologize. There's been some trouble here, that's all, and someone seems to know what's going on in my house. I'm just trying to find out—"

"Enough said, ma'am. I don't care to come to a house where I'm suspected of spying. There's plenty of calls on my time."

And ignoring her repeated apology, he turned and left. After a minute or so, she heard the back door slam.

She sank into her chair again. Everything about this business was hateful; and she was so tired.

ELLIE'S YOUNG man Sidney, Dr. Talbot's groom, had made an appointment with her for eight o'clock that night. They both liked the music hall, and there was a new bill at the Britannia in the High Street. Monday wasn't the best night to go—the house was always a bit thin—but they could sit and hold hands in the warmth, and have a little drink. He was a liberal man, Dr. Talbot—like Miss Lockhart; nothing strict or harsh about him, very free with granting an evening off, not like some employers.

In the interval between the two halves of the bill, Ellie told him all about the knife man. He'd heard about the intruder the other night and been seriously concerned; he said they ought to have a man in the house and offered to sleep there himself. Ellie told him to give over; she wasn't falling for that one. But he was in no doubt about the knife man.

"He's a wrong 'un," he said. "Stands out a mile. Them smooth-talking ones, they're the blokes to watch. Got an answer for everything, I'll be bound."

"If he was innocent, though, he would, wouldn't he?" said Ellie.

"No. That's where you're wrong. I made a study of police court cases, I have, and it's a proven fact that your average innocent party *doesn't* have his story all pat. People don't, do they? They forget things. It's only natural. Where were you on the night of the fourteenth of August? See, you can't remember. But your crook, now, he'd tell you straight out, look you right in the eye, butter wouldn't melt in his mouth. Worked it out beforehand, see. You can always tell. This stuff about Mr. Pratt—it's a lot of old blarney. Who's this Tremble geezer you was talking about?"

"Oh, Mr. Molloy. They calls him Trembler. Just in fun, really. He used to work for Mr. Garland in the old days. He runs a lodging house now, in Islington. Miss Lockhart went up there today. . . ."

It was nice, talking to Sidney. He knew a lot, and he was always willing to listen, not like some young men she knew, all mouth and trousers. Course, he was a bit saucy, but she liked that in a man—showed he wasn't just a stuffed shirt.

And he had a serious side. He'd been sympathetic about Miss Lockhart from the beginning, followed all the doings.

As the band filed back in (wiping the beer off their whiskers, Sidney said, and a couple of them were, too) he gave her hand a squeeze.

"You can depend on it," he said. "It's that knife man what's behind all this. You're well rid of him, if you want my opinion. It's them smooth Johnnies every time. It's us awkward, shy, forgetful blokes as is the honest ones. . . ."

He slid his arm behind her, and she smiled.

"You're forgetting yourself now, Sidney," she said.

"What did I tell you? Proves I'm honest, doesn't it?"

She let him keep his arm there. They watched the second half companionably.

9

The Eminent Q.C.

WEDNESDAY MORNING DAWNED COLD AND BLUSTERY. BY THE time Sally left for the City, the rain was teeming down and the wind was tearing twigs from the bare treetops. She got to the office chilly and wet, with red-rimmed eyes from an anxiety-haunted night.

The day didn't get much better. During the morning she discovered that she'd made a mistake in a letter she'd sent to her stockbrokers, which had resulted in a client's money being wrongly invested. Luckily no great sum was involved, and as things turned out the investment hadn't lost money, but it was a kind of carelessness she'd thought herself above. And it was exactly the sort of thing the firm could not afford. She had a partner now to be responsible to, after all.

She ate a hurried lunch—sandwiches made by Mrs. Perkins, an apple from the orchard, coffee from the recalcitrant fire—while poring over the financial columns of *The Times* and the weekly *Financial Chronicle*. There a name caught her eye in a leading article urging the government to take a strong line and expel foreign agitators who abused the traditional hospitality of Britain in order to stir up hatred and dissent. The name was that of Daniel Goldberg, and it seemed that Goldberg was a well-known figure in continental socialist circles, and that he'd been exiled from Prussia and then again from Brussels. In calling for his expulsion from Britain, the journal was concerned to emphasize that, of course, it upheld all the traditional liberties of speech and thought for which this country had long been a beacon to others, but that . . .

Sally read it without feeling anything on one side or the other. And that was worrying; she didn't like this neutrality of feeling that colored the world gray. She ought to feel something about socialism, because it raised some vital questions. She even knew what it was she ought to feel, but while she was hating and fearing what Arthur Parrish was doing to her, she had no energy left to dislike an economic theory.

She put the paper aside, made some notes on share movements, paced up and down, made some more coffee. Finally Cicely Corrigan, the gentlest of souls, lost her patience.

"For goodness' sake, Miss Lockhart, why don't you go out and go for a walk or something? There's nothing else to do here, and you're only fretting yourself. Go and get good and wet and cold and worn out and then when you go home you can have a hot bath and feel a lot better. I'll clear away and lock up."

"All right," said Sally. "Perhaps I will."

She put her cloak and hat on, took her boots from where they'd been drying on the hearth, and without a backward glance at the papers on her desk, left.

It was still drizzling, with a thin, mean, half-misty chill in it, but she took no notice and marched briskly past St. Paul's, down Ludgate Hill, and then along the embankment all the way to the houses of Parliament. The tide was going out, exposing the far bank of the river, muddy and gray and littered with fragments of rubbish. Wharves, timber yards, sawmills, foundries, lead works stretched out dismally under the low sky; the steam cranes opposite Whitehall Stairs rose and fell meaninglessly. Westminster Bridge, now that the tide was low, looked awkward on its long, narrow piers. Everything was wrong. The world was crazy.

Sally shook her head as Big Ben struck three, and set out across the bridge at a smart pace. On the south bank, she turned right toward Lambeth, and for the next two hours she just walked hard. She didn't know this side of the river, and before long she was lost. That suited her; if she didn't know where she was, no one else would either. Long terraces of mean little dwellings, railway bridges, a prison, a hospital, chapels, a grand square of elegant eighteenth-century houses, an engineering works, a market, a workhouse, a theater, houses, houses, houses; a cricket ground, a gas works, a brewery, a stable, a builder's yard, a railway station, a school; grim blocks of artisans' dwellings, more houses, an asylum for the blind, a printing works . . .

She'd had no idea of the vastness of London, despite having lived in the city for so long. After all, she usually passed through it on a train while reading a newspaper or making notes; she knew London as an idea, not as a reality. In each of those houses there were real people. In each of those businesses there were decisions being made. Behind that door people were falling in love, or dying, or giving birth, or freezing into years of married hatred. That little boy limping: why was he limping? He didn't look well, he was poorly dressed; had someone beaten him? Or had he been born lame? Or had he suffered from rickets? That old woman with her tray of matches . . . that old Jew in the bazaar there, turning over the books at a secondhand stall . . . that woman who might be Sally's own age, who had lost all her teeth, whose face was marked all down one side with a burn scar . . . Sally felt something stirring in her heart for these poor, anonymous people. They were only anonymous because of her own ignorance; they each had a life inside them, just as she did.

So she wandered, looking and absorbing and feeling, until a church clock somewhere near St. George's Circus told her it was five o'clock. There was a cab rank nearby. She found a hansom waiting and told the driver to go to the Temple.

Blackfriars Bridge was crowded, and it was after twenty past five when Sally paid off the cabdriver at the bottom of Middle Temple Lane and hurried up toward Pump Court, where Mr. Coleman, Q.C., had his chambers. It was dark, and the windows overlooking the little court glowed yellow in the heavy mist. She hesitated, wondering which door to enter, and a figure detached itself from the darkness on her right and hastened toward her.

"Miss Lockhart! I was becoming distinctly anxious."

It was the solicitor, Mr. Adcock. He was bareheaded, so he'd left his hat inside, and he was clearly agitated.

"I am on time, aren't I? Wasn't our appointment for half past five?"

"It is nearly that now. It would be extremely unfortunate if we were late. Mr. Coleman is so very busy—"

He opened the door for her, and she went up the step and into a corridor, where a porter was waiting to show them into a warm office. Three clerks were working in silence, scratching with steel pens under bright gaslight.

A clerk took them through another office and knocked deferentially at a door. There was no reply. He opened it carefully and stood aside for them to go in.

"Mr. Coleman will arrive in just a minute or two," he said in a soft voice, a voice with slippers on. "Please be good enough to wait in here."

Sally went in, conscious now in the luxurious warmth of how wet she was, how bedraggled she must look. Her boots left puddles on the polished floor. Mr. Adcock had acquired his hat from the porter and was twisting its brim between nervous fingers.

The clerk withdrew. Sally saw no reason why she shouldn't sit down, so she sat.

"I've discovered something about Mr. Beech," she said. "Are you not going to sit down, Mr. Adcock?"

"Beech? Beech?" he said, sitting in the other upright chair which faced the desk.

"The clergyman who signed the marriage register," she said.

"To be sure. What have you discovered?"

"That he was resident for some time in—"

But Sally got no further, for the door was thrown open and

a large man, gown flying half-off one shoulder, entered briskly and dumped a fat pile of papers on the desk. Coarse black hair was trained over a bald crown; coarse reddish whiskers grew down his cheeks. His fleshy nose, puffy eyes, and heavy, brutal mouth were fit for carrying no expression at all except harsh, bullying scorn.

Mr. Adcock was on his feet in a moment, bobbing forward automatically, hands pressed together as if in supplication.

"Mr. Coleman, your clerk showed us in. We took the liberty of waiting for you—"

The barrister grunted. He took no notice whatsoever of Sally, but sat down and began turning over his papers.

"Well?" he said after a moment or two, without looking up.

"Er—my client Miss Lockhart was desirous of an interview, Mr. Coleman, if you recall. It was her feeling that, er, it might possibly clarify one or two minor—"

"Waste of time," said Mr. Coleman.

"I beg your pardon?" said Sally, startled.

He looked at her as if surprised. His small eyes radiated scorn.

"I said it's a waste of time. I've read all the papers; there's nothing to be gained from a meeting. Still, here you are."

He looked back at the papers in front of him and scanned the next one before making a note with a pencil. Sally could see that they concerned some commercial case—not hers at all.

"I was about to tell Mr. Adcock of a discovery I've made concerning the clergyman who—"

"Too late for that. You're not going to win this case by going around grubbing up so-called evidence."

"It may be important."

"It will only be important if it makes a difference and it won't."

"Then what will make a difference? How am I going to win this case, Mr. Coleman?"

"By not interfering with your counsel."

"I see. And will he win it by himself?"

His hot glare came up to seek her again. She met it with contempt. Beside her, Mr. Adcock was nearly melting with nervousness.

"I think Miss Lockhart would be anxious to affirm that—" he began, but the barrister spoke over him.

"Your case is a very poor one," he said gratingly, "and I do not hold out much hope of success. If you take the line that you are taking with me, I guarantee you will lose. Pertness and sarcasm do not impress me, and they will certainly not impress the court. Your only chance is to remain silent, to answer the questions you are asked as shortly and simply and politely as you are capable of doing, and not to presume that you know more than your betters about how to conduct something as subtle and difficult as a legal defense."

Sally was robbed of breath. She closed her eyes a moment, clenched her fists, heard him turn over another paper. She was aware of Mr. Adcock rocking gently back and forth beside her in an agony of apprehension. Then she took a breath and said, "And may I presume to ask what line you are going to take in my defense?"

"Not your business. I have read all the papers. That's all you need to know."

"If you have read all the papers, you will know that the issue of whether or not I was truly married to Parrish is central to the case. And if—"

He stood up, hooked his thumbs in his waistcoat pockets, and glowered down at her.

"The issue is one of morality," he said. "Of decency. And don't think for a moment that any sleight of hand with marriage certificates and signatures is going to alter that for a moment. You come before me, a woman who by her own admission has given away her virtue, who has behaved in a manner no better than a common prostitute, who seeks to deny the bastard she has conceived the dignity and benefit of a legitimate name and a home. That's what you look like: lascivious, greedy, weak-minded, and mean-spirited. Oh, stop

trying to protest. Your only chance of keeping your child is
to allow me to persuade the court that you are contrite. That
you're ashamed. That you bitterly regret your rash and
thoughtless action in abandoning your home. You keep quiet
and cry a little, and the court might be persuaded with the
help of my arguments that it would be in the unfortunate
child's interests to remain with you rather than with the father. I do not want to be prevented from making the best of
a bad job by your sentimental drivel about evidence—as if
this were a sensational novel to amuse idle women. You know
nothing about the law; it's not a woman's business. Stop fill-
ing your head with stuff you don't understand and then wasting my time with your stupid vaporings. Keep quiet and look
ashamed, and let me get on with the business of defending
you."

Sally sat unmoving for a few seconds, and then smiled
sweetly.

"How much am I paying you for this experience?" she
said. "On second thought, don't bother to answer. Gentlemen don't discuss money. Tell me: what will happen to my
child if I lose tomorrow?"

"You will be required to hand him over to his father at a
time and a place that the court will decide."

Sally's eyes opened wide involuntarily, and she caught her
breath. Plainly she wasn't as imperturbable as she'd thought.

"And you have, as you say, read the papers," she said
with a shaking voice.

"Of course," he returned contemptuously.

"A pity you failed to notice the many references to the
fact that my child is a girl, not a boy," Sally said, getting up.
"Thank you for making things clear to me. I have every confidence that you will perform in court as effectively as you've
done in here. Good day to you."

Without looking at Mr. Adcock, she turned and went out.
She heard the solicitor begin to gabble an apology, heard the
Q.C. cut him short, heard his hurrying footsteps leave the

building and hasten after her through the little passage into Middle Temple Lane.

She stopped at the end of the passage and let him catch up to her.

"Mr. Coleman," he began breathlessly, "is one of the most eminent, one of the most respected barristers in the kingdom. Had I thought that you would treat him to a display of—I'm afraid I must say it—pertness and insolence, I should never have—"

"Pertness and sarcasm, I think he said," Sally cut in. "That's wrong, anyway. If he didn't know my child was a daughter, he had no business to claim he'd read the papers."

"A detail."

"Oh, she's a *detail*, is she? That's lawyers' language for my child? I've heard enough lawyers' language for one day, thank you, Mr. Adcock."

She turned away, but felt his hand on her arm and stopped.

"Miss Lockhart, Mr. Coleman's intention, believe me, was to simulate for you the stress, the . . . discomfort that you will face in court tomorrow. It was a very valuable insight, a very helpful illustration of the kind of things which the other side will indubitably want to face you with. And if you recall, it was at your own insistence that I made this appointment for you. Mr. Coleman's time is so exceedingly valuable . . ."

"Good night," she said, and removed her arm from his grasp and walked away.

TWO HOURS LATER, thoroughly cold and wet, she arrived home. A hot bath, a sandwich, a glass of Webster's whiskey and hot water, some letters, a peep at Harriet, a sleepy kiss, bed. For the first time in weeks, she slept perfectly well. Her mind was made up. She knew just what she had to do.

10

Custody

CICELY CORRIGAN SAT AT THE BACK OF THE COURTROOM, on the public benches, trying to make sense of what she was hearing. She was nearly alone. At the other end of the bench there was a dark-haired man huddled up in a large gray overcoat, who spent the entire time scribbling in a little pad. Perhaps he was a starving poet, she thought, who spent his days in the law courts for the sake of a dry place to sit.

The case didn't take long. In the absence of the lady, the result was a foregone conclusion. Sally's counsel made a perfunctory effort to claim that she was so overcome with remorse and regret that she'd decided to mend her ways, and made an appeal to the court to put off the judgment for six months, during which time his side would attempt a reconciliation. But Mr. Parrish's counsel argued against that; the time for that had long gone, he said, and in any case Mr. Parrish had made numerous attempts both in person and through his solicitor to bring about a reconciliation already, to be met with nothing but contempt and rejection from the other party. Details and letters were, of course, available, should the court wish to examine them. The court did not. Mr. Parrish sat there looking modest and regretful, and rather noble, all things considered.

So not twenty minutes after it opened, the case was over and done with. The process of dissolving this invisible marriage was begun; and custody of the child Harriet Beatrice Rosa Parrish, known as Harriet Beatrice Rosa Lockhart, was granted to her father, Arthur James Parrish. Sally's lawyers were given notice that she was to produce the child at the chambers of Mr. Parrish's counsel before five o'clock that afternoon, the time now being eleven o'clock in the morning. If she didn't do that . . . They didn't spell it out, but Sally knew, and she'd explained it to Cicely: she'd be in contempt of court and in danger of arrest. The die was cast.

"BUT WHAT are you going to *do?*"

"Hide," said Sally. "And then prove him wrong. Have another teacake."

They were sitting in a tea shop in the Strand. Sally had been busy elsewhere all day, but she'd arranged to meet Cicely there at half past four. Margaret was with a client, or she'd have come as well. Cicely was still shocked by this new vision of her Miss Lockhart: the *mother* of a *child*. . . . She took the last teacake automatically and tried to stop staring at her.

"Where's the . . . where's your . . . where's Harriet now?" she said.

"With some friends. Quite safe. We'll be all right there for a day or so, and then I'll look for a place of our own."

"In London?"

"Well, if I can't hide in London, I won't be able to hide anywhere. I've thought about nothing else for days; I'm sure I'm right. If I go abroad I won't be able to find out what's behind this; I need to be on the spot. I need to do some detecting. It would be the same if I went to, I don't know, some village in the country or something. And I'd stick out like a sore thumb there, wouldn't I? But no one notices people in London. We're all anonymous. It's the only place to be. I'm only sorry I'm throwing such a burden on Miss Haddow. And on you. I'm terribly grateful, Cicely. . . ."

Miss Lockhart had changed. She wasn't low anymore; her eyes were bright, her cheeks were flushed, it looked as if she was happy, of all things. She finished her tea and called for the bill.

"Tell Miss Haddow I'll write to her tonight. I daren't come to the office, because they're bound to be watching, but I'll let her know where she can find me. I'll need to give as much time to this business as I can—she might need to take on extra help—but I'll say all that in my letter. Thanks for doing all this. It's not part of your job at all. . . ."

She left Cicely finishing her teacake, and pulled the fur collar of her cloak high around her neck and cheeks before going out into the damp afternoon.

It was nearly dark, and the streets were crowded. Sally waited for an omnibus, and when it came she sat in the crowded, swaying interior between a fat lady with a muff and a gentleman with a wet umbrella, turning over in her mind what she was going to do. Supper for Harriet first, and then she'd put her to bed and tell her they were going on an adventure in the morning, like Uncle Webster and Jim, and then they'd have their favorite nursery rhymes and Harriet would say her prayers.

And then when Harriet was asleep Sally would arrange with Mr. and Mrs. Molloy for them to act as a halfway house, a place where she could retreat to if she needed to, a place where she and Margaret could meet, a place to which Sarah-Jane Russell could relay any news from Twickenham. And then supper, and then bed. She wasn't tired, but she knew she'd sleep.

The omnibus stopped. She squeezed her way out and into the street. It was completely dark now; the street lamps glowed in the mist like huge ghostly dahlias. Passers-by hurried along with their heads down, huddled in their upturned collars and mufflers. A little crossing sweeper hovered near the cabmen's shelter, waiting to dart out and clear the road if anyone wanted to cross. At the corner of the square she was turning into, a hot-chestnut man stood hunched forlornly over his brazier, not even bothering to cry his wares and only stirring the chestnuts over the flame when they threatened to catch fire.

Sally entered the square. She'd lived here herself for some

time, before Harriet was conceived; the boardinghouse belonged to old friends of hers, a man called Trembler Molloy and his wife. Trembler had worked for Frederick when Sally had first met the Garlands, and when his wife had inherited a bit of money, Sally had advised them how to buy the house and set up in business.

The house itself was on the far side, beyond the trees in the little central garden, and she couldn't see it until she was halfway along one side. When she did, she stopped at once.

There was a cab outside the door. Two men were standing on the step, and one of them was a policeman.

Sally felt something clutch her heart. They couldn't have found her already, surely. . . . She shrank back and took a step down into the area of the nearest house, watching through the railings.

Mrs. Molloy's shape was visible inside the lighted doorway. She looked at something the policeman was showing her and shook her head. The other man moved up a step and seemed to be arguing, but again Mrs. Molloy shook her head. Sally couldn't hear a word they were saying, because of the rumble of traffic in the street behind and the constant heavy drip of moisture all around. It was like watching three tiny figures in a peep show.

Oh, keep them out, Sally was saying under her breath. . . .

Then the two men turned away, the policeman speaking over his shoulder. Mrs. Molloy shut the door with a bang that Sally did hear as they got into their cab.

The driver shook the reins, and the cab came away from the curb and headed down toward her. She retreated farther down the steps, conscious of the lighted kitchen window behind her, and drew the high collar of her cloak across her face.

As soon as the cab had turned the corner and disappeared from sight, she ran out of the area and flew along the pavement, slipping on the wet stone, grabbing the railing to get her balance again, and ran up the steps to hammer on the Molloys' door.

"It's me!" she called through the letter box. "Mrs. Molloy—it's me—"

She heard the lady's footsteps. A moment later the door opened, and Sally burst into the little hall.

"Is she safe? She's still here?"

"Good Lord, miss, what d'you take me for?" said Mrs. Molloy. "I wouldn't let 'em in, don't you fear. But he said they'd be back in half an hour with a search warrant. You'd best—"

"Half an hour? I must go. I'll take her now. Could you help me—could you put her outdoor clothes on? I'll go and throw some things in a bag, and perhaps Mr. Molloy could call a cab—"

"But where are you going to go, miss?"

"I don't know. Anywhere. I'll think about that in the cab. Please, Mrs. Molloy, in case they come back sooner—"

The lady, stout and firm-hearted, nodded agreement, but her face was full of doubt. Sally hurried up the stairs to her first-floor bedroom, seized the carpetbag she'd brought with her from Orchard House, threw in some clothes, some washing things, some shoes, and then her writing case from the bedside table; and finally a little package wrapped in oilskin, which dropped heavily into the nest of clothes in the bag. In it was the pistol.

She looked around, but she hadn't brought much with her anyway. Her purse—here it was; her checkbook, her keys.

Holding the bag shut, she hastened downstairs to find Mr. Molloy, mufflered and bowler-hatted, coming in through the door.

"There's a cab waiting, miss," he said. "It's a four-wheeler; it's a bit brisk for a hansom, and if you're going any distance . . ."

"Bless you," she said. "Is Harriet—?"

"The missus is seeing to her. It's a big adventure for her, I suppose. Though I don't know, they take a lot for normal, kids do, not knowing what normal is anyway. Nothing surprises 'em. Where you going to go, miss?"

"I honestly don't know. But I'll write as soon as I can and let you know where I am."

"Don't you worry, miss, we won't give you away. You could stay here if you wanted, you know."

"If they're going to come back with a warrant, they'd find us sooner or later."

A door opened, and a little shape came through, followed by Mrs. Molloy carrying a large paper bag.

"Mama," said Harriet, and then added in a muffled voice as Sally bent swiftly and embraced her, "Bikkits! Look."

She twisted impatiently out of the embrace and took the bag.

"I put some fresh-baked in," said Mrs. Molloy. "You never know, eh?"

"Let me take your bag, miss," said her husband.

Mrs. Molloy stooped to kiss Harriet, who absently returned the embrace while clinging tightly to the biscuits. She was so bundled up in her hat, coat, gloves, and boots that she could hardly waddle. Sally picked her up and put her own hat on with one hand, before snatching up her astrakhan purse-muff and hooking its cord swiftly around her neck.

"I pottied her and changed her diaper just a little while ago," Mrs. Molloy said in a whisper. "She won't need changing yet. Here, don't let me forget, they're all nice and aired, and there's all the washing things in there as well. . . ."

She picked up a big linen bag bulging with folded diapers and gave it to her husband, who just appeared in the doorway again. Sally wanted to say a hundred things, but there was only time for one.

"Thank you," she said. "I don't know what I'd have done. . . . I'll write to you tomorrow. Good-bye."

Harriet, peering out regally from under the brim of her fur hat, realized what was happening and transferred the biscuits to her left hand so as to wave good-bye with the right. Then, in a confusion of looks and thanks and clumsy movements, Sally and Mr. Molloy got the linen bag down and into the cab and Harriet seated inside next to the window.

"Where to, ma'am?" said the driver.

"Oh. Er—Charing Cross," said Sally.

She shut the door and sat down, taking Harriet on her lap. The driver called softly to his horse and released the brake, and the cab rolled away. Sally leaned forward, looking back and waving for as long as she could, until the cab turned the corner and the warm little doorway vanished.

BOOK TWO

II

Villiers Street

She found some lodgings in Villiers Street, a narrow little place beside Charing Cross Station. The lady of the house was German; she displayed no interest at all in anything but Sally's money. Sally paid a guinea in advance for a week's rent of a bedroom and parlor. Coals and candles were extra, and Sally paid for them; washing was to be sent out; meals could be provided by arrangement. Sally arranged them.

"Your name, please?" said the landlady, having noted down all the points they'd agreed on. They were standing in the chilly, dimly lit hall, with Harriet watching suspiciously, still clutching her bag.

"Mrs. Marchbanks," said Sally, off the top of her head. She kept her left hand in the muff: she must buy a wedding ring. What did widows wear? She'd have to be a widow; anything to be inconspicuous. There was so much to find out.

"Does she make wet the bed?" said the landlady.

"Oh, no. That is—not usually. Sometimes."

"I give you an oilcloth. Put it on the mattress, please. Come this way."

Carpetbag under her arm, linen bag of Harriet's things in her hand, Harriet on her other arm, Sally followed the landlady up the narrow stairs to a second-floor door. The landlady put down the lamp she was carrying on the window sill and took a key from a bunch, unlocking the nearest door.

"Here it is," she said. "I get you the oilcloth. Do not forget, please."

Sally entered the cold little parlor and sat Harriet on a sofa.

"There is only one bed," said the landlady. "She will have to sleep with you. I get some candles and fire. You wait."

She disappeared. Sally put down her carpetbag and went to the window. Villiers Street gleamed wetly in the light spilling from the pub next-door and the half-dozen street lamps; up to the right, the Strand was busy with the trundle of wheels, the clop of hooves, and the crying of two rival newspaper sellers outside the station. It was noisier here than in Islington, noisier by far than the near-total quiet of Orchard House.

"Mama," said Harriet. "Dark."

Sally turned and sat down, taking the child on her lap. She unfastened the fur bonnet and took it off, smoothing down the fair curly hair that was almost as stiff as her father's had been.

"Yes, it's dark, but the landlady's bringing some candles for us, and then we'll make it light. And we'll have a fire to keep us warm, and we'll have some biscuits, shall we?"

"All bikkits."

"We'll keep some for tomorrow. And then we'll put you to bed."

"*All* the bikkits."

"We'll see. Look, here comes the fire. . . ."

Harriet craned around to look at a lanky boy with a red nose who brought in a coal scuttle and a bucket containing a few hot coals and put them in the hearth. Without taking any notice of Sally or Harriet, he produced a candle from his waistcoat pocket, fitted it into the candleholder on the mantelpiece, and struck a match. Once it was lit he shoveled a few lumps of coal into the fireplace and then emptied the bucket onto it. He stirred the red coals into the rest and drifted out again.

"I hope that'll catch," Sally said. "I haven't got any matches. He might have brought some wood. . . ."

She got up and arranged the fire more purposefully. The

room looked a little more welcoming in the candlelight, though not by much. Harriet settled back in the sofa and tugged off her glove so she could put her thumb in her mouth.

"Tired, little one?" Sally said.

"Mmm."

"Don't go to sleep yet. Wait till we've got you undressed and in bed. Won't be long."

Presently the landlady came in with more candles, a little bundle of kindling wood, and a stiff oilcloth. She agreed to provide some milk for Harriet and some tea and bread and cheese for Sally; and five minutes later, the fire was burning brightly, the candles were glowing, the curtains drawn, and the door shut.

While Harriet sat at the table with her milk and biscuits, Sally took a candle into the bedroom. It was chilly, and the bed felt as if it hadn't been aired; there was a smell of dampness. Sally took off the blankets and sheets and brought them to warm in front of the fire, and then unfolded the stiff, crackling oilcloth and laid it over the mattress.

"You'll have to grow up quickly, little one," she whispered.

There was a chamber pot under the bed, a bathroom and water closet on the next floor down. Sally took the jug from the washstand in the bedroom and brought up some hot water, and then took out their washing things.

Harriet had finished the milk, and when Sally undressed her she found that she was still dry, which was a mercy. She was very sleepy; her cheeks were flushed, and she was chewing her thumb. Sally sat her on the pot and then washed her and put her nightdress on and brushed her hair, and then made the bed again with the sheets a little warmer now.

When she carried her to the bed, Harriet suddenly began to cry—desperate, howling sobs.

"What is it? What's the matter, dear?"

"Lamb! Lamb!"

Since the loss of Bruin, her woolly lamb had become her necessary bedtime toy. And they'd left him at the Molloys'.

Sally sat down on the bed and held Harriet close, rocking her gently as the child pressed her face into Sally's shoulder.

"Hush, darling, hush. Listen, we'll write a letter to Mrs. Molloy and ask her to give Lamb to the postman to bring here, shall we? We'll put the letter in the post tomorrow. We're having an adventure. Lamb's . . . Lamb's staying to look after Mr. and Mrs. Molloy for tonight. Because he's such a brave lamb. But look"—an idea came: she put Harriet down so quickly that her crying stopped from sheer surprise—"look, here's a mouse!"

Hoping she could remember how to do it, she swiftly took a handkerchief from the bag, shook it open, and folded it over, twisting and pulling and knotting until there was a rough-looking thing with two ears and a tail. Her father had shown her how to do it when she was young.

Harriet took it and clutched it to her chest with one hand, the other thumb still firmly in her mouth. Sally kissed her and laid her down on the crackly sheet and blew out the candle. A little light came through the open parlor door, and Sally could just make out the glint of tears on Harriet's cheeks. A wave of such powerful tenderness overcame her that her own eyes filled with tears and she felt a lump in her throat.

After a moment she controlled it and stroked Harriet's head and quietly sang a nursery rhyme.

> *"Lavender's blue, dilly, dilly,*
> *Lavender's green,*
> *When I am king, dilly, dilly,*
> *You shall be queen . . ."*

She remembered lying ill with her father sitting patiently in the darkness beside her, his deep voice singing those old songs, telling her stories, making her well again, keeping her safe. She'd never known her mother. He'd been father and mother to her, as she would have to be mother and father to Harriet.

Presently the child was asleep. Sally tucked the blanket around her and tiptoed into the parlor.

The fire was nearly out. She knelt and attended to it, feeding it a screw of newspaper, a stick or two, a fresh coal. When it was safe she stood up again and looked at her hands. There was no water to wash them in without going downstairs again; she brushed them on her skirt and sat down wearily at the table, pushing her hair out of her eyes with a wrist.

She took a deep breath and let it out slowly. Then she brought the candlestick a little closer, took a small exercise book and a pencil out of the carpetbag, and began to write.

25 October 1881

I don't know what to do. I don't know enough about washing her and feeding her, and I certainly don't know how we're going to manage, but many women do, after all. I'm so used to Sarah-Jane doing it all (*Mem:* Send her money for a month—should be over by then?), and I just didn't realize how much there was to do and think about.

What am I going to do?

We've got £10 or a little more in cash. I must go to the bank tomorrow and withdraw some more and open a new account in another name. And buy a wedding ring. Don't widows wear it on the other hand or something? Who can I ask? Why don't *I* know? I think we can live easily enough—we'll find somewhere nicer than this—but I mustn't—*must not*—have any contact with Orchard House or the Molloys or the shop or the office or anyone. Except letters.

Am I going to have to stay like this for the rest of my life?

Especially no contact with the lawyer. Will he be appealing against the decision? *Can* you appeal? I suppose I could write to him. But I think I've burned all my bridges there.

What I must do, since I can't prove H. is not his daughter, is find out why he's doing it and what's behind it. Behind him.

Find out everything I can. If he's doing anything criminal, they wouldn't give him custody.

And that clergyman. Mr. Beech. (*Mem:* Let Rosa know new address as soon as we're safe.) That's his weakest point, that lie in the register. If I can find out why

She broke off, hearing Harriet stir, but she was only muttering in her sleep. She put another couple of coals on the fire and sat down again.

then I'll know how to beat him. It's the only chance.

A LITTLE EARLIER in the evening, Ellie had heard a ring at the door of Orchard House. She looked up from the game of patience she was playing at the kitchen table and said, "Who can that be?"

"You'll never know if you don't go and see," said Mrs. Perkins, who was dozing over her newspaper in the rocking chair.

Ellie got up uneasily. She'd already had an awkward interview with the police, and so had Sarah-Jane Russell; she was beginning to wonder if she hadn't said too much to someone about where Sally had gone. Perhaps the sergeant had thought of some more questions, or perhaps they had a warrant to search the house.

But it wasn't a policeman. It was a dark-haired young man in a rough-looking overcoat. She took him at first for a tramp, especially as he had a funny accent of some kind, but he seemed polite enough.

"I am trying to find Miss Lockhart," he said. "Is she at home?"

"No, sir," said Ellie. "I don't know where she is."

"Who is in charge in her absence?"

Ellie heard Sarah-Jane behind her and looked around.

"May I know your name?" said Sarah-Jane.

"Daniel Goldberg. I'm a journalist. I know what's happened to Miss Lockhart, and I think I can help her, but I'll have to talk to her personally."

Ellie stood aside. Sarah-Jane didn't come any closer to the door; they were both a little afraid of strangers now.

"I can't tell you where Miss Lockhart is because I don't know," Sarah-Jane said. "She hasn't been home since this morning. I don't know when she's coming back. I don't think I ought to tell you even if I did know, but I really don't."

"May I leave a message for her here?" said the stranger.

"I suppose that can't hurt," said Sarah-Jane. "You're not going to write about this, are you? Is it going to be in the newspapers?"

"Not yet." He was scribbling something in a pocket book. He tore the sheet out, folded it, and wrote Sally's name on the back. "Please see she gets this. It's important. Good night."

He raised the wide-brimmed dark hat and turned away. Ellie shut the door after him.

Sarah-Jane was looking at the note dubiously.

"D'you think he's telling the truth?" said Ellie.

"I don't know. I just don't know anything. I suppose I could send this on to Mrs. Molloy's. . . . But if she's not there either, like that policeman said, she won't get it anyway."

"Better leave it, perhaps," said Ellie. "Till we hear from her."

Sarah-Jane nodded. She put the note on the hall stand, and Ellie went back to the kitchen.

12

The Bank Manager

SALLY WOKE UP SEVERAL TIMES IN THE NIGHT, FOR HARRIET was restless and the bed was narrow. Once she cried out, but Sally's warmth soon lulled her into quiet again.

When she judged it was time to get up, she got out of bed stiff and tired, putting on her dressing gown and leaving Harriet to sleep on while she lit the fire and put a kettle on to boil. Was it going to be possible to continue like this for long? she wondered. It was all so temporary. They must find a better place as soon as they could; then she could send for Sarah-Jane and start looking seriously for whatever lay behind this business.

She made some tea and then went back to wake Harriet. In that little time, she'd wet the bed. Sally stood indecisively. What did Sarah-Jane do? She couldn't remember. Well, what should *she* do?

She pulled back the covers to keep them dry and then lifted the child out. Harriet protested and struggled to go back, but Sally took her into the parlor and stood her by the fire before taking the sheet off the bed. Now what? She'd have to wash her, but could she leave her by an open fire while she fetched some water? Next time she'd know: have the water ready before she got her up. And make the tea afterward; it would be cold now before she drank it, and she could have used that water to wash her with.

"Stay there, darling," she said. "Mama's going to get some water. Don't go near the fire. . . ."

Taking the jug, she hurried down to the bathroom. It was occupied. More indecision; and then a door opened next to the bathroom and a man came out, dressed in an overcoat and a bowler hat. He looked at her, in her dressing gown, in open-mouthed amazement before looking away and going downstairs. She stood there blushing. Then the bathroom door opened and another man came out, also fully dressed. He paused like the first man and looked as if he'd say something, but frowned and went downstairs without a word.

She gritted her teeth and went in quickly, filled the jug from the gas heater, and hurried back up to Harriet, shutting the door firmly behind her.

"Come on, Hattie-face, let's get you clean," she said, pouring the water into the basin.

"No," said Harriet sleepily, and stamped her foot, nuzzling into Sally's thighs.

Sally removed the wet, clinging nightdress and sponged Harriet clean, and then wrapped a towel around her while she searched for clean clothes. But they'd left in such a hurry that she hadn't packed any stockings for Harriet.

"You'll have to wear yesterday's," she said. "Today we'll buy some more. And I think Mama will have to wear yesterday's as well. Come on, stand up now. . . ."

She coaxed the child into her clothes, and then saw that the fire had gone out. There was no more paper to relight it with.

"Oh, Hattie-face, this is going to be difficult, isn't it?" she said, sitting Harriet in the armchair.

The child looked at her with eyes that were still half-asleep, and then closed them as if in disdain, shrugging herself around to get comfortable on the cold, slippery leather.

"Yes, you stay there for a while," Sally said. "Mama will get dressed and then we'll . . . I don't know. We'll have breakfast."

She mopped the oilcloth on the bed dry with the sheet she'd taken off, and then got dressed. She'd go down and get some more water and then wash, but she didn't want any more encounters on the stairs in her night clothes. She must have more privacy.

And cleanliness. Until they found somewhere that was more their own, where they could settle for a while and send their washing out, she'd have to buy several pairs of stockings for both of them, and underclothing. Make a list after breakfast. Find another place.

She dressed, fetched water, undressed, washed, dressed again, and then felt a little better. Her watch told her it was eight o'clock, and the morning outside was damp and misty. She could hear the traffic from the Strand, and she lifted Harriet up to the window sill, holding her close, to point things out.

"Listen!" she said. "Can you hear the train?"

An engine was whistling somewhere behind the black wall of Charing Cross Station across the way. Harriet pointed down the street.

"Tommy!" she said.

A man with a milk cart was pouring milk into two large jugs held by a maidservant. His horse stood placidly by and shook its head.

"No, it's not Tommy, but it looks like him," Sally agreed. "It's a different milkman. It's the Charing Cross milkman."

There was plenty to see out of the window: a crossing sweeper, a news vendor, lots of cabs. Harriet liked the hansom cabs best, because of the stylish way they swung along. Then there was a policeman, big and fat as they should be, and two sparrows, and a pigeon, and a lady with a little black bouncy dog that made Harriet laugh. And then by pressing their faces to the glass they could just see the Strand and read the advertisements on the sides of the omnibuses going past. At least, Harriet thought she was reading them; she looked at them and said something while Sally spoke them clearly.

At half past eight there came a knock on the door, and the landlady came in with a tray of tea and toast and butter and marmalade. Harriet, not sure again where they were or who this was and not liking frowns, sat very still and suspicious while Sally explained about the sheet and asked for some paper and wood to make the fire.

Then they went into the bedroom. Harriet looked at the tray. It was very thin toast. She wondered if it tasted like thick toast, or different. Then Mama and the lady came out of the bedroom, and Mama's face was angry, and the lady was carrying the wet sheet and her face was cross. They were cross with her, thought Harriet, and felt frightened.

But then the lady went out and Mama came and kissed her and they had some toast. It didn't taste different, but the marmalade did, and so did the milk.

What had happened was that the landlady had told Sally of various complaints she had received, to the effect that Sally had appeared improperly dressed in front of several gentleman lodgers. This was an intolerable state of affairs and she would have to leave that very day.

Sally's protests had done no good at all. The landlady's mind was made up, fixed, resolute, even to the extent of refunding Sally's rent for the rest of the week. Sally would have to leave as soon as the two of them had had breakfast.

Once the row (very decorous, no raised voices, grim politeness on both sides) was over, and she was sitting down buttering Harriet's toast, Sally felt almost light-hearted. *Kismet,* she thought. *Fate. We didn't like this place anyway.*

"We're going to find another house today," she said to Harriet. "And then we'll send for Sarah-Jane to come and live with us, shall we?"

"And Lamb."

"Oh, and Lamb, yes. Of course. We'll write to Mrs. Molloy, and she can give Lamb to the postman, remember? Eat up now. We'll pack all our things and then we'll go and do that. We've got all day this time."

THREE QUARTERS of an hour and a frosty exchange with the landlady later, Sally and Harriet found themselves in the

Strand. It wasn't quite drizzling, but it was cold and damp, the air so saturated with moisture that Sally saw it condense and settle on the fur of her purse-muff even before they'd left Villiers Street.

She wanted first to go to her bank, the London and Counties, which was only a few hundred yards away. Clutching the bags tightly in one hand and holding Harriet with the other, she made her way through the jostling crowd—newsboys, bootblacks, clerks hastening to work, ladies shopping, commissionaires on duty, messenger boys racing through the throng like fish through gray weeds—conscious all the time that Arthur Parrish's office was not far from here, and that she must not be seen.

She told herself that that was ridiculous, that in a busy street like the Strand she was as safe as anywhere in the world, but still she felt nervous; and conspicuous, too, with her heavy bags.

She reached the bank and turned inside, and sat Harriet on a chair beside the luggage.

"You look after that," she said. "Mama's going to get some money."

There was two hundred pounds in her account. If she withdrew it and opened another account somewhere else in another name, she'd be able to take out a year's lease on a small house or a flat and live quite comfortably. She wasn't altogether happy about the idea of carrying around that much cash, but there was no need to go far—there were plenty of banks nearby; and if she asked for a check to be drawn, they might be able to trace her. Cash was untraceable.

She went to the cashier and explained what she wanted. She was about to write a check when she saw his expression.

"Excuse me a moment, Miss Lockhart," he said, and stood up. "I must just check something with the manager."

With a curious glance at her, he left for an inner office. Sally felt alarm bells ringing in her heart. She looked around; Harriet was playing quietly, counting the rings on the turned mahogany leg of the table beside her. The doorman, resplendent in his uniform, stood benevolently by, lifting his cap as he opened the door to a lady going out. Would he stop her if she had to run out with Harriet?

"Miss Lockhart?"

The manager was standing behind the counter, together with the embarrassed-looking cashier. The manager was a middle-aged, balding man with a condescending smile; Sally had spoken to him on only two occasions before, neither of them in the last year.

"I want to draw some money out of my account," said Sally. "Is there anything the matter?"

"I think I should speak to you privately," he said. "Would you be kind enough to come into my office?"

Sally thought: *This is bad news. He's going to tell me something bad.* The cashier exchanged a glance with the manager and then went and spoke to the doorman, as if he were sharing a joke.

She picked up Harriet and followed the manager through the door at the end of the banking hall. He sat down behind his desk before he spoke. Sally sat opposite, Harriet on her lap, feeling frightened.

"What is it, Mr. Emes? Why can't I have my money?"

"There is no money in your account," he said. "In fact, the account is now closed."

She felt her jaw drop. *It really does drop,* she thought foolishly, and then gathered herself.

"I beg your pardon? What's happened to my money? There was two hundred pounds in that account. Where is the money now?"

"Your, ahem, your husband came in as soon as the bank opened this morning, with documents from the court empowering him to . . . I was not in a position to, you understand . . . He was accompanied by his solicitor, and—"

"You gave him my money?"

"His money. In the eyes of the law, a wife's personal

property is the husband's, to dispose of as he will. Unless there was a marriage settlement, that is to say. And the solicitor—"

"But I'm not married to that man! I never have been! He is not my husband!"

Harriet was looking up at her, wide-eyed, alarmed. Sally stroked her hair automatically.

"Miss, er, Miss Lockhart, there was no possible doubt. The solicitor had all the necessary papers. I was astonished when the, ah, information first came to me, as you can well imagine. But I have taken every step I could to make sure I was doing the right thing."

"You mean you knew about this before? Well, why in heaven's name didn't you tell me?"

"You were not here."

"But *my money*—" Sally swept her hand across her face and found herself helplessly shaking her head.

"Legally, his money. I must remind you of that. The bank has done nothing wrong."

"You let that man—that stranger—walk out with all my money?"

The shock was too much for anger. She sat there breathless and dazed.

"Hardly a stranger, I think," he said. "It is a well-established principle of law that the husband—"

"How long has he been preparing this?"

"Naturally the bank would not part with a client's money on the spur of the moment. We have had notice of this for some time. It required only the production of the necessary papers for the formalities to be completed, and with yesterday's court order—"

Sally stood up. In the middle of her shock, she had remembered the cashier and the doorman. Was he giving the man a message? Parrish's office was only a street or two away; he might be hurrying there at this very minute. She gathered up Harriet and held her close.

"You've behaved abominably," she said to the manager.

"I can't find the words or I'd tell you how disgusting you are. You allow that man—that thief—to steal all my money; you hand it over the counter to him, and you don't even warn me about it. You squalid little cheat, you coward . . ."

His pinched face looked as mean as a rat's. His cheeks gleamed sweatily, but his smile was as bland as ever. She turned swiftly and walked out. The cashier was standing in the entrance to the bank as if watching for someone; the doorman had gone. She'd been right. As she marched toward the door, the cashier made a half-hearted movement as if to stop her going out, and she stood still.

"You lay a finger on me," she said clearly, "and you'll regret it as long as you live. Now get out of my way at once."

People turned; Sally was conscious of astonished faces, craning heads. She took a step toward the cashier, and he fell back. She opened the door and went out, and a minute later she was two hundred yards away in the crowded anonymity of the Strand.

AND HARRIET was tugging at her hand. She wanted to whisper something. Sally bent down and listened, but she couldn't hear what the child was saying. She picked her up, but there was still a roaring in her ears; she just kissed her swiftly and walked on. Harriet fell silent. Normally Sally chatted and Harriet burbled, and though it wasn't really a conversation, they were conversing all the same. Sally, tight-lipped and tense, wasn't talking this morning, so Harriet wasn't either.

It wasn't ten o'clock yet, she saw from the clock over a tobacconist's shop. Perhaps she should sit down, have a cup of coffee, talk to Harriet, calm herself a little.

That was a good idea. There was a tea shop, just over the road. Within five minutes they were sitting at a corner table, and Harriet was clutching a large glass of milk while Sally watched the waitress pour some steaming coffee from a silver jug.

"Could you bring me a newspaper?" she said.

"Certainly, ma'am," said the girl.

Ma'am again. She'd have to get used to it. She was Mrs.
. . . oh, Mrs. Jones. And she was exhausted already, and it
was only ten o'clock. And all that money . . . she was trembling. What could she do? Well, there was enough left in her
purse to find another lodging house and last for a couple of
weeks. And that would give her time to write to Margaret
and arrange to sell some shares.

"Mama?"

"Yes, dear?"

"I want Lamb."

"Yes, I know. As soon as we're in our new house we'll
write for him, remember?"

"What new house?"

"Well, we didn't like the house we lived in last night, so
we're going—thank you," she said to the waitress bringing
the paper. "We're going to look for another one. A nice one."

"And Sarah-Jane," said Harriet firmly.

"Well . . . not at first. But soon. Soon, I promise. We've
got to find a nice house. And we will. But Mama's got to
look in the paper to see where to go."

"Why?"

"Because . . . because that's where you have to look. In
advertisements. Now hush while Mama looks."

Harriet subsided, though she was far from satisfied. She
pulled off her gloves and ran her fingernail along the raised
pattern in the tablecloth. The smells here were nice. She
couldn't remember not liking the house they'd lived in last
night. She couldn't remember much of it at all, though she
remembered her own proper bedroom with the rocking horse
and Bruin's lair that Uncle Webster had made, and the dollhouse. She suddenly wanted the dollhouse very much.

Then Mama made a coughing sound, like the cough she
made when she got a crumb in her throat. And her eyes were
big and wet, and her cheeks were red. Harriet watched, interested.

The story Sally had seen read:

MISSING
FLIGHT OF WIFE AFTER COURT'S JUDGMENT

Following a decision in the High Court yesterday, a wife and child have vanished for the second time.

Mr. Arthur Parrish, a commission agent, of 24, Telegraph Road, Clapham, brought the action against his wife, suing for custody of their child. Mrs. Parrish had left their home some months before.

Custody was granted yesterday by Mr. Justice Hawke. Almost at once, however, it was found that Mrs. Parrish and her daughter Harriet, age 2, had flown from the address where she was known to be staying. Their whereabouts are still unknown.

Mrs. Parrish is 24 years old, with fair hair and brown eyes. She may be using the name of Lockhart, which is the name she assumed when she deserted the matrimonial home on the previous occasion.

Police have instituted a search and have taken out a warrant for her arrest on a charge of abduction.

Sally thrust away the paper and looked around blindly with eyes that she had to mop. How many people had seen this? And what was wrong with the laws of England, that they let a woman be hunted for kidnapping her own child?

Fiercely she reached out to Harriet and lifted her onto her lap, hugging her. Harriet wriggled around to look up into her face.

"Mama?"

"What is it, little one?"

"Want a bun. Effant bun."

"Oh—" Sally found herself laughing and mopped her eyes again. "An elephant bun. Like the ones we gave the elephant in the zoo, yes? Well, what have you got to say?"

"Please."

"That's better."

Sally called the waitress and asked for a bun and some more coffee. Thank heaven for tea shops, she thought. If you had a few pennies you could stay there as long as you liked, and they brought you food and drink and newspapers.

She looked out at the crowds passing. It wasn't possible that anyone would recognize her, was it? Perhaps they should go abroad after all. Perhaps she should dye her hair.

When Harriet had finished, Sally paid the bill and gathered the bags once more. Harriet came placidly, taking it all for granted.

She thinks I know what I'm doing, Sally thought.

Miraculously, an empty cab appeared as soon as they were outside. She hailed it and asked the driver to take them to Bloomsbury. Within a minute they were bowling along the southern side of Trafalgar Square, and Harriet was clinging to Sally's hand and watching the horse's gleaming back, glossy with dampness, and the reins leading down from the driver's seat above and behind them, shaking to the right as they turned out of Cockspur Street and up into the Haymarket.

Why Bloomsbury, Sally couldn't have said, except that she'd found safety there once before, in the photographer's shop. Harriet had been conceived there on the night Fred died. Bloomsbury was safe, somehow. She wondered that she hadn't thought of it before.

She paid off the driver in Russell Square, and she and Harriet stood there like newly disembarked passengers.

"Which way shall we go?" she said.

"Go home," said Harriet.

"We're going to find a house," Sally said. "That'll be our home. Where shall we look first? This way? Across there? Down that street? You choose."

Harriet considered. The square was very big. Sally picked her up so that she could see more, and she pointed to a street on the east side.

"All right," said Sally. "We'll look down there. Be a good girl and keep close while we cross the road."

The bags were getting heavier. Harriet trotted obediently

beside her as they moved down the street she'd chosen: tall brick houses, classically simple, but all rich-looking. There was nothing for them there.

Sally turned down a narrower street, and then into a little court closed off from traffic by a gate. It was called Wellcome Passage.

"This looks nice, Hattie-face," she said. "Let's knock on a door. Which one shall we knock on?"

Harriet pointed. Sally knocked. A young maid-of-all-work answered, peering around the door at both of them as Sally said, "I'm looking for lodgings. Do you know if anyone in this court keeps rooms to let?"

"Mrs. Parker at number five, ma'am," said the maid. "I dunno if she's got any spare rooms, mind. Just over there."

Number 5 was a shabby-looking place, tall and narrow like all the other houses thereabouts, with a battered-looking front door and a knocker that hadn't been polished for years. But it was smooth with use, so the house wasn't unvisited, and the window sills were crowded with flowers.

Another maid, older this time, less tidy, less curious, came to the door.

"Yes'm, there's a room free, 'm; I'll get Mrs. Parker, 'm. Come in out the damp."

The narrow hall was crowded with an umbrella stand and a bicycle, and the walls were crowded with pictures—bad watercolors, clumsily framed. The house smelled of cabbage.

After a few minutes the lady of the house, a little, round, bustling woman with bright eyes, came out of the kitchen wiping her hands on an apron.

"Good morning," said Sally. "I believe you have a room to let? I'm looking for lodgings."

"Yes . . . yes," said Mrs. Parker dramatically, standing back and gazing at Sally as if measuring her for a costume. "Oh, yes." Her voice was deep and dramatic, with a touch of cockney. "We have met before."

"Have we? I don't think—"

"On the plane of souls. As an adept, I recognize the signs. You are young in the spirit, my dear, so you probably wouldn't. What name are you going by in this incarnation?"

That question was uncomfortably close to the mark. Sally blinked and then remembered. "Oh—Mrs. Jones. And this is my daughter Harriet."

Harriet was poking at the bicycle pedal. Sally picked her up in case she made it fall over. Mrs. Parker gazed intensely at Harriet, who stared back stolidly.

"She has a wise soul," said Mrs. Parker. "And you—you have a young soul. You are troubled, my dear. You have secrets. Come this way. . . ."

She led the way up two flights of stairs. The place was unevenly clean, with varying patches where it smelled intensely of furniture polish or cigar smoke. On the second landing Mrs. Parker unlocked a green-painted door.

"The Green Room," she said. "The colors we see in the physical world are emanations from the infinite, you know. Their vibrations act on the soul. For you, Mrs. Jones, I should really prescribe blue, only a commercial gentleman's got the Blue Room for six months. You won't come to no harm in green, though."

The room was shabby but comfortable. There were more dire paintings on the wall; they looked like imaginary landscapes, with lots of green in them.

"Er, how much—?"

"A guinea a week," said Mrs. Parker. "With meals, twenty-seven shillings and sixpence. Coals and gas extra, washing sent out."

"There's only one thing. My daughter"—she put Harriet, who was starting to wriggle, down on a chair and went on quietly—"well, she sometimes—"

"In here," said Mrs. Parker, opening the bedroom door and showing Sally through. "Bed-wetting?" she went on. "One of the minor inconveniences of the physical world. Don't you worry about that, my dear. We'll slip this India rubber sheet over the mattress. Admiring the paintings? My son Rodney does 'em. He guides my hand, that is to say, him being in the spirit world. Our meals here, Mrs. Jones, are strictly vegetarian—you won't mind that I'm sure—and they're taken in the dining room. How long was it you wanted the room for?"

"Oh, a week. To start with. I've just come to London, you see. We shall be looking for a more permanent place. . . ."

"Widowed?" said Mrs. Parker cheerfully.

"Harriet's father died before she was born."

"He sees her now, my dear, he sees her now. Luncheon in twenty minutes. Lizzie will make up the fires and the beds. I'll trouble you for a week's rent in advance."

Sally paid for the week's rent and meals, and for coal and for the gas she'd be using in the lights; and discovered that as well as all the spiritual privileges on hand, she and Harriet would have exclusive use of the bathroom and lavatory next-door, there being no one else on this floor.

"I do believe in the desirability of hygiene in all kinds of personal affairs," said Mrs. Parker at the top of the stairs, nodding briskly to a lanky youth emerging from a door at the foot of them.

"Oh, so do I," said Sally.

When the lady had gone, Sally went back into the bedroom and took off her hat and gloves. Harriet was playing with the wardrobe door, looking at herself in the mirror that backed it. Sally sat down on the larger of the two beds in the tiny room and, overcome by weariness, lay back and closed her eyes.

Only a minute later, it seemed, Harriet was shaking her hand.

"Mama! Mama!" she was saying.

Someone was knocking at the door. Sally struggled up and hastened to open it.

"Mrs. Parker says luncheon is being served," said the maid wearily.

"Thank you," said Sally. "We'll be down directly. Come on, Hattie, let's wash our hands."

As the maid slumped off downstairs Sally hastily took off Harriet's coat and hat, brushed her hair, took her to the lavatory, washed her hands, and then—remembering—took the rest of her little stock of money from her coat pocket and tucked it into the bosom of her dress. Then they hurried downstairs.

Luncheon consisted of curried vegetables, potatoes, and batter pudding and jam. Harriet refused to eat it, making Sally uncomfortable: Should she insist and make a scene? Should she allow her to leave it for the sake of peace? She found herself feeling, among all her other emotions, ashamed that she knew so little about her own daughter's eating habits. Sarah-Jane Russell had taken charge of all that sort of thing so efficiently and so discreetly that Sally had hardly noticed that she herself was doing nothing. She was noticing now, with a vengeance.

She made Harriet eat up all her batter pudding, which entailed staying at the table after the others had left. When they'd finally done, she set off back to their rooms, only to meet Mr. Parker on the stairs.

He looked around conspiratorially, stuck his tongue in his cheek, and, leaning close, said quietly, "Anytime you want a meat pie—nice little shop around the corner—got an interest. I sometimes slip out for a meat pie of an evening—don't tell Mrs. P. Bring you back one, if you like."

Twinkling with his immense hidden enjoyment, he went on down.

Sally found that the beds had been made up, and as Harriet was yawning, she decided to let her sleep for a while. She found the handkerchief-mouse at the bottom of the carpetbag and remade it, and Harriet clutched it to her at once, closed her eyes, and fell asleep.

Sally went into the parlor, shut the door, and sighed with such a deep weariness that it turned into a yawn that felt as if it would never end. Then she sat down, took out her exercise book, and wrote:

Moved already. I can't write about the other place; too beastly. This is shabby but friendlier. Oh, and the money . . . For an hour or so I haven't even thought about it. But for him to take it like that—and the manager to let him get away with it, planning it for days, not telling me.

She broke off there. She was crying with anger. She rubbed her eyes roughly and went on:

No good crying. I've got three pounds and six shillings, and food and lodging paid for a week.

Things to do:

Immediately

1. Write to Margaret—messenger? Sell Anglo-Egyptian, Grand Trunk of Canada—hold it in *her account.* Or money belt, carry cash.
2. Write to Molloys—Lamb.

Later

3. Find somewhere to live.
4. Bring Sarah-Jane to help—can't go investigating Parrish while looking after H.
5. Find out why.

She put the pencil down and shivered, and then realized that she could light a fire if she wanted to. The gray afternoon was still and chilly outside, but at least it *was* outside. She realized with a shock that it was less than twenty-four hours since she'd seen Cicely in the tea shop. Only this time yesterday she'd had a home and a daughter and money. What was she now? A refugee?

She made up the fire and lit it, and then washed her hands and began to unpack.

13

The Tea Shop

AFTER HE HAD TAKEN SALLY'S MONEY FROM HER BANK AND deposited it prudently in his, Mr. Parrish went to his office. He looked in at Rubinstein, the tobacconist downstairs, and wished him good morning; he checked the postbox; he greeted his two clerks, and having cast a careful eye around, he sat down to a profitable morning's work.

When his gold-plated American Watch Company time-piece told him it was twelve o'clock, he took his coat and hat and set out again. He walked briskly along the Strand and up Fleet Street, and went on past St. Paul's Cathedral and the Bank of England and into Cornhill. He enjoyed the walk. He swung his arms and breathed deeply, using his diaphragm, according to the method advocated by Dr. Alver, of the Swedish Institute of Sciences, whose lectures on hygiene he had attended the previous spring.

In Cornhill he consulted a newspaper and looked around for number 14. When he found it—an office building bearing a discreet brass plate on which were the words ARTHUR C. MONTAGU, PRIVATE INQUIRY AGENTS—he went straight in.

There were a number of such inquiry agents in London then, and Montagu's was the biggest: a thrusting, dynamic, go-ahead firm, with twenty years' experience, a large and well-trained staff, and all bathed in the utmost discretion. If you wanted to find out who'd run away with your husband, or why your chief clerk was looking so uncommonly prosperous just when you were finding the tills emptier than they should be, Arthur C. Montagu and his discreet staff would deploy their twenty years' experience, find out, and send you the bill. They advertised—discreetly—in *The Times,* which was where Mr. Parrish had first come across their name.

He was soon sitting in a neat, modern office, bristling with voice tubes, pneumatic message pipes, and typewriting machines. A keen young operative was taking notes.

"Wife—description? Ah! Photograph. Capital. And daughter—age? Name? Picture? No? Pity. Vanished when? Yesterday. Posing as Lockhart, of Garland and Lockhart, photographers, Twickenham. Any reason to think she might have gone abroad? We have instant communication by telegraph with offices in Paris and Berlin, Mr. Parrish. And the new telephone system will be installed any week now. No? Still in London, possibly? Possibly not. Any names of associates, friends . . . Taylor . . . Garland . . . Bertram: Hon. Charles Bertram—who's he? Partner of Garland, at present in South America. She wouldn't have gone there, would she? Office in the City, financial consultancy—dear me. Enterprising lady, your wife, sir. Yes, of course, rather she didn't, quite so, unbecoming, yes; but this is the new age, what? Emancipation! Eh? Very well, Mr. Parrish, we'll set some inquiries in train. You understand—can't promise—big place, London. Still, Arthur C. Montagu's good, confounded good, dashed good. Arnold! Circulate this description at once, and send in Mr. Billings."

Mr. Billings was the agent who was going to do the actual searching. He looked suitably tenacious, with enough of a bloodhoundlike droop to his expression to inspire confidence.

Mr. Parrish paid a deposit against Mr. Billings's expenses and went on his way, having pocketed a leaflet explaining Arthur C. Montagu's scale of charges. There was another call he had to make, in accordance with the advice he'd once heard given by Gentleman Jack Draper, the famous middleweight: when they're on the ropes, hit 'em hard, all at once, with everything you've got.

MR. BILLINGS was a methodical man, even more methodical than Mr. Parrish, despite his lack of acquaintance with the scientific business principles on which Mr. Parrish's success was founded. Shortly after leaving the office, he was turning into Bengal Court, a narrow little place between four churches. Sunlight never penetrated here; everything wore an air of grim moneymaking duty, covered in dust. Number 3 was as dark and austere as all the rest. Mr. Billings, despite his face and his calling, was a cheerful man at heart, and he looked around with some distaste. No place for a woman, he thought as he entered number 3.

There was a porter on duty behind a sliding window, who referred Mr. Billings to the third floor; and when he reached that level, he found the air lighter and the aspect altogether more pleasing, for the window sill on the landing bore a cheerful plant of some kind, and the window itself looked out at a fine church tower with an absurd little dome on top of it, and beyond that to the Mansion House.

There was a door with a sign saying S. LOCKHART, FINANCIAL CONSULTANT, at which he knocked.

"Come in," said a female voice.

As easy as that? he thought. *Surely not . . .*

The young lady at the desk was in her early twenties and was not Miss Lockhart, or Mrs. Parrish. *She* was pretty, according to the photograph he was carrying; this one wasn't. At least, not at a first glance. She had an expression full of a kind of amused confidence which Mr. Billings didn't like above half, since she looked too damn shrewd. The last time Mr. Billings had seen a look like this was when his aunt had caught him smoking a cigar behind the garden shed. He wouldn't be able to put much past this one.

Still, he could try.

"Miss Lockhart?" he said.

"No, I am Miss Haddow. Miss Lockhart is away. Can I help you?"

"Ah, well, it's really Miss Lockhart I wanted to see. I represent Messrs. Gillray and Gillray, solicitors, and it's in connection with a will. Miss Lockhart's been left a sum of money, and—"

"May I see your card?"

Brisk, too. He found a card in his waistcoat pocket and handed it over, and was slightly dismayed to see her reach for a *Kelly's Directory* from the shelf behind her. If she looked up the address on the card, she'd find it listed as an accommodation address, and only a step or two's more research would disclose that the tenants were Arthur C. Montagu, private inquiry agents. *Better play it straight*, he thought; *she's too quick to fool, this one.*

But before he could say anything, there was a knock on the door; and that was the point at which Sally's luck ran out.

Miss Haddow opened the door and said, "Would you mind waiting just a moment? I'm busy with a visitor—"

"Message from Miss Lockhart, miss," said a military voice.

Mr. Billings could see through the open door: the visitor was a commissionaire. An idea struck him.

"Just a moment, miss," he said, and stepped forward. They were all three clustered around the door now, but the other two were momentarily nonplussed, and a moment was all he needed. "There've been a number of cases lately of men in commissionaires' uniforms imposing on members of the public. Have you got your ticket book?" he demanded of the man.

The commissionaire, a stout, gray-haired man with several medal ribbons on his breast, was about to reply, but Miss Haddow cut in sharply: "Employers are entitled to inspect ticket books. I'm not aware that anyone else is."

"That's all right, miss," said the commissionaire. "I'll show my ticket book to anyone."

He produced a folded booklet. Mr. Billings took it from him, looked at it swiftly, and then said, "Good afternoon, miss." He thrust the ticket book back at the commissionaire and set off downstairs.

Margaret Haddow watched him go, perplexity turning into

annoyance. She felt she'd been outmaneuvered, though she couldn't see how, and she took the letter from the commissionaire, tipped him, and sat down to read it.

"CAB! CAB!"

Mr. Billings was in luck. An empty hansom happened to be passing; the driver heard him and turned abruptly, causing a crossing sweeper to skip onto the curb for dear life and release a jet of language, some of which was new to Mr. Billings.

"Office of the corps of commissionaires, in the Strand," called Mr. Billings, leaping in. "I don't mind how fast you go."

The driver was a sporting kind of a man; he'd winged one or two crossing sweepers before, and he was always willing to bag another. He shook the reins, flicked his whip, and urged the hansom out into a narrow gap between a four-wheeled carriage and a builder's wagon, raising a cry of alarm from the first and a volley of curses from the other. Then they were clattering and swaying and bouncing like a Roman chariot down Lombard Street. Mr. Billings clung to his hat approvingly, blessing the strict rules of the corps of commissionaires.

The corps was formed of retired soldiers and sailors, and you could hire a commissionaire to go on an errand, or take a message, or carry a parcel, or deliver circulars, or take money or check tickets at a door, or watch over an empty building at night—do more or less anything, in fact; and there was a regular tariff for all these jobs, which was printed in the ticket book Mr. Billings had demanded.

Also printed in each commissionaire's ticket book was his personal number, which in the case of imitation or fake commissionaires, they had not got. Mr. Billings had noted the number of this genuine example of the species. He was hoping, now, that he'd beat Miss Haddow to the punch.

The cab drew up with a fine flourish of the whip, a tug on the brake, a skid of the wheels; and Mr. Billings leaped out, threw a coin to the driver, calling out "Wait there!" and raced into the building.

There was a sergeant on duty at the desk, waxed and polished and whiskered. Mr. Billings wasted no time.

"Commissionaire number three eighteen," he said. "A corporal. Can you find out where he is now?"

"Why, sir?"

"Urgent. Police business. We need him as a witness in a murder case—oh, beg pardon: my card. Solicitors. Apparently your number three eighteen can vouch for our client's alibi—it might make the difference between getting him off and seeing an innocent man hanged. Where is he, quick?"

The sergeant was as willing to be impressed by the gallows as anyone. He turned to a large appointment book and leafed through it, licking a finger to help turn the pages.

"Three eighteen—Corporal Lewis," he said. "Message to be taken to an address in Bengal Court, in the City. On behalf of a Miss Lockhart, number five, Wellcome Passage, Bloomsbury. He set off at—"

"I'll find him," said Mr. Billings, and dashed out again, leaving the sergeant still poised with his finger over the appointment book.

MARGARET HADDOW crumpled Sally's letter and swore. It was a word she'd heard a cabman use once, and she judged it appropriate now.

She *had* been outmaneuvered. That bowler-hatted bloodhound would have discovered Sally's address by now—or he would very soon, and what then? The only thing to do was go there herself at once. And she had an appointment in twenty minutes: a client who was coming to see her, and he'd been put off once already. They couldn't really afford to lose him, but equally she couldn't let Sally down.

She looked through into the other office, where Cicely Corrigan was filing some letters.

"I've got to go out," she said. "Emergency. Now, listen— Mr. Patten's coming in about twenty minutes. You'll have to give our profound apologies and make another appointment for him. I'm sorry to let you in for—"

"That's him now, isn't it?" said Cicely.

They listened. There were voices outside. Margaret closed her eyes in exasperation and thought swiftly.

"You'll have to go yourself then," she said. "It's *very* important. Get your coat and hat and take a cab to Wellcome Passage in Bloomsbury—got that? Go to number five. Keep the cab waiting. Miss Lockhart's there. Tell her to go to the . . . oh, to the British Museum, that's not far, and meet me in the Assyrian Room. She mustn't stay at that address, Wellcome Passage. I'll be along as soon as I can. Oh—money for the cab. Here you are. Use it to come back here when you've taken her to the museum. Quick now—it's desperately important."

Bewildered but willing, Cicely struggled into the shabby coat and last year's hat and took the money, while Margaret hastened to open the door.

As Cicely hurried down the stairs, Margaret turned to her visitor and was slightly disconcerted to find that there was someone else there besides Mr. Patten. That someone else was the result of Mr. Parrish's remembering Gentleman Jack Draper's advice; but Margaret wouldn't know that for a few minutes yet.

MR. PARRISH was transacting some business on behalf of a missionary society when Mr. Billings rushed into the outer office and spoke to his clerk.

"I hesitate to interrupt Mr. Parrish in the execution of his duty," said the clerk, a fish-faced young man of high moral standards. "He has with him at the moment the national secretary of the United Missions to South India and Ceylon. I don't think—"

"Take him this, son," said Mr. Billings, scribbling the words I HAVE MISS LOCKHART'S ADDRESS—EZ. BILLINGS on an Arthur C. Montagu card. "Go on. Don't stand there gaping."

The clerk gulped and knocked at the inner door. Mr. Parrish

didn't like being interrupted at the best of times, but he could only try. . . .

His employer took the card, eyed it narrowly, and stood up at once.

"Is he outside?" he said.

"Yes, Mr. Parrish."

"Tell him to wait. You'll have to excuse me, Mr. Pryor; urgent business. We'll discuss the furnishing of your mission another day. But in the meantime we'll have those Bibles and solar topees shipped out to Madras on the very next steamer. Good day, sir. See Mr. Pryor out, Blake, come along."

The missionary, who had been looking forward to thinking about mosquito nets and punkahs, found himself hustled out and given his hat, and a moment later Mr. Parrish was donning his own.

"Where?" was his only word to Mr. Billings.

"Bloomsbury. I got a cab waiting."

"Good man."

A minute later they were bowling up Drury Lane. The cabdriver was enjoying his afternoon.

CICELY CORRIGAN, more than a little nervous, ran to the cab rank in King William Street. She'd never taken a cab on her own before, though she'd been in one with her father once; how much should she tip the driver? She'd heard they were terribly abusive if you didn't give them enough. . . .

She wished she had Miss Lockhart's ease or Miss Haddow's assurance; they were both so grown-up. Was it going to university that did that for you?

Well, she'd have to do her best without it. She ran to the cab at the head of the rank and said, "Bloomsbury, please. Number five, Wellcome Passage."

"Right you are, miss," said the cabbie as she got in, and flicked the reins. They moved away.

That was easy enough. And after all, she could always ask Miss Lockhart about a tip.

But he didn't seem to be going very fast. Of course, the traffic was heavy; they were stuck behind a slow-moving omnibus, which itself was held up by—she craned sideways to look—a hearse, of all things; and as they reached Ludgate Circus, they had to stop altogether while a policeman allowed traffic through from Farringdon Road on the right.

It seemed to take ten minutes, but finally they were moving forward again. Gradually the traffic began to move more freely, and soon the hansom was bowling along Fleet Street. Right into Chancery Lane, the tall distinguished lawyerlike buildings austere in brick on right and left; out into Holborn, past the ancient gabled buildings leaning four stories and more over the street; right again into Southampton Row, and then they were in Bloomsbury. Cicely didn't know this area, though her father had once taken her and her brother to the British Museum.

The driver slid back a panel behind her head, making her jump.

"Where was it, miss?"

"Oh! Wellcome Passage. I don't know where that is."

"Have to ask."

He jingled the harness, and the horse slowed to a walk, and then the cab moved in to the pavement. A tall policeman, as grand as a monument, was strolling along.

"Wellcome Passage?" said the cabbie. "Know where that is?"

"That's odd," said the constable. "Second cabbie in five minutes to ask me that, you are. Over there, mate—down the street, first on the right. Can't get the cab in there, though."

"Ta," said the cabbie, flicking the reins, and they moved off in the direction he'd indicated.

Cicely sat up. Someone else was looking for Wellcome Passage. This was what Miss Haddow was worried about.

The cab turned down the street, came to the barred entrance to Wellcome Passage, and stopped. Another cab was waiting there already.

Cicely got out and came around to her driver. Something was wrong. She didn't know what it was, but she felt suddenly anxious.

"Can you wait here for a few minutes?" she said. "I'll be coming out with another lady, and we'll want to go to the British Museum."

"I'll need paying first," said the driver.

"Oh, sorry. How much?"

"One and sixpence, love."

Cicely fumbled at her purse, found the coins and handed them to him, and then blushed as the driver looked at them and raised his eyebrows. What should she give him? What would Miss Lockhart do?

"If you're still here when I come back," she said boldly, "you'll get a tip."

The man nodded. Cicely ran past the barrier as the other cabbie eyed the competition with interest: was there going to be a race?

Cicely found number 5 and knocked at the door. It was opened by a cynical-looking maidservant with dusty hair.

"Is there a Miss Lockhart here?"

"Lockhart? Oh—you mean Jones. Mrs. Jones. There's two more waiting for her upstairs. D'you want to join 'em?"

"Two more?"

"Two gentlemen. Just arrived. This is like Piccadilly Circus this afternoon. D'you want to go up or not?"

"Isn't she there?"

"She's gone out, with the baby. Kiddie. Back soon, I shouldn't wonder. You coming in or not? It's blooming cold with the door open."

This was a very unusual and familiar kind of servant, clearly, and it wasn't the sort of house she pictured Miss Lockhart in at all.

"Do you know where she went?" Cicely asked.

"Haven't the faintest idea, and I'm cold, besides," said the maid.

Cicely looked around undecidedly.

"I'll wait here," she said.

The maid shrugged and shut the door.

Cicely felt even more anxious. Those men upstairs—they'd come in the other cab, which was waiting, as hers was, to . . . what? To take them away? To take Miss Lockhart away?

She could see both drivers at the end of the passage, watching her: hers sourly, the other with a twitchy kind of eagerness. She beat her fists together softly and looked the other way. The dull gray afternoon was closing in on the little passage, with a chilly mist in the air around the roofs. Suppose Miss Lockhart had gone for good? How long should she wait? How long would the cabbie wait?

But as it happened, it was only a minute later when Miss Lockhart came around the corner. She had a basket on one arm and a small child on the other, and she looked tired. She saw Cicely with a start.

"Oh! Miss Lockhart! Thank goodness—" Cicely began.

"Cicely, what are you doing here? Did Miss Haddow get my message?"

"Yes. She sent me because Mr. Patten—you know, the client—he arrived just as she was about to go, and she said I was to come quickly. Miss Lockhart, there's two men up in the house waiting for you. I thought I'd better wait outside in case. . . . Oh, and Miss Haddow *is* coming. She said to wait in the British Museum and to leave the house. I suppose because she knew about those men, perhaps. You're to wait for her in the Assyrian Room. I've got a cab."

"Oh . . . oh. Thank you, Cicely. We'd better do that, then. Come on, Hattie-face."

"Mama," said the child, and whispered something.

Miss Lockhart nodded and handed Cicely the basket without a word. Grim-faced, she took the child to a narrow gap between the houses, lifted her skirt and petticoat, and let her relieve herself into the gutter. Cicely felt her head swim. She nearly fainted with embarrassment and mortification. In fact, for a moment she scarcely felt real at all. Knowing that

Miss Lockhart had had a child was shocking enough, but to let her do that in the open street—

She didn't know what it was costing Sally.

A minute later all three of them were in the cab, Harriet on Sally's lap, swinging out of Russell Square and down toward the entrance of the British Museum.

Cicely explained as well as she could what had happened. Sally nodded. It was clear enough. That meant she'd have to move yet again. How much longer could Harriet keep this up? How much longer could *she?*

She looked pale and tight-lipped. And tired. The child sat on her lap, cheeks flushed, thumb in mouth, head leaning on her shoulder, gazing at Cicely with wide, dark eyes like her mother's.

The cab rolled to a halt, and Sally got out and lifted Harriet down and then took the basket from Cicely.

"The Assyrian Room?" she said. "I hope she comes soon. They close in twenty minutes. But—thanks, Cicely."

She smiled briefly and hurried through the gate. Cicely collected herself and slid open the panel behind her.

"The City again, please," she said. "Corner of Cornhill and Gracechurch Street."

As they rolled away she found herself trembling, but she didn't know whether it was shock or shame or cold. She did feel shame, though she hadn't the least idea why; she felt as if she'd suddenly seen how much more grown-up Miss Lockhart was even than she'd thought before, and how being grown-up meant having to cope with things that she couldn't even have put a name to without blushing. Miss Lockhart seemed less goddesslike now—distinctly so. She seemed older and more tired and even *lined*, perhaps. Not ideal at all. Holding the child over the gutter like that . . . And yet more real, somehow. Stronger. How extraordinary things were when you saw behind them. . . . And she'd forgotten to ask how much to tip the driver; well, she could hardly bother Miss Lockhart with that, under the circumstances. She'd have to grow up a little herself.

SALLY LET Harriet walk to the steps, but then picked her up and carried her to the entrance. The attendant at the door said, "Closing in fifteen minutes, ma'am."

She nodded. "Can you tell me where the Assyrian Room is?"

"On the left, ma'am. Just carry straight on through."

She put Harriet down again, but she protested.

"Hattie, you've got to walk, darling, because Mama's arm's tired—"

"Don't want to!"

Sally looked around. The attendant was eyeing her unfavorably, and so was a man at a desk just inside the entrance.

Arms aching, she carried Harriet through the Greek and Roman galleries, the cold white statues looking chilly and complacent; through the Egyptian Room, past colossal stone gods and pharaohs and obelisks which had never looked so alien to her as they did now; and into the Assyrian Room. Huge, cruel faces with spade-shaped beards, a gigantic bull, figures marching flatly sideways along slabs of stone for some brutal, boastful purpose forgotten thousands of years ago. . . .

There was no one else here. She put Harriet down, then put the basket down too. There were some new washing things in it—soap, a good towel; and a bag of ginger biscuits. Harriet was looking fretful and flushed. Sally gave her a biscuit, hoping no attendant would come and throw them out for defiling the Assyrians with crumbs. Why didn't they put a seat in here? Harriet stood leaning against her legs, one arm around her, the other hand holding the biscuit. If they were at home now Sarah-Jane would know what to do: she'd give Harriet a glass of milk and put her to bed, since she had a touch of fever, Sally thought.

She'd have to assume that she couldn't go back to Mrs. Parker's, because someone would be watching for her. So she'd lost all she had—her clothes, Harriet's clothes, everything except what was in the basket and what they stood in.

As she saw the enormity of what she was trying to do, and the way luck was playing against her, she felt overwhelmed by fear and by weariness. How she longed to sleep, and sleep safe! And how Harriet longed for it too: the poor little thing was leaning into her, hardly able to hold the biscuit. Sally bent down and picked her up, holding her tight, letting her head rest on her shoulder. Harriet closed her eyes at once. Sally thought, *I mustn't lean against anything. I must stand upright. If I stand up and don't lean till Margaret comes, we'll be all right.*

She walked slowly up and down in the dim light that filtered through a dusty glass roof. The cruel old stones loomed on either side, their carvings of slaves and battles and lion hunts like the memory of a bad dream that wouldn't go away.

The biscuit fell from Harriet's sleeping fingers. Sally stooped, keeping her back straight, and dropped it into the basket, letting Harriet settle more comfortably into her arms.

More to herself than to the child, Sally whispered, "All right, little one, we'll get through. We'll be back in our home soon, and everything will be all right. We can play with Lamb and Sarah-Jane, and Jim will come home and Uncle Webster, and you can sleep in your own bed again. . . . Oh, where is Margaret? They're going to close soon. . . ."

She wandered to the door and looked down the long passage with its ghostly old statues. A lady and a gentleman were walking slowly along, examining inscriptions; a young man was sketching; an attendant looked at his watch. There was no one else in sight. Then the attendant put his watch back in his pocket and spoke to the lady and the gentleman, who nodded and turned their slow steps toward the way out. The young man put away his pencils.

Sally withdrew, hoping that she'd be overlooked and that they'd have somewhere to shelter, even if there was only a floor to sleep on; but after a minute or so the man looked in and said, "We're closing now, ma'am."

Her heart didn't sink; it could hardly sink further. She nodded and picked up the basket, and set off back through the obelisks, the pharaohs, the Venuses and Minervas.

Outside, she stood at the bottom of the wide steps and

felt like weeping. Harriet was lying awkwardly; Sally's feet ached; she felt dirty and sticky and dusty and cold and afraid. She began to walk heavily toward the gates.

A cab rolled up and stopped. Margaret got out, thrust some money at the driver, and turned and saw Sally. They ran toward each other.

"Oh, thank God—"

"What's been happening?"

"Have you got—"

"Let me carry—"

Confused words tumbled over each other, and then Margaret had the basket, and Harriet was awake again, hot, heavy-eyed, thumb in mouth.

"We'll have a cup of tea," said Margaret.

She led the way around the corner and into Duke Street, a quiet little thoroughfare with an inviting tea shop on the corner.

"I'm spending more time in tea shops . . ." Sally said, but didn't know how to complete the sentence. She let Margaret take charge and order tea and crumpets, and sat back, exhausted.

Margaret explained why she'd been delayed. And it was serious. She'd dealt with Mr. Patten easily enough, but there'd been another man there—with a writ.

"A writ? What sort of writ?"

"I didn't look at the details; I wanted to get here quickly. The main point is that Parrish has taken out an injunction to stop you from getting at your money. Your shares, everything—you can't touch them. And he's applied for some authority or other to allow him to dispose of them himself. Oh, Sally—"

"He can't," said Sally, and her voice was so faint that she herself could hardly hear it. "He's already taken all the money out of my bank. . . ."

"*What?* You mean this fanatic's lied and perjured himself, and now he's doing all this to you as *well*—how much have you lost?"

"Two hundred pounds. . . . I was going to sell the, I don't know, Grand Trunk of Canada perhaps—just for some cash—but . . . And there's the partnership. If he can do this, it might make that uncertain, legally. Oh, Margaret, I'm just so afraid. . . ."

She spoke quietly, but Harriet didn't seem to be listening. She was sipping her milk carefully, intent on not spilling it. Margaret reached for Sally's hand and squeezed it.

"Stop being frightened and drink your tea," she said. "We'll decide what to do in a minute. Harriet, would you like a crumpet if I cut it up for you?"

Sally breathed deeply until her hands had stopped trembling, and then sipped her tea.

"If only I knew *why*," she said. "I thought if I got my money I could—I don't know—rent a place and keep secret, keep hidden, or something, and then start to fight back, and find out why he's doing it. But he's too quick, Margaret. He's shut me out of this new place now, and they were so kind, and I daren't go home to Twickenham, they'll be watching it—and now I can't get at my money. . . ."

She had to stop.

"What's your lawyer doing?" said Margaret. "This is intolerable persecution. He ought to be able to have it stopped."

"He can't. All we can do is tell the truth. If Parrish lies, and keeps on lying, and has documents to back him up, and if it all seems to hang together as it does, then . . . I mean the judge was bound to . . . It's just my word against his, and he's a respectable man, isn't he? A churchwarden, and all. According to my lawyer and the courts, I'm an immoral woman living in God knows what den of terrible vice with two unmarried men. What else would you expect? I thought you could hide in London, but, my God, it's like living behind glass."

Margaret took out a notebook and a little silver pencil.

"Immediately," she said, "you need the following: money, shelter—"

"And a bath," said Sally.

Margaret wrote it down in the neat shorthand she'd acquired after university.

"And in the longer term you need—"

"Time to investigate. Safety. I mean I need to know that"—she nodded at Harriet—"is safe. It's too difficult to trail her about, poor lamb; I've done nothing but look after her all day long and feed her and all that sort of thing. I mean that would be all right, I suppose, but not if I'm going to fight. I can't do both. So I need that: time and safety, really. Money. It comes back to that."

"That's not too bad, then," said Margaret. "We'll find a hotel for you tonight. You could stop with us, except that my cousins are there at the moment, and there isn't room. Tomorrow I'll—"

Suddenly she gripped Sally's hand. "Don't look," she said. "He's out there now—Parrish and two other men."

For a moment Sally sat still. Then she snatched up Harriet, who was too startled to protest, and looked around for the kitchen door.

Margaret swiftly took a handful of coins from her purse and thrust them into Sally's hand.

"Just *go*, get away, now."

Sally darted for the kitchen door. She heard a man's voice behind her, raised in a cry, and heard Margaret calling loudly for the police, and then she was through the door and in a tiny kitchen where a young woman was buttering teacakes at a table.

"Excuse me," said Sally. "Emergency. Does this lead to the street?"

The girl was too dumbfounded to do anything but gape. Sally shoved at the door and found herself looking out at a dark little courtyard with high walls. Harriet, frightened, had begun to cry.

Sally shifted her quickly from right arm to left and reached into her basket, putting her back against the wall.

The kitchen door burst open again, and the serving girl

screamed. The man in the doorway lunged forward—and then stopped short, looking at the pistol in Sally's hand.

"Yes, it's loaded," said Sally. "And I'll fire it too. Put your hands in the air and walk through the door again. Miss, hold it open."

They did as she said. She didn't recognize the man: an ordinary mustached face, with ordinary clothes. He backed slowly through the door, and Sally followed.

The tea shop, full of nervous interest a moment before, had fallen silent. Behind the first man stood two others—Parrish himself and one she didn't know. Margaret was standing, as were two other customers, nervous and wide-eyed. When they saw her pistol, two more stood up and backed against the wall.

Silence for a moment, and then Parrish said, "Sally, my dear, this isn't the way to—"

She turned on him like a tiger, her finger tightening on the trigger. She felt the blaze in her eyes, and he fell back a step before it.

Sally said, "Where's the manager?"

"I am the manageress," said a woman in black at the cash box.

"Have you got the key to the door?"

"Yes, I have."

"Come outside with me, please. If you move," she said to Parrish, "or if either of those men do, I shall shoot you dead. *You*. Parrish. I'll kill you."

Parrish and his men stood and watched without moving as the manageress detached a key from the bunch at her waist. Sally couldn't look at Margaret. She backed toward the door, still covering the men with her pistol.

"Come outside with me," she said to the manageress. "Everyone else is to stay where they are."

The woman did so. The men locked inside rushed to the door and rattled the handle; the customers peered nervously through the windows.

"Give me the key, please," Sally said, and dropped it into her bag. "And the others," she added, thinking there might be a duplicate on the bunch. The manageress handed them over without a word, and Sally flung them as far as she could down the street, and heard them splash into the mud somewhere in the darkness.

"I'm very sorry," she said. "There was no other way out."

The men were pounding on the door. Carefully letting down the hammer, Sally put the pistol back in her basket and gathered up Harriet before hurrying away around the corner. One or two bewildered passers-by had stopped to stare. It wouldn't be long before those men smashed a window, she thought; get a cab, run, hide, do anything. . . .

An omnibus came trundling along, heading for Holborn. She pushed her way through the crowded pavement and pulled herself and Harriet up onto the open platform at the rear, and then jostled past the men coming down the steps from the upper deck and, ducking her head, shoved inside and sat down, taking Harriet up on her lap.

She watched through the window, but there was no sign of pursuit. Shop windows were lit now; New Oxford Street was crowded with shoppers, businessmen going home, newspaper boys, flower girls. The afternoon had gone, and darkness covered everything.

"All the way, please," Sally said to the conductor, handing over fourpence. She took her ticket and sat back, beginning to tremble again now that she had relaxed.

She smoothed Harriet's hair under her bonnet with an automatic hand.

"We'll hide, won't we, Hattie?" she whispered.

"Want to go home," said Harriet.

Sally couldn't answer. She sat still, holding her daughter close, as the stream of traffic bore them to the East End.

14

The Graveyard

SALLY AND HARRIET STAYED ON THE OMNIBUS TILL IT stopped. Harriet was asleep, Sally stiff and cold and desperate for sleep herself. She picked up the basket, settled Harriet more comfortably in the crook of her left arm, and stood up.

"Where are we?" she said to the old conductor.

"Whitechapel Road," he said. "Near the London Hospital. We don't go no farther. This is the end of the line."

She climbed out and stood on the busy pavement, getting her bearings. It was early evening, and the road and pavement were crowded; the air was full of the rattle of traffic, the smell of fried fish, the flare and dazzle of naphtha lights. Harriet rubbed her eyes. Sally put her down for a moment, and she clung to Sally's skirt and cried. Sally was looking in her purse. She had three shillings and sevenpence, and that was all.

Minute to minute, she thought. *Don't look too far ahead. There'll be a pawnbroker's not far away; what can I sell?*

She wore very little jewelry. She had a locket on a chain that Frederick had given her, and she wasn't going to part with that, but she had no earrings or brooches or bracelets. The only thing salable was her father's gold watch.

All right then, pawn it, she told herself. *He'll keep it for a year and a day—he's not allowed to sell it before then—and long before that's up this'll all be over and you can go and buy it back.*

And there was always her pistol. . . .

No. She'd needed that this afternoon, and she might need it again. A watch she didn't need, not in London, where every tall building sported a clock, some of them agreeing with each other.

"Come on, let's go and see the pawnbroker," she said to Harriet, taking her hand. She looked along the street for the three brass balls, and sure enough, there they were, only a hundred yards away.

Since it was Thursday night, and the week's wages were beginning to run out, the place was busy. Many poor families would pawn an item or two to bridge the gap between the end of one week's money and the beginning of the next's.

Sally found a queue of women waiting in the musty shop while the pawnbroker and his wife dealt with the pennies and shillings and issued tickets or shelved the items they took in: pitiful things like saucepans, a child's shoes, a framed engraving of the late prince consort.

Sally felt out of place in her warm coat and hat, and Harriet looked around wide-eyed, a little frightened by the crush, the dustiness, the smell of stale clothes and unwashed bodies, the darkness of the shadowy shop. The other women stared curiously and held themselves a little away, talking in quiet voices.

Then it was Sally's turn at the counter. The pawnbroker, a white-haired old man with a calculating eye, said, "Don't take long, please, I've got a lot of customers waiting."

"I want to pawn a watch," Sally said. She'd never done this before; she wasn't sure how much to expect or how to behave. "A gold watch," she added.

"Well, let's have a look then," said the old man.

"Of course. Sorry." She fumbled for it and nearly dropped it from her gloved hands. She and Harriet had the only gloves in the shop. She handed over her father's watch, still faithfully ticking, and watched as the man's indifferent hands held it to his ear, flicked it open, tapped it with a fingernail, held it up close while he peered into the works.

"Five bob," he said.

"Five shillings—" She swallowed a protest. The watch was worth something like five pounds, twenty times as much.

But he was already looking impatiently over her shoulder, and someone was jostling, and she sensed that five shillings represented a lot of money to any of the women around her. He had all the power, and she had nowhere else to go. So she said, "All right."

He numbered a ticket, tore it in half, tied half to the watch and gave the rest to her. She tucked it carefully in her glove and watched as he dropped the watch none too carefully into a drawer. Then he handed over a half crown, two shillings, and a sixpence, and she took Harriet's hand again and made for the door.

"Cheer up, love," said a stout woman carrying an umbrella.

Sally smiled; the woman was so jolly-looking, and Sally felt her spirits lift a little. But five shillings! She'd hoped for something like three pounds. . . .

Outside in the busy street she suddenly felt hungry. Nowhere to sleep, but plenty of things to eat; jellied eels from that stall at a penny a dish, oysters over there, fried fish at that shop beyond.

"Hungry, darling?" she said.

"Want to go home," said Harriet.

"In a little while. Let's go and find some supper."

She wandered along, holding Harriet's hand, and the child came willingly enough. She was sleepy, and still flushed in a way that Sally didn't like, but she was fascinated by the lights and the bustle and the shouting, as long as she was close to Mama.

Sally felt her tugging, and turned to watch a butcher, his face ghastly pallid in the light of a naphtha flare, cheerfully slicing some anonymous beast in two, hacking and slashing like a pirate in a picture, while his mate bawled out, "Cheapy cheapy! Name yer price, lady, name yer price! Given away! Look at this lovely fat bit of flesh—not you, love, the old cow here. No, not *you*, neither—given away! Name yer price!"

Next to him, a greengrocer was rolling great knobbly potatoes into someone's basket, and a little farther on there was an old-clothes man's shop, with racks of worn coats hung up outside and a tub full of shoes. Sally and Harriet wandered along like tourists. So this was how people lived in Whitechapel? They pawned broken umbrellas, they ate jellied eels, they wore someone else's old shoes. They slept—

No! Don't think of where we're going to sleep yet. One step at a time. Food first.

There was a warm-looking eating house next to the old-clothes shop. Through the windows Sally could see people sitting down, and appetizing smells wafted out.

She pushed open the door and they went into a narrow, steamy place with little boxlike stalls on either side. There was an empty one on the left, with dirty plates still on the table, but it was the only one free. Sally lifted Harriet up onto the wooden bench, and she scrambled along to make room.

People were staring; was she so different from them, then? A grizzled workman in the stall opposite, shoveling a great pile of mashed potato steadily into his mouth, could hardly take his eyes off them. She wondered how long it would be before she was inconspicuous. Maybe they shouldn't have come to the East End.

And then a waiter appeared, in a long apron that had once been white. He swept up the dirty plates and cutlery and the empty beer bottles, wiped the table with a filthy cloth, and said, "Yus?"

"Is there a menu?" said Sally.

"A what?"

"What have you got to eat?"

"Same as usual. Sausage and mash. Stewed eel. Fried herrings. Tuppenny pie."

"A tuppenny pie, please. And—"

"Mash?"

"Oh. Yes."

"What about the kiddie? Eh? What's your name, then?" he said to Harriet, who was gazing up at him.

She hid her face in Sally's sleeve.

"She's Harriet," said Sally. "We'll share the pie and mash, if I could have a spoon and fork for her, please. Oh, and a cup of tea and a glass of milk," she added, hoping that those beverages would be available.

The waiter nodded, winked at the emerging Harriet, and hurried away. Sally discreetly counted her remaining money: eight shillings and sevenpence. And only yesterday—if she'd had the forethought to take her money out then . . .

No. Don't think of that.

Their tuppenny pie, when it came, was enormous. There was beef in it, Sally supposed, and the piecrust was thick and the gravy was fragrant and the plate was hot; so it was possible to eat, and they wouldn't starve. Moment by moment. She cut some pieces off the pie and put them on one side of the plate to cool for Harriet.

Harriet had come fully awake again, in that bright-eyed, hot-cheeked way that ends in fretful sleeplessness. *A moment at a time*, Sally thought; *just be grateful she's awake.* She blew on one of the pieces of pie to cool it quickly and gave it to Harriet on a spoon; never mind table manners now.

Between them they could only just finish the pie, but they had to leave some of the potato, for they had no room for it. Sally lingered as long as possible in the little booth, reading out a music hall poster on the wall line by line to Harriet, following it with her finger and telling her what a prestidigitator was, what Señor Chavez the Mexican Boneless Wonder did. Harriet sat happily and listened to it all; she probably understood about a tenth of it, but it was her mama's voice and they were warm and close together.

"Puddin', me lady?" said the waiter. Sally looked up; he was addressing Harriet, who was staring back, puzzled. "We got plum duff, roly-poly jam puddin' and custard, spotted dick—"

"No, thank you," Sally said. "But we enjoyed the pie. May I have the bill?"

"Eh? Oh, right you are. Tuppenny pie and mash—gravy—tea—milk . . . fivepence, love," he said.

She gave him a sixpenny piece and told him to keep the extra penny. He raised his eyebrows. She thought, *I shouldn't have tipped him—they don't tip here—or was it too little? Should I have given more?*

But he dropped the money in his waistcoat pocket, took up the plate and the cutlery, and said quietly, "Good night, love. Here—you don't mind if I say summing? It ain't yer clothes as gives yer away—it's yer voice. Talk a bit rougher, and you won't stick out. You'll get used to it."

She opened her mouth to reply, but found nothing to say; then closed it again and nodded. With a flick of his dirty cloth around the table, the waiter was away to the kitchen.

Well, out again, she thought, and picked Harriet up. She was heavy, full of pie, or Sally was tired. And she knew very well that her voice gave her away. But she'd never learned to speak cockney; never had to. Never 'ad to. 'Ave to now. Nah. No, it was silly, she couldn't pretend, it would sound even worse.

So what were they going to do?

Harriet was quite content to be carried about by Mama and gaze at the busy stalls, the pubs, the shops, the press of people buying and selling and gossiping and quarreling. And Sally was content for the moment to drift with her, because out there in the darkness of the street where only the flaring lamps cast any light she felt invisible. Hardly anyone looked at them. She felt safe.

But so tired. Tiredness made you feel drunk, she supposed, who had never been drunk. Though she had once succumbed to the fumes of opium, and this extremity of weariness had the same dizzying helplessness about it.

She didn't know how long they wandered; she didn't know where they were. The only thing was, they were free. Occasionally they passed a house with the word LODGINGS on a board outside, or ROOMS FOR TRAVELERS; and once a card in a window saying simply LOGINS. In the dim gaslight they all looked unsavory: dark, narrow places, with filthy windows.

These shops and stalls stayed open very late. But it was

dry now, and the sky had cleared. They passed an old-clothes shop with some folded blankets in the window. On impulse she went in, taking no notice of the reek, and paid four-pence for two of them. That was tenpence gone, but they'd eaten and they could keep warm. She couldn't remember, when she came out of the shop, what she'd said to the old man or what voice she'd said it in, but he hadn't registered any surprise.

There was a church or something opposite, with trees overhanging darkly, and a bench, was it? In the dimness it was hard to see. Yes, she found, it was a bench, and it was dry, being under a thick canopy of yew.

She shook out one of the blankets and spread it on the bench, Harriet looking on doubtfully. Then she sat down and took Harriet on her lap and wrapped the other blanket around them, and then tucked the first one around the outside, and leaned back.

"Oh, Hattie," she whispered. "What would your papa say to see us like this? D'you know what he'd say? He'd say, 'Lockhart, you're insane. The whole of England to hide in, and you sleep on a bench in the East End.' He'd say, 'Out-face them, that's what to do. Stand firm and show them' . . ."

Harriet lay close, thumb in mouth, soothed by Sally's whispers, warm on her breast. After a moment Sally went on, her breath hardly stirring the fur on Harriet's hat: "Fred, what shall I do? It seems as if there are too many enemies to fight, and I don't know who they are or why—why they want . . . They're not ever going to have it, you know that, don't you? You know I'd never give her up? You know I'd die first? You do know that? Oh, Fred, all that silence where you are. . . . That money, Fred, this morning . . . that was four years' wages for some of the people who live around here. They'd never believe their eyes if they saw that much money. Those poor women, Fred, pawning saucepans for pennies. . . . And it's all gone. . . ."

"All gone," muttered Harriet sleepily.

"All gone," Sally said, stroking her cheek. Then, whispering again, "All gone. But the other money's more important still. If Margaret could have sold some stock for me we'd still have been all right. A little house in, I don't know, Hampstead or somewhere, and Sarah-Jane to come and look after Harriet—change my name—Mrs. Jones—then start to fight back. I could, Fred. I've done it before, haven't I? Fought and won? But I had you then. And I knew who I was fighting. . . ."

She looked out across the dim graveyard. The street seemed a long way off now, the cries of the street traders muffled by distance, leaves, weariness. A figure stumbled into the graveyard, drunk, and fell over a stone, and lay there cursing quietly. Then it got up, so swathed in rags that she couldn't tell whether it was male or female, and fumbled toward a doorway in the church wall. But it was just going to settle when another figure—just a shadow among shadows—rose up and shoved it away. It fell; Sally heard the sound of vomiting, and then a muffled curse.

She watched all this without surprise. Little by little she became aware of other shapes huddled in the darkness, in the doorways, behind gravestones, on the other bench farther off into the shadows.

"There's a lot of people here," she whispered silently. "All of them asleep, like I should be. Why was this bench free? I can see two—or it is three?—on the other bench. Huddled up like Harriet and me. Oh, Fred, I've done wrong to come here. I shouldn't expose her to this. But I didn't know what to do. Me, the great independent woman—oh, I used to be so proud. I cruised along earning money and organizing businesses and thinking I was so clever, and then *this* comes at me and all of a sudden I'm huddling on a bench with only seven shillings in the world, and a couple of old blankets. . . ."

Suddenly she caught her breath. There was someone else on the bench with her. Harriet didn't stir, but in a moment

Sally was awake and prickling all over with tension. A man's shape, that was all she could tell, and he was looking at her.

And then she heard footsteps: heavy ones, steady ones, coming down the gravel path, and she knew why this bench had been empty. The footsteps came to a halt nearby. The policeman was wearing a cape and carrying a lantern, which he shone full in her face.

"What you plannin' on doin'?" he said. " 'Cause you can't stay there. You ain't no vagrant."

And before she could reply, the other man spoke, the shadow man.

"It's all right, officer," he said in a deep voice, a voice with a strong accent—Russian? Polish? "My wife speaks no English. We are resting. We have just arrived at the docks from Hamburg."

"You got somewhere to go, then?"

"Oh, yes. I have a cousin in Lamb Street, Spitalfields. But we had to rest a moment."

"Better be along, then. This ain't no place to stop for long."

He watched as the man gently took Sally's arm. She let herself be helped up, and draped the blankets high around her neck, holding Harriet close to her.

Saying nothing, she accompanied the man along the gravel path, through the gate, and turned left along the street.

"Who are you?" she said when they'd gone far enough to be out of earshot of the policeman.

"A friend," he said. "A friend of a friend. My name is Morris Katz. Forgive me for referring to you as my wife; it seemed the safest thing to do. The policeman is watching us. Will you come with me?"

15

The Mission

HE WAS OF MEDIUM HEIGHT, HEAVILY BUILT, AND DRESSED in a shabby overcoat and a black hat which he took off as he spoke to her under the sputtering gaslight on the wall. He had a thick black beard, and his expression was a curious mixture of mildness and understanding and determination.

He replaced his hat, and the shadow fell back across his face.

"I've never heard of you," she said. "If you're a friend, then you'll know my name. What is it?"

"Your name is Lockhart, and the child is Harriet."

"How did you know who I was? Have you been following me?"

"Yes. For some time. You have thought you were in danger, and so you are, but you have friends as well that you do not know about."

"Friends . . . who? Who's the friend of a friend you mentioned just now?"

"I don't think his name would mean anything to you. It is not Mr. Parrish, in case you are wondering. Now it would be safer to come with me, because the policeman is watching."

She turned to look, and there was the policeman, still standing suspiciously outside the churchyard.

"Where, then?" she said.

"A house not far away. There is a bed. You will be safe."

He walked on. Sally, shifting Harriet from one arm to the other, followed. She was bewildered. If this was a dream, as it felt like, then she'd go with it; because Mr. Katz seemed trustworthy enough for the moment. And besides, there was really nothing else she could do.

From time to time, when a drunk man or a gang of children or two fighting, shrieking women threatened to knock Sally off the pavement, he drew close and took her arm, putting himself between her and the threat. He didn't seem particularly pugnacious, but his hand was strong, and his pace was steady. She let him lead her.

Not very much later, in a quiet old street somewhere in Spitalfields, Sally's guide stopped and rang the bell of a tall house with remnants of the eighteenth century still in its windows and the fanlight over the door. The door was opened by a middle-aged woman who stood aside silently and let them in.

Sally found herself in a dimly lit, shabby hall with an institutional smell of boiled cabbage everywhere. There were no pictures, no carpets, no linoleum, but the bare boards were clean.

Her aching arms prompted her to put Harriet down, but the child was fast asleep and she cried as she felt Sally moving. Wearily Sally changed positions yet again, and then felt with a sigh that Harriet was wet. No fresh clothes. What to do?

Her guide was speaking quietly to the woman who'd let them in. When he'd finished, he turned back to Sally.

"I shall leave you here," he said. "You'll be safe. Sometime soon I shall come back and we shall talk. But now I must go."

He raised his hat, and again she saw those disconcerting black eyes. Then he was gone. The woman said, "Come this way, miss. Miss Robbins will see you now."

"But who—?" Sally began, but the woman was already climbing the stairs ahead of her. Sally followed, and was shown into a room. The woman announced her name and then left, and Sally looked around.

It was a large, Spartan room, nearly empty except for a couple of chairs and a large desk littered with papers, government reports, and various political journals. Seated at the desk was a woman whom Sally took to be Miss Robbins: forty or so, with a stern, almost cruel expression, and solidly built. She was wearing a severe dress and had scraped her hair back into a bun with no attempt at softening her appearance. The white of her eyes showed all around the iris, giving her a disconcertingly predatory look. She stared at Sally for a few moments, and then stood up and offered her hand. Sally shook it.

"Sit down, Miss Lockhart," said the woman. "My name is Elizabeth Robbins. This is the Spitalfields Social Mission. I have been expecting you."

More astonishment. Sally sat, holding Harriet carefully.

"Expecting me?" she said stupidly.

"Mr. Katz has told me of your history. A man called Parrish has claimed that you are his wife, and that he is the father of your child. Is that correct?"

"Yes—but who is Mr. Katz? And how does he know about me? Miss Robbins, I don't understand—"

"No doubt Mr. Katz will explain when he sees you. For the moment, you need night clothes for yourself and for your child. Susan will show you to a bedroom in a minute or two. You would like to wash, I don't doubt. You are welcome to remain here as long as you need, but you will have to help. I understand that you are a professional businesswoman?"

"I am a financial consultant," said Sally. "That is, I was. But I—today I found out that . . . What I'm trying to say is that I haven't any money, Miss Robbins, none at all."

"You can work. You're strong and healthy. Pitch in and make beds. Cook. Help Dr. Turner. Do whatever needs doing."

Sally nodded. "Yes. Anything. Perhaps I could help with the accounts."

"That would take ten seconds. You're not a socialist, by any chance?"

"No . . . why?"

"Just curious. Don't worry, we won't try to convert you. I'll call Susan and she'll show you upstairs."

She rang a bell and then turned back to her papers, ignoring Sally. When the woman knocked and came in, Miss Robbins told her to put Sally in the guest bedroom and find some night clothes, and then wished Sally a brusque good night.

Sally followed the woman upstairs and into a narrow little room, where she lit a stump of candle and turned down the covers on the one small bed.

"I'll see if I can find you a hot-water bottle, miss," she said. "There's towels in the cupboard. Bathroom's next-door."

She left, and reappeared a minute later with an earthenware hot-water bottle, almost too hot to touch, and two thin cotton nightgowns, one for her and one child-size. Sally took them gratefully. The woman was taciturn and didn't want to stay and talk, so Sally was able to concentrate on getting Harriet undressed. The child was cross and flushed with sleep and fretfulness, but she let herself be washed and dried without doing more than grizzling and shivering. Sally had wrapped the small nightgown around the hot-water bottle; it hadn't been aired, and there was a smell of dampness about it.

"We're going to be sharing the bed, little one," she said. "Like we did last night in Villiers Street."

Was it only last night? This had been almost the longest day of her life. She tucked Harriet in, kissed her, sang a nursery rhyme or two, watched her eyes close and the thumb go into her mouth, stroked her strong hair back off her forehead (*haven't got a brush; must buy one tomorrow. What with?*), and sat by her till she was sure she was asleep.

Then she yawned. She felt it coming from a long way off, this yawn, and when it arrived it held her jaw open so wide she thought she'd never close it again. When it had subsided she sat with her elbows on her knees, drained of everything except exhaustion.

And she might have fallen asleep there and then, but there was a disturbance in the corridor. Someone was shouting; something was banging the floor. She jumped up and looked out.

A third woman, whom Sally hadn't seen before, was dealing with a drunken woman whose head was bleeding profusely—trying to pull her along to the bathroom, by the look of it. She saw Sally standing there and called out, "I say— lend a hand, will you? Light the gas in the bathroom."

Sally hurried out and did that, and then came back to help with the drunk woman. She was shouting incoherently and struggling, and she smelled vile.

"Let's get her in there, clean up that wound. Come on, Mary, there's a good girl—no sense in struggling. Here we are, now let's have a look at you."

The nurse, if that was what she was, kicked a stool smartly into the back of Mary's knees so that she sat down, and then held her head with two strong hands and looked at the wound. Sally could see even through the woman's tangled hair that her scalp was alive with insects.

"She needs a bath," said the nurse. "We'll have to disinfect the bed if she sleeps in it in this state. Can you help?"

She was a brisk, red-faced woman a little older than Sally, with a cheerful manner and a cultured voice. She was already running the water.

"Well, yes, of course," said Sally.

She helped the nurse undress Mary, who was still struggling but more weakly now, and who resorted to slumping suddenly to the floor and then springing up again. Sally learned, in between the struggles and curses, that Mary had almost certainly earned the money she'd drunk from prostitution; and that she was suffering from syphilis. Sally stood back hastily.

"Oh, it's all right," said the nurse cheerfully, soaping Mary's filthy head and shoving it under to rinse it. "You won't catch it. My goodness, if that's all she's got, I'll be surprised. She won't"—she lowered her voice while vigorously soaping Mary's ears—"she won't last long. This time next year she'll be dead. Alcoholic poisoning, that's my bet, though half a dozen other things would do it. That's a nasty cut on her head, but I bet whoever gave it to her came off worse. I don't *think* she'll die from violence. . . ."

Mary, dazed perhaps by the hot water and the vigorous washing, was nearly unconscious. Sally helped her out of the tub and dried her as best she could while the nurse swiftly applied a sticking plaster to her forehead.

"Put her clothes in a heap," she told Sally. "We'll wash 'em and bake 'em and then she can have 'em back. Who are you, anyway?"

"Sally Lockhart. Miss Lockhart. But I hardly know . . . I mean, what is this place? Are you a nurse?"

"Name's Turner, and as a matter of fact I'm a doctor," said the other. Sally blushed. She knew that there were qualified women doctors now, but to find herself of all people assuming that a woman doing a medical job must be a nurse. . . . But Dr. Turner didn't seem to mind. She went on, while helping Mary into a nightgown: "And this is a mission. Not a religious one, though. We're not here to save souls. Don't know what a soul is, actually. Enough to do saving bodies. Socialist, you know. Miss Robbins is president of the East London Socialist Women's League. I'm just here to mop up the blood and dish out the pills and potions. What brings you here?"

"A man called Katz," said Sally, trying to ease Mary's arm into a sleeve. "But to tell the truth I don't know why. I mean, I'm very grateful, but . . . I was going to sleep on a bench. I just didn't know what to do."

She found herself pathetically near to tears. Dr. Turner looked at her curiously, and then at her obviously expensive clothes, and decided to say nothing.

"Let's get Mary to bed," she said. "She'll sleep like a log. Come on, Mary, beddy-byes. Up the wooden hill to blanket fair. . . ."

This large, loud cheeriness was exactly right, Sally thought.

Dr. Turner was the sort of hearty Englishwoman who in other circumstances would have ridden to hounds or explored the upper reaches of the Zambezi. It was hard to imagine anyone more capable of dealing with the East End. Sally helped her get Mary to bed (in a narrow room where two other beds were already occupied), and then carried her filthy clothes down to a scullery behind the kitchen.

"Leave 'em in the corner," said Dr. Turner. "With a bit of luck they'll have walked out by the morning. Better cut along now and wash your hands."

Sally did, and then found herself yawning again. Who was this Dr. Turner? Who was Miss Robbins? Who, above all, was Katz? *Can't think now; can't write my diary. Find out in the morning. Harriet's here. Safe for the moment. Move over, baby, move over. Let Mama sleep.*

AMONG THE ROWS of filthy tenements, squalid courts, and malodorous alleys of the East End were some corners of elegance and beauty: a row or a whole street of tall old brick houses built for the Huguenot silk weavers who'd fled to London from the French persecutions, at a time when builders couldn't put up an ugly house if they tried.

One of these corners of Spitalfields (only a stone's throw from the mission) was called Fournier Square. The nineteenth century had hardly touched it. Clear that hansom cab out of the way, shoo that butcher's boy out of sight, take down that placard advertising the merits of Brand's Essence of Beef, and you could people it with perukes and swords and three-cornered hats and sedan chairs, and if the great Dr. Johnson came back to dine, as he'd once done at number 12, Fournier Square, he'd never know the difference.

Number 12 was busy. Lights blazed at most of the windows; a clutter of dishes, a fragrance of smoky steam, came from the basement kitchen and floated up the area steps; the figures of servants could be seen moving to and fro inside the rooms, carrying lamps, drawing curtains, arranging furniture.

Outside, a large coach had just unloaded its passenger. Grooms were busy folding some large metal apparatus back underneath it and signaling the coachman to move away. One of them swung the coach door shut: wider by far than the door of a normal carriage, as the vehicle itself was larger and more massive. It was the coach that Jacob Liebermann had seen in Riga, that Bill and Goldberg had seen in Amsterdam, and it had brought the Tzaddik to his house in London.

Inside the hall, a valet was deftly removing the dark rug from around his master's legs. A footman lifted the top hat off the man's head with a swift and apprehensive flick, and then, watching every second, unfastened his cloak and lifted it away. The reason for his apprehension was the little malevolent shadow, the *dybbuk* which had so frightened the few people who'd seen it. It sat in plain view on the invalid's right shoulder, clinging with sharp little fingers to his hair and his ear, and chattering in a savage undertone. It was a gray monkey.

No one spoke. All these well-rehearsed movements were carried out in silence. When the master's rug and cloak and hat had been put away, a footman opened a double door into a cloakroom, where a basin of hot water and scented soap were laid out ready. The valet wheeled the chair through and washed his master's face and hands, drying them tenderly on warm towels, and then pressed a bell. From the towel rail the monkey watched, its fierce little eyes never leaving the hands of the valet.

The door opened, and a footman wheeled the chair through the hall again and into a warm, glittering dining room. As soon as they were near the table, the monkey sprang off its master's shoulder and stalked through the dishes and glasses, rounding the silver centerpiece and the crystal saltcellar, brushing the candelabrum with its uplifted tail and seizing an apple from the great bowl before running with it to the place next to its master's and devouring it with small, busy nibbles.

The master laughed. The butler was pouring wine, the

valet at the sideboard putting turtle soup into a plate from a silver tureen.

"The lift," said the master. His voice was deep and oddly accented.

"Yes, Mr. Lee," said the butler at once. "It is installed and working perfectly. We tested it yesterday, sir."

"Good. You may go; Michelet will serve me."

The butler bowed. The valet, a plump man with a small, red-lipped, pursed mouth, placed the soup in front of him and broke a bread roll into small pieces. The monkey put down the apple.

Mr. Lee made a soft chittering with his tongue, and the monkey seized one of the pieces of bread, dipped it messily in the soup, and conveyed it to its master's mouth.

He ate, and as soon as he'd swallowed it, another sopping morsel was thrust in with those hard, black-nailed little hands.

"Michelet, you have not been quick enough with the napkin," observed Mr. Lee quietly to the valet, and the man paled and shook out a stiff white cloth at once, dabbing his master's chin solicitously before tucking it around his neck. Meanwhile, the monkey had splashed another piece of bread in the soup and was pushing it into Mr. Lee's mouth—swift, rough, abrupt.

After half a dozen mouthfuls, Mr. Lee said, "Eat, Miranda."

The monkey thrust the next morsel into its own mouth, chewing with quick, vicious little bites as it crouched on the table by his plate, its tail dangling over the edge.

The valet removed the plate and substituted a dish on which some pieces of turbot in a cream sauce had been arranged. The monkey followed the same procedure, thrusting the pieces home with an urgent fierceness, and the valet stood poised, ready to wipe Mr. Lee's chin when a drop or two of sauce didn't reach his mouth. That didn't often happen, for Miranda was too quick to drop much. The valet himself conveyed the wine to his master's mouth.

After the fish, a saddle of lamb, cut up small for the monkey's paws, with vegetables similarly treated; and then some melon; and then a Scotch woodcock—anchovies and scrambled eggs on toast. The monkey ate a mouthful or two of everything but the anchovies.

After the meal, a glass of port, and some nuts cracked by the valet and delivered by the monkey; and then Mr. Lee said, "Enough. Take me to the drawing room."

Miranda heard, and leaped from the table at once, clinging to his lapels; and then remembered the apple, sprang back to fetch it, and came back to his bosom, where she nestled, chewing and nibbling fiercely as the valet wheeled the chair out and into the drawing room. When he was positioned at a comfortable distance from the fire, when coffee and brandy had been poured, when the monkey was curled up asleep in his waistcoat, Mr. Lee spoke again.

"You may show the secretary in," he said, his soft voice rumbling and making the monkey click her tongue in her sleep.

The valet bowed and left, and a minute later came back with a tall man whose blond hair was cut short and brushed upward in the Prussian style. He put down a briefcase beside him, clicked his heels, and bowed slightly.

"Welcome back, Mr. Lee," he said. "I hope you had a good journey."

"Good evening, Winterhalter. Yes, thank you, it was enjoyable. Please sit down."

Coffee and brandy were offered, coffee was accepted, and the valet withdrew.

The strange voice had wakened the monkey, which now sat on Mr. Lee's shoulder, darting glances of hatred at the visitor. He took no notice; he sat upright, occasionally, at Mr. Lee's request, lifting the coffee cup or the brandy glass to his employer's lips. The monkey watched his hand every inch of the way.

"Well now, Winterhalter. How much has Parrish collected for me?" said Mr. Lee.

"I've banked seven thousand eight hundred and forty-six pounds, seven shillings and threepence since your last visit, Mr. Lee. That's in addition to the proceeds from the sale of the white goods to Argentina, which came to three thousand four hundred pounds. That's eleven thousand two hundred and forty-six pounds, seven and threepence. Expenses are a little higher this quarter, mainly on account of the police. Mr. Parrish's contact, Inspector Allen, has been unfortunately removed from his duties, and—"

"He won't talk, I take it."

"We have taken care of that, sir."

Mr. Lee nodded. "Good," said the invalid. "Good. Now to other business. I had a useful journey to Russia. The possibilities are enormous, and I have begun to organize already. I am pleased with the application shown by this man Parrish. I am going to reward him with more responsibility. By the way, is his domestic matter proceeding well?"

"There was a favorable judgment in the court only yesterday, Mr. Lee. Favorable to Mr. Parrish, that is. The matter should be resolved any time now. Oh—we have acquired this."

He reached into the briefcase and took out something small and soft. The monkey hissed with hatred, and Mr. Lee chittered softly until she calmed down. Winterhalter set the object up beside the lamp. Harriet would have recognized it; it was her woolly bear, Bruin.

"Ah," said Mr. Lee. "We shall put that in a safe place. Miranda is jealous. Excellent work, Winterhalter. Excellent. Now, the Russian business. Attend closely, if you will, and feel free to take notes. It is a complex matter."

The secretary flicked open a notebook, took out his silver pencil, and sat up attentively. The monkey caught the glint of silver; its hard black eyes followed every movement as the two men talked. It sprang from the armchair to the carpet, to the curtains, to the mantelpiece, never still for a moment. In the red firelight, it looked like an imp playing in the palace of the Prince of Darkness. Once it sprang up next to the woolly bear, but Mr. Lee growled and Winterhalter lifted the toy out of its reach, for all the world as though they were saving it for later.

16

Playing with Blocks

WHEN SALLY AWOKE SHE COULD HEAR VOICES AND FOOT-
steps and the sounds of a busy house going on around her.
She had no idea what time it was. Harriet was fast asleep
and still dry. Sally lay for a minute or so, collecting herself,
and then got up and drew the thin curtains. There was a
church tower at the end of the narrow street, and the clock
said ten to eight.

She woke Harriet and washed and dressed her, and they
went downstairs and found their way to the kitchen, which
seemed to be the center of the house's life. Dr. Turner was
there, eating breakfast at a large table with six or seven other
women in various stages of shabbiness. The maid who'd let
her in the night before was cooking eggs at a range. Mary,
the woman with the cut on her head, was not there. Dr.
Turner looked up and greeted her.

"Ah! Miss Lockhart! Come and have some brekker. There's
porridge and toast and there's some tea in the pot and—
hello! What's your name?"

Harriet was introduced, and they sat down. The other
women looked at them curiously, but only for a moment or
so. There was a democracy here that Sally was comfortable
with: it reminded her of the old days in Burton Street. As
they ate the watery porridge and the burned toast, Dr. Turner
quietly explained a little more about the place.

"Miss Robbins inherited a lot of money from her family's
firm—they make chocolate, I think, or cocoa or something—
and set up the mission five years ago to spread progressive

ideas through the East End—you know, socialism, secular-
ism, what have you. Soon found out that that wasn't what
they needed just yet. So she turned it into a shelter. A place
for women to go when they've got nowhere else. As for me,
I was going to be a missionary in Africa, would you believe.
But I heard about Miss Robbins and came here to have a
look, and here I still am. Not sure about God anymore. Think
he's turned his back. We've got to look after *bodies*, you know.
Souls can take care of themselves. But this woman needs
medicine now, and then she might be alive next week, and
she can think about her soul then. Or that child: he needs
shelter tonight before his father kills him. When he's learned
to trust an adult for more than a minute at a time, then
someone can tell him about Jesus. Waste of time till then.
That's what I think, anyway. Of course, this is a drop in the
ocean. We don't do much good in comparison to what there
is to be done. There are thousands, thousands out there
starving and . . ." She fell silent, and then shrugged. "You'll
find Miss Robbins's bark pretty fearsome," she went on, "but
she's fair. Don't give her cause to bite you, though, or you'll
lose a limb. I think she said she had a job for you this morning. If you want to leave Harriet here, she'll be perfectly
safe. I don't know what your situation is, but she'll be all
right with us."

SALLY HAD a hundred qualms about leaving Harriet. While
Parrish was still hunting for her, she didn't want to let the
child out of her sight. On the other hand, having seen Dr.
Turner at work, she'd trust her with her life. If anywhere
was safe, she decided, the Spitalfields Social Mission was;
and it was time she began to pay them back for their hospitality.

An hour later, having settled Harriet with Susan the maid,
Sally was walking with Miss Robbins down toward Wapping.
She seized the chance to ask about Mr. Katz.

"Mr. Katz is a friend of the mission. He's helped many
refugees—Jewish mostly, of course. He's a clockmaker by

trade. His own house is full just now, or I daresay he would have taken you there."

"But how did he know about me?"

"I don't know. He has many acquaintances among the socialist groups in London."

"He said there was a friend we had in common. But I can't think who it might be."

"Nor can I," said Miss Robbins. "You will have to ask him. Now, about this problem. There's a woman down in Rowley Court. We helped her last year when her husband was ill-treating her. He was out of work. It's got better now; he's got a job and he doesn't drink so much. We keep records, you see. Need sorting. Job for you. But she remembered us and came to ask for help. Here we are—on the left. Keep your skirt clear of the ground, I should."

She folded the street map she was consulting and turned into a dark alley. It was a clear, cold day, but as Sally followed her between the high brick walls she felt as if she'd left the sky behind forever and would never smell fresh air again.

She gasped at the stench and held her sleeve across her face. It was more than a stench—it was an invisible being that leaped at her and almost tangibly forced her backward. As they rounded the corner into the court she saw what was causing it. The privy in the court, the only one between all eight dwellings, was blocked and overflowing; the stones on the floor of the court were covered with a lake of sewage. A child squatted on one of the house steps, naked from the waist down. She was hardly bigger than Harriet, though her pinched face was like an elderly monkey's.

"Ma!" she shrieked when she saw the visitors, and vanished on dung-spattered feet.

"Hitch your skirt up under your belt. Never mind your boots—they can be cleaned. Don't waste time feeling sick. Take notes. That's what you're here for," said Miss Robbins.

Sally fumbled at the skirts of her coat, doing as Miss

Robbins had advised, and then took out her notebook and pencil.

"Miss Robbins—you see how it is?" said the woman who came to the door. "It's been like this three weeks now, miss. We asked the landlord, and he says it's nothing to do with him, it's the water board. Only I dunno where to go, miss, nor what to say or nothing. . . ."

She was hollow-cheeked and thin, and under one eye was a livid bruise. Her clothes were hardly clean, but they showed evidence of careful mending, and there was a spark of liveliness in her eyes still.

Sally was finding it difficult to avoid being sick. That anyone could stay for more than a few minutes in this noxious atmosphere, far less live in it, was incredible, yet here people were. She concentrated hard, taking down the woman's words, trying not to breathe.

Then Miss Robbins insisted on an inspection of the privy itself.

"No good complaining if I don't know what I'm complaining about," she said. "We want facts, the more of 'em the better. Can you remember the date it became blocked? And what you did, and when you spoke to the landlord?"

She quizzed the woman thoroughly. When she'd found out all she wanted to know about that topic, she touched the woman's bruised cheek and said, "How did you come by that, Martha?"

"Oh—I fell in the dark and hit it on the stair rail, miss. Honest. The candle blew out, and I couldn't be bothered to go back for the matches."

"Is your husband still working?"

"Yes, miss."

"How much does he bring home?"

"Nineteen shillings last week, miss. Twenty the week before."

"And you manage on that?"

"Just about, miss. We're better off than some. I'm up to date with the rent, and that's a great thing, miss."

"Indeed. One might think that the landlord would agree. And your children, how are they?"

"Fit as fleas, miss. You'd think this'd make 'em ill, but they're all right so far. But there's typhoid just along the street. Just two courts down. It won't take long to get here, and once it's in the court . . ."

"Very well. Leave it to me. I'll see that something gets done. By the bye, if your husband hits you again, you will let me know, I hope?"

"Course I will, miss," she said in a subdued voice.

They said good-bye and left. Sally felt pale and found herself damp with the effort of controlling her urge to vomit. Miss Robbins uncapped a bottle of smelling salts and passed it to her without a word; the stinging shock helped Sally recover a little.

"I hope you took notes of everything," she said. "You can write it up for me later, but we'll need it before then. Come along."

She led Sally briskly under the arches of the London and Blackwall Railway and up Leman Street toward Whitechapel. It was shabby here, but at least the air was clear of that stench, though it bore traces of others: a sickly heaviness from the sugar refinery on the left, a choking whiff of smoke from the animal charcoal works a street or two away on the other side.

In Colchester Street, Miss Robbins scanned the brass plates by the doors until she found the one she wanted, and then walked straight in without knocking. Sally followed, notebook ready.

A fat man in an office was making entries in a ledger, while a thin man was counting out coins on a table.

"Cooper?" said Miss Robbins. "Are you responsible for the rents in Rowley Court?"

"I beg your pardon?" said the fat man. The other man stopped counting, hand in midair.

"The drain is blocked in Rowley Court. The tenants complained to you on . . ."

"The twenty-fifth of last month," said Sally.

". . . and you have done nothing. The place is now in an atrocious condition. Have you referred the matter to the Metropolitan Water Board?"

"I may have done, yes. But I fail to see—"

"By letter? May I see a copy?"

"No, you may not. How dare you come in here and demand—"

"How dare you expose your tenants to disease and filth? How dare you allow children to remain in conditions like that? How dare you take rent from people while doing nothing to remedy that appalling state of affairs? How long d'you think it'll be before typhoid arrives? Or cholera? I'm glad to have met you, Cooper. I shall know you again."

"Please, please, just a minute, madam—let me explain. They're not my properties; I'm only the agent. I did pass on the tenants' observations to the owner, madam—that would be directly after I became aware of the problem—but more than that is not within our competence. It's the water board's responsibility entirely, and what Mr.—I mean, what the landlord has done with regard to the, to informing the, er, the water board, I couldn't say."

"Who is the owner?"

"Ah, well, that's a company, madam, not so much an individual."

"The name?"

He made a pretense of checking it inside a ledger, though he must have known it as well as his own face in a mirror.

"The East London Property Company, madam."

"Is that incorporated?" said Sally.

"I beg your pardon?"

"Is that a private company, with limited liability? Is it registered as a company? Does it exist as a legal entity, or doesn't it?" Sally went on.

"I beg your pardon, miss, but I don't understand."

"Very well, what is the company's address?"

He looked troubled. "Angel Court, just off Throgmorton Street. Look here—"

"Good day to you," said Miss Robbins, and swept out. Sally followed.

"What's this about incorporation? What did that mean?" Miss Robbins asked.

"If a company is incorporated, then it's a legal entity just as a person is, and it can be sued. If it isn't, you'd have to sue the individuals, if you could find out who they were. Do you want to find out?"

"We'll see. We'll tackle the water board first. I haven't got money to sue people with."

Nor have I, now, thought Sally as they walked on in silence. It was a more companionable silence than before, though; she felt as if she'd passed a test.

The offices of the Metropolitan Water Board were in Bishopsgate, half a mile away. There they found themselves confronted with a smooth official called Mr. Hanbury.

"Rowley Court . . . Rowley Court . . . East London Property Company . . . Ah, I have a note here from a Mr. Cooper concerning a report of . . . yes, we sent an acknowledgment of that information. Look, I've got a record here."

He smiled gently and showed them a letter.

"And is that all you're going to do? Send a letter? Mr. Hanbury, I think you ought to put your hat and coat on and come with us."

He looked gently puzzled. "I beg your pardon?"

"Have you seen the state that place is in?"

He spread his hands. "Madam," he said, "I don't know who you are or what your business is, but matters like that are, after all, the landlord's responsibility entirely. Besides, I'll be perfectly frank with you: decisions as to which improvements are to be effected are not mine to make. The water board has a program of improvements planned—"

"I'm not talking about improvements; I'm talking about repairs. This one is urgent. The people in Rowley Court are having to walk ankle-deep in filth. When are you going to repair it?"

He raised his eyebrows and gave a little helpless shrug. Then he looked around and lowered his voice.

"You see, the trouble is that very often these places are full of Jews—aliens—people of the lowest class. Their ideas of cleanliness are very different from ours. I can well understand your being offended by the sights and smells, but believe me, what they're used to is a great deal worse. I could take you to—"

"That will be enough," said Miss Robbins. "We shall note your remarks and include them in our letter to your superior, with a copy to the member of Parliament for the Tower Hamlets. Good day to you."

And once again she swept out. Before she left, Sally had time to notice the man's elaborate show of unconcern.

"What will they do?" she asked, as they set off back to the mission. "Will they mend it?"

"Yes, they will now," said Miss Robbins. "But you shall write those letters, if you please, and post them directly."

"Do they always use that excuse about the Jews?"

"Oh, very often. Immigration has increased vastly in the past year or so; it's easy to blame incomers for bad conditions. And some of them *are* filthy. They've had little chance to be anything else."

THAT AFTERNOON, as there was no one else to help, Sally occupied herself with supervising the five children who were sheltering temporarily at the mission. Their mothers—each in her twenties, each looking twice her real age—had fled home because of their husbands' violence. One of them was a drunkard and had found that morning enough liquor to become stupefied by noon. The other was a quiet, thin Irish woman called Bridget, who'd been given a pile of mending to do by Miss Robbins.

She sat with Sally in a big empty room at the front of the house, watching the children occupying themselves with a few building blocks and a battered doll or two. Sally was doubtful about Harriet's playing with the others: fears of disease, of dirt, of she knew not what—of bad manners, she found herself thinking, and blushed for it—rose up like specters, to be pushed away again by the thoughts that firstly, it wouldn't be for long, and secondly, she was no longer in any position to be snobbish.

One of Bridget's children, a stunted little boy of three or so, was moving awkwardly, and Sally asked her what the matter was.

"His father beat him with a poker, ma'am," she said. "Look at his back."

She called the boy over and lifted the ragged shirt and undershirt he wore. His back was raw. There were three great wounds with pus oozing from under thick scabs, a mass of red welts, and near the base of his spine a great flaring wound with bare red flesh and puckered skin.

"That one," she said, pointing to it, "he held a red-hot poker to the lad. 'Twas the drink, it wasn't him in himself. He's a good man, but when the drink gets in him he's not a man at all."

Sally could hardly find her voice.

"Have you seen Dr. Turner? Has she seen his back?"

"Oh, yes, indeed. She put some ointment on, but it's best to leave them open, she says. Let them heal in the air."

The little boy toddled away stiffly. His face had been expressionless, as if he were an old man who didn't understand a word of English.

"Have you been to the police?" said Sally.

"About my man? They won't interfere."

"But the child—surely, can't he be punished for that?"

"D'you know what happened before, ma'am? When he put the poker to him? They took him to the police court and the magistrate fined him, if you please—fined a poor man with no money! So we all had to go hungry for weeks to pay his fine. At least he couldn't drink during that time. That was a mercy."

Sally watched the boy, Johnny, as he sat on the floor a

little away from the other children. Harriet was holding a tea party with two bemused little girls; a boy was off on his own with a couple of toy soldiers. In the gray afternoon the air was cold and still. There was a small fire in the grate. There were four chairs in the room, and a table, and the battered toy box, and that was all. The children were playing on the bare boards; Bridget was sewing next to her, and everything was quiet.

And Sally felt as if the world had been poisoned. Who could let these things happen? No wonder Dr. Turner felt that God, if there was a God, had turned his back. But she, Sally Lockhart, was here now. What was she doing? Was she any better?

Awkwardly she unclasped her hands and smoothed her skirt, and then got up and clumsily knelt down beside Johnny.

"Would you like to play?" she said.

He looked at her. She tried to smile, but it faltered before his hard, dead eyes. She turned aside and pulled some of the building blocks toward them. There were big wooden cubes and smaller brick shapes made of some heavy composition material. They were all chipped and battered.

"Shall we build a house?" she said.

He watched as she set out some blocks and began to build them up.

"Wouldn't you like to put some there?" she said. "Look, that big one could go at the corner. . . ."

She showed him. Slowly he joined in, but always by doing what she suggested; either he was unwilling to take the initiative, or he genuinely had no idea what to do.

Very soon, because there weren't many blocks, the house was made. There was a door but no roof, and only one window.

They knelt and looked at it.

Now what should we do? thought Sally. *What can we play?*

Because he didn't know what playing was. He had never played in his life before. And as Sally looked into that bleak little eternity three years long, she felt stricken with tears that she could do so little for him: because she didn't know how to play either.

She had no more idea than he did what you could do with a pretend house.

At home it was always Sarah-Jane who played with Harriet, and Sally who looked in, smiling at the pretty sight, and went away again. Or it was Jim who took the child hunting toffees in the garden, having carefully hidden them beforehand; and it was Webster who built the swing and who gave her rides on the little camera railway. All Sally did was watch briefly and then go back to something more important, such as reading a financial journal or advising someone how to make money.

And now she couldn't show this little boy how to play.

The empty house stood primly between them. She put out a hand and pushed gently, and it all fell over.

THAT EVENING Mr. Katz came for her.

She had written those letters for Miss Robbins, put Harriet to bed, eaten a supper of bread and cheese, and helped Dr. Turner in the dispensary—cutting up old muslin for bandages, washing medicine bottles. She hadn't had a moment to herself, though she knew that sometime soon she'd have to think through the problem of her money, and write to Margaret, and let Sarah-Jane know where she was, and then get back to the mystery of why Parrish was persecuting her. For the time being, it was enough to feel safe.

At eight o'clock the maid, Susan, came to the dispensary to say that a visitor was waiting downstairs for her. Sally's heart pounded until Susan added that it was the same gentleman who'd brought her there yesterday. Sally dried her hands and felt the color come back to her cheeks as she saw Dr. Turner watching her.

Mr. Katz was waiting in Miss Robbins's office. He stood up when Sally entered. In the light she saw him more clearly than she'd done the previous night, and noticed his threadbare cuffs and scratched boots. But the deep rumbling voice was reassuring, and the look in his eyes was courteous and friendly. They shook hands.

"Mr. Katz, I owe you many thanks," she said. "But I hope you can tell me who you are, and how you know about me."

"I am going to take you to a man who needs your help," he said. "He will tell you what you need to know."

"*My* help? I'm hardly in a position to help anyone!"

"You'll give him your help when you hear what he has to say. You have a cloak and a hat? As I remember yours from last night, they are distinctive—can you borrow some others? We won't be spotted, but it does no harm to take precautions."

"Borrow mine," said Dr. Turner, coming in breezily. "Dull old things. No one'll spot you in my togs. Don't worry about Harriet; we'll keep her safe."

She tugged a rusty brown cloak off a peg by the door and tossed it over to Sally, who put it on. The hat followed—a little big for Sally, but it shadowed her face. Then she fetched her basket from the bedroom, and she was ready.

"Where are we going?" she said.

"Soho," said Katz.

HE SAID little on the omnibus, little on the crowded pavement of Oxford Street where they got off, little on the way down Dean Street, and only when they were outside the lodging house would he tell her who they were going to see.

"His name is Jacob Adler," he said, "though he's got other names besides. You see, he's wanted by the police in some countries—not for what you would consider a crime, I think. In this house, in this country, and for now, he's known as Goldberg. Daniel Goldberg."

"The journalist?"

She'd been about to climb the steps. Now she paused.

"You've heard of him. Then you'll know why he's not popular."

"I'm not going to speak to a journalist. Especially . . ."

"Especially a socialist one?"

She didn't reply. She felt caught: whatever she did now would be foolish. But having come out, it would be wrong not to see him; and as for the socialism, what she'd seen today had made her uncomfortable about many things, and that was one.

"Very well," she said.

"Have you enough money to get back to Whitechapel? I shall not come in: I have other calls to make."

"Yes. But why—?"

"You'll find him in the room at the top of the second flight of stairs. That's his window there." He pointed up to a small window which was lit; she could see a shadow moving across the ceiling. "Just go in. This is a meeting place; people are always going in and out. No one will take any notice. Good night to you."

And before she could say anything, he had vanished into the crowd outside the little theater next-door.

She turned back to the house. The door was open, and as Katz had said, people seemed to be coming and going. A placard by the steps announced a lecture in English and in a language whose letters she didn't recognize—not Russian; Hebrew?

She climbed the steps and pushed through the crowd outside a room where a short, bearded man in a plum-colored jacket was addressing a packed meeting. His voice was rich, his gestures operatic, his eyes magnetic, and the audience was applauding, cheering, whistling, hooting with laughter— and eating and drinking and smoking and arguing with the speaker, with each other, with those outside who couldn't get in.

On the first floor Sally saw a room with a number of men and women sitting at tables reading newspapers, or writing, or playing chess. It seemed more like a club than a lodging house. She heard three languages she recognized and several she didn't; and no one took the least notice of her.

She climbed the second flight of stairs. It was darker here, and quieter. She felt her heart beating fast: suppose it was a trick? They'd duped her—Katz had lured her here and then gone back to Whitechapel and taken Harriet—

What had possessed her to come here? What a fool! Would she never learn?

Her fingers sought the pistol under the shawl in her basket. It was there, firm and heavy and loaded. She took it in her hand, rested the handle of the basket on her wrist so that she could shoot freely, and knocked at the door with the line of light underneath it.

"*Ja,*" came a voice. "Yes. Come in."

She opened the door and slowly went in.

17

Just a Man Working

GOLDBERG LOOKED UP. SHE STOOD IN THE DOORWAY, trembling, intent as a tigress, an electric nervousness in every line of her. Her clear eyes glittered; her fair hair shone. She was extraordinary: desperate, frightened, but undaunted. And, he saw at once, so pretty. No, far too weak a word: she was magnificent.

He'd never seen her before, yet he knew at once who she was. He stood up.

"Miss Lockhart, come in. Welcome. Do you know how long I've been looking for you?"

"I . . . a man called Mr. Katz brought me here. But—"

"I asked him to look after you. Did he take you to Miss Robbins's mission?"

She nodded helplessly. Goldberg brought forward a chair for her and turned to the sideboard.

Sally looked around, bemused. The room was full of life; she felt it to be thronged with busy people, like the Stock Exchange, the House of Commons, backstage in a great theater. The place was glowing with activity, alive with excitement and energy and purpose.

And yet it was only a man who'd been writing at a table.

He turned from the sideboard and said, "You'll take a glass of wine?"

Without waiting for an answer he poured two small glasses of something rich and gold. His desk, she saw, was littered with open books and journals, and the floor was covered with paper, for he had a simple system: as soon as one sheet was written (one side only), he dropped it on the floor and took another. He was halfway through one now; strong, swift writing, blots and splashes of ink. . . . A fist-sized stone held down another pile of papers, and a mug full of pens and pencils stood beside them.

He handed her the glass and sat down.

He was younger than she'd expected Daniel Goldberg to be: late twenties, she thought, with a mass of rough dark hair in which were blended some streaks of gray at the temples. He was strongly built, with powerful shoulders and hands that looked capable of tearing one of those official reports in half; and his expression made her think he'd enjoy doing it. His eyes were dark, the network of laugh lines around them already complex. His nose was powerful, with flared nostrils, and his mouth was wide and mobile. He was hardly handsome; but he was more alive than anyone she had ever seen.

He held up his glass.

"Confusion to our enemies," he said.

She sipped. The wine was intense and sweet.

Then they both spoke at once, and smiled, and she let him say, "The child—is she safe?"

"Yes, she is. But . . . how do you know of me? And our enemies, you say . . . is Parrish your enemy, too? Please, Mr. Goldberg—just what *is* going on?"

"Parrish is a criminal. I'm investigating a fraud, a colossal plot against Jewish immigrants. Someone's defrauding them by selling them fake steamship tickets, by making them pay for couriers who don't appear, by forcing them to pay non-existent taxes and transit charges and God knows what else. God? *I* know what else—a hundred and one little cuts that bleed and bleed, thousands of people swindled and robbed and cheated. I've seen it working from St. Petersburg all the way to Wapping and Hull and Liverpool, and I know it goes beyond, to New York. The Russians don't need much encouragement to persecute the Jews at the moment, but I believe that this—oh, conspiracy, organization, plot, whatever—is even engaged in stirring up pogroms to start off another wave of immigration. You know what a pogrom is? Looting, terror, destruction.

"All right, now someone is organizing this. I've seen him, but I don't know his name. They call him the Tzaddik—it's a Yiddish word, it means righteous man, holy one. Ironic, you see. Now the Tzaddik has agents in every European country, and no doubt in America, too. And his agent in London is your Mr. Parrish."

Sally caught her breath. "Go on," she said.

"He's ideally placed. A commission agent—it's such a vague title, such an open kind of job, no?—with money flowing in and out all the time, so it would be hard to prove he was doing anything wrong. But he is. For instance, when they arrive in London, some immigrants have an address to go to—a cousin, a brother, something like that. But many haven't. Parrish has men at the docks, who lead them—for a fee, of course—to a landlord who lets them have a room for a high rental, a month in advance. Next week, maybe next day, they find out from neighbors or relatives what a fair rent should be. But it's too late, they can't get it back from the landlord, and when they leave—pah! Plenty more on the next boat. There are many, many kinds of fraud and extortion he's running, and he hasn't even begun to move into the sweatshops yet, though he's planning it.

"But he's got other golden geese besides the Jews. There are six houses in the West End which pay him each week something between sixty and seventy pounds each. To rent a house this size, say, would cost what? Two guineas? Three guineas? But he takes sixty, seventy pounds a week from each of them. Gambling, of course. Prostitution. I know about them because I arranged for his rent collector to be robbed a couple of weeks ago." He saw her expression and said cheerfully, "Oh, yes, I'm in the criminal business, too, as well as journalism. I haven't killed anyone yet, but I wouldn't want to make it a principle. The money in this case went to the Jewish Shelter in Wapping. What I wanted was this—the rent book."

He opened a drawer and took out the greasy little book which Bill had taken from Mr. Tubb. Sally looked through it: details of money passed over for months back, addresses. . . . She looked up, dazed.

"But we've got him!" she said. "With this, I can—if he's a criminal, they'll never let him have Harriet! And he'll have to give my money back—"

"You'd testify against him, would you?"

"Of course, with this!"

"Think again. In the court's eyes, you're married to him."

"Oh . . ." she realized bitterly. "A wife can't testify against her husband. But surely—"

He took the notebook back. "I'm keeping this safe. We shall use it, but not yet."

"How . . . why did you become interested in me and my . . . situation?" she said. "I've got nothing to do with Jewish immigration."

"Anything that concerns Parrish is interesting to me. And when I heard that he was applying to divorce a wife and gain custody of a child, I naturally wondered why. So I looked into it, and I found out about you: an independent woman, a person of intelligence and character and strength, and I compared you with him; and the deeper I looked, the more crazy it seemed."

"It *is* crazy," she said. "I thought I was mad. Why? Why me, why Harriet? There was no explanation at all unless, I don't know, unless it was somehow true and I'd forgotten it. . . . People *do* forget the most extraordinary things; I know, it's happened to me. But to forget *that*, I'd have to be insane. . . . No. Harriet's not his child. Her father's dead. I was never married. And anyway—"

"Anyway, a woman like you would never marry a man like Parrish," he said flatly. "Of course not. It doesn't make sense."

"But what does?"

"This," he said. "It's not Parrish's own idea to do this crazy thing. There's someone else behind him, someone else

who wants to punish you by taking your child. Parrish is doing
it for the money; he's nothing; he's a pawn. Anyone else
would have done as well. Forget Parrish. The man behind
this is the Tzaddik."

She sat silently. She'd thought through possibilities like
this a hundred times, without having a name to put to the
shadow behind them, and it had all been fantastical and empty
and speculative. Hearing it from this man made it solid; it
meant that she wasn't mad. It meant that she had an ally.

"Now, do you see why I wanted to find you?" he went
on. "Because I want to find out who the Tzaddik is. I know
a little. But if he's someone who hates you—then if you can
think who that might be, well! We've got him. And *you've*
got free, because with that you could go to the law again. I
should choose a better barrister next time, by the way. I saw
him in court. A jackass."

"I will. Mr. Goldberg, that's the most cheering news I've
had since . . . oh, for weeks. But this man, the—what is
he? Tzaddik? What is he? Who is he?"

Goldberg told her what had happened in Amsterdam. She
listened intently. Her eyes widened as he told her of the
strange paralyzed bulk of the man, the evil, skipping shadow
of the monkey, the girl in the carriage who'd screamed and
chosen drowning rather than . . . than what? She felt a chill
of fear. And *this* was the man who wanted Harriet?

But who could he be?

"I think he's in London now," said Goldberg. "I'm not
sure. But a man I know saw that great black carriage being
unloaded in the docks a day or so ago. And it would make
sense for him to be here in time for the result of the court
case, no? They must be angry now, with you in hiding."

"They nearly caught me yesterday," she said. "I had to
. . . well."

She took out the pistol. He whistled.

"A heavy weapon," he said. "You fired this?"

"I was ready to yesterday." She told him everything that
had happened from the moment the divorce petition arrived

that morning in the garden to the moment Katz found her on the churchyard bench. He interrupted only once, when she told of the boy who'd stopped her at the entrance to Middle Temple Lane.

"That was Bill," he said. "A protégé of mine. He told me how you'd looked. He said you were fierce, that you'd have killed him. You were like a tiger. I wanted to see you for myself, and now I have. Please, go on."

They looked at each other clearly for a moment, and then she lowered her eyes and continued. When she'd finished he sat quite still for a moment, and then put both hands flat on the table and stood up.

"Well," he said. "Well . . . you deserve some more wine."

He took her glass and filled it again.

"Tokay," he said. "From my country."

"You're Hungarian?"

"I was once. Now I'm . . . This is where I live, this is where my work is. I write in English. So perhaps I am becoming English. Downfall to the Tzaddik!"

They drank. And Sally found herself becoming tongue-tied. It was the sudden relaxation, the relief at finding an ally; but more than that, it was the nature of this ally—the magnetic presence of the man, his troubling vitality. There was the sense that invisibly, all around him, played gales and storms of electric life and meaning. It was simply that he had work to do, and he was doing it with all his life and being, and that was something she loved in anyone; and so she felt like a girl again and didn't know what to say.

But you're not a girl, she told herself. *You're grown-up. Find something to say.*

"In Parrish's notebook," she said, indicating it on the desk, "there's the phrase *white goods.* What does that mean?"

He looked at her steadily and said, "Girls sold into prostitution. That's a pleasant little part of the Tzaddik's business. Or Parrish's. They employ a number of women—Yiddish-speakers, often—to go to the docks and look out for single girls traveling alone. They offer them somewhere to stay, and when the girl is safely out of the way of help, with no one who speaks her language within a mile, they make it clear what the price of shelter is. The girls who work in these filthy houses of Parrish's—half of those will be refugees, poor Jewish girls who arrived alone. When they become diseased or worn-out, they're taken abroad and sold to brothels in seaports. South America is a favorite destination. That's the sort of people we're dealing with, Miss Lockhart: men who do that."

She sat silent; she couldn't find her voice.

He went on: "You see why I need your help? We must find out why the Tzaddik would be interested in hurting you. If we find that out, we find out who he is. Then maybe we can destroy him. Now, then—practical things. You need first of all what? Money?"

She gathered her wits. "Yes. And to let my child's nurse know where we are. And my partner, Miss Haddow. . . . Those are the three most important things immediately. Then to find the clergyman who signed the marriage register."

"Very well." He took a fresh sheet of paper and wrote it down; his hand reached for the pen and ink without his having to look, and he jabbed the pen at the bottle with an action as accurate as a bird's. "You must write a note—now— to your child's nurse and to your partner, and I shall take them, so they'll know me and trust me. As far as I can tell, Parrish doesn't know of me. He knows that someone's after him, but not who it is. Come, write those notes."

He stood up and offered her his place. She did as he said, and sealed each of them in an envelope while he leaned on the window sill and watched her. She was aware of his gaze and didn't mind it; there was even a sense in which it was flattering to be looked at by such a man. But she pushed that thought to the back of her mind, intending to come back to it later.

"Finished?" he said. "Good. Now I'm going to accompany you back to your mission. All right, you've got a gun, I know, but I want to do it anyway. Apart from being with you, I want to see where it is, so I can come later and find out about Miss Robbins and her work. It will make an interesting article when all this is over. Some of my comrades disparage the work of middle-class reformers who go to the slums to do good. I don't. Of course, there should be no slums, and of course the most important work is to abolish them. But while they're still there, and your friends are doing this work, then tonight there's a dozen women who have a safe place to sleep in, or a little medicine for their coughs. Your hat . . ."

"Thank you," she said. "Not mine, in fact. It's too big. I borrowed it."

She was well aware why she told him that: it was vanity. But it was so long since she'd enjoyed looking pretty. Not now, she told herself. Not now. Another thing to think about later.

They didn't talk much on the omnibus, and he gave her only a swift smile as they shook hands outside the mission in the light from the gas lamp over the door. But later, when she'd kissed Harriet and slipped down into the narrow bed beside her, she allowed herself to dwell on the cause of this strange apprehensive exultation that she sensed flickering at the edge of her mind: it was the fact that in Daniel Goldberg she'd seen the rarest thing of all—a man whom she knew at once, and without any qualification, to be her equal.

ONLY A MILE AWAY, the Tzaddik sat in his drawing room, waiting for Mr. Parrish to explain why he'd lost Sally.

The monkey was crouched on his shoulder, turning the kernel of a Brazil nut over and over in her little black hands before nibbling at it swiftly. Mr. Parrish would have been nervous but for the fact that he was applying the principles of Oriental mind control, as expounded by the great mystic Wu Shu-Fan in a book Mr. Parrish had purchased the previous spring. Deep breathing was involved, and a spiral movement of the psychic energies around the spinal column.

His psychic energies corkscrewing briskly upward, his

breathing profound and diaphragmatic, Mr. Parrish faced his patron with equanimity and told him what had happened.

"She had a pistol, Mr. Lee," he explained. "It was quite clear what was going to happen. She'd've shot me first, because I was in her sights, and then if need be she'd've shot the other two, and in the panic she'd've escaped, like she did anyway. Now, I shouldn't like the inconvenience of being wounded, but the embarrassment of being dead would be far worse, especially for the court case. No possibility of claiming the child then. What we did was to smash the tea shop window and follow her. She caught an omnibus to the East End. It was crowded—streets full—busy time of day—but I got a cab and followed it and watched closely to see where she got off. Unfortunately, the traffic being thick, I lost sight of the vehicle. But I did notice it was a dark green one, and that line terminates in Whitechapel."

"Did you take her belongings away from the lodging house in Bloomsbury?"

"The landlady—a Mrs. Parker—refused to let anything leave the house. So I don't know what she's got there. I could have it burgled, if you like, Mr. Lee."

The big man considered. The monkey finished her nut and climbed down, head first, to fetch another from the bowl of nuts the butler had shelled earlier. Mr. Lee gave a soft command, and instantly the monkey brought a walnut to his lips and thrust it between them.

When he had chewed it slowly and swallowed it all, he spoke again.

"Do not burgle the lodging house. Continue to search. However, I am not impressed with what you have done so far. You are not sufficiently self-critical. The money in her bank account you may keep; all her shares, all the property she owns in stocks and bonds, you will make over to me. If it is you who finds her, you may have it all back; if she is found by another agency, you will not see it again. Do that at once. I shall require evidence as soon as is practicable tomorrow morning that all the stocks, shares, and bonds which

were once registered in the name of Veronica Beatrice
Lockhart and then claimed as his due possession by Arthur
James Parrish have been transferred to my ownership."

"I understand, Mr. Lee," said Mr. Parrish, the Oriental
mind control shaken badly. "You intend to call in another
agency, then, sir? May I inquire which one I shall be—as it
were—competing against?"

"Yes," said Mr. Lee. "The Metropolitan Police. On your
way out you may show in the gentleman who is waiting in
the hall. He is Assistant Commissioner Bushell."

The psychic spiral sagged entirely. Mr. Parrish got up and
was about to say something else, but looked at his patron's
impassive face and thought better of it.

"Good night, sir," he said, endeavoring to sound positive
and project an impression of vigor and efficiency. "I shall
bring you that financial information tomorrow morning, sir.
Good night."

Assistant Commissioner Bushell was a middle-aged man
with a dry cough and a deferential manner—deferential to
Mr. Lee, that is; to Mr. Parrish he was dismissive.

He sat down and listened carefully as Mr. Lee explained
what he wanted.

"A woman called Lockhart—Miss Sally Lockhart—is in
hiding, probably though not certainly in the East End, with
a child of two years old, a girl called Harriet. I want you to
find her. She is blond, pretty, in her early twenties. She has
very little money, as far as I know. She is already the subject
of a police hunt; the newspaper on the table to your right
will explain why. Miranda, another nut . . ."

The monkey sprang at once to the bowl, snatched a walnut, and thrust it into Mr. Lee's mouth while the senior policeman read the passage Sally herself had seen in *The Times*
the day before.

Mr. Bushell finished reading and folded the paper neatly.

"I was not personally aware of this business," he said. "As
a senior officer, naturally I do not concern myself with day-
to-day operational matters. It would be difficult, indeed, to

do so without attracting attentions which would be perhaps a little unwelcome. . . ."

"Do it," said Mr. Lee flatly. "Cover it up how you like. The alternative is that I tell your superior—and the newspapers—about your connection with the houses. I have all the details of every visit you have ever made, times, payments, money you have won or lost, all the girls you have seen. You knew there would be a price, Bushell. Here it is: put every man you can onto it, and find that woman."

Mr. Bushell, unacquainted with the mysteries of Oriental mind control, wilted visibly. Then he nodded, sighed, and rose to go.

"One more thing," said Mr. Lee before his visitor reached the door. "Somewhere in Soho there is a man calling himself Goldberg—a journalist. It's come to my attention that he is misusing his position as a guest in this country by spying on various legitimate commercial operations. It would be an act of decency and patriotism to find out exactly where this scoundrel is hiding, and let the Home Secretary know what he's doing, so that he can be deported. He is, as a matter of fact, under sentence of death in Hungary; the authorities there would be pleased to have him back. See to it, would you?"

18

The Order of Sanctissima Sophia

MR. PARRISH HAD MANY CONTACTS ON THE UNSAVORY SHORES of the underworld, and it didn't take him long to set the search for Sally in motion. He did it scientifically, following the principles outlined in Abner T. Handley's capital work, *The Young Man's Friend: A Guide to Business Success*, which he had spent many profitable hours studying. Abner T. Handley was eloquent on the subjects of prudence and resourcefulness, and Mr. Parrish felt that he'd set new standards in those departments, because he'd offered a reward of fifty pounds for news of Sally's whereabouts—the money, of course, being Sally's own. What could be more elegantly economical than making the quarry pay for the hunt?

Simultaneously, Assistant Commissioner Bushell was instructing the superintendents of the Whitechapel, Stepney, and Thames divisions of the Metropolitan Police to divert as many men as possible to the search. They had a total of 1,235 men under their commands, and while privately each of them thought it was a quite extraordinary and unwarranted interference from the old man, who ought to stick to pushing paper around in Scotland Yard, they were nonetheless each determined to look good by catching her; so they returned to their divisions and set a good number of those 1,235 to work.

Nor did Assistant Commissioner Bushell forget Goldberg. He had his own views on foreign agitators, socialists to a man, or communists, or anarchists, or worse, and he had an agent who'd done this kind of work for him in the past; so

he summoned him to Scotland Yard and told him to look for
this political scoundrel and report back as soon as he'd found
him.

Sally, that morning, went out with Miss Robbins again.
They went this time to visit a family of matchbox makers.
Miss Robbins was compiling statistics for a report on social
conditions in the East End, and Sally went with her because
she wanted to see a sweatshop.

It was a family of five: father, mother, two daughters in
their teens, and a sick little boy of seven all crammed into a
room no bigger than twelve feet by eight. The boy lay on a
mattress in the corner, scarcely breathing. The rest of them
worked around a table in the dingy light from the window.
The air was thick with the smells of sickness, of sweat, of
fish, of glue. The family's hands moved without ceasing,
pasting strips of wood to strips of magenta-colored paper,
standing them on one side to dry, then folding them into
matchboxes. One of the daughters, a bright, rebellious-look-
ing girl, was tying bundles of completed boxes together. They
got twopence farthing from the factory for every twelve dozen
boxes they made, said the father. Sally could hardly believe
it, but Miss Robbins confirmed what he said. Furthermore,
they had to buy their own string and paste. By working all
the hours of daylight and late into the night, they could make
just enough money to keep starvation at bay.

"Not really a sweatshop," Miss Robbins said as they came
away, "because they're working for themselves, in a sense,
not for a small employer who owns the premises and orga-
nizes the work. But it comes to the same thing: exploitation.
By the match factory, in this case. That girl, incidentally,
will leave home soon. The one tying the bundles. She's being
enticed away by a woman who runs a brothel in Devonshire
Street. She'll earn money quickly there, and then die of disease."

"You can't know that for certain," Sally said, feeling that
she had to say something on the side of hope.

"Perhaps not. Perhaps a kindhearted gentleman with five

hundred pounds a year will fall in love with her and marry her. Perhaps an angel will come down and take her straight to heaven. Perhaps she'll be run over by an omnibus. I can't predict the fate of an individual. But what's undeniable is that in a thousand other sweatshops there are girls as pretty as that, as lively and quick and frustrated as that, and of those a large number will end as I describe. Nothing is more certain."

Sally couldn't argue. The pity of it made her dumb, so she turned back to what she knew about—money and profits and costs; and she began to wonder how many clients she'd advised to buy shares in Bryant and May's, the match manufacturers. Why, she owned some herself.

THERE WERE three letters waiting for her at the mission, but she didn't have time to look at them until after she'd helped in the kitchen, giving out soup and bread to the women and children sheltering there. A dark gentleman had brought the letters; that was all the maid could tell her. Sally put them into her pocket to read later, but she felt her heart leap at the sight of the bold, black writing on one of them.

After Harriet had eaten, and they'd cleared up and washed the dishes, Sally took her up to rest. She was clinging and a little flushed and fretful, and Sally fussed over her, cuddling her to sleep before laying her gently in the bed and covering her up.

Then in the thin afternoon light she took out the letters. She recognized Sarah-Jane Russell's handwriting, and opened hers and read:

Dear Miss Lockhart,

I do hope you are safely hidden. There have been three men watching the house since yesterday, and a policeman called with a warrant to search it. I had to let him in. He says there is a warrant to arrest you. I could not believe it; it sounds dreadful, but if he said it it must be true. He took away a lot of papers and things. I tried to stop him, but he said his warrant empowered him to do it. I do so wish they would come back from South America, but there is no news.

Mrs. Molloy came today to see what news there was; she is dreadfully worried. I do not wish to make things more difficult, but the cook and Ellie will need paying tomorrow, and I have no money.

I send on the letter from Oxford with Mr. Goldberg. He came before, but I did not know who he was and could not tell him anything.

I will do whatever I can to help. Please kiss darling Harriet for me and give her my love. I hope so much that this will all soon be over.

With all my love,
Sarah-Jane.

The letter from Oxford was in Nicholas Bedwell's handwriting.

My dear Sally,

I think I've found your elusive Mr. Beech. A chum of mine who used to be the chaplain of Exeter College is now—well, it's a long story, but the gist of it is that there's an establishment in Hampstead (Rolfe Road) known as the Order of Saint Sophia. The full name's longer than that, but I'm in a hurry to catch the post, and you'll find it.

It seems to be a brotherhood of priests or monks or something. *Sophia* means "wisdom"; it's a precious-scented sort of flummery that I haven't any time for myself. There's a lot of it in Oxford; aesthetic undergraduates giving each other extravagant titles and performing fanciful rites. It's Roman Catholic, not Anglican, but my chum Reggie Routledge tells me that it includes a number of converts; and one of them is a Gervase Davidson Beech, who spent some time convalescing, for want of a better word, in the community of St. Anselm's, Norwich.

If I might suggest it, a frontal attack (just go there and come straight out with it) might be the best bet. Don't give him time to think of an excuse. I hope I'm not misjudging the man; but the nature of the affliction which took him to St. Anselm's for a cure makes it only too likely, I'm afraid, that I'm not. But perhaps you would like me as a man of the cloth to see what I can find out from him?

I have seen nothing in the papers regarding your court case. I need hardly say that you and dear Harriet are in our prayers. Let me know what you would like me to do.

> Most affectionately yours,
> Nicholas.

She put it down simultaneously elated, touched, and exasperated: because if Nicholas knew what this affliction of Mr. Beech's was, and if it had a bearing on the case, why on earth didn't he name it?

However, in an hour or so she could ask the man himself. *Thank you, Nick,* she thought, and resolved to write to him as soon as she came back.

Then she opened Goldberg's letter, observing that her hands were shaking.

Dear Miss Lockhart,

I was sorry not to find you here when I arrived, but the excellent Dr. Turner was kind enough to agree to pass these letters on to you. I hope they contain news which will cheer you.

I'm going now to visit Miss Haddow. I hope to call again at the mission this evening.

> In haste,
> Daniel Goldberg.

She felt deflated, for some reason, and foolish for feeling so. She made arrangements for Susan to look after Harriet, and hurried out.

A DARK GREEN omnibus to Tottenham Court Road, then a yellow one to Haverstock Hill; sixpence altogether, and three quarters of an hour after she left the mission, she was walking down Rolfe Road looking for the Order of Saint Sophia.

It was a quiet suburban road with secluded houses sheltered by trees, and large gardens. She had no idea what to look for, but it wasn't long before she saw a painted sign on a wooden gate. It said in small red gothic letters:

THE MOST NOBLE AND SACRED ORDER
OF THE EMANATION
OF THE BLESSED AND HOLY SANCTISSIMA SOPHIA

The house was well looked after, and the garden was tidy, if rather austere. She rang the doorbell, and after a minute the door was opened by a thin man dressed as a Catholic priest.

"Good afternoon," she said. "I've come to see Mr. Beech."

He looked a little pained.

"Mr. Beech is . . . well, he is in the house. . . . Is he expecting you?"

"No, but he'll know who I am when he sees me," she said. "My name is Lockhart."

She spoke as pleasantly as she could. There was something narrow and fastidious about this man, with his slightly preposterous gold medallion on its chain around his neck, and his amethyst ring. She didn't want to have the door shut in her face. He made up his mind and stepped aside.

"Well, you'd better wait in the hall," he said.

Dark, oppressive furniture, meticulously cleaned and polished; a scent of incense in the air; a feeling of impersonality. The priest awkwardly gestured to a chair for her and vanished up the stairs. She sat and waited. Apart from the incense and the oddly institutional feeling, there was nothing to mark this house as being the headquarters of the Order of the Most Holy Sophia's Emanation, whatever that was.

Five minutes went past, and then she heard someone coming downstairs. He reached the bottom and turned: a thin, sallow, elderly-looking man, dressed like the one who'd let her in, and with the same golden device on a chain around his neck.

"Mr. Beech?" she said.

"I am," he replied. "I am afraid I don't know who you are, Miss Lockhart. I am not sure how I can help you."

"Were you once the rector of St. Thomas's in Portsmouth?"

"I was, but for some time now I have . . ."

His voice sagged. She looked at him in alarm, for he looked as if he was going to faint. He'd suddenly realized who she was.

She wasn't going to help him. She watched as he struggled to a chair. He looked as though he wanted to sink onto it, but he held the back and stayed upright.

"You had better come into the library," he said in a voice that was hardly more than a whisper.

He opened the door for her. The library was not much of one; a few shelves of books, a table, some chairs, and over the mantelpiece a painting in the symbolist manner, full of people with halos, and golden rays, and ecstatic expressions.

She sat down, and he shut the door.

"You know why I've come," she said.

"Yes."

"You falsified a marriage register to make it look as if I'd married a Mr. Parrish."

"I . . . yes."

He was standing brokenly by the table, twisting the golden medallion between his fingers. In the clearer light of the library Sally could see that it wasn't gold at all, but brass. It consisted of a vaguely female shape surrounded by rays, as if she were giving off light.

"What is that?" she said, after a few moments' silence.

"The symbol of Sanctissima Sophia, the Most Holy Wisdom."

"And what is this . . . order of yours?"

"A group, a band of . . . of initiates devoted to the understanding, the propagation, so to speak, of the Holy Wisdom."

"The Holy Wisdom? Is that different from the everyday kind?"

"It . . . naturally, there is an esoteric aspect which I cannot . . . degrees of initiation . . . It is a complex system, based ultimately on the idea of salvation through, through, through knowledge. . . . A very ancient doctrine . . . Gnostic . . ."

"So if you know the right things, you go to heaven. Yes, well, I can understand that. The opposite is *not* knowing things, and that's pretty hellish, Mr. Beech. I didn't know for three years that I was married to Mr. Parrish, for instance. Is that an example of the secret knowledge you're so devoted to?"

"Miss Lockhart, I beg you to allow me to explain. . . ."

"That's exactly what I've come for."

He pulled out a chair and sat down across the table. His skin was loose, papery, and yellow; he looked as if he'd been profoundly ill. Nicholas's *Crockford's Clerical Directory* had revealed that he was in his early fifties, but he looked eighty. His eyes were watery and bloodshot. She had never seen such guilt, such weakness, such misery, such—what? There was a cunning stubbornness in his face, too, which she did not like.

"Well?" she said.

"It was something which occurred when I was not altogether in my full health," he said. His eyes would look at her a moment, and then flick away again. "Since I was a young man, as a missionary in the tropics, I have been subject to a . . . a . . . an affliction which renders me, from time to time, perhaps . . . ah . . . less sure in my judgment than I should be. This incident . . . to my intense regret, my profound embarrassment . . . it fell in one of those periods."

"Why did you do it?"

"I have explained. I cannot be sure of my actions at such times. It was a deplorable lapse, truly deplorable. I admit it freely."

"I asked *why*. Why did you do it? Did he make you?"

"He?"

"Parrish, of course."

"It is hard to be sure, at this distance. . . . Please believe me, I was not acting from malice; I had no idea that there was really anyone of your name. It was of the nature of a jest, a sportive essay in . . ."

"Oh, stop lying, Mr. Beech. Have you any notion of what this has led to?"

"Please, Miss—er—Lockhart, please keep your voice a little lower, I beg you—"

"I have a daughter. Yes, an illegitimate daughter, but mine, and I love her. Her father is dead. I have never met Mr. Parrish in my life. Suddenly I was served with papers saying that he was suing me for divorce and custody of my child. He was able to tell this—this fantastic lie because of what *you* did three years ago when you entered a false record in the marriage register. I've been trying to find you ever since I saw it there, and now I've finally tracked you down, you're going to have to testify in court that you made that false entry. You're the only person who can say with absolute certainty that Parrish did not marry me that January. If you . . ."

She stopped, aware that he was shaking his head. She stared. He looked down.

"You're going to have to," she said again.

"No. I cannot."

"*Why?* Why are you doing this to me? My *daughter*—you'll let a complete stranger take her away from me? *Why?*"

He swallowed several times, tried to speak, made as if to get up. She reached across the table and seized his papery wrist, aware of the urgent strength in her fingers and quite willing to snap those frail bones if that would have helped.

"Please—you're hurting me—"

"Why did you do it? What hold has he got over you, for God's sake? Why won't you admit it's not true?"

"I cannot—I cannot be spoken to like this—"

The door opened. Mr. Beech looked around like a guilty schoolboy.

"May I ask what is the occasion for this extraordinary display?" said the priest who'd shown Sally in.

She let go of Mr. Beech's wrist, and he sank backward, sniveling, his lower lip quivering, tears in his eyes.

"I am trying to persuade Mr. Beech to do what he knows is right. He has grievously harmed me and endangered my child, and only he can make things right. Mr. Beech, I ask you again: Will you testify in court that you made a false entry in that marriage register?"

"I cannot be compelled. . . . It would be quite incompatible with my, my, my work for the Order of Sanctissima Sophia for me to be submitted to the cross-examination of a—"

"Very well. Will you sign an affidavit saying it?"

"I cannot do that. It would be improper for a man of, of the cloth to commit himself to, to an oath of any kind."

"Mr. Beech has made his position clear, it seems to me," said the other man. "I think you will not gain anything by adopting a threatening manner. I must ask you to leave."

He moved toward her, and desperately she said, "Very well, I shan't threaten Mr. Beech with anything. I'll even withdraw my request for his help in court. He can stay here undisturbed. But you must see that I need to know *why!* Why did you do it? Was it Parrish who made you, or someone else? What did they do to make you sign that register?"

"No, it was not! I don't know anyone called Parrish!"

"You wrote a letter to a clergyman in Clapham recommending Mr. Parrish. You must have known him."

"I was ill!"

"Who was it, three years ago? Who came to you and got you to sign the register?"

They were all three standing, and none of them moved for some moments. Finally Mr. Beech made a convulsive little shudder and began to cry. His shoulders heaved, the tears ran thickly down his cheeks, his hands mopped helplessly at his nose and his eyes. The other man turned and let him out the door; Sally heard his frail footsteps mount the stairs.

The priest shut the door again.

"I do not know what is best in this case," he said heavily. "Mr. Beech is of course subject to the disciplines of this order, which he joined recently, but they do not include the power to force brothers to reveal anything they wish to keep private. . . . But there is another involved, namely yourself, and if I understand you correctly there is a child in danger. This is very difficult."

He looked at the tawdry picture over the mantelpiece as if for inspiration.

"What I can do is this. It did not come to me in the confessional, and I don't consider it especially secret; the housekeeper knows, and the gardener's boy knows, and better you should hear it from me than from someone of that sort. Mr. Beech has been suffering for years from a condition which he contracted as a young man. He told me when he first joined this order that he had recovered from it, but to my sorrow I discovered that that was not true. He was receiving packages brought to him and left in the care of the housekeeper, as I say, or the gardener's boy. So I can make a guess that the sender of those packages was the same person who made him do whatever it is that has hurt you—the same person who is still in control of him."

"Still?"

"Oh, yes. Mr. Beech is unhappily still a victim; I fear that at his age . . ."

"But what *is* this illness of his? And why should it give anyone else a hold over him?"

"Oh, I beg your pardon; I should have made it clearer. Mr. Beech is a victim of morphine. He is addicted to the consumption of opium."

OPIUM . . .

Sally had shivered when she heard that. She'd had expe-

rience of what opium could do, and now she understood
Nicholas Bedwell's curious reference in the letter: because
his twin brother had been trapped, as Mr. Beech was, into
helpless dependence on the drug.

So it was blackmail: sign that register, or we'll expose you.
His will weakened by years of addiction, he'd signed. All
that Sanctissima Sophia nonsense was an attempt to forget,
to cover up, to distract his guilt by flinging mysticism in its
face. How many other weak little crimes had he committed?
How many other lies had he told?

But they were still supplying him with the drug. That was
interesting. It was why he didn't want to say any more, of
course; they might cut off the supply. There was something
in this opium connection that made an alarm bell jangle
somewhere in Sally's mind. The hair on her neck was bristling, and she didn't know why.

SHE SPENT the early part of the evening playing with Harriet
and cutting bread for the supper which they all shared. Harriet
was definitely not well. She had a slight fever, and she couldn't
concentrate on any game for long without becoming cross
and tearful, and Sally was torn between her desire to fuss
over Harriet and her awareness of the much worse sufferings
of some of the other children.

When she had a spare moment, she went to the dispensary
to see if Dr. Turner could reassure her about the fever; and
to her surprise she found the doctor alone and in tears.

"Oh—silly—can't help it, damn it. But it always takes me
like this—oh, when will we be able to *change* things?"

Sally put her arms around her and let her sob. It seemed
that a woman with tuberculosis had come to the mission earlier, and Dr. Turner had had to send her away. She should
have gone to the London Hospital in the Whitechapel Road,
not far away, but she'd refused.

"They know it's a sentence of death—they only go there
to die, they all say that, and they won't go in. She begged
me to let her in here, but, oh, I can't let disease in—I just

daren't. Any infection will spread and spread. She's just going to sleep in the street, I know it—"

Sally let her cry; she was so strong, so honest in her tears, that Sally had to cry too, for Dr. Turner, for the little boy Johnny, for the woman with consumption, for all those poor stunted lives. And all her own fears and problems seemed not separate for once but part of them, part of this great ocean of unhappiness that was lapping at the door of the mission.

"I'm no use to you," Sally said.

They looked at each other, each tear-stained and red-eyed. Dr. Turner shook her head. Then she stood back and blew her nose and sighed.

"Come and listen to Jack Burton tonight," she said. "He'll cheer both of us up."

"Who's he?"

"A docker. He's trying to get all the dockworkers behind the union, so the union can help all the workers. Unless they're united, you see, they can be exploited so easily. Jack Burton's so cheerful, such a powerful speaker, he lifts my heart, makes me think it's all possible. Do come, Sally! May I call you Sally? I'm Angela."

"I'd like to. I'd love to. This is a new world to me; I'd never dreamed of things like this, troubles like this—those matchbox makers I saw this morning. But . . . I'm worried about Harriet. She's got a slight fever, and I don't think I ought to go out. Anyway, there's someone coming to see me. About the business involving Harriet, you remember. I'll tell you more about it soon; I found out something today. I think I'm on the track."

"You'll come another time? Sally, I can't tell you how much strength there is, how much wasted talent and imagination and all those qualities like intelligence and courage and leadership and vision. They're all there, in working men and women. They don't need middle-class do-gooders like me! All they need is the *chance*. . . ."

"They don't respect you because you're middle-class, for

goodness' sake, Angela; they respect you because of what you are yourself. You're a doctor. How many doctors choose to work here? Think how valuable that is! And you're a woman who struggled to become a doctor—and people know how difficult that is and how determined you must have been to do it. You *know* how valuable your work is. And you know how well you do it. Don't you? Don't let *them* corner all the pride. You've got things to be proud of too."

"Them?"

"The enemy. The landlords, the factory owners."

"The capitalists?"

"Yes. Including me, I know. But I'm not one of *them*. And I'm learning all the time."

Angela nodded, blew her nose again, and smiled briskly with her red-rimmed eyes.

"Now, what's the matter with Harriet?" she said. "Let's go and have a look."

BILL WAS BUSY. The *melamed*, Mr. Kipnis, had found a surge of energy in some bottle or other and was making Bill work hard at his tattered copy of Webb, Millington, and Co.'s *New Indestructible Pictorial Lesson Book.*

"I bought that for you personally," he said for the tenth time in their acquaintance. "I went looking down the Farringdon Road. Spent hours till I found it. Cost me three-pence. There's a lot of wear in that book. Do your best, now. Do that one there, that wossname, that bird."

His trembling fingers fumbled the book open. Bill looked down at a picture of an owl and frowned as he tried to make out the words below it.

"*The* . . . that's an owl, innit? *The owl—is to be—found—among—old* . . . *old* . . . I can't do that one, Mr. Kipnis."

"Giss a look." The old man peered at it. "*Ruins*, boy. See, there's a bloody great *R*, then you go *oo*, and then you got *ins. Ruins.* Go on. You do it."

"*Ruins, and in—holl* . . . *hollow trees.*" Bill felt a sense of relief at every full stop; it meant he'd got a bit further. Already the little words were becoming transparent: he could see through them into the text, like a lot of little windows into a house. And day by day more light got in, so that the big words were beginning to look familiar too, and he felt more able to guess what they might be, and got more of his guesses right. It wouldn't be long now before he'd be able to go straight to the *Communist Manifesto*. "*It feeds on . . . on . . . young . . . hares, rabbits*—here, look, Mr. Kipnis, there's *rabbits* on this page and all. That's *rabbits*, innit?"

"That's right, boy. You're doing well. It's a good book, this 'un. Lot of wisdom in this book. Here . . ."

Mr. Kipnis looked around blurrily. They were in the lodging house in Dean Street, and Goldberg was out. The *melamed* beckoned Bill closer and leaned over to say quietly: "Summing I heard today. You tell Mr. Goldberg they're looking for him. The coppers. He ought to lay low for a bit. They're after him, that's what I heard. You tell him, all right?"

"The coppers? What for?"

"I dunno that, do I? But he wants to keep out of the way. No sense in provoking trouble if you can run and keep out of it."

"Suppose he don't want to run?"

"That's what Jewish people always have to do, son. We're not wanted anywhere. The best we got to hope for, it's just keeping down, keeping out of trouble. Course, it'd be different in Jerusalem. In Eretz Israel. But that's not for the likes of us, not in our lifetime." He sighed melodically; his ancient eyes were moist. His fingers fumbled for the tin flask in his pocket, and he nodded to the book. "Go on, boy, that whatchamacallit, that owl. Don't stop."

Frowning, Bill picked up the book again. Running away, keeping out of trouble—that didn't sound like Goldberg. Or Kid Mendel. There must be Jews who didn't run away. What kind of respect would the great Bridie Sullivan of Lambeth Walk have for him if he turned and ran? She had fellows like Liam to compare him with.

"Don't forget, now," said Mr. Kipnis. "You pass it on, what I said."

"All right, Mr. Kipnis. But he won't run—you watch. *It feeds on . . . young hares, rabbits, rats, mice, and birds. It—seeks its food when—night comes on. . . .*"

AT EIGHT o'clock that evening, the maid opened the door of the office where Sally was filing some letters and said, "Lady to see you, miss."

It was Margaret. Sally gave a little gasp, and then embraced.

"Did you get—did he come—?"

"Oh, Sally, you've no idea—"

Margaret's expression was troubled. Sally pulled out a chair and let her talk.

"Ever since Thursday—all yesterday in fact, and all this morning—there've been men in the office, accountants, going through everything—every letter, every file, every single thing. They came first thing yesterday morning. They were going to take it all away. They had a warrant, but I read it very carefully, and it didn't say anything about taking things away, so I ran down and got the porter to lock the door while I ran next-door to that odd little lawyer—you remember him, the man with the limp? He was *excellent*. He came straightaway and looked at the warrant. They were about to smash the door down, and he said if they'd done that he'd have sued them for damages. At any rate, I engaged him at once, and he made sure they didn't take anything away, but had to do all their searching there. Sally, they're taking our business to pieces! Mr. Wentworth—he's the lawyer—he's discovered that it's not just your money they're after. It's the business itself, and according to the papers he's seen, they're applying for some order to make us stop trading on the grounds that the company's improperly registered. It all comes back to the marriage claim. The idea is that since you didn't reveal that you were trading with your husband's money, all our activities are illegal. They're just—helping themselves. . . . I've been there all day trying to answer questions, trying to stem it, and I think they've done all they can for the moment. Mr. Wentworth has been wonderfully industrious; he's understood everything and worked as quickly as anyone could hope. He's applied for every kind of stalling process—injunctions, writs, I don't know, everything possible—and it's held them up until Monday. But he can't do any more without your authority to act. If he can look at the papers in your case against Parrish, he might be able to find another way through. But, oh, Sally, they were so arrogant. They seemed to think they had the right to just walk in and take anything they wanted. I know now how you felt—corrupted, invaded—it's horrible. . . ."

Cool, ironic Margaret, talking like this, showing her helplessness. Sally was shaken.

"But what's been happening to you?" Margaret went on. "How did you get here? What *is* this place? Who's the man who came to the office? Oh, don't worry, we didn't speak in front of the men. And how's Harriet?"

Sally told her everything that had happened. Only a couple of days, and it felt like an epic. She finished with the strange, unsatisfactory, but tantalizing interview with Mr. Beech and the revelation about opium.

"Margaret, I don't know why, but I keep coming back to that. There's something there that's not right. But would this lawyer, Mr. Wentworth, would he really be able to take on my case? Do you trust him?"

"Yes, I do. He's quick and he's clever and he's honest. He hasn't got many clients, I think. I mean, he's not very prepossessing. Perhaps people choose their lawyers for their looks; and his office is very shabby. But, yes, seeing what he's done, I'd trust him with anything now. The only thing is this: You'll have to give yourself up to the police."

"But—absolutely not! I couldn't possibly—"

"*Listen.* He can't help you if you're in hiding. He'd only get into trouble himself, and then it *would* be impossible. He's got to act within the law. But if you once give yourself

up and appoint him, he can get you bail for the gun business—you know, in the tea shop—get Harriet made a ward
of court to keep her safe from Parrish for the time being, get
all the papers from your previous solicitor and start work right
away. Unless you do that, he can't act."

Sally got up and walked to the window. It overlooked the
street, and there was nothing but darkness out there now,
with one or two dim gas lamps to hold it back. Much of
Whitechapel—the main streets, at least—was lively during
the early evening, with pubs and market stalls doing a fine
trade, but this was a quiet street, and no one was out at all.

She leaned her forehead on the cold glass. If she had a
good lawyer working for her, he might be able to fight it off,
this evil craziness. Parrish's claim would be dismissed, Harriet
would be safe, she'd get her money back, the business would
be rescued.

But farther off in the darkness lay the Tzaddik. He was
the source of it. If Parrish were disposed of, it wouldn't make
any difference; the Tzaddik was too well concealed, and there
wouldn't be the slightest trace to connect him with Parrish.
Furthermore, he'd be warned by what happened and withdraw even farther.

And out there in the dark, he'd be able to mount another
attack. And like this one, it would be so well prepared, so
long in coming, that the blow, when it fell, would be deadly.
Perhaps there was another trap already prepared in case this
one failed; from the thoroughness with which he'd set this
one up, she didn't think he'd fail to cover every possibility.
Her life might already be surrounded invisibly by dozens of
traps, all ingenious and deadly and just waiting to be sprung.

No: her fight was with the Tzaddik, and her best chance
of winning it was to stay in hiding and for the moment let
Parrish do his worst. If it were just her property, though,
she'd give it up without a thought; but there was Margaret
to consider; and if once they found out where Harriet
was . . .

She turned around, intending to say . . . she didn't know

what—tell Margaret about the Tzaddik, perhaps; but before she could speak, the door opened, and there stood Goldberg.

And having seen Goldberg, she looked back at Margaret and realized, from Margaret's expression, what look there was on her own face. And she was swept by confusion and blushed as she'd never blushed before.

Goldberg nodded courteously to Margaret.

"Good evening," he said. "Your lawyer Mr. Wentworth is a good man. I have spoken to him. But later for that. Miss Lockhart, you're needed now. Down on the river. Is the child safe here? Then come. Miss Haddow . . ."

Another nod and he went out, leaving the door open for Sally. With a helpless look at Margaret, she followed.

19

Rebecca's Story

THEY WALKED DOWN ROYAL MINT STREET TOWARD THE Tower of London. Goldberg was urgent and preoccupied, and in answer to her questions he said only, "We're going to meet a ship. I'll tell you more when we're on the river."

The streets were crowded, and the pavements narrow, and he took her arm as if he had a right to, walking steadily and swiftly beside her. She was aware, through her hand pressed against his side, of his tension, and of his strength, too; there was something implacable about him. She felt baffled by the strength of her own feelings, and even more baffled as to what those feelings were.

They turned down toward the river. The great bulk of the Tower of London rose darkly on their right. At the end of the street, before it turned left, a narrow opening led to a flight of stone stairs that went down to the water. Before they went through, Goldberg stopped and pointed toward the dock gates farther down the street.

"See all those cabs?" he said. "And the hangers-on?"

Sally could see that the road was blocked. A policeman was trying vainly to organize the cabs into a line, and people were jostling and shouting. They looked like a flock of greedy vultures eager to get at a kill, and she said that to Goldberg.

"Exactly what they are," he said. "They're waiting to prey on the Jews who come ashore. The first boats will be arriving very soon; we'd better hurry."

He led her through the opening and down the steps. They were lit only by a feeble gaslight at the angle of the warehouse that stood on the left, and the steps were wet and slippery. She took Goldberg's hand.

At the foot of the steps a man was waiting in a rowboat. He had an old-fashioned horn lantern, and he held it up as they came down toward him. Sally saw a dirty, gray-bearded face and caught, even before she was close, a powerful drift of spirits.

"Evening, Mr. G.," said the boatman.

"Evening, Charlie. We're going to bring back one passenger, and we want to come ashore here."

"Right you are, sir."

The old man held the boat steady as Sally got in. Goldberg settled himself down with her in the stern, and then the boatman fixed the lantern on a pole at the bow and took up the oars.

"Where are the crimps working from?" said Goldberg.

"Off the Pier Head, sir. St. Katharine's Basin. See, there's sixty, maybe seventy people to come ashore, maybe more. They offload 'em at the Pier Head, then they can get away straight up Little Thames Street. You seen all them cabs? The cabmen got wind of this trade in the last month or so. They put a copper there regular now, to control 'em. There was nearly a hundred there last week."

He pushed off, then slipped the oars into the oarlocks and started to pull away with short, light strokes.

"What are crimps?" said Sally.

"Parasites," said Goldberg. "Swindlers. Minor criminals. Those vultures you saw back there."

Their voices sounded different on the open water, away from the enclosing cliffs of brick.

"Them cabs," said the boatman, "they're the worst. Even if they got somewhere to go to, the people coming in, they can't speak English, most of 'em, so they just repeat the address till the cabbie gets it. Then they're off. Some of them cabbies'll take 'em all over the place, out to Walthamstow, Leyton, Wanstead Flats, drop 'em there and charge a fortune. There'll be plenty of that tonight, this being a Rotterdam boat. They don't bother with the Hamburg ones. It's the sweatshops that do for the Hamburg passengers. Looking for greeners."

"This is a new language to me," said Sally. "What are greeners?"

"Newly arrived workers. Blokes without jobs who don't know their way around. Green, yer see."

It was a still night, and the water slid under the boat like oiled silk. Goldberg sat quietly beside her, and the gin-flavored old boatman looked half-asleep, only those quick light strokes, as regular as clockwork, showing that he was in command. Sally felt suspended—between sky and water, past and future, danger and . . . and what? She looked at Goldberg, but she wasn't sure of his expression under the wide brim of his hat.

"What have you brought me here for?" she said. "Is there something you want me to do?"

He nodded. "There's a young woman traveling alone. She has some news of the Tzaddik, and I want to be sure we hear it as soon as possible. And we have to be quick. At the ship there will be women like the ones I told you about, probably several of them, watching out for single girls. They speak Yiddish, Russian, German. They pretend to come from Jewish charities—anything to take them in."

"The white goods?" said Sally.

He nodded. "We must find Rebecca Meyer—that's this girl—and keep her out of their hands. The problem is, she's expecting to be met by a woman. If you find her and stay with her, she'll come with us. Will you do that?"

Sally nodded. "How will I know her?"

"I have a photograph. Here."

He handed her a tattered photograph and struck a match for her to see it by. The girl was pictured standing on the front step of a house in, she supposed, Russia; dark, heavy-featured, suspicious, with a shawl covering her hair. She was holding a broom and looked like a servant of some kind. The match went out.

"Does she speak English?" said Sally.

"Not much. Some German, I think. Show her the photograph if you need to. It's going to be difficult; you'll have to make her trust you. I won't be with you; I have other work to do on board. But you can do it."

I hope I can, thought Sally. She tucked the photograph into her glove and sat back beside Goldberg as the boat moved out farther into the middle of the stream.

Then she saw the steamer. It sat some way off in a forest of masts, with lights glowing at the portholes and the bridge, and a swarm of smaller vessels—rowboats and dinghies like the one they were in, a steam launch or two, and many others she couldn't make out—clustered around it like bees. As they moved closer she saw that the deck was crowded with dark, huddled figures, and some were already swarming down the dimly lit, swaying stairs that hung alongside. Hands reached up to help them down, seized ragged bundles and swung them into the bottom of the boat before helping the owner down briskly and reaching up for the next.

Charlie, the boatman, kept the dinghy level with the steamer and a little way off, and Sally noticed for the first time that the tide was flowing strongly in.

One of the boats, laden and leaning over, moved away sluggishly, and another darted in to take its place. There seemed to be no order about which came next to the foot of the stairs—it was first come, first served, and the boatmen who jostled for position filled the night air with shouts and curses.

The boat that had just succeeded had two men in it, one to row and one, as Sally heard, to interpret. He was calling up in Yiddish to those on the deck, and Goldberg told her that the man was offering passage to the Pier Head, guaranteed cab journey to a clean Jewish lodging house, and an introduction to the landlord for no more than ten shillings. Sally drew breath at this, for the passage all the way from Rotterdam cost only a pound. Still, people were crowding down the ladder. Perhaps they didn't know what ten shillings was worth.

"Ah," said Goldberg. "Look who's arrived."

A steam launch was next to reach the ladder, sweeping aside a couple of smaller boats and leaving them rocking in its wake. A large, round-faced man in a top hat and Inverness cape was getting out and climbing the swaying stairs with difficulty, followed by a smaller man in a bowler hat carrying a dispatch case.

"Who's that?" said Sally.

"It's the famous Arnold Fox. If you haven't seen his name in the papers, you will. An anti-Semite. He's making a stir, trying to get Parliament to keep out the Jews. All right, Charlie, take us in. I want to see what he's up to. Ready, Miss Lockhart?"

Sally nodded. Hardly seeming to make any effort, the old boatman turned the dinghy and darted in skillfully between the stern of Arnold Fox's launch and the bow of the next.

As soon as they touched, Goldberg seized the railing and held it while Sally stepped over the side of the boat and onto the swinging narrow staircase. She was conscious of the stares from above, the jostling and shoving, the other boats crowding the dark water, and conscious too of Goldberg close behind her. She felt his hand on hers for a moment, looked down and met his eyes, and then turned back to the top.

Once on deck, in the harsh light and strong shadows thrown by the kerosene lamps, he leaned close and spoke quietly.

"As soon as you see her, move in. There'll be others eager to do the same. Look over there—I know that old witch; I've seen her before. A brothel keeper called Mrs. Paton. Look what she's doing."

He indicated a woman dressed in expensive-looking furs, her face heavily made-up. She was in her fifties, Sally supposed, with a narrow trap of a mouth and eyes as cold as coins. She was stroking the lapel of a pretty dark-eyed girl who was holding a bundle of luggage, helpless, bewildered, polite, as the older woman spoke wheedlingly into her ear.

The beringed hand moved up from her lapel and stroked her cheek. The girl said something, and the woman glanced over to a man by the rail and nodded. The girl moved away with them toward the stairs.

Sally wanted to dart forward and hold her back, but she found Goldberg's hand on her arm.

"We attack the roots, not the leaves. You want to see more? Watch that man."

He nodded at one of the passengers, a big man with a fur hat. As she watched, Sally saw that he was acting just like a sheepdog. The struggle for places, the jostling at the rail, the confusion weren't random at all. He was selecting some passengers to go down and holding others back, according to which boat was waiting at the bottom, and doing it so skillfully that it looked as if he was merely helping to keep the stream flowing.

"Who is he?" said Sally.

"He's one of the crimps. Look at the boatmen. Some are in the organization, some not, and they'll have a password, some kind of signal, something like that."

They watched over the rail, but in the darkness and the swift movements of the shouting boatmen below it was hard to see any signal they were making.

"Who's he picking out?" said Sally.

"The wealthy ones. That's to say, those with a few rubles left. The ones with not much, he doesn't care about. Imagine this, all the way from Russia; parasites every inch of the way. But now you must look for Rebecca Meyer. I'm going to leave you for a little while, but I'll find you again. Good luck."

She nodded. He moved away into the crowd, and she looked around and got her bearings. There was plenty to see.

Bundles everywhere—rough canvas sacks tied at the neck, small parcels carefully wrapped in calico, rolled-up mattresses and feather eiderdowns bulging out of the cords that held them together. Hats: no bowlers here, no top hats but

Arnold Fox the anti-Semite's, no tweed caps or deerstalkers; but Russian-style caps with leather brims, moth-eaten fur hats, one sumptuous article in astrakhan, and shawls; all the women wore shawls tied over their heads. Children: hollow-eyed, white-faced, ill after the crossing or lethargic through hunger. The men and women: foreign faces, all the men bearded, all the women broad of cheek and dark of eye.

And the smell. Dirty clothes, dirty bodies, filthy boots; smells of fried fish and of seasickness; smells of illness and poverty and long, weary travel.

She was standing near a well-lit doorway into the inner part of the ship. A gray-bearded man in uniform was standing in the doorway, blocking the path of Mr. Arnold Fox and his companion, who had a notebook and pencil in his hand.

"Captain van Houten, I insist that you answer my question," came the high, rich voice of Arnold Fox. "I am conducting a survey on behalf of the British Parliament, and I must have an answer. Has the customs officer been on board or not?"

"Of course," said the captain impatiently. "He came aboard at Gravesend, like always."

"And did he count the passengers? Or did he merely accept your numbers?"

"You mean my numbers are incorrect? You mean I can't count?"

"I must know, Captain van Houten. What number did you give him for the aliens on board?"

"Sixty-three. And that's correct."

"And did he count them?"

"I don't care if he looked or not. That's for him to say. Why don't you ask him? Why are you bothering me?"

"Be assured, I shall ask him," said Arnold Fox. "I would like to see your official returns, please."

"You got no authority for that. I give the documents to the collector at the report office. You want to see them, you go and ask him."

"Captain, I would remind you that this is an official parliamentary report."

"You a member of the government?"

"No, but—"

"You a member of Parliament, even?"

"I hardly see—"

"Don't waste my time. Any fool can say he's making an official report; it means nothing. Go and play somewhere else."

"Have you no concern for the plight of these unfortunate people?"

The captain snorted and turned away. Arnold Fox, quite unabashed, turned and called out over the noisy, teeming crowd on deck: "Anyone—here—speak—English? Anyone—on board—English?"

He moved through the throng, his large white nose wrinkling involuntarily as he tried to find an interpreter.

Sally moved away too, glancing at the photograph again to remind herself of Rebecca Meyer's appearance. But it wasn't a large photograph, and the girl's features were wrinkled against the sun, and in any case she had the same kind of build and look as many of these women. It wouldn't be easy.

She picked her way through the confusion on deck, ignoring the stares as best she could and looking carefully at every solitary woman or girl she could see. In the crowd, though, it was hard to see who was on her own and who wasn't. More than once she thought she'd found Rebecca Meyer, only for the woman concerned to pick up a nearby child or turn to a man behind her and say something, obviously part of a family.

Having moved through the whole throng as far as the bows, stepping over canvas bundles and mattresses and cracked and broken boxes tied together with string, she turned and looked back. Goldberg was nowhere in sight, but the man in the fur hat was busily at work by the stair, pretending to help by signaling for boats and organizing the queue at the top. Sally watched him for a minute and saw how he did it: he was beckoning the boatmen with four fingers for one sort of passenger, one finger for another. But how he sorted the passengers out, she couldn't tell. Arnold Fox, high voice braying over the bustle, was interrogating someone nearby, with his companion jotting down everything in his notebook. A little way off, the brothel keeper, Mrs. Paton, was talking to a young woman in a dark shawl, hand on her arm, exuding kindliness while—Sally could see—eyeing her figure.

But wasn't the young woman Rebecca Meyer?

Sally looked at the photograph again: it could be. It could easily be. Sally was too far off to be sure, so she quickly moved forward to be closer. Out of the corner of her eye she saw Mrs. Paton's male companion reach the top of the stairs and exchange a word with Fur Hat; perhaps Fur Hat had a cut in the business.

She got within three or four yards of Mrs. Paton and the young woman and stopped. It was so hard to know. Mrs. Paton was talking in a sympathetic voice, stroking the rough cloth of the girl's sleeve, and the girl was looking down expressionlessly at the deck. But as Sally watched, the girl looked up and wrinkled her face with what seemed like despair, looking around as if for an escape from Mrs. Paton, and Sally had no doubt.

She hastened forward.

"Rebecca!" she said, and before the girl could react she leaned forward to kiss her, whispering *"Ich bin deine Schwester . . . I am your sister."*

Rebecca's hands found hers, and a flash of understanding entered her eyes. Sally turned to Mrs. Paton.

"Please," she said. "My sister will come with me."

The older woman looked at her with steady hatred, and then quite calmly pursed up her mouth and spat deliberately on Sally's sleeve before moving away, shrugging to her companion at the stairway.

Sally, shocked, didn't move, but Rebecca took a handkerchief and wiped off the old woman's spittle. She was younger than Sally had expected: hardly more than eighteen or so. But something had marked her soul, for her eyes were full of pain.

"I come with you?" she said in German.

"Yes. Herr Goldberg is here. We'll go with him in a minute."

Sally looked around, but couldn't see him. Only a yard or so away Mr. Arnold Fox, his fact-finding completed for the night, was calling down to his boatman and gathering the tails of his coat about him fastidiously as he prepared to climb down the stairs. His bowler-hatted secretary was close behind, thrusting his notes into the dispatch case.

Sally had an idea; could she do it without being spotted?

She edged forward, and then, under cover of the crush, she nudged the dispatch case out from under the man's arm just as he was about to step onto the ladder. With a cry of dismay he grabbed for it, but too late: it struck the railing and burst open, and the papers swirled and fluttered out into the darkness, to float and sink and drift among the jostling boats. Sally enjoyed the secretary's horror almost as much as Arnold Fox's goggling rage.

Rebecca was watching, a puzzled smile somewhere behind her expression.

"An enemy," said Sally.

"Ah."

"Bravo," came Goldberg's voice from behind her. She turned, and then he said something in Russian to Rebecca, who responded guardedly.

"Let's go," he said, and waved over the side to Charlie the boatman. Sally saw the dinghy slip easily through the press of boats and reach the foot of the ladder, and then they were hurrying down and moving away, back on the dark water.

LESS THAN an hour later, they were in a house in Spitalfields, drinking tea. It was the home of Morris Katz. His wife and their daughter, a young woman of Rebecca's age, welcomed Rebecca with embraces and a warm cloud of Yiddish, and

bore her away to wash and to find some clean clothes while
Goldberg and the heavy, bearded Katz talked quietly for some
time. Sally sat apart, aware of the warmth and the welcoming
protectiveness of this home; or was it the Jewishness? Whatever the source, she wondered how she fitted in. It wasn't
that she felt excluded; but it was a world she didn't know.

Presently the door opened and Rebecca came in. She was
wearing a different dress, with a belt around the waist on
which was hung a little purse of faded maroon velvet. She
looked softer now, less tense, more tired, and she smiled at
Sally and clasped her hands.

"I've got to go," said Goldberg. "Morris, Miss Lockhart
is going to stay and talk to Rebecca."

He nodded to Sally, who watched him go, surprised as
ever by his abruptness, the sudden shifts from warm to cold,
friendly to distant, stern to vulnerable. She felt oddly dimin-
ished as the door closed behind him.

Rebecca sat down at the table across from Sally. She was
a strange mixture; she looked at first sullen and heavy-featured
and slow-witted, and then her face would come alive with
intelligence and feeling for a short while before it sank into
immobility again. At those moments she was almost beautiful; for the rest of the time she could have been any Russian-
Jewish peasant girl, accustomed to docility and deference.
But all the time, sparkling or not, there were shadows in her
eyes.

In a mixture of Russian and Yiddish, which Morris Katz
translated, and German, which Sally understood, Rebecca told
them her story.

She had come from the *shtetl*, from a desperately poor Jewish community in the Russian provinces. She was the daughter of a dairyman. When the rest of her family was killed in
one of the waves of slaughter that swept that world, she became a maidservant in the household of a more prosperous
Jew, a merchant, who bribed his way out of the province and
settled in Moscow. As Rebecca grew she learned to read and
proved to be intelligent, and she attracted the closer atten-

tion of the merchant; eventually she became pregnant with his child. That was the point at which she ceased to be attractive to him, so he dismissed her. She drifted into a circle of students and artists, earning a living as a painter's model. When her child was born she lived briefly with a student called Semyonov, a socialist, who was soon exiled to Siberia. Shortly afterward the child died. But while living with Semyonov, Rebecca had absorbed some of his ideas and had begun to study for herself. She had read as much as she could—including Goldberg's articles, which were appearing in various forbidden journals.

And like many others, she'd become aware of the shadowy figure of the Tzaddik, this brooding parasitical presence haunting the lives of those who wished to leave. All kinds of rumors swept the superstitious communities in the *shtetl:* the man was not human, but an animated mass of flesh brought to life by a corrupt rabbi; he had an evil spirit bound by magic to do his will; his agents enticed young girls into his house, where he ate them in an attempt to absorb their youth and strength. . . .

Sally remembered Goldberg's account of the girl in Amsterdam who drowned herself. It would be easy to believe crazy horror stories like that.

And as Rebecca continued with her story, Sally found her respect growing for this quiet, unimpressive, stolid-seeming girl; for she had found out the Tzaddik's Moscow address and found work with the neighboring household.

"I wanted to get close and see for myself. I'd thrown away superstition; I didn't believe in *dybbuk*s and *golem*s and all that old-fashioned folklore stuff. I just wanted to find out and maybe do something about it. I made friends with one of his maidservants. And I found that he had houses all over Europe, but that he spent most time in Amsterdam. He speaks many languages, but Dutch seems to be his native tongue.

"I saw him go in and out once or twice. He always travels by night. He is huge, gross. And paralyzed. He can speak and move his head, but none of his limbs. That's why he has that monkey; it goes everywhere with him. It sleeps in his bed. He has electric bells instead of a bellpull, so the monkey can press the switch to call the servants.

"And he has one special servant, a valet called Michelet, who does everything for him that the monkey can't do—washes him, dresses him, and so on. He's an abominable man. Because he's so close to the Tzaddik, he's got power over all the other servants, and he uses it, especially on the women.

"The servant told me all that. And she told me about the whistles."

"The whistles?" Sally said.

Morris Katz nodded. "I've heard those whistles. In Kiev and Berdichev, and other places, too, the rioters who loot Jewish shops and houses are controlled by whistles. Someone blows a signal, and what looks like an innocent crowd turns into a raging mob. Then the whistle blows again, and they stop and melt away. Once you know what the whistle means, it's terrifying when you hear it. And he had something to do with it?" he said to Rebecca.

"Yes," she said. "He dictated a letter to his secretary, to be sent to one of his agents in Byelorussia. He described the whole system. He dictated it in German and the secretary translated it, but the Tzaddik can't read Russian, and he doesn't trust anyone, so he got someone else to translate it back for him. The maid overheard. And then . . . she stole it and gave it to me. I've got it with me."

Katz smiled, the smile of a man proud of a comrade's achievement. Sally found herself hoping for the chance to do something worthy of a smile like that; but Rebecca looked down as if she was ashamed. She went on: "But then the Tzaddik found out that the maid was speaking to someone and had her punished. He gave her to Michelet. . . . I don't know what he did to her, but I never saw her again. And I know they inflicted terrible punishments. The Tzaddik had one of his servants flogged with the knout. They hardly ever use that nowadays, even in government prisons. That man died, apparently. But no one lifted a finger to protest."

She stopped to sip some tea, and went on: "I was friendly with that maid, and I wanted to do something to avenge her. I knew the Tzaddik was going on a journey soon, and I didn't have much time, so I broke into his house and . . . well, I don't know what I thought I was going to do. His luggage was stacked in the hall. I'd only just found it when an alarm went off. Men came running from all over the house. They took me down to the basement."

She stopped again. Her face was expressionless. Sally reached over the table and took her hand, and Rebecca held it tightly.

"After a while they'd had enough, I suppose. They threw me out into the street. I never saw the Tzaddik, then or afterward. So I'd failed. Except—"

There was a pounding at the street door, and she stopped at once. Sally felt through her hand a great bolt of fear strike Rebecca, and squeezed hard. They all sat frozen.

Morris Katz put his finger to his lips and stood up. Footsteps were running down the stairs, and then the door opened and Mrs. Katz, breathless with fear, looked in and said something in Yiddish. Katz closed his eyes a moment and nodded. His wife withdrew.

"It's the police," he said quietly. "We'll have to let them in. Come on—the cellar."

He pulled aside a low curtain behind the rocking chair. The pounding on the front door was getting louder, and shouts were coming: "Open up! Police!"

Katz shoved Sally and Rebecca in front of him.

"Down!" he said.

Behind the curtain was a door about three feet high. Katz pushed it open, revealing a stairway down into darkness. Sally crouched low and followed Rebecca down the first couple of steps—and then there was a crash from somewhere outside.

"The front door—" said Sally, turning back.

But all she saw was Katz, outside, putting his finger to his lips, and then shutting the cellar door.

Sally found Rebecca's hand, and they sat balanced uneasily on the stairs in the pitch dark, listening.

A hectoring voice was saying "Mr. Morris Katz, I believe that you are sheltering a wanted person—"

A torrent of Yiddish followed in Katz's voice, but the first man cut in: "Enough! I'm looking for a man called Goldberg. Is he in this house?"

Sally gripped Rebecca's hand. She'd thought they were looking for *her*.

"No, he is not," said Morris Katz. "And have you got a search warrant?"

A rustle of paper.

"Satisfied? All right, Constable Bagley, you take the upstairs. I'll have a look around down here. Did you know you'd been sheltering a fugitive from justice, Mr. Katz? And a murderer, what's more. There's a death sentence waiting for him back in his own country. What do they do in Hungary, Mr. Katz, d'you know? Do they hang 'em? Or is it the guillotine?"

20

Henna

"But what's he done?" Sally said, her voice shaking. "What's this crime?"

It was half an hour later. Sally and Rebecca had sat in the darkness for most of that time, not even daring to whisper as the heavy feet moved about overhead and the loud voices called up and down the stairs. Eventually, with a warning to Katz, the police had left, but he didn't open the cellar door for another five minutes.

Sally couldn't think of anything except this new threat. What would she do if Goldberg was captured? And—her fear coming alive again—*was* he a criminal?

"It's politics, not crime," Morris Katz was trying to explain, though he didn't know himself exactly. "They say he's not legally in this country—he should—I don't know—"

"But a death sentence?" She could hardly speak.

"In England you don't kill people directly for politics. Other places . . . they pin any crime on you; it doesn't matter to them what the excuse is."

"But they said he was a *murderer* . . ."

"They would say anything. Goldberg is not like that. A fighter, yes, but—"

Then Sally remembered something Rebecca had been about to say when the police arrived. She turned to her urgently.

"Rebecca, when the police came you were telling us about what you'd done, and you said *abgesehen von*—except for . . ."

"*Abgesehen von—Ah! Der Tzaddik, ja?*"

"Yes, that's it. You said you'd failed, except for something. . . . And then the police came. Remember?"

Sally was clinging hard to Rebecca's story, because even through the mist of fear about Goldberg she felt that something important was almost in reach, just beyond the edge of her vision.

"Ah! I know what it was. I said I'd failed, except for one little thing. When I was in the Tzaddik's house, before the men came, I saw his luggage."

"I remember. And?"

"And there were labels on it. I took one. I brought it all the way—it's here in my purse."

She fumbled in the shabby little purse, and a second later she had found it. It was crumpled and torn, but still legible were the words H. LEE, ESQ., 12, FOURNIER SQUARE, SPITAL-FIELDS, LONDON.

"So that's his name," Rebecca said, "or one of them. Lee. *Esq.* is not part of the name, no? And this address—Spital-fields . . ."

The name sounded odd on her lips, all its sounds came from the front of the mouth, unlike the sounds in the words she was used to speaking. But Sally didn't notice that. Her fists were pressed together and she was shaking them back and forth as if that would help her remember.

"Sally? What is it?"

Then she had it. Mr. Bywater, the lawyer's clerk, all that time ago, telling her about the case his friend had reported to him. *Lee v. Belcovitch*—how Lee had dispossessed the man Belcovitch of his business and set up Parrish as manager—how Mr. Bywater had said that that proved that Lee was the man behind Parrish. How had she forgotten that? And the address in the case—a square in Spitalfields with a French-sounding name that began with *F*—

"It's him! That proves it!"

More struggle then, to explain what she meant, and how she was involved at all; about Harriet, and Parrish, and her flight and refuge in the mission. It took a long time, but

Rebecca looked at her after it with a new understanding, and with a complex expression: part envy, part compassion. And Sally remembered that Rebecca had had a child, and it had died.

But all the time part of her mind was desperately beating, frightened, at the question of Goldberg, and as soon as she'd finished explaining her own case she came back to it.

"We must find a lawyer. There might be a way to stop them from sending him back. Has he got a lawyer? Do you know anything about him, Mr. Katz? I hardly know a thing. . . . But we must find a lawyer."

Morris Katz shrugged. "There is a man at Dean Street in Soho—but whether they have a lawyer . . ."

"Mr. Wentworth!" Sally remembered the name of the lawyer Margaret Haddow had told her about—the one who'd helped, when was it? Only that day?

She stood up too suddenly, and she felt faint and had to clutch at Rebecca's hand for support. The other girl stood too.

"I'm going to find a lawyer for Mr. Goldberg," she said after a dizzy second or two. She thanked Mr. Katz for his help, then put on her cloak and bonnet. Everything moved too slowly—her shaking hands fumbled at the fastenings, and she felt paralyzed with cold.

Rebecca came to the door, and the two of them clung tightly and kissed like sisters.

Bengal Court by moonlight looked ancient, villainous, and secret. Shadow lay like a great curtain across half the court, and Sally hesitated to enter it; but she had to. Her key turned in the lock.

She climbed the familiar stairs in the dark and let herself into the office. There she lit a candle from the supply in the filing cabinet and scribbled a quick note to Margaret. Could she tell Mr. Wentworth that Sally would like to see him on a matter of the most extreme urgency as soon as possible in the morning? She would wait for him (not being able to go to the office, in case it was still watched) in—she hesitated—St. Dionis Backchurch, nearby just off Fenchurch Street.

By going to meet him, she was risking her safety; she knew that he'd be obliged to insist that she give herself up to the police. But she'd deal with that later. Getting a lawyer for Goldberg was the most important thing now.

She left the note, looked around for a moment, and noticed the large map of London on the wall behind Margaret's desk. It took her some time to find Fournier Square; it was only a street or two from where she'd been sitting earlier that evening, in Morris Katz's house. The street directory on the shelf confirmed it: at 12, Fournier Square, lived H. Lee, Esq.

And where did that leave her? Better informed, was the answer. And with the germ of an idea that made her tremble. She blew out the candle and sat in the dark thinking it through. The more she thought, the more frightened she became, and a great heaviness crept around her heart.

After a while she left silently and went back to the mission. She reached it as a nearby church clock struck two. Harriet resented being taken out of the warm bed to go to the lavatory, and grumbled and screwed up her face as she always did, and it was all so dear and familiar that when Sally cried herself to sleep, it wasn't for apprehension about Goldberg or fear of the mysterious H. Lee; it was for love of her child. The fear and the apprehension came later, in her dreams.

St. Dionis Backchurch was one of Christopher Wren's churches: tall and dark and dignified, and empty at nine the following morning. Sally brought Harriet with her, and they sat in a pew near the back and read the inscriptions on the nearest tombs.

Only five minutes after they'd sat down, the church door opened and in came a short, shabby figure who removed his hat and then limped briskly to her pew.

"Miss Lockhart, I'm Wentworth. This is Harriet? Good

morning, Harriet. Uncommon numbers of policemen about this morning, eh? Noticed? Mmm. Now then, you've decided what you want to do?"

"It's not about me, Mr. Wentworth. My case can wait for the time being. It's about someone else."

He nodded intently, like a bright-eyed bird. Harriet was fascinated by him. He had an ugly, gnomelike face with a wide mouth and bushy red eyebrows, and his hair was fiery, too, but his expression was so lively and vivid that the effect wasn't ugly at all. He sat in the pew in front of them and hooked an arm over the back.

"Go on," he said.

"If someone was accused of a crime in another country— a citizen of that country—and he took refuge here, would he have to be sent back?"

"Which country?"

"Hungary."

"Yes. There's a treaty of extradition between Britain and the Austro-Hungarian Empire."

"But if he was innocent? If it was just a trumped-up charge, and they really wanted him for political reasons?"

"The court here can't decide on the merits of the case; that would have to be decided in the Hungarian court. But if it was clear that the offense was political, extradition would not be competent."

"You mean . . ."

"It wouldn't apply. They couldn't send him back."

Sally felt a great rush of relief. She sank back against the pew for a second, realizing how tense she'd been. When she opened her eyes, the lawyer was looking at her calmly.

"Consider carefully before you tell me anything," he said. "Remember, I'm obliged to obey the law myself."

Sally looked at him in return. She noticed that his cuffs were frayed, his collar dingy, but his eyes were clear and steady, and she felt the confidence she always felt in the presence of people who knew what they were doing.

She took a breath and told him everything she knew about

Goldberg. He didn't speak except to ask for clarification, but jotted it all down with a pencil in a tattered notebook.

When she'd finished, he shut the notebook with a snap. Then he looked up at her, his gnome-face serious.

"And the other business—your own problem? You're sure you want to do nothing?"

"I . . . I've got one or two things to find out first. I think I know who's behind it. But if I move now it'll warn him, and he'll find some other way of attacking me."

He looked skeptical. She went on: "It's a man who's responsible for defrauding and exploiting immigrants. And . . . and for enticing girls into prostitution. That's how I met Mr. Goldberg, because he's investigating that side of it."

"Hmm," he said. "I'll repeat what I said to Miss Haddow: I can't help you while you're hiding from the police. In strict honesty I should report you now; there's a warrant for your arrest on a charge of kidnapping, and if I don't turn you in I could be considered an accessory after the fact. I won't, but I should. Now then, you know where my office is. Here's my card if you need to reach me at home. I'm going to look at my books and brush up on extradition. The moment you hear anything more—if Mr. Goldberg is arrested, say—get in touch with me, and we'll apply for a writ of habeas corpus."

"Habeas corpus?"

"It's a writ requiring the jailer to produce the prisoner in person and state the reasons for holding him. If the court decides the reasons aren't good enough, he goes free. What it'll do in this case is to delay the whole process and give us time to establish a political motive."

He got to his feet and solemnly shook Harriet's hand.

"And as I said a few minutes ago," he said, "there's an uncommon number of policemen about this morning. That's all."

He shook Sally's hand, nodded to both of them, and limped out as briskly as he'd come in. She realized with surprise that he hadn't once said how difficult it would be, how awkward it was to take on a case like this, what a problem she was causing him. Anyone less like the helpless Mr. Adcock was hard to imagine.

Mindful of his warning, she slipped out of the church by a side entrance and looked both ways before turning left into Lime Street and setting off back to Spitalfields.

At the mission, there was work to be done. Someone had brought in a vast pile of old clothes, and Miss Robbins wanted someone to go through them and sort out the wearable from the worthless. Sally spent the morning doing that, with Harriet playing busily nearby, and wondered all the time about Mr. Wentworth and extradition and habeas corpus; but even more about something else.

After their lunch of bread and cheese, and after washing the dishes for the three or four women and children who were there with them, Sally took Harriet upstairs for her nap. When the child was in bed, Sally sat down beside her and stroked her head.

"Hattie?"

"Mmm."

"You're being a good girl. Can you be a brave girl, too?"

Harriet lay looking up at her, right thumb in mouth, left hand tugging gently at her right ear: her sleepy posture. Sally knelt down and laid her own head beside Harriet's on the pillow. She whispered, "When Mama was a little girl like Harriet, her papa would take her into the forest or up in the mountains, and we'd live in a little tent, and we'd cook our food over a campfire and drink water out of the river. And both of us had to be very brave because of the tigers and the snakes and the wild monkeys. But even when Mama couldn't see her papa, she knew he was there, close-by, and she wasn't afraid. Now, Hattie, my sweet, you're going to be brave too, aren't you? Because Mama is going to go somewhere else for a while. But we'll take you to a friend who'll look after you. And you won't see Mama, but she'll be there, close by. And soon afterward we'll go home. . . ."

Harriet was asleep. Sally's voice faltered. Very gently she stroked the hair off Harriet's face and looked at the child for a minute or so, marveling at that intense firmness, even in sleep, the concentration, the Harriet-ness.

Sally bent to kiss her, and then got up quietly, wrote a note to Angela Turner and another to Miss Robbins, and set off for the bathroom.

"BUT SALLY—what have you done? Your hair—*dein schönes Haar . . .*"

"I want to change my appearance. But cutting it short isn't enough—I want to change the color, too. I wondered if you could help me?"

Rebecca turned to Mrs. Katz and her daughter Leah, who was holding Harriet, and they spoke rapidly. Sally heard the words *mit Henna färben,* and Mrs. Katz nodded and went out.

"With . . . henna? I don't know the word," said Rebecca. "It will make it red, maybe. Browny-red. Yes, we can do it. But why, Sally? What are you going to do?"

Seeing that Harriet was occupied with a little wooden dog, Sally spoke quietly. "It's what you told us yesterday. I had an idea after I left, but I'll need to disguise myself. And I'll need somewhere safe for Harriet to stay. I can't leave her in the mission; they're too busy, there isn't anyone who can look after her. But I thought perhaps you might be able to . . . and Mrs. Katz and Leah are so kind . . . I don't like to ask. But I can't think of anything else."

It was the first time in her life she had asked for something without being able to pay for it. She felt quite naked, and not only because of her newly cropped head. Rebecca looked at Leah, and the other girl, small and birdlike and lively, nodded at once.

"Of course," Leah said. "Of course we can. But what are you going to do?"

Sally felt sick. Each time she thought about it, it felt worse; but she was set on course now, and she wouldn't turn back.

"I'm going to get into his house. I want to see him for myself. If I can do something to stop him, then I will. But I need to look different. He knows what I look like—or Parrish does—and they won't be expecting someone dark-haired. They won't be expecting anyone at all. So . . . well, that's what I'm going to do."

They looked at her without speaking. She thought for a moment that they hadn't understood, but Leah's English was good, and Sally had tried to translate as she went along anyway. No, they understood all right.

"But *how?*" said Leah.

"I don't know yet. I'll find a way. But it might take me some time, and that's why . . ."

She looked at Harriet, who was oblivious to everything except the little wooden dog. Rebecca stooped and picked her up, taking Harriet on her lap.

"She'll be safe," she said. "We'll take care of her. But have you really made up your mind?"

They were understanding each other more easily now— half in German, half in English. Sally nodded.

"Absolutely. I must. Not only for Harriet and me but for Mr. Goldberg. I've thought it through. Why should they suddenly want to arrest him now? He hasn't been in hiding; he's a journalist, he's well known. It's only now he's started investigating the Tzaddik that the police come after him. No, Rebecca, I've got to do this. But I need you to tell me everything you can remember—every *detail*—about him, his servants, his habits . . . everything."

Mrs. Katz came into the room with a bowl of hot water, a towel, and various things in a brown paper bag. She said something to Leah, who translated: "It will take two hours. You have to put up with hot water, says Mama. And your hair is so blond that it might not go very dark. But we'll make it as dark as we can. You'll need to loosen your dress— put this towel around your neck so it doesn't stain. . . ."

As Harriet watched, curious, Sally bent forward over the bowl and Mrs. Katz began to work.

AND REBECCA told her everything she remembered. The maid she had known was a Russian girl, and she had been on the permanent staff of the house, not the Tzaddik's personal staff. Like a monarch, he traveled with a court. There was his secretary, a German called Winterhalter; his cook, a Frenchman whose name Rebecca didn't know; his personal physician, also a German, Dr. Strauss; his coachman and the servants who dealt with the business of moving him about; and, most important of all, his valet, Michelet.

It was Michelet's job to see to dressing and washing the Tzaddik and to all his other personal needs. He was the most powerful person in the household apart from the Tzaddik himself. He was a vain man, Rebecca thought, trying to remember what she'd heard; capricious and plump and greedy for chocolates and little sweetmeats and scented cigarettes. He was the only person in the household who could manage the monkey, which bit anyone it wanted to without punishment. It had fastened its teeth into Michelet's hand once, and instead of trying to shake it loose or pry its jaws open, he had calmly puffed at his cigarette to make the end glow and then stubbed it out on the monkey's head. The monkey had screamed and fled, and had been terrified of him ever since.

And as for the monkey itself . . .

"It's evil," said Rebecca, as she rubbed something pungent into Sally's hair. "I don't care what they say about animals being innocent, not knowing good or evil, Adam and Eve, the tree of knowledge, blah blah—that monkey is not innocent. It knows evil, and it does evil. If I believed in all that folklore stuff about *dybbuk*s and *golem*s, I'd think it was an evil spirit, not an animal of flesh and blood. When the Tzaddik wants to punish a servant he sometimes tells the monkey to attack him, and it does. The servants daren't defend themselves—except Michelet that one time. And one other thing she told me, the maid Olga: she said the monkey is getting old. The Tzaddik has tried to replace it by training younger ones, but they won't take to it. One day soon it will be too old to do anything, and then it'll die, and what he'll do then, God knows . . . there. Now we rinse again. Put your head over the bowl."

Sally absorbed it all, letting Mrs. Katz and Rebecca rub and rinse and dab on the paste and swathe her in towels and rinse again. Mr. Katz came in halfway through, threw up his hands, and went out again, but came back to play with Harriet.

Time went past, and they had some supper of beetroot soup and pickles and black bread, and then Sally (with her head still turbaned) took Harriet up to bed in the cot they'd made up in Rebecca's room. Mr. Katz had often sheltered refugees before; his business was prospering, and there was always room in the house for anyone in need of help. Besides, he liked children.

They left Sally alone to say good-bye to Harriet. The child was sleepy and no longer curious about the towels that swathed her mother's head.

"Good night, my little sweet one," Sally whispered. "Remember what Mama said about being brave?"

"Tigers," said Harriet.

"That's right. Even if you can't see Mama, she won't be far away. Now close your eyes, my baby. Be a good girl and a brave girl . . ."

She kissed her forehead, and then her cheeks, and then hugged her close. As she laid her down, tears fell on the pillow beside her; but Harriet didn't notice.

And then downstairs again, and the towels came off, and there was her hair, dark red, cropped. She didn't recognize herself in the little looking glass Mrs. Katz held up for her.

"Thank you," she said. "That's . . . well, it's just what I wanted."

"Die Augenbrauen!" said Rebecca. "The eyebrows—they should be darker. Your eyes are dark already—that's strange, isn't it? Eyes so dark with hair so fair. But the eyebrows ought to match."

Leah found a pencil, and Sally licked it and darkened her eyebrows. Now she was completely someone else. She realized she needed another name.

"Louisa Kemp," she said. "That's what I'll call myself.

I'm . . . a maid-of-all-work. Or something. Thank you all for what you're doing."

"Sally, you mustn't forget, he's *dangerous*. He kills people," said Rebecca.

"How long shall we leave it before coming in to get you?" said Leah.

"I'll get a message to you somehow. If I don't . . ."

"And what about Mr. Goldberg?"

Sally hesitated, and then shrugged. "If he turns up . . . I don't know. Tell him I've seen a lawyer. . . . Look after Harriet."

"She'll be safe," whispered Rebecca.

They kissed. Sally wrapped her cloak around her, put on her bonnet, and left.

BOOK
THREE

The Valet

IT HAD BEGUN TO RAIN.

It came down steadily and heavily. There was a depression over the whole of southern England; clouds hung low over London, their heavy bellies turning into mist where they touched the high points of Crouch Hill, Streatham Hill, Hampstead, and Highgate, and discharging themselves copiously and endlessly into the drains, the gutters, the soil.

The new sewers under London had been designed to cope with exceptional rainfall. When there was too much water for the main interceptory sewers, it flowed over weirs into storm relief sewers and thence into the Thames. These weirs were on the courses of the old rivers that laced subterraneanly through London: the Fleet, Stamford Brook, the Walbrook, the Tyburn, and so on. Most of these rivers were known and mapped and accounted for, though few of the pedestrians and drivers and passengers who moved about above them had any idea they were there.

But in the older parts of the city there were dozens of springs and streams that had been completely forgotten. Not more than trickles, for the most part, but some of them carried substantial volumes of water—much more after a rainfall, when the water had had time to soak into the soil. And along with the springs and rivers, there were hundreds—maybe thousands—of ancient sewers, some blocked and crumbling, others still just flowing, but all of them crusted with filth and slime and alive with frogs and rats and eels.

One of these lost rivers had been called the Blackbourne.

It rose deep in the ground under a spot in Hackney where there had once been a monastery, but which by Sally's time was occupied by a pickle factory. It flowed meanderingly south and eventually slouched into the Thames somewhere near the Tower of London. By the thirteenth century it was already an open sewer, flowing not only with household wastes and dead dogs but also with the by-products of paper mills, tanneries, and soap boilers along the banks, so that Blackbourne water became a synonym for unspeakable filthiness. By the seventeenth century it had been built over and lost, but it still flowed on, and in 1646 a heavy rainfall caused three houses to collapse into it. Fifteen people were drowned, and three more never found at all in the putrid swamp. Soon after that it was built over again and forgotten.

But it still ran. The forgotten sewers still emptied their filth into it; and the various abominations that had trickled into it since then had made it no sweeter. All kinds of things contributed. A leaking drain under a slaughterhouse in Stepney allowed vast quantities of blood to seep into an ancient culvert running below it, and thence into the Blackbourne. A dye works in Shoreditch discharged all its waste chemicals into a convenient pit in the yard behind, which absorbed them gratefully and conveyed them through various channels into the river. The brick wall built roughly in 1665 to shore up the side of a plague pit had begun to crumble, and the Blackbourne was leaching out the essences of several dozen long-dead plague victims to add to the mixture. All in all, it was a powerful brew, and when it moved sluggishly in dry weather, it released gouts of nauseating stink through crumbling bricks and loose flagstones into a hundred cellars; and little by little, it scoured away ancient mortar and lime and cement when it was swollen after a storm.

And if you were below ground, you could hear it.

"What's that noise, Charlie?" said a painter and decorator to his mate as they cleared up after a job.

Charlie listened.

"Sort o' rumbling," he said. "It's them hydraulics." He

jerked his thumb at the new pipework bearing high-pressure water from the London Hydraulic Company to power the lift in the corner of the basement they were working in. "I don't trust 'em."

"No, it ain't," said the first man. "It's coming from down under the floor. Listen . . ."

He knelt laboriously and applied his ear to the parquet flooring.

There was a clatter as the iron cage of the lift rattled open, and Herr Winterhalter, the Tzaddik's secretary, got out. He looked at the kneeling workman.

"Have you finished?" he said stiffly.

"Oh, yeah—sorry, guv. Thought I heard a noise."

The workman got to his feet as the newcomer handed both of them some coins.

"That, I believe, is the sum we agreed," he said. "You seem to have completed the work satisfactorily. When will the paint be dry?"

"Best give it thirty-six hours," said Charlie. "Not much ventilation down here. All them doors want keeping open."

They gathered their tools and went up by the narrow staircase, the lift evidently being out of bounds to tradesmen. So was the front door, so they left by the area steps.

Sally watched them from the shelter of a cab rank across the square. The house was full of activity; every window was lighted, with servants passing to and fro carrying things or adjusting curtains. Soon she would have to make a move.

Clutching her basket, she gathered the cloak about her and ran through the teeming rain to the area steps. Was her story ready? Then down.

The kitchen window lit up the little sunken area, but it was streaming with moisture both inside and out, and no one looked through as she knocked at the door.

Before anyone could stop her, she opened it and stepped inside, and stood blinking the rain out of her eyes.

"Here—"

A portly woman was looking up from the saucepan she was

holding over the range. A maidservant stopped in midstride, holding a tray of dirty plates, and a footman stared from the door, where he was about to take out a large covered silver dish.

"*Remuez! Remuez!*" came in a sharp voice from the fourth person, a dark-featured man in a cook's white hat. He was cracking eggs into a bowl and watching the stout woman's saucepan. She looked at him blankly. "Stir it! Stir it!"

She turned back, but it was too late; the sauce boiled over and hissed on the range, and the smell of burning came to Sally's nostrils.

The French cook released a volley of curses, but he couldn't move for the eggs in both hands. It was Sally's chance. She saw a dishcloth nearby and darted forward to mop up the mess, letting the stout woman turn and shout back at the Frenchman.

The maid carried her dishes through to the scullery, the footman went out, and the moment passed. The stout woman took back the saucepan from Sally and said, "Ta, love. I'll see to it. Blooming fancy rubbish—I can't understand what he's on about. You the girl from the agency?"

Sally had only a second to think. "Yes," she said.

"Put down your basket there for now, then. We'll get your uniform sorted out later. See if you can give Monsewer a hand; I don't know what he wants."

"If you please, ma'am, I speak a little French. There was a French cook at my last situation—"

For some reason, her voice came out slightly Yorkshire. She let it, happy to go with the flow of events while they were favorable.

"Thank Gawd for that. I can't understand him . . . stupid man."

Throwing off her cloak and bonnet, Sally hastened to speak to the cook. Within five minutes she had become indispensable, relaying brisk orders to the stout woman (who, she learned, was the cook-housekeeper, Mrs. Wilson) and the kitchenmaid. It was the busiest time of the evening; apparently there were some important guests, and dinner was in progress upstairs. The cook, M. Ponsot, fussed over sauces and pastries in a lordly, arrogant way that made Mrs. Wilson fume with irritation, and Sally exchanged little sympathetic glances with her. What a piece of extraordinary luck, to come in just now; could she use it? And what was this agency?

Little by little, in between the translating and the whisking and the heating and the grinding coffee, she tried to find out more about what they assumed her to be.

"When did you send to the agency, Mrs. Wilson?" she said during a lull.

"Only this morning. We had to dismiss the other girl. She drank."

"Oh, dear."

"That's why I was surprised to see you. We wasn't expecting anyone till tomorrow."

That was a relief. There wouldn't be a genuine claimant turning up for a few hours yet, then.

"Er, no," Sally said. "It just happened that I was there at the time, sort of thing."

"Where d'you come from?"

Sally was glad her voice had decided to be Yorkshire; any deficiencies in her accent wouldn't be spotted so quickly by Londoners. Again she had to think quickly.

"From Bradford. But I was in service with a lady and gentleman who did a lot of traveling, and I spent some time abroad, one way or another."

"Lady's maid?" said Mrs. Wilson. "We sent for a general housemaid."

"I was a lady's maid, yes. But I'm happier with the general work."

"Good thing. No ladies in this house."

"Oh?" Sally thought she might realistically be a little curious now. "Who's the master?"

"A gentleman called Mr. Lee. Ever so wealthy. Paralyzed, you know. He can't move a muscle."

"Really? How awful."

"And there's two sorts of servants here, you'll find. There's us, under Mr. Clegg, the butler, and there's the master's own personal servants. His valet, especially. Mr. Michelet. He attends the master everywhere."

Her voice was noncommittal, but her dislike of the valet was easy to read. Sally thought it sounded like a fine recipe for resentment and discord.

She was about to probe a little deeper when the kitchen door opened and an austere-looking man came in. He had an expression of distaste that seemed to be built into the bones of his face. From his clothes she took him to be the butler, and if her interpretation of things was correct, he would be feeling as put out by the influx of new, superior servants as Mrs. Wilson was.

"So you're the new girl. Name?"

"Louisa Kemp, Mr. Clegg."

"Character?"

Sally was ready for this. No servant could get a situation without a character, which was a reference from her previous employer.

"My last situation was with Lord and Lady Islip, and if the master here was to write, I'm sure they'd supply a copy, Mr. Clegg. It's my own fault, I'm sure, but all my things was in a fire. It was only 'cause I'd been with the agency before and they knew me, and when this come up . . ."

"Lord and Lady Islip," he said, making a note. "Address?"

Sally told him. Lord Islip was the older brother of Charles Bertram, Webster Garland's partner; Sally knew he'd cooperate, but it meant writing—or telegraphing—to him first thing tomorrow. Solve that problem when the time came; for the moment, be modest and helpful.

Mrs. Wilson was telling the butler about Sally's command of French, and Mr. Clegg nodded.

"Could be useful," he said. "All right, you're here now. Foster there"—nodding to the kitchenmaid—"will take you up to your room after supper. Supper, by the way, we take after the master's personal servants have had theirs. So we all have to wait. No doubt it's good for the soul. Rules: Most importantly, you never go near the master, not unless he sends for you personally. All his wants are seen to by Mr. Michelet, his valet. So everything that needs doing—cleaning and suchlike—has to be done while he's nowhere near. If you're sent for, if you answer a bell or some such, you don't knock and enter, you knock and wait. Mr. Michelet will tell you more about that, I daresay. Remember, the master don't want to see you. He's a gentleman with a huge burden—Mrs. Wilson will have told you, I expect. He suffers considerably. Don't add to it."

Sally nodded, trying to look respectful and humble.

"And you can speak French, eh? Well, that'll be useful. I daresay Mr. Michelet will enjoy having a conversation with you."

She couldn't interpret that remark; she took it to be another example of the tension between the household and the court, as she thought of them.

Supper was a brisk, plain meal, which was served to them by the kitchenmaid and the youngest footman. There were eleven servants altogether. She thought that although they were a little formal and distant with her, they all seemed honest enough. They knew nothing, or said nothing, about their employer's business; all she could gather was that he did a lot of traveling and was in this house about one month in three.

Little by little the relationship between these servants and the others became clear. While Mr. Lee was in residence, his valet took over the use of Mr. Clegg's private sitting room, so the butler had to sit with the lower servants in the kitchen. That, she thought, was the source of their stiffness; he was the sort of frowning, austere man no one can relax with, even when he's trying to be friendly. The other housemaid whispered to Sally that he had a ferocious temper, and she'd have to mind how she spoke to him.

She knew little of the formalities and routines of a servants' hall, and she had to remind herself constantly to be careful to be modest and retiring and polite to everyone. It seemed to be working; they took little notice of her, apart from the interested glances from the menservants, the frank stares at her figure. She knew that if she'd come into this house as a guest, they'd never have dared to look at her in that way.

She found out more after supper, when the other housemaid, Eliza Foster, took her up to see the room they were to share, and to find her a uniform from the servants' linen cupboard. Eliza was a plain, dumpy girl with freckles. As soon as they left the kitchen, Eliza carrying a candle, she whispered, "Watch out for that bloody valet. Mr. Michelet."

"Why? What's he like?"

"His hands go all over the place. Not only hands, either. That was why Lucy had to go."

"The other maid? I thought Mrs. Wilson said she drank?"

"She wouldn't tell you straight off, would she?"

They were on the first-floor landing of the back stairs. Eliza stopped and listened. Her eyes widened, and she put her finger to her lips. "Sssh! He's coming now. . . ."

A door had opened below, and someone came up carrying a lamp. Eliza hastily set off upward, but a voice from behind said, "Aha! Who is this?"

Eliza stopped. Sally could sense her reluctance. Sally turned and waited as the man came up to them, but kept her eyes modestly on the floor till he said, "And what is your name?"

"Louisa Kemp, sir," she said.

"Ah! Not sir! Mr. Michelet," he said. "Or if you like, *Monsieur* Michelet. Look at me, child."

She looked up. He had a plump, greedy face, somehow soft and hawkish at the same time. He held out his hand. She shook it, and he retained hers, bringing it up close to his face.

"Soft hand," he said. "You are housemaid, Louisa?"

"Used to be a lady's maid, s—Mr. Michelet."

"Ah. Very soft hand. Very pretty face. Well, Louisa, I am glad to make your acquaintance. We will talk together, I hope."

"Yes, I hope so, Mr. Michelet."

But he wouldn't let go of her hand for some seconds. When he did, she made a little bob that might have been taken for a bashful girl's embarrassed half-curtsy.

"Come on," said Eliza.

Sally followed her, conscious of his eyes on her as far as the turn in the stairs.

When they were in the bedroom, a poky little place under the roof with two narrow beds and one chest of drawers, Eliza made sure he was nowhere near before saying "I hate him. It's only 'cause I ain't pretty like you or Lucy that he never does more than touch me. Poor Lucy—I dunno where she is now. . . ."

"What happened?"

"The usual thing. I tried to warn her, I really did. She'll have her baby, and then she'll have to leave it in the foundlings' home or summing. She won't find it easy to get another situation without a character. But you daren't say no to him, that's the trouble. He'd go to the master and then you'd be out on yer ear anyway. It's so much better when he's not here."

"What's he like? The master?"

"He gives me the creeps. The way he just sits there looking. I ain't seen him much, mind you, 'cause he likes us to keep out the way. Poor man though, being paralyzed. And having to depend on that bloody Frenchman for everything—washing, dressing, all of it. No, it's him you want to watch out for."

So it was clear that Sally's route to the Tzaddik had to lie through Michelet. One step at a time, she told herself in bed, shivering under the thin blankets. She felt like a soldier on campaign. Coolness under fire. Keep your powder dry. Don't shoot until you see the whites of his eyes.

SHE SLEPT dreamlessly and woke up at once when Eliza shook her at six o'clock. The uniform she was to wear was a little loose, but by tightening the apron she managed to make it fit.

"We got to make up all the fires, all through the house," Eliza told her, "same as a normal house, except that he has 'em all burning all day. Shocking expense in coals. Just had this new lift thing put in to take his chair up and down; you'd think they'd put a lift in for the coals, but, oh, no. Up and down the bloody stairs, same as anywhere. We got to clean extra-thorough—he's that fussy; a speck of dust and there's all kinds of trouble. You do the dining room first, then the drawing room. I'll do in the library and the hall, and then we'll do the upstairs. Breakfast at half past seven."

Having washed in cold water and cleared and refilled four fireplaces, Sally was feeling dirty and uncomfortable by the time the servants sat down to their breakfast. However, it had given her time to think what her next move should be, and she said quietly to Mrs. Wilson as they sat down to the porridge and tea: "Mrs. Wilson, ma'am? Could I ask a favor? I know I ain't been here for five minutes, but it's me old mum—I said I'd let her know directly I had a situation. She's waiting for a bit of money, and if I slip out for five minutes I can catch the post at half past eight around the corner. I'll make the time up, ma'am. . . ."

Mrs. Wilson looked doubtful. Sally dreaded her saying that someone else would post it later, but she just nodded and muttered, "Mind Mr. Clegg don't see you. It's your own risk."

"Thank you, Mrs. Wilson," Sally said.

She bolted the porridge, which was palatable enough, though thin, and waited for Mr. Clegg to leave before slipping out. There was a good deal of coming and going, breakfast not being so formal a meal as supper, and within five minutes she had run through the rain and was standing at the counter of the post office around the corner. Again her luck held. Not only did they accept telegrams here, but there was no queue. It didn't take long to write on the telegram form the words:

AT ALL COSTS SEND FAVORABLE REPLY TO FORTHCOMING
REQUEST FOR SERVANT'S CHARACTER STOP NAME OF
LOUISA KEMP STOP DESPERATELY IMPORTANT STOP
EXPLAIN LATER STOP SALLY LOCKHART.

She handed it in, paid the fee, and was back in the house within five minutes.

That left the other problem: what to do when the girl turned up from the agency. Well, there was no point in holding back. She waited till she knew the valet was alone in the drawing room, and then slipped in and shut the door.

"What are you doing—ah! Louisa! But you must not be in here after this hour—"

She held her finger to her lips. His eyes glistened. He came closer, and she said softly, "Monsieur?"

"*Vous parlez français? Mais—*"

"Only a little. Please, Mr. Michelet, can you help me?"

"What do you want?"

She was looking up at him, she hoped appealingly. He came still closer. She smelt his eau de cologne.

"I shouldn't be here. The thing is I don't come from the staff agency. I was only in there when the message came from here, and I was desperate, so I came last night. They said they'd send someone today. Another girl. I don't know what to do. . . ."

"Ah . . . you want me to send this other girl away?"

She looked up at him, and then down, and then shyly up again. He licked his lips. Then he traced the outline of her cheek with his finger.

"Well, Louisa. The household staff is not for me to arrange. It will be difficult. However . . ."

"I'll do something for you one day, monsieur."

"Yes," he said. "You will."

He twisted his hand slowly into the short hair on the back

of her head and began to pull her toward himself—and then something screamed on the ceiling.

She started and looked up. Michelet let go with a curse. There, leaping from cornice to cabinet to bookshelf to mantelpiece, was the monkey she'd heard about: a little gray flash, screeching with hatred and gnashing its yellow teeth. It leaped—clung—swung on—leaped again—and it had something with it in one arm, a little brown bundle—

Michelet reached up and snatched it out of the air like a cricketer catching a ball.

Immediately it fell quiet and lay motionless in his hand. The object it was carrying had dropped unregarded beside the wall. He brought the creature slowly, threateningly, to his mouth as if he would bite it, and it lay as limp as a rag doll, its eyes closed.

Then he dropped it to the floor. Like a cat, it twisted the right way up in midair and landed on its paws, and scuttled away through the door and out. She could hear it chittering angrily in the hall.

"Oh, Louisa," Michelet said softly. "You must be very wicked for the creature to hate you so much! You saw how she was making with her teeth? Very sharp teeth, Louisa. She would like to bite you. . . . But I can control her. She is afraid of me. You mustn't be frightened, Louisa. You have to be cruel, and then they are afraid."

He slipped out quickly, leaving the door open.

She leaned on the back of a chair and took a deep breath. There was worse to come. Well, let it. She could face it. But she had her eyes shut, and when she opened them again, she saw the object the monkey had dropped; so she reached down automatically to pick it up and found herself holding Harriet's toy bear, Bruin.

He was unmistakable. His left ear was torn, and Sally had mended it with scarlet thread once when Sarah-Jane was on holiday and she couldn't find anything else. Her heart leaped with recognition and love, and she clutched the battered little thing to her breast helplessly. But this was *proof.* . . .

They *had* stolen it. She wasn't wrong, the trail did lead here; it was all true. But to give it to a *monkey* . . .

Michelet opened the door. She put Bruin down at once, and he took the toy from her.

"She must not have this," he said. "She hates it. She was going to destroy it, and the master would not want that to happen. A good thing we saved it, no?"

And he took it and left.

What did they want with Bruin if he wasn't for the monkey? It must be for Harriet. It must be to make her feel at home when they brought her here. *No, don't think about that; one thing at a time.*

But she'd crossed two bridges this morning, and now she was safe for the time being. She'd better act like a housemaid, though, or she'd be dismissed for incompetence—and that would be ironic, to say the least.

So for the rest of the day she labored diligently wherever Mrs. Wilson sent her: polishing silver, ironing linen, replacing all the candles in the great chandelier in the dining room, dusting, fetching coals . . .

In the late afternoon she was sitting down for five minutes in the kitchen when a bell rang. She looked up at the row of little bells beside the door and saw the one labeled LIBRARY still bobbing on its spring. There was no one else in the kitchen; it was her job to answer it.

She stood up, smoothed down her apron, made sure her cap was on straight, and hurried up the stairs and through the green baize door.

Don't knock and enter—knock and wait, she thought. She expected that Michelet would open the door, but instead a deep voice called, "Come in."

She entered and gave a little curtsy to the man in the invalid chair, keeping her eyes modestly on the floor. There was nothing she wanted more than to look at him, but she managed not to. She had the impression of a dark, still bulk, and saw another man there out of the corner of her eye, standing by the window.

"Some tea for us," said the deep, cracked voice of the man in the wheelchair.

Something profound stirred a long way down in Sally's memory, but only for a moment, like a great slow fish moving a fin; and then it vanished.

She was about to turn and go when he said, "Wait. You are new. What is your name?"

"Kemp, sir."

She looked up then, because at the sound of her voice something made a chittering sound. She looked into his vast moon face briefly, registering only his impassive eyes, and then to the implike malevolence perched on his shoulder, baring its monkey teeth at her.

"Kemp. Very well. Go."

She curtsied again and turned to go, and as she did so the man at the window turned around, and she found herself looking into the eyes of Arthur Parrish.

He didn't react, apart from casting the usual automatic glance at her figure. Then he looked away, ignoring her, and she managed to get out without shaking.

It works, she thought triumphantly. *They can't see me!*

It was either the hair or the servant's dress, or both, or the fact that it was the last thing they'd have expected. She felt jubilant as she walked back to the kitchen. And she thought of Parrish's glance. *When I was a lady*, she thought, *no one looked at my body so openly. Now that I'm a servant they all do. . . .*

Mrs. Wilson was in the kitchen when she got back. She explained that the master liked his tea placed on the low table near the fire; the guest would pour for him.

When Sally took the tray back the two men were talking. They took scarcely any notice as she set the tray down carefully on the low table.

She curtsied and heard Parrish say, "No, sir. I'm afraid she'd flown the coop. We got there just too late."

"What was this place?" said the Tzaddik.

"Some kind of socialist settlement in Whitechapel. There's

no doubt she was there, with the kid as well. But we're working on another lead at the moment. The Jews . . ."

She couldn't stop to hear more. As it was, she feared that her shaking hands would give her away. When she shut the door, she pressed her ear against it; but all that came through was a confused mutter, and then she heard Mr. Clegg coming. She smoothed her apron and went back to the kitchen.

JAMES WENTWORTH knocked at the door of the office in Bengal Court. Cicely Corrigan, who opened it tentatively, sighed with relief and let him in.

"Miss Haddow!" she called. "It's the lawyer—Mr. Wentworth. I'm sorry sir," she said, turning back to him. "We've been upside down today."

"Come in, Mr. Wentworth," said Margaret, and the lawyer limped through, leaving his hat and coat with Cicely.

Margaret poured him some tea without needing to ask whether he'd like any. He was pale, she thought, and he sat down as if he were aching in every limb.

"Well, it took all day," he began, "but I've held them off for the time being. I won't go into the technicalities, but you can write checks again, on your number-one account at least. They've agreed to honor them on your signature alone, provided that you don't exceed twenty pounds a time."

"Then the first thing I'll do is pay your fee," she said.

"I haven't finished the job yet."

"If I don't pay you when we've still got money, I certainly won't be able to pay you when we haven't," she said, opening the checkbook. *Besides*, she thought, *you need it, by the look of you.* She wrote a check and tore it out.

"Have you any idea where Miss Lockhart is?" he said.

"None. I'm very worried, Mr. Wentworth. You know the shelter's been raided?"

He raised his eyebrows. "Raided? By whom?"

"This morning. By the police. They ransacked the place from attics to cellars. She wasn't there, of course. The woman in charge admitted nothing, but she told me afterward she didn't know where Sally was anyway. According to the doctor, last thing yesterday Sally cropped her hair short and left. So she must have somewhere else to stay."

"Cropped her hair? Is she hoping to disguise herself? She'll have to do a good job. I've seen an excellent photograph of her only this afternoon, on display outside a police station. She's in serious trouble, Miss Haddow, and I can't help her till she asks me to."

"And gives herself up."

"Just so."

"She won't. You don't know her; she'll fight."

"I hope you don't mean that literally."

"I do. She's got a pistol, and she's used it."

He was silent. He looked grim.

"I know there are better ways of solving her problems," Margaret went on, "but she's tried them, and look where they've got her. Do you realize how everything's been stacked against her?"

"I'm beginning to. And it makes me all the more convinced that she shouldn't add to the problem by shooting anyone. Tell me—you don't know anything about this Mr. Goldberg, do you?"

She shook her head. "I've seen him once or twice. I . . . I'd trust him . . . in a sort of gallant-highwayman way . . . a musketeer or something. I don't know how *serious* he is."

"I think I've found out enough to know that he's serious. I must say I quite admire what I've heard. But it's a dangerous business, facing a murder charge."

He was quiet and authoritative, this ugly little limping man. Margaret, like Sally, valued competence when she saw it; it was one of the reasons they liked each other.

She turned her head, hearing voices outside: Cicely's and another girl's. The newcomer sounded agitated.

Margaret took a step toward the door, but it opened before she got to it. In the doorway stood a girl of eighteen or so, who looked as though she'd been crying.

"Miss Haddow? I don't know who else to come to. I'm from Orchard House, miss; I'm Harriet's nurse—"

"Sarah-Jane Russell. Of course I remember you. What is it? Have you seen Miss Lockhart?"

"No, miss—but they've thrown us out—"

She was trembling, whether from cold or distress or both. James Wentworth offered her his chair.

"I'm a lawyer, Miss Russell, and I'm acting for this firm. What's happened? Who's thrown you out?"

Sarah sat helplessly. "Some men came to the house today. They had papers—warrants—I don't know. They said that the house belonged to Mr. Parrish now, and everything in it was his as well; and they paid us a week's wages and told us all—that's me and the cook and Ellie, the maid—told us all that we were dismissed and we had to leave at once. They had a locksmith with them and he's changing all the locks. I'm just . . . I don't know what to do. . . . Oh, miss, what's going to happen?"

The Cellar

SALLY DIDN'T HAVE TIME BEFORE SHE WAS IN BED TO THINK of Goldberg, or even much of Harriet, though as soon as her head touched the hard pillow all her anxieties returned. And it was unbearable, because her little child was crying for her.

Sally felt such a tug of anguish that she couldn't repress a sob of her own. She lay still, clutching the pillow to her as if it were Harriet, and letting the sobs shake themselves out of her throat as quietly as she could.

But Eliza was awake.

"Louisa, you all right?" came a whisper from the other bed. "What's the matter, love?"

Sally swallowed hard. "I were just . . . thinking about my mother," she whispered. It was hateful to lie; it felt like denying Harriet. But she knew she had to.

"Mrs. Wilson said summing about you and your mother earlier."

Good, thought part of Sally's mind. *The deception's building up*.

"She's not well, you see," she whispered back, "and I were that desperate to get her a bit of money. I put it in the post this morning. . . . It were the last I had."

She sniffed. Her face was wet with tears, but the real sorrow was curiously muted now. How strange it was that by acting one kind of feeling you could subdue another!

She reached for a handkerchief to dry her tears.

Eliza whispered, "She's not bad, Mrs. Wilson."

"She was kind to me."

"She can be a bit sharp, but she's all right. Mr. Clegg's all right, really. It's that valet I can't stand. All them others, come to that. He's real taken with you, Louisa. You know, since I bin here, it's the first time in me life I was glad I weren't pretty. It's not only him, neither. It's the master. . . ."

Sally's skin crawled. "What d'you mean?"

"Well . . ."

There was the sound of the bed creaking as Eliza rolled over to a more comfortable position. It was too dark to see her, and the rain lashing on the roof not far above their heads made it hard to hear whispers.

"No one'll tell you anything about the master. If you ask they'll warn you off. It's as if he didn't have no life at all outside whatever he wants doing at the moment. In me last place, Sir Charles Dyhouse's, we was gossiping all the time in the kitchen about how Sir Charles was doing in Parliament or who was coming to stay—all that kind of thing. When there was a party staying one time there was a gentleman called Mr. Priestley, and he used to creep along to Lady Dyhouse's room and back again first thing in the morning. We got up extra-early once, three of us, just to catch him in his nightshirt. Each of us popped up around a corner with a bucket of coals or an armful of linen; he'd just got past one when he came on another of us. 'Good morning, Mr. Priestley!' we'd say, nice and loud and cheerylike. He went ever so red. He give us a nice tip, though, so we didn't do it next time he came."

Sally laughed and blew her nose.

"I remember shooting parties like that," she said. "You could tell who was, you know, 'cause the mistress knew and arranged their rooms so they didn't have far to go."

"Yeah, and you talked about it, didn't yer? 'S only natural. But not here. We don't say a word about him. Sort of as if we was all afraid. Anyway, what I was going to say, I ain't spoken to anyone in the kitchen about him—the master. Only Lucy, her as was here before you. She told me once she saw

Mr. Michelet take a girl down to the master. In the cellar. One of *those* sort of girls, you know. And Mr. Michelet told her afterward, and she told me, what the master does is he just looks at the girl. Just looks at her for hours on end. Then Mr. Michelet pays her a bit of money and shows her out. He'd've had Lucy down there, too, her being pretty, only Mr. Michelet took care to keep her away from the master so he never saw her, and Mr. Michelet had her to hisself. Didn't do her any good, mind you."

"Where did he take her? To the cellar? What's down there?"

"I don't know. Mr. Michelet does all the cleaning hisself down there; the house staff ain't allowed. They just put a new hydraulic whatnot in. They used to have to lower the master down in a sort of hand-operated one. There's all kinds of new things been put in; there's wires been brought to the house and down into the cellar—you know, telegraph wires or summing. There's probly all kinds of things down there, but we'll never see 'em."

"Has he ever spoken to you?"

"The master? No, nor set eyes on me. Except when I takes the tea in or fetches coals or whatever he wants. It's like a hotel, this place, this staff. Not like his own, sort of thing. He don't know our names; it don't matter to him."

"Where does he get his money from?"

"Gawd knows. No, it's not a bad place, all things considered." Eliza yawned. "Listen to that blooming rain. We'll have washing all over the kitchen to dry if it carries on."

She turned over. After a minute or two Sally heard a gentle snore. She lay still, the tears dry on her face, her mind and body fully awake.

This room, like the other servants' rooms, was on the top floor under the attics. Below this were the rooms belonging to the master's own staff, the secretary, his physician, and so on, whom Sally had only glimpsed distantly. Below that was the master's own bedroom, dressing room, and bathroom, with the valet's room close by. Then there was the ground floor, and below that, the kitchen—and, she now knew, the cellar.

Well, she'd come here to find things out. There was nothing for it but to go and look.

She slipped out of bed, put on a pair of dark stockings, and then (with second thoughts) another pair as well on top of those. Her nightdress was white, but her cloak was dark brown, and if she tucked the nightdress up and put the hood over her head, nothing light would show.

She had some matches in her basket. She took them, and the stump of candle from the candlestick between the beds, and opened the door.

She heard a church clock striking twelve. The house was silent and absolutely dark. The thick clouds and heavy rain meant that there was no light from the sky, and the street lamps below were so feeble that nothing of their glimmer came through the narrow landing window. She'd have to navigate by feeling her way.

She set off down the back stairs. She knew them well enough by now. She didn't stop on the next floor down, but when she came to the floor where the master and his valet slept, she pushed open the baize door that separated the servants' stairs from the rest of the house. A gaslight hissed quietly on a bracket outside the double door to the master's bedroom. This was opposite the lift, which was kept open at whichever floor he happened to be on. Right next to the servants' staircase was the valet's room. Sally could see a glimmer of light under the door, and closed the baize door silently.

She went down to the ground floor and looked briefly through. The only light came from the gas lamp on the landing above. She went down the half-flight to the kitchen, taking immense care not to make a sound. Once she'd made sure there was no one there, she came back up to the ground floor again and went out into the hall.

She was glad of her double stockings, because the floor

was cold. Dining room—drawing room—library—lift; was the lift the only way down to the cellar, then? Surely not, because there must be another way out in case it failed. Somewhere there must be a staircase. But it wasn't in the hall, and there was no way down from the kitchen.

She went silently across to the drawing room. All the rooms had double doors, to let the wheelchair through, and they were all in good order and well oiled; none of them squeaked. She slipped in quickly and shut the door behind her with a click that sounded very loud in the silence.

The blinds were shut, but the faintest of glimmers still came from the embers in the fireplace. When her eyes had adjusted, and when she had located the main pieces of furniture, she moved around them carefully, looking for a way down to the cellar which she might have missed before.

There wasn't one. She turned to go and listened intently at the door before opening it and going back into the hall.

For a moment she thought they'd discovered her and turned the light up, because even the faint light from upstairs was bright in comparison with the firelight in the drawing room. Her heart leaped, but there was no sound, no movement, nothing; she was still alone and undiscovered.

She felt more vulnerable than ever, though. She was frightened: she couldn't deny it. But it was no good going back.

She opened the door to the library, slipped through, and closed it again in a moment. This was totally black; the fire had gone out. A smell of cigarette smoke hung in the air.

Should she light a match? Well, what else was she going to do?

She found the candle and struck a match with trembling fingers, shaking it out when the candle was alight and throwing it in the grate. A stream of hot wax instantly coated her fingers, but she took no notice, moving swiftly around the room, looking between the bookshelves and past the large glass-fronted cabinet that contained Chinese porcelain.

And then in the corner she saw a door. It wasn't shut—in

fact, a wedge held it open. A narrow flight of steps led down into the darkness, and a strong smell of paint came from it. Pausing only to listen and make sure there was no one coming, she set off down the steps.

They turned sharply at the bottom, where another door was propped open. The smell of paint was even stronger.

The first room was bare. A freshly laid wooden floor, bare white-painted walls, and nothing else. A door led from that into a much larger room, which was furnished, though dust sheets covered the chairs and table to keep them from the paint. The great iron cage of the lift occupied the very center of the room, with its pipework from the London Hydraulic Company and its iron grille both newly painted.

There was one other room beyond, again with an open door. She was moving toward that when she felt rather than heard a faint, very distant rumbling, like the sensation of a great engine running some way off, or like water rushing over a weir. It seemed to come from the brickwork itself, and she was tempted to put a hand on the wall to see, but remembered the wet paint in time. Instead she knelt and put her hand to the floor, and, yes, it was trembling ever so slightly.

What did that mean? Was there some engine farther below? Impossible to guess.

Then the lift moved behind her.

She gasped, and her hand shook so suddenly that the candle fell from her grasp and went out at once.

Simultaneously, she saw a light at the top of the stairs—so she couldn't go out that way. Desperate with fear, she swept her hand across the floor for the candle—couldn't leave it there—found it and the pool of wax that had spilled from it, got up, felt for the other door (never mind the paint now), and was in the next room just as the lift reached the bottom and sighed to a halt.

She stood behind the open door, next to the wall, and held her breath, conscious of the sharp, hot smell of the snuffed candle. In the silence, the lift doors clattered open, and someone stepped out into the room.

EARLIER THAT EVENING, a meeting had taken place in the hall of the Whitechapel Ethical and Temperance League. This was a body so high-minded that it believed censorship was abhorrent, and would hire out its premises to anyone, even if they wanted to advocate the force-feeding of infants with stolen whiskey.

The members of the Ethical and Temperance League had done a lot of deploring in their time—taking their visitors' money while wringing their hands over the regrettable things they were saying—but they had their work cut out that night, for Mr. Arnold Fox was on the platform.

He was addressing a meeting on the subject of alien immigration, as if he ever spoke on anything else. The audience knew what they were going to get, but no one minds having a prejudice confirmed; and he was in good form, his high, rich voice throbbing with sincerity as it told them how noble they were, how rich and pure was their English stock.

But they liked it best when he got onto how low and verminous were those outside, how filthy their habits, how rotten their bodies with every sort of disease. That was what the audience had come for, and the loathsome, subhuman life forms seemed to throng and gibber in the air as he described them: those red-rimmed eyes, those rotten teeth, those greasy locks, those fleshy noses, that foul stench. . . . The audience sighed and shivered with delicious horror.

Then he excited them even more.

"Purity!" he throbbed. "Purity . . . an English girl's birthright, an English rose's most precious possession, the holy temple of her womanhood, her most sacred jewel—ravished! Torn asunder! Plundered and defiled by these bestial monsters of lust and every kind of depravity. . . ."

There's nothing like sex for steaming people up. It always works.

At the back of the crowded hall, a dark-eyed man with a cloth cap and a gray muffler stood and watched. Not the speaker—he'd seen him plenty of times before; he was watching the audience, and he didn't like the craziness Fox was summoning up. He turned to the man beside him and said softly, "Call 'em off, Dick. Breaking up an ordinary meeting's one thing, but these people are going mad. Best thing tonight is find out all we can. Watch him—listen—trail him. See who's paying. But no violence."

"The boys are ready for it, Mr. Goldberg," said the other man.

"Then unready them," said Goldberg, his dark eyes cold. "Can't you see the stewards? Didn't you see the coppers outside? Which would you rather—be reckless and lose, or be clever and win? Don't bother to answer; you'd get it wrong. Just do as I say. I'll fix him, you'll see."

The other man nodded mournfully and slipped away to pass on Goldberg's message. Goldberg turned back to the platform, only to feel his sleeve tugged on the other side. He looked around to find the slight, anxious figure of a young man in spectacles.

"Reuben Singer?" he said quietly, under the rant of Fox and the ugly clamor from the audience. "You're Katz's apprentice, aren't you? What are you doing here? This is dangerous!"

"*You're* here, Mr. Goldberg, and there's a price on your head."

"I'm used to it. And don't say my name aloud again. Come on, what do you want?"

"It's the woman with the child. Mr. Katz thought you ought to know, but no one could find you."

Goldberg's eyes suddenly blazed, and Singer shrank back slightly under the intensity of his expression.

"What about her? Have they found her?"

"No. She's left the child at the Katzes'; Rebecca Meyer's looking after her. Miss Lockhart's disguised herself and gone to spy on the Tzaddik—working as a housemaid. They couldn't persuade her not to. And of course they didn't know . . ."

Singer expected dismay or fury; so when a broad smile of mischievous admiration spread across Goldberg's face, the young man was disconcerted.

"What a girl!" said Goldberg. "Magnificent! Who'd have thought of that?"

"But doesn't it make our plans more difficult?"

"Considerably. It means we'll have to get her out. If only she has the sense to go carefully. . . ."

And it was winter again in Goldberg's face. Singer wished he wouldn't do that; you couldn't expect to go about disguised if your face was that expressive. What was more, the men nearby had heard them whispering through the rant from the platform and were turning to stare.

But Goldberg was equal to that. Beaming with rapture at the starers, he turned his face to Arnold Fox, nodding and clapping his hands together softly in silent ecstasy.

He's mad, Singer thought. *Like the English girl Lockhart; she must be mad too. . . .*

SALLY DIDN'T MOVE. The footsteps moved slowly away from the lift—toward the door she was hiding behind—and stopped.

A voice said in English: "Do the servants clean down here?"

It was not a voice Sally knew; German, she thought, precise and prim. But she knew the next voice.

"Of course not," said Michelet. "They are forbidden to come here, Herr Winterhalter."

The secretary, Sally thought.

"You clean it yourself?"

"That is so."

"Not very well, I observe. You have dropped candle grease on the floor."

"I have never used a candle down here. It must have been the workmen."

"Mr. Lee will not be pleased. See to it at once."

Sally prayed that the wax would have hardened by now and wouldn't give her away.

After a moment Michelet spoke again.

"May I ask, Herr Winterhalter, has Mr. Lee made provision for a nursemaid?"

"A nursemaid?"

"For the child. If she is to be kept down here, she will need someone to attend to her. I am merely inquiring."

"Not your concern, Michelet."

"I beg your pardon, Herr Winterhalter, it is precisely my concern. The care of every aspect of Mr. Lee's personal life is in my hands. If this child is to become part of the household, and introduced into a . . . well, some kind of relationship with Mr. Lee, it is my duty to make sure that she does not—for instance—die of neglect or starvation."

"She will be fed. Do not be ridiculous."

"And by whom?"

"One of the servants. It does not matter. Her training will be in my hands."

Sally could hardly breathe. This was *Harriet* they were talking about. . . .

"No doubt you know best, Herr Winterhalter," said Michelet silkily.

"I do. Do not concern yourself with the matter. It is not in your province."

"The care of Mr. Lee *is* my province."

"The regulation of the household is mine."

"The regulation of that animal is my concern. No one can manage it but me. The child must be mine as well."

"Yours?"

The single word was loaded with contempt. Sally stood horrified; some bargain was being struck—some disposal of her own daughter was being argued over—but what it was, she daren't think.

"Yes! *Mine*. If she is to replace that animal—to feed him, wipe his mouth, wash him—those are *my* responsibilities. It must be *I* who trains her. Only *I* know how to do it. And he will back me up!"

"You think so?"

"I know it!"

"He has told me to assume authority. There is no disputing it. I am in charge."

"You know nothing. All you know is correspondence, business, money. He does not want a little ape-secretary; he wants something to replace that monkey when it dies. A little charming creature who will feed him, clean him, hold his cigarettes, please him. *I* know those arts. You do not. She must be mine to train."

"Too late, Michelet. Mr. Lee himself will confirm what I say. The training of the child will be in my hands."

"Impossible!"

"Certain."

"You will destroy her with your demands."

"These things are scientifically determinable. The precise degrees of pain, punishment, reward are known and calculated. There are tables, charts. Nothing will be left to chance, or instinct, or sentimentality, or whatever qualities you could manage to bring to it. And remind me, Michelet—what was the offense for which you served three years in prison?"

Silence.

"I think children came into that, did they not?" the secretary went on. "It was something, at any rate, that would make it undesirable to let you have charge of a child. Very well, we understand each other. There is no more to be said. Stand aside, please, and let me look in the other room."

The light moved toward the door and stopped in the doorway, inches away from Sally as she stood holding her breath behind the door.

"Will this be the child's bedroom?" Michelet asked, his voice quiet now.

"Possibly." The secretary sniffed. "Strange. There is the smell of a candle here."

He moved into the room. Sally could see him clearly; if he'd turned around he would have seen her. He touched a wall, looked at his fingers, dabbed them on a handkerchief in his pocket, turned back.

Sally kept her head still, the hood shading her face.

Winterhalter moved back to the door and through into the other room.

"The paint is not quite dry yet. The doors will have to remain open until the smell is gone. Give me the key, please."

A jingle of keys, and a moment or two later the clatter of the lift doors opening. Then the sighing of the hydraulics, and the light vanished as the lift moved upward.

Sally felt a stream of perspiration trickle down her back. She wanted to lean against the wall, but dared not because of the paint; instead she sank to her knees and let her head rest on the cold floor till she stopped trembling.

Think about it later, she told herself. *Get back to bed first.*

After waiting for what felt like a long time, she got to her feet and felt for the door. The darkness was complete. Striking a match was out of the question: she'd have to feel her way out of the cellar, risk the crossing of the hall, and get back up the servants' staircase. Supposing the paint was dry, and he'd locked the door. . . .

It took her the best part of an hour. As she closed the green baize door behind her out of the hall and set foot on the first steps, she heard a church clock strike two. She was cold, bone weary, and aching in every limb from the day's hard work and the effort of not making a noise.

Only three flights of stairs now. She reached the top of the first, turned to go up the next—and her heart slammed into her ribs with fear.

Someone was standing there, waiting for her.

He struck a match. In its flare she saw the plump, greedy face of Michelet.

"So it was you," he whispered. "Louisa. The naughty Louisa. Well, mademoiselle, you had better come to my room, hadn't you? We will have a nice conversation. I look forward to it very much indeed."

23

NO JUWES

ONCE INSIDE HIS ROOM, HE STRUCK ANOTHER MATCH AND lit a lamp. Then without any warning he seized her and kissed her full on the mouth. She could taste cigarettes, Parma violets, eau de cologne.

He was holding her awkwardly. Her neck was twisted; she couldn't breathe. She pushed him away and gasped.

"Quiet," he hissed. "Mr. Lee is only next-door. His hearing is very acute. Well? What is your explanation?"

"My explanation, sir?"

"Of how you came to be in the cellar. You may count yourself very lucky I did not give you away to that imbecile Winterhalter."

"I'm sure I don't know what you mean, sir. I didn't know there was a cellar. I've just been down to the kitchen—to the icebox, sir. To put some ice on my head, because it was aching so. I know I shouldn't have done, but it was unbearable. I don't know who Mr. Winter . . . I just don't know what you mean, sir."

His eyes were narrow.

"You were there. I saw the match you threw in the library fireplace, and I saw the drop of wax on the steps. Winterhalter missed that. And what about this?"

He lifted her cloak. On the hem was a vague smear that might have been white paint.

"I did that in the post office this morning; they'd just painted the walls. . . . Why are you questioning me like this, Mr. Michelet?"

She tried to look innocent, puzzled, hurt. At the same time she let her cloak fall open slightly at the throat. She saw his eyes move there and thought for the first time that she might be able to get away with it.

He let the hem fall and reached up slowly to her jaw. He tilted her chin up and stroked his fingers down her neck to the hollow at the base of her throat. She willed herself to keep still as he traced the length of her collarbone from left to right and back again.

She saw that his eyes were becoming glazed, and coughed slightly, as if she felt ill.

"Please, sir . . ." she whispered.

"Louisa, you have been a bad girl," he said in a low, soft voice, almost as if he were mesmerized. "You must not tell me lies. What did you hear him say down there?"

"I didn't hear no one, sir—honest."

Steeling herself, she put one hand timidly on his chest. He seized it and crushed it to his mouth, and then pulled her to him a second time and ran his hands down her sides under the cloak. She was trembling: *Let him think it's nervousness*, she thought. He couldn't suspect it was loathing.

"Oh, Mr. Michelet . . . please may I go to my bed, sir?" she whispered into his ear. "Another time . . . I'm not well, sir."

"Louisa," he said, and his voice was thick. "You're beautiful. One more kiss."

He pressed his mouth on hers, busily working away like a greedy child with a sweet. She held her breath, making herself loose and passive and doll-like. Presently he stopped.

"Soon," he said, and his eyes were lost. She'd never seen a man so nearly at the edge of his control, but she sensed his fear, too, holding him back: fear of Winterhalter, fear of Lee, fear even of her.

Because he really wasn't sure now whether she'd heard them or not. And he couldn't afford to guess.

He pushed her away. He was clearly the kind of man to like his women frightened, nervous, unwilling. If she had offered herself blatantly, he'd have turned away with loath-ing. She must let him think that he was the masterful pur-suer and she was the timid victim.

The last she saw of him before she left the room was his puffy eyes, still hot with desire, still hooded with fear.

SALLY HAD LITTLE more than three hours of sleep. Of all the images that haunted her dreams, none was worse than the idea of little Harriet imprisoned in that cellar and trained to act as the Tzaddik's . . . what? Nursemaid? Putting food into his mouth, wiping his chin . . .

She felt sick when she thought about it. That, and her lack of sleep, made her look pale, and Mrs. Wilson com-mented on it at midmorning, when Sally was summoned to take a tray of coffee to the library.

"No, it's nothing, Mrs. Wilson," she said. "My head's been aching, but it'll clear up."

There were three cups on the tray. Once again the Tzaddik called for her to come in, and once again she tried not to look up as she brought the tray to the table by the fireplace. She let her eyes flick across to the door she'd gone through to the cellar, inconspicuous in the corner of the room. It was closed.

She curtsied briefly to the Tzaddik and was about to leave when he said, "Stop. Your name is Kemp, is it not?"

"Yes, sir," she said, glancing at him swiftly.

"Be so good as to pour some coffee for my guests."

"Very good, sir."

She felt the three of them watch her as she set out the cups and poured the coffee. Who they were she didn't know until she handed the cups around. As one of the men took his cup without acknowledging it, he spoke to the other, and she recognized his voice: it was the man she'd seen on the immigrant ship, Arnold Fox.

She looked up involuntarily then, and saw that the other man was Arthur Parrish, and he was looking at her with a little frown, as if he was puzzled. But he turned away to answer Arnold Fox, and she breathed again.

Taking as much time as she reasonably could, she poured the second cup and listened.

"You see, the danger in a full-scale pogrom, so to speak, on the Russian model," Parrish was saying, "is that Jews presently on their way to England would be tempted to miss it out altogether and go straight to America. Oh, I know you'd welcome that," he went on as Mr. Fox seemed about to interrupt, "but look at it from a business point of view."

He took his cup from Sally, who turned back to the Tzaddik. The monkey wasn't there, she noticed.

"Pour some for me," the Tzaddik told her.

That voice—oh, there was something in the softness, the depth, the cracked thickness of it. . . . She'd heard it before, or dreamed it in a nightmare. Thankful for the excuse to stay, she poured another cup as Fox replied, "I have higher considerations than business, Mr. Parrish. I am concerned with the purity of the English race."

"You are a vain, pompous man whose main concern is getting himself elected," said the Tzaddik. "I am supporting you with my funds only to the extent that you are useful. The moment you cease to be so, I shall drop you. Kemp, bring me the cup. Lift it to my lips."

"It's hot, sir," she said, aware of the subdued fury on the face of Arnold Fox, the cheerful blandness of Parrish; and aware too of the stillness of her hands as she held the delicate porcelain to his lips.

He sipped noisily once, twice, three times. His bulk, so close to her, was massive and nearly shapeless; the suit he wore, though immaculately tailored, could not disguise the fact that his arms and chest were no more than inert lumps of fat. This close, she could hear him breathing, and see the huge chest inflate with effort and sigh itself empty again. And she could see how the sleek reddish hair was plastered to the scalp with some scented pomade, and how the helpless fingers, huge and dead in his lap, were perfectly manicured.

"Again," he said, and she put the coffee cup to his mouth, feeling despite her fear and loathing a desperate pity for this man imprisoned in his vast hulk of flesh, utterly unable to make the slightest movement.

Arnold Fox put down his coffee cup with a shaking hand and stood up. Sally was careful not to look at him, but held the cup out of the way for the Tzaddik to face him as Fox said in a throbbing voice, "I shall do as you say. I have no choice. But, Mr. Lee, I am not afraid to label your change of mind as hardly less than a betrayal. Instead of the fine gesture of righteous anger the British people would wish to make, you reduce the affair to a . . . to little more than a drunken brawl. But you know best; doubtless you know best, sir. I am obliged to both of you. Good day."

And he left. Both men watched him indifferently, and when the door had slammed behind him the Tzaddik said, "Good. That makes the decision for us. I am happy to accept the will of heaven, Parrish."

Mr. Parrish smiled. "So now we press ahead, sir?"

He stopped and looked up at Sally, who could feel his eyes on her but kept hers modestly cast down.

"Thank you, Kemp," said the Tzaddik. "You may go."

"Thank you, sir," she said, curtsying, and left.

In the hall she looked around quickly. No one in sight, and she knew Mr. Clegg was busy in his pantry, and Mrs. Wilson was in the kitchen, and . . .

She bent down and pretended to be adjusting her boot-lace.

Parrish's voice came through the door: " . . . the whistles?"

"Not yet," said the Tzaddik. "The English mob is not disciplined enough. It has lost the taste for rioting, besides. It will have to be educated."

"But you want a full-scale riot?"

"I want deaths, and lootings, and I want an entire street

burned down. A street of Jewish houses. That will create the most panic and resentment. And it will look as if Mr. Fox was behind it, and he will try to stop it, thinking that's what we want, and he'll fail. The press will blame him for encouraging it; we will blame him for not stopping it. So we discard him at once, and pledge our support for Jewish charities and reconstruction and so forth. . . . They will come to us voluntarily, Parrish. The little fish will swim into the net!"

"Magnificent," said the other man. "What date did you have in mind, Mr. Lee?"

Sally leaned closer to the door to hear.

And then a hand clasped her mouth, and an arm encircled her waist and lifted her clear of the floor.

For a second she struggled, until she realized that the hand over her mouth was wearing a white glove. It wasn't Michelet—it was one of the footmen. Suddenly she let herself flop, as if she'd fainted.

Startled, he loosened his grip. She fell forward, but found her balance and whipped around to face him.

"What d'you think you're doing?" she hissed.

"Just having a bit of fun—"

He was a strapping, swaggering sort of fellow, with a broad, confident grin. But he was looking a little uneasy now in the face of her anger.

"How dare you touch me like that?" she said, keeping her voice low so as not to be heard through the door. And as she looked, she saw a different expression come into his face, and realized that she'd made a mistake.

"Who *are* you, anyway?" he said. "You're not a bloody maidservant—I can see that now. What are you doing here?"

What she'd done was to act like a lady: to do what a person of her class would naturally do if a man behaved as he'd done. She'd assumed that any girl would have done the same. Now, in a split second, she recalled the different way men looked at her when they thought she wasn't a lady, and realized that a real servant wouldn't have had the option of being ruffled and indignant. She should have been wearily contemptuous.

But as soon as she realized that, she saw a way of winning back the initiative. She'd have to move fast, though; keep him off balance.

She put a finger to her lips, hushing him, looked around, and then beckoned him to follow her into the dining room next-door.

Intrigued, as she knew he would be, he followed. She shut the door behind him and looked around before whispering "What's your name? Is it John?"

"John's the other footman. I'm Alfred. But—"

"Listen, Alfred, I want your help. You're right—I'm not here as a maidservant. I'm here because of my cousin. . . ."

She was standing close, looking up at him, hoping she looked appealing and desperate. His expression was still suspicious, but he was interested now too, and not unwilling to stand close to a pretty girl while she confided in him.

"Your cousin?"

"Yes. Lucy. You remember—she had to leave because of that Frenchman—that . . ."

Understanding dawned. "The valet!" he said. "Ah."

"Yes, the pig," she said. "She told me everything. How he promised to marry her, how he swore he'd look after her, everything. It broke my mother's heart—that's Lucy's aunt, see. We was like sisters. And I swore I'd get even with him, the swine. So . . . but no one's got to know. 'Specially him."

"What're you going to do?"

"I don't know yet. I'll find something. I'll destroy him, I will. She was such a sweet girl. . . . And she's ruined now; she'll never get another situation. . . ."

He nodded. He wasn't very bright, she thought—vain, conceited, like all footmen, fond of showing off his broad chest and his manly legs in their white stockings; but good-hearted, on the whole, if she was any judge. And he knew what happened to servants without a character.

"So, please, Alfred, can I trust you? There's no one else here I can say a word to."

"Yeah," he said. "I won't give yer away. I hates that prinking French popinjay, anyway. We all do. Nasty bit o' work. We all thought you was making up to him."

"I was! I want to trap him, see! I want to catch him and pay him out. You don't mind me telling you this, do you, Alfred? I don't want to get you into trouble."

" 'S all right. I'll stick up for yer. They was wondering about you in the kitchen—them others. 'Cause you don't seem like a housemaid—too ladylike. You bin a lady's maid? Thought so. Well, that explains it. If you don't want to stick out, you want to act a bit more natural-like. Have a laugh. Then you won't seem so out of place. You don't *look* like your cousin."

"She took after her pa. Oh, Alfred, I *am* grateful."

She laid a hand on his chest, but only for a moment. She felt him stir with a chivalry that probably took him quite by surprise.

"Where is he now?" she said quietly. "Mr. Michelet?"

"He'll be upstairs, with the secretary. Second floor. That's where the master works most of the time. The master's own staff, they have their sitting room up there too. Next to the lift."

"Do the household staff clean up there, or is that Mr. Michelet's job, like the cellar?"

"Who told you about the cellar?"

Careful, she thought. "I saw the open door in the library when I took the master's tea in yesterday. I asked Eliza about it."

"Ah . . . no, he cleans down there, but not upstairs. You'll be doing that. Here—what you going to do to him?"

"I don't know. I just need to get close to him first, get his confidence, let him get all sweet with me like he got with Lucy. I need to find out—oh, everything, what he does for the master, when he has time off, what he likes to eat . . .

everything. Alfred, I'm trusting you—you won't let me down, will you?"

He looked down at her, tall and confident and masterful. Then he winked and tapped his nose.

"You leave it to me," he said.

Then before leaving she did something she'd never have believed possible before all this began: she stood on tiptoe and kissed his cheek. It was just a swift, hurried brush of the lips, but it seemed to fulfill some expectation of his, and it cost her nothing. And it might help save Harriet.

"Mama! Mama!"

Harriet was inconsolable. Rebecca tried to pick her up, but Harriet squirmed away and threw herself down on the worn carpet. Ever since she'd woken up the morning before and Mama hadn't been there, she'd alternated between helpless indignant rage and gasping, tearful suspicion. It might have been easier for Rebecca if it hadn't been raining, because then they could have gone into the little backyard where Morris Katz had fixed up a plank and a rope as a swing for Leah when she was younger. But the rain was incessant.

Rebecca had sung to her, drawn pictures for her, played with the wooden dog for her, tried to pick her up, tried to put her down when she finally started dozing, tried to feed her, tried to make her drink: but Harriet's rage and unhappiness were enormous, unbounded, as deep as the foundations of the earth.

"I never heard a child cry like that!" said Leah admiringly. "She's got lungs like a prima donna."

"What can I do to stop her?" said Rebecca helplessly.

"Join in," said Leah.

"I feel like it. Sally left me looking after her, and all I do is make her cry. What a noise . . ."

Just then they heard another voice in the hall, and Mr. Katz came in. It was unusual to see him there at midday.

But here he was, and he hadn't even taken off his apron. His deep voice filled the room—and Harriet stopped crying.

She looked up, tear-stained, at this big, rumbling bear, with his dark whiskers and his dirty apron, and he looked down at her little frown and determined, trembling lip, and he swept her up in a moment.

Too astonished to protest, she stared at him in amazement as the strange, urgent words tumbled out of those nearly hidden lips. He was serious: she could tell that from his eyes. But he was strong, and she was safe: she could tell that from his solid arms and his deep voice.

Then he stopped talking and turned his eyes to her. And, weak with sorrow and fear, tears still wet on her eyelashes, she had enough energy left to wonder where his mouth had gone, so she reached up and lifted the mustache to see if it was still there.

When she found it, it was smiling. What a surprise! She looked up, uncertain, and saw his dark eyes smiling too. So she smiled back. She couldn't help it.

"Eh, *bubeleh!* What an eloquent silence!" said the big man in Yiddish, and his deep voice rumbled in his chest. She could feel it as she leaned against him.

She gave a long, shuddering, exhausted sigh, and her thumb came up to her mouth. She gazed at him solemnly.

"Look at that!" said Mrs. Katz. "The injustice of it! There's Leah and Rebecca spent all day yesterday and all day today trying to stop her crying, and he comes in and lets her play with his whiskers and she stops in a moment."

"There's nothing for it, Rebecca," said Leah. "We'll have to grow beards. But, Papa, what is it? What have you come home for?"

"Trouble," said Morris Katz. "Isaac Feinberg's son was attacked by some roughs in Mile End yesterday. They left a note pinned to his coat saying NO JEWS. And the synagogue was painted with the same slogan. They can't spell *Jews*, either. They write it *Juwes*. Someone threw a brick through the window of Bloom's, the baker's. . . . I don't want you to go out alone until things are calmer, d'you see?"

"But—are you talking about a pogrom, Morris? What do you mean? Is it that bad?"

"I don't know yet! I just don't like the feel of things, that's all. If Goldberg was free to move around, maybe he could rally the Jews, keep us together. We're all splitting up into factions. But Reuben Singer said he saw him last night—at Arnold Fox's meeting, of all places."

"The man's mad," said Mrs. Katz decisively. "He's as bad as these crazy men from Hibbat Zion. They're everywhere now; you hear their talk all over the place. You haven't been listening to them?"

Hibbat Zion was a movement of Jews who wanted to encourage a return to the Holy Land. Morris Katz waved impatiently.

"To hear what they say, of course I've been listening! D'you think I buy my opinions ready-made? And I'm not so sure they are crazy, Hibbat Zion. They sound to me as if they're talking a lot of sense."

"Goldberg would know better. He wouldn't waste his time with them."

"One minute he's mad, the next minute he'd know better! Make up your mind. Anyway, you're wrong. Goldberg would argue with them, but he'd listen first. That's what you people don't understand about him—"

"You people! Who's *you people?* His own wife he calls *you people?*"

"Oh, I can't stop now," said Morris Katz. "I've got a shop to run. Rebecca, take the child. Remember what I said—don't go out alone. Keep the door shut."

He embraced his wife and daughter more warmly than he usually did, and hurried out. Harriet knew nothing of the move from one pair of arms to another. Rebecca sat down with her, marveling at the lightness and softness of this creature who only a few minutes before had been howling, kicking, screaming in fury. Her little face was drenched with sleep. She was at home, in Orchard House, and they were all there—Uncle Webster, Sarah-Jane, Jim, Bruin, and Mama, and she was with them, commanding them never to go away again.

LIKE MANY immigrant Jews, Morris Katz belonged to a *chevra:* a religious organization not quite a synagogue but more than a club, where services were held, discussions and arguments and learning of all kinds took place, and where poor men worn out after their day's toil could go and refresh themselves in the fountain of the Talmud, the collective wisdom of Jewishness. For many immigrants the *chevra* was a link with the past, with the society and fellowship of the town or the village they'd come from, and they clung to it in this strange land as something familiar.

And when Morris Katz visited the *chevra* that evening, he found that his wife's guess about Hibbat Zion was right, for there was a visitor in the room, a pale, intense young Russian Jew whom Katz had never seen before.

"My brothers," he was saying in a passionate, musical voice, "what is happening all over Europe? Shall I tell you? Every nation is coming to a consciousness of itself—realizing who and what it is—and as it does so, it expels all those who don't belong. Russia throws us out of Russia; Germany doesn't want us in Germany; Poland can't wait to hustle us out of Poland.

"But aren't *we* a nation too? Isn't every Jew a member of a nation—but one without a country?"

This question had been posed many times, and many of the men there had argued it back and forth. But the young man went on. "I say to you that, yes, there is a Jewish nation, and, yes, there is a country which is ours, given to us by the Lord—given to Abraham, given to Isaac—yes, I'm talking about Eretz Israel, the land of Israel!"

Morris Katz had heard that before too. Talk like this was being heard more and more, among the eastern European Jews in particular. And in spite of what he'd said to his wife, he really wasn't sure what he thought about it, which was why he liked to listen to the arguments.

"But . . . we've settled here," said one of the men. "We have businesses here, homes here. And what would we do in Eretz Israel? I'm not a farmer. . . ."

"No, our visitor's right," said another. "You can be born here and die here, but they'll never think of you as English; you'll always be a Jew first—an alien—"

"It's the same in Germany—"

"It's the same everywhere!"

"Wait, wait, wait!" said another objector. "Every nation has its own language. Right? That's one of the things that makes it a nation. So what language would your Jewish nation speak? Yiddish? German? Polish?"

"Hebrew," said the young man.

Shrugs, nods, vigorous head shakings, and a dozen voices at once. Morris Katz listened with half an ear, obscurely troubled. He knew that Dan Goldberg would have a dozen arguments to beat this one; but Goldberg wasn't there, and intense believers like this young man were becoming more and more influential.

The room they were in was narrow and dark, and extremely hot and stuffy from the iron stove in the corner. Morris Katz hadn't meant to stay for long, and he was about to get up and leave when there was a sudden, shocking crash of glass.

All talk stopped. The talkers froze. On the floor among their feet was a scatter of glass and a brick, and chalked on the brick were the words NO JUWES.

It took a moment for the men to gather their wits. Then those nearest the window, Morris Katz among them, leaped up and peered out into the rain. Across the street, under a gas lamp, two young men made an obscene gesture and ran off laughing.

As two of the Jews made for the door to try and catch them, as others hunted for a broom to sweep up the glass and a patch of cardboard to put over the window, Morris Katz met the eyes of the visitor. The young man looked determined and frightened and triumphant all at once.

"Well?" he said. "It's beginning, Morris Katz. You're going to have to choose. Are you with us, or against us? It's not going to get better. It's going to get worse. Do you want the Jews to have a country? Or do you want them to vanish?"

Morris Katz didn't reply. He felt the choice wasn't as simple as that. He didn't like these crude certainties; and more than ever he wished Dan Goldberg was there, to help them all see what the truth was.

24

The Entry in the Ledger

THAT SAME NIGHT, GOLDBERG HELD A CONFERENCE ON THE fourth floor of a tobacco warehouse in Wapping. It was a place he'd used before; a sovereign to the night watchman, and the place was his. Once the windows were covered with sacking, no lights could be seen from the street, and provided no one dropped a match and burned the warehouse down, they were perfectly safe.

Kid Mendel, the Soho gangster, was there, and so was Moishe Lipman, the leader of the Jewish gangs in Bethnal Green; and so, looking far from easy, were the young Russian from Hibbat Zion and several other representatives of Jewish causes. There were some of the earnest socialists, too, and Reuben Singer, and Bill—about twenty men in all, and they eyed each other warily, waiting for Goldberg to speak. Warily, that is, except for Kid Mendel, who sat on a bale of tobacco with one immaculately shod foot resting on the opposite knee, looking around with urbane curiosity.

When they had all arrived, Goldberg began. He spoke in English, translating into Yiddish and Russian as he went along.

"I've called you all here, gentlemen, because we have to make a decision very soon about the violence that's going to erupt in our midst. We know it's coming; we've been seeing the signs for weeks. We have to decide how we're going to meet it. And what we decide will have a great effect on the lives of all of us.

"Now, as you look around you'll see men you know, men

you don't know, men you trust, men you wouldn't give the time of day to. There are capitalists here, and there are socialists. There are those who want all Jews to live in Palestine, and those who are prospering in London. The only thing we have in common is that we're Jews.

"But for the moment that's the important thing, because that's what we're going to be attacked for. Now, you've all put aside your other concerns and come to this meeting, and I'm very glad to see you. What we'll do to start with is go around briefly and compare our observations about how things are in our different areas. Then we'll decide what to do about it. Who'd like to start? Mr. Mendel?"

"With pleasure, Dan," said Kid Mendel. "But I've got a question for you first. You're no fool, and we all know there's a price on your head. How do you know one of us won't turn you in as soon as we leave here?"

Goldberg smiled, and his eyes glittered with pure innocence. "D'you know, I hadn't thought of that?" he said, and no one believed him for a moment. "Tell you what, Kid—if you know who's going to turn me in, ask him to leave the room, and I'll tell the rest of you how I'm going to spike his guns. Then he can come back in, and we'll get on with the business."

Smiles all around, the broadest from Kid Mendel himself. He nodded.

"All right," he said. "I suppose I'll have to trust my fellow Jews, even the law-abiding ones. The situation in Soho's like this, gentlemen. . . ."

SALLY WAS too tired to explore that night. Instead she lay listening to Eliza's faint snores and reviewed what she'd discovered so far.

First, the business with the footman. She'd been foolish to expose herself so easily to getting caught, but if they thought that her real target was Michelet, they wouldn't think her curiosity about the Tzaddik was suspicious: she'd be just

trying to find a way to Michelet through him. On the whole
she'd come well out of that encounter, after a few moments
of panic.

Second, Michelet himself. Every time she saw him now
she found herself remembering the secretary's words: Michelet
had been convicted of an offense involving children. Images
of what that might have been, and images of Harriet connected with it, strained insistently to come into her mind.

Third, the secretary himself and those offices on the second floor. That was where she must go next.

Fourth, the matter she'd overheard them discussing—and
that was the most urgent of all these urgent things. The
Tzaddik, through Parrish, was planning to start a riot—an
attack on the Jews—and unleash who knew what savagery
and hatred. . . . She had the sense of some huge earth
movement, a landslide, beginning to move under her; and
all she could do was hold back a few pebbles.

But somehow the key to it all lay in that bloated, inert
mass of flesh, the Tzaddik. Somehow the way to stop him
was to find out who he was—or who *else* he was; and the way
to find that out was to understand the plot against her and
Harriet.

Why had he picked on her, out of all the women in London
with a small child? He was so hooded, so guarded, so mysterious that even when she was holding a cup to his lips she
could sense nothing but his deathly helplessness. And the
fact that the malevolence that victimized her came out of
such infantile weakness made it all the more chilling. *Out of
the strong came forth sweetness.* . . . She remembered Samson's
riddle. Out of the still came forth poison. Out of the dark
. . . Out of the past . . .

She fell asleep.

ALL OVER Whitechapel, all over Spitalfields and Mile End
and Wapping, the rain fell unceasingly. The sewers were en-
gorged; the drains and gutters brimmed, choked, over-
flowed.

In the pubs, in the Mechanics' Improvement Societies, in kitchens and parlors and eating houses, the word was spreading that there was going to be trouble.

Dockers who were out of work, factory hands, brewery workers, toilers in warehouses and tanneries, laborers of all sorts: anyone who felt cheated, dispossessed, done out of a living or a home or a bit of space. . . . Parrish's men moved among them, buying drinks, lending an ear, letting the poison drip.

The Jews do all right for themselves, don't they?

They don't go short . . .

They got the markets all sewn up.

Disease. They spread disease. . . . Their women are rotten with it.

There's more and more of 'em coming over on every boat. . . .

You can go down their end of Brick Lane and not see a proper English face for an hour at at time. Hanbury Street—Fashion Street—they're just as bad; Flower and Dean Street . . .

That Hungarian case—it was in the papers—they stole a Christian child and killed it to use her blood in their rituals. It's true—witnesses—they confessed—

There was a case like that in Germany.

Christian children? What, they kill 'em?

It's been proved time and time again.

There's a Jewish girl in Montagu Street with a stolen child.

Get away. . . .

It is! Not Jewish, neither. . . . Not with fair hair . . .

"Montagu Street?" said Mr. Parrish. He was in a pub in the Whitechapel Road—a grand mahogany place, with polished brass and glittering mirrors and plushly upholstered barmaids. Cigar smoke hung thickly in the air, and Parrish was buying the drinks.

"Yeah," said his informant blurrily, through his eighth pint.

"Have you seen this child? What is it, by the way—boy or girl?"

"My old lady has. It's a girl, she reckons. Crying all the time. Stands to reason they stole it."

"Your wife familiar with the street, is she?"

"She oughter be. She was born there. Afore them bloody Jews come in. She was going down there yesterday, and she hears this kid yelling and screaming. Smart house it was—lick of paint, clean curtains; must be a bit of money in there, eh? They don't go without, do they?"

"I expect they're living nice and fat," said Mr. Parrish. "Go on about the child."

"Oh, aye. Well, she hears this yelling and carrying on and looks in through the window, and she sees it—nice little fair-haired kiddie struggling to get away from this Jewish gel what was holding it. The gel sees her looking and drags it away from the window. Bound to be stolen, my old lady reckons. Course, she didn't know about this blood business. . . . Is that true, then?"

"I wouldn't be surprised. What number house was that?"

"Oh, blimey, I dunno. Smart-looking place. Potted plant in the window. Think they're a cut above the rest of us. . . . I hates 'em. Ta, guv, another pint for me. . . ."

As THE REST of the men were leaving the tobacco warehouse, Goldberg asked Kid Mendel and Moishe Lipman to stay behind. Bill stayed too, and when Goldberg was sure they wouldn't be overheard, he offered them each a cigar and said, "Gentlemen, we've got another problem to deal with. I didn't want to bother the meeting with it; it's your particular expertise I want."

The two gang leaders said nothing. They were very different: the sophisticated, elegant Mendel was dressed in the height of fashion and looked like a prince on holiday, whereas Moishe Lipman, who'd been a fairground boxer in his youth, could have auditioned for the part of Frankenstein's monster in a theater company that wasn't fussy.

The two men knew each other; their feelings comprised equal parts of respect and mistrust. Bill, watching them, marveled at the magnetic personality of Goldberg, who'd drawn such different kinds of steel together.

"Well?" said Lipman harshly, when they were seated again.

Mendel blew a stream of smoke toward the candle, making its flame waver and flare upward in the gloom.

"Let me guess," he said before Goldberg could answer. "It's the woman."

Lipman's heavy eyes left Goldberg and turned to his rival. "What woman is this? Is this connected with the business we came here for?"

"Very closely," said Goldberg. "She's the one person who can sink the Tzaddik." In a few sentences he told them about Sally and Harriet. "Now I'm afraid she's put herself in real danger. I want a watch kept on that house; and the moment there's any sign of trouble, I want it raided. Second, the child. She's safe where she is, but I want a guard there. Twenty-four hours a day."

Silence. Kid Mendel raised an eyebrow; Moishe Lipman scowled.

"Expensive," he said after a moment or two. "Why bother?"

"Because that child's mother is the only way we can beat the Tzaddik. If the child is caught, we lose everything; he'll be stronger than ever, because the mother's disguise won't last a moment. In any case, I'm afraid of something worse."

"The blood libel?" said Mendel, but it wasn't really a question.

Goldberg nodded.

"He'd do that and blame it on the Jews?" said Lipman. "But why on earth—?"

He didn't finish, because there were running footsteps outside, and a pounding on the door. Lipman jumped to his feet, fists clenched; Mendel turned to watch with elegant curiosity. But first on his feet, quicker even than Bill, was Goldberg, and his hand was in his pocket.

Bill opened the door, and it was Reuben Singer who fell in, breathless.

"The child—they've got her. . . ."

Goldberg was at his side in a second. The young man was bleeding from a split lip, and one of his eyes was closing rapidly.

"A bunch of roughs—not police, no—no warrant, nothing—a dapper little man in charge of them, called himself Parrish. Rebecca knew what he wanted and tried to get the child out the back way, but they had men in the yard, too. And Mr. Katz"—he broke off to gasp for breath—"he's unconscious," he managed to say. "They beat him with sticks. Rebecca, too. I think her arm's broken. But they've got the child. . . ."

"All right, Dan," said Mendel. "You with us, Moishe?"

Lipman's brutal features glowered in the flickering light.

"They're not hurting kids," he said. "Jewish, goy, Hottentot, whatever. Tell us what you want, Dan."

Goldberg thought swiftly. "Three places he might have taken her to: the house in Fournier Square, or Parrish's own house in Telegraph Road, Clapham, or the place he's taken over in Twickenham. Moishe, take some boys and go to Fournier Square. Kid, you do the same in Twickenham. Orchard House—big place by the river. I'll go to Clapham."

"What do we do?" said Mendel.

"Stake it out. Keep watch. The second you see her, move in and snatch her."

"Ever seen a kidnapping?" said Lipman. "It won't be easy without hurting her."

"We'll do it," said Mendel.

"We'll need a place to contact," said Goldberg. "My place in Soho is watched, now there's a warrant for me. Any ideas?"

"I've got a telephone," said Mendel. "Number four-two-one-four. I'll put a man on the line full-time. Call in as soon as you can when the exchange opens at nine o'clock, and he'll pass on the news."

"Good," said Goldberg as the two gang leaders hurried out. "All right, Reuben? You're going to have to look after Mrs. Katz and the others. Come on, let's go. . . ."

Then he was off, leaping down the dark stairs and out through the slashing rain, with Bill following close behind.

HARRIET SAT very still. There was a horse, because she could hear it, and it was cold and smooth under her hand, like the seat in the cab she and Mama had ridden in.

There were men talking. It was dark. Mama had said she must be brave, so she was being brave, like Mama herself in the jungle with the bad monkeys.

There was no Rebecca. She wanted Rebecca suddenly. The men hadn't wanted Rebecca to come, and they'd hit her. They'd hit Mr. Katz, too.

It was cold. Her thumb came up to her mouth, and she sucked it hard, but she didn't cry. She just had to sit still.

SALLY WOKE UP suddenly from a confused, painful dream and lay biting her lip in the darkness. Eliza was breathing heavily, obviously asleep, and a clock was striking one, unhelpfully. It was no good; she wouldn't sleep anymore.

Well, she knew what the target was this time: the offices on the second floor. There must be something incriminating there, if only she could find it.

She put her feet over the side of the bed, shivering as they touched the cold boards, and felt for her stockings. Then she paused and felt in her basket till she found the heavy coldness of the pistol.

She was very tempted. She could carry it in the pocket of her cloak, and of course she wouldn't use it, but it would make her feel safer. . . .

It was heavy and swung awkwardly at her side, and halfway down the stairs she wished she hadn't brought it. Still, there it was. When she opened the door on the second-floor landing, the butt of the pistol knocked against the jamb, and she stood still for nearly a minute, hardly daring to breathe.

But nothing happened, and she moved on through. The light outside the Tzaddik's bedroom on the floor below fil-

tered up and showed her the dim outlines of doors and ban-
isters, and she tiptoed along the linoleum-covered floor to
the door at the front, where she knew the secretary worked.

Would it open? Yes.

The chilling thought, suddenly: Was the monkey on this
floor? Or was it asleep with the Tzaddik?

Don't stop to think. Look around. Move quickly, but be careful.

The blinds were open, and a dim light from the gas lamp
in the street below made its way in through the rain-splashed
windows—enough for her to see shelves behind the desk,
and on them the bulky shapes of something familiar: ledg-
ers. Perhaps she was being lucky at last, finding something
she understood. Could she risk lighting the candle?

The pistol gave her confidence; if worst came to worst,
she could fight her way out. She lit the stump of candle in
its enamel holder, set it on the desk, and took the first ledger
from the shelf.

It seemed to be a record of payments to the domestic staff:
nothing unusual or irregular here. She scanned it quickly and
put it back. The next she took down concerned share deal-
ings; the Tzaddik evidently had a large and diverse portfolio,
and it was being managed, she could see, very efficiently.
But again there was nothing that any wealthy gentleman would
have needed to hide. She put that one back and took another.

She looked through five more, and found nothing more
than the records—immaculately kept—of a successful import
and export business. Then in the eighth she saw something.

It seemed to be an account of payments received from
various sources. The amounts varied and were in several different currencies; but one of them consisted of weekly payments in sterling of amounts around two hundred pounds.
There was something familiar about that figure, but she
couldn't place it until she noticed that each kind of entry
was identified by a letter. The one for the payments which
had caught her eye was *P*.

Parrish.

It was the money Goldberg had told her about—the money Parrish collected from the gambling houses and brothels in the West End, the money those poor girls from the immigrant ships were making. And Goldberg had the book that Parrish had entered the weekly totals in! If that tallied with this . . .

If it did, she had him.

She found a pair of scissors in the drawer and very carefully cut out the page, cutting as close as she could to the stitching so as to make it inconspicuous. They'd find it soon—but every little bit helped.

Then she replaced the ledger and heaved a sigh of achievement. She folded the page and tucked it into her stocking for safety.

Bed?

She hesitated. This was an important discovery, but perhaps she ought to force things further. It would be hateful, but so was being without Harriet, so was the whole business. And the heaviness in her soul when she thought of the Tzaddik . . . No, she couldn't avoid it.

She left the office, her heart beating hard, and crept down the stairs to Michelet's door. And there she hesitated again, and for longer, like a nervous swimmer on the brink of a river that she knows will be cold and deep and dangerous.

But the longer she stayed, the worse it would be. She swallowed hard, turned the door handle, and stepped softly in.

As THE CAB rattled over Blackfriars Bridge, Bill said, "Why'd you go for Clapham, Mr. G.? Wouldn't he want to take her straight to his boss?"

"No, not if I know Parrish. He'll want to do a little bargaining. Damn it, Bill, this is my bloody fault. I should have moved quicker."

He peered ahead through the teeming rain. There was little traffic—one or two carts lumbering north toward the great markets, another late cab, a strolling policeman swathed in rain gear.

"Listen," said Goldberg. "I'm going to stop the cab in Lambeth. I want you to go and round up as many of your Irish mates as you can find, and bring 'em on down to Clapham. Those boys you keep telling me about—good fighters, are they?"

"The best," said Bill.

"They'll have to be smart as well as headstrong. Now, listen: I've been to look over Telegraph Road, and there's a little alleyway between the houses—a passage through to the backyards of the houses on the other side of the road from Parrish's. I'll be waiting in there. Go discreetly—don't get yourselves followed. By the time you get there I'll have worked out what to do."

"Can I promise 'em a fight?"

"If Parrish is there, yes, we'll have a fight. Cabbie!"

He slid back the partition behind his head and told the cabdriver to pull over. Bill looked out at the bulk of Bethlehem Hospital.

"Bedlam," he said. "See you later, Mr. G."

He leaped out and ran off into the dark. The cab rolled on toward Clapham.

HARRIET HADN'T cried once. The man beside her was cruel. He shouted at the other men and made them run out of the carriage and open something, and then he picked her up, but not properly, and it was hurting her. She struggled to get up straight in his arms, but he was squeezing too tight. She struggled harder, and he shook her and said something fierce, and then she felt the crying come, but she didn't let it and didn't let it and clenched her mouth and her eyes.

And they were inside somewhere, and there were stairs and a door. He put her down on a bed, and it was dark— very, very dark. And he said something fierce to someone else, and then the door shut her in the darkness.

They didn't know what to do. They didn't know how to do anything. They hadn't taken off her boots, even.

And then she knew what was going to happen, and it did,

and she couldn't stop it, and the warm wetness spread all through her underclothes and soaked the dress and the coat and the bed; and then she knew that no one would come to wash her, that there were no clothes to change her into, that no one would help her ever again, that she was alone in the dark forever, because Mama had lost her.

At last, with a little shuddering whimper, she began to cry.

MICHELET WAS stroking her hair. He had sprinkled some eau de cologne on his hands and rubbed it on his neck, his chest, his arms, and the sweetness of it was making her feel queasy. So were his greedy little kisses.

"Is he awake?" she whispered. "Is that why we got to be quiet?"

"He wakes very easily. The doctor gives him a sleeping draught, but nothing keeps him asleep for long. He has severe pain from his back. And that monkey is restless too. . . . Don't think about him, Louisa."

"Poor man. I can't help it. How does he dress? How does he wash?"

"I do it for him. Everything. Another servant helps me to lift him up, but everything he needs, I do for him."

"How did he get paralyzed like that?"

"Why are you asking? Never mind him, Louisa. *I* am not paralyzed. Nor are you. Look at the pretty way your skin takes the light of the candle. . . . There. Let me kiss your pretty arm. . . ."

A dull continual throb, like a muffled drum, beat through Sally's body. It was the hidden thing she was going to find out; it was the secret she'd come to uncover. And she was fighting back the suspicion that lurked inside her—the suspicion that she'd known all the time, but hadn't wanted to look at. . . . It was like being in a railway without a driver. She'd touched a lever and the locomotive had begun to move forward, and she didn't know how to find the brake, and now that it was moving she felt compelled to push more levers, move it faster, drive it forward, because even a crash would be better than this inexorable helpless rolling. . . .

Michelet's eyes were glazed. He was lost. For the first time since the notion had come to her, she began to understand the real danger she'd put herself in, because the man was crazy. She began to wonder whether she could reach the pistol if she needed to. Where was it? Just out of reach—

And then the Tzaddik spoke from the room next-door.

"Michelet, come here," said the thick, deep voice.

With a heavy, slow shudder, Michelet pulled himself back to clear consciousness. He stood up, brushing his hand across his eyes, and shrugged himself into a dressing gown before opening the door between the two rooms.

Sally lay still as the Tzaddik said, "I cannot sleep, Michelet. Light me a cigarette and bring me the brandy."

Michelet moved through. She heard him strike a match and saw the glow of the gaslight around the edge of the door; and then there was the sound of another match for the cigarette; and then he went out to go downstairs for the brandy.

The time had come.

She felt for her cloak, with the heavy gun in its pocket. She swung it around her shoulders and stood up. With shaking hands, shaking feet, with fear drenching her from head to foot, she moved through the door and into the Tzaddik's bedroom.

It was large and luxuriously furnished. The bed was immense, reinforced by an iron frame that extended above it at the sides and the head. Handles and pulleys were suspended from the frame, and the monkey sat up on the corner of it, watching her with eyes like stones.

The Tzaddik lay on his back under a silk coverlet, and his great head was turned toward her. In his eyes, which glittered in the lamplight, she could see a reflection of that knowledge which was pounding insistently at her own heart.

He said nothing as she came toward him. The monkey chittered softly. She caught a drift of the smoke from the cigarette in the ashtray, and picked it up and inhaled, feeling the shaking subside as the smoke calmed her.

He lay there helpless and watched.

All the knowledge she had was crowding forward, pressing at the front of her mind; the train was moving faster. Almost lethargically, as helpless as he was, she reached down and pulled away the silk coverlet, the blankets, the sheet, exposing his huge inert chest in its nightshirt. Still he didn't speak. Still his eyes blazed at her.

She unbuttoned the front of the nightshirt to the waist. Now she was shaking again, so that she had to clasp her hands together and close her eyes as if she were asking for the blessing of heaven on what she was doing.

Then she pulled the nightshirt open. His flesh, so much of it, so still it was hardly human, lay in a pallid mass. She forced herself to look—and there it was, the little mark that had brought all this about, all this suffering—

A bullet hole just under his breastbone. A little puckered scar. A wound that she had made.

"Ah Ling," Sally whispered.

Her knees buckled, a great weakness spreading through all her limbs, as if all the blood in her body had drained out at once. She clutched the iron frame, and the two of them looked for a moment like a patient and his tender, solicitous nurse.

And still the monkey watched, and still the cigarette smoke drifted upward. . . .

Why didn't I see it before? His eyes—those half-Chinese eyes— those hands, huge and freckled and gold-haired—that voice—the opium and Mr. Beech—I didn't want to, I couldn't bear it, didn't want to look—

"I thought you were dead," she said, her voice hardly audible, even to herself. "I thought I killed you. That night in the cab, by the East India Docks. . . . You were alive all this time?"

"You call this alive, do you?" he said.

There was a roaring in her ears. "What happened?" she whispered.

"The bullet went through my spine. My men from the ship nearby carried me away at once. And from that day to this I have never moved and never been free of pain. You should have killed me once and for all. Have you come to finish the job? I see you have a pistol in your pocket. There's nothing to stop you now, after all."

She fumbled for the heavy gun and dragged it out, tearing the edge of her pocket, and pulled back the hammer, but for the first time in her life her hands failed her. They shook and trembled with weakness, and she knew why, knew she wasn't going to shoot him, knew she couldn't; because his very helplessness protected him better than armor.

And beating through the hatred and the anger and the fear like a pulse in her head was a new knowledge—or rather an old hidden suspicion confirmed and clarified: as clear as a scarlet thread of blood, it was the sight of her own part in his suffocating imprisonment. She'd pitied him; well, she'd caused it.

She couldn't hold the gun. With a cry of anger and pain she hurled it away from her with all her might. It crashed into a mirror and fell among shattered glass to the floor.

The door opened.

"You will find a pistol on the floor, Michelet," said Ah Ling. "Pick it up and shoot Miss Lockhart with it."

She looked through the baffled tears and saw the valet's face, blank with astonishment and then flooded with a hideous glee. She was too weak to move; she sank to her knees beside the bed as Michelet put down the tray with the decanter and glass and stooped to pick up the gun.

And turned his back on the monkey.

It moved almost too quickly to see. It sprang down to the bedside table, seized the burning cigarette, and then leaped just as Michelet stood up. It landed on his neck, seized his hair with one hand—and stabbed the cigarette into his eye.

An explosion as the gun went off. A scream from Michelet,

as he staggered back against the frame of the bed, crashing into Sally and knocking her to the floor. She lay half-stunned; her head had struck something. She couldn't find the strength to get up—

Then Michelet tore the monkey loose and flung it with all his might against the wall. It fell like a rag doll, dead.

And the door opened, and there were the secretary Winterhalter and the doctor, in dressing gowns, and a man-servant—was it Alfred?—and Ah Ling's heavy, unmoved voice: "This woman came into my room to try and kill me. Winterhalter, take a servant, escort her to the cellar, and lock her in. Doctor, see to Michelet."

Michelet was crying with pain, crouching on the floor beside her, blood leaking between his fingers. Hands seized Sally's arms and dragged her up and out of the door, and into the lift, and down, and down, and down. Whether it was the footman Alfred who was holding her she couldn't tell, because she was conscious of only two things in the world: that little puckered circle of flesh where her bullet had entered his breast, and the single page from the ledger, tucked in the top of her stocking.

They reached the bottom, threw her out, ascended again. Like Harriet, she was locked in the dark, alone.

25

The Battle of Telegraph Road

DANIEL GOLDBERG STOOD IN THE LITTLE PASSAGE BE-
tween two of the houses in Telegraph Road. The rain from
the flooded gutter above fell like Niagara in front of him.

There was a light burning behind the curtains in the front
room of Parrish's house. The upstairs was dark, front and
back. The houses backed onto the row behind, and Goldberg
had reconnoitered along there already, moving silently like a
cat along the wall between the backyards. They were mean,
stunted little houses, hardly bigger than those in Whitechapel,
and distinguished from them only by the bay window and a
bit of fancy molding above the front door.

It was half past one. Goldberg had just decided to give
Bill another twenty minutes when there came a whisper behind him: "All right, Mr. G.?"

He turned to see half a dozen shapes, maybe more, clustered behind Bill in the little passageway.

"Well done," he said. "How many?"

"There's ten of us," said a quiet, hard Irish voice from
the darkness.

"This is Liam," said Bill. A hand came forward, and
Goldberg shook it. "We got shivs and jimmies and knuckle-
dusters."

Goldberg looked past Bill and made out the form of a girl
of sixteen or so.

"Is that the famous Bridie Sullivan?" he said.

She said nothing, but lifted her head dangerously.

"It's all right, Bridie," said Liam. "This feller's all right, don't you mind him."

"I've heard you're a good fighter," said Goldberg. "You'll need to be, too. It's that house over there with the light on. There's a small child inside, probably upstairs, and we've got to get her out unharmed."

He stood aside to let them peer past him out of the little entrance.

"Can you get into the backyard?" said Bill.

"There's a passage like this farther down on the right. There's a privy or a coal shed against the house—like the one behind us now—and a window above that with the curtains drawn. You could reach it from the roof of the privy. What I don't know is how many men there are inside."

Bill and Liam went back to look over the wall into the backyard of the house beside them.

"Got a weapon, Bridie?" said Goldberg.

"I use a shiv," she said. Her voice was low and soft and musical—the voice of an Irish angel, velvet, peat smoke. The weapon she mentioned consisted of the blade of a razor set in a wooden handle.

Bill appeared beside him. "Half a minute, that's all it'll take," he said.

"Right," said Goldberg. "Liam, who's your best man with horses?"

"Dermot," said Liam at once, shoving forward a skinny boy of twelve or so.

"Dermot, there's a jobmaster's stable at the south side of the common. Take a couple of boys and pinch a four-wheeler and a decent nag, and get back here double-quick."

Three boys peeled off at once and slipped away down the road, and Goldberg beckoned the rest of them closer as he began to explain his plan.

THE BATTLE OF Telegraph Road was celebrated for years afterward by the Irish gangs in Lambeth. Those who'd taken part heard their names becoming legends; those who hadn't wished they had, and began to bend the legends in their own favor. There was nothing like it till the rise of the great Pat Hooligan himself, who gave his name to the species.

Goldberg divided the forces into three. Bill and Liam, as the most experienced cracksmen, were to get into the back-yard, climb onto the roof of the privy, and wait till the others created a diversion before getting in through the window.

But it was no good creating a diversion if they couldn't get the door open, because that was the way they'd have to take Harriet out; so Goldberg and Bridie would knock at the front door, and Bridie would pretend to faint on the step.

As soon as the door was open, Goldberg would shout— which would be the signal for two more boys at the back of the house to start hammering at the back door as loudly as they could. Under cover of that noise, Bill and Liam would get to work above them, while Goldberg and the four re-maining boys would rush in from the front. Goldberg and Bridie would hold the hall clear, and the boys would rush the stairs and deal with anyone up there, distracting atten-tion from the window where Bill and Liam were climbing in to look for Harriet.

Goldberg and Bridie and the boys who were going to take the front waited while the others ran across the road, swift, dark shadows in the rain, and vanished through the passage-way on the other side. A couple of minutes went by, and then Goldberg said, "All right. Time to go."

The boys ran over and crouched down behind the little wall of the garden. Goldberg and Bridie stood outside the front door.

"Ready?"

She nodded. He knocked on the door, and she leaned against him as if she was about to faint.

The curtains in the bay window stirred, and a face looked through. Goldberg made a gesture of helplessness, and Bridie slumped against him.

"Here he comes," Goldberg muttered, hearing a door open.

The curtain fell back into place as the front door opened.

Instantly Bridie fell across the threshold, and the man there
stepped back quickly. Goldberg knelt beside her, keeping
his head down, and pretended to be trying to lift her.

"My wife—she's been taken ill—help me get her inside,
for God's sake," he said.

The man stood there doubtfully, looking back—and then
Arthur Parrish came out of the front room, and his eyes met
Goldberg's with a shock of recognition.

"Scream, girl," said Goldberg, and Bridie screamed like a
banshee, and he yelled, "Go!"

And several things happened at once. Goldberg leaped
forward, slamming the first man into the wall, and Bridie
sprang after him, her knife flashing. A violent hammering
came from somewhere at the back of the house, and then
the four other boys were in through the front door like eels.

Another man came out of the front room behind Parrish,
and the first boy ran for him, burying his head in the man's
stomach with a *whoosh* of air that could have been heard across
the street. Goldberg's fist met his man's chin, and the man
collapsed across the umbrella stand, unconscious.

"Upstairs!" Goldberg yelled to the other boys, and they
sprang up the staircase three steps at a time, yelling with
glee.

And Parrish had a gun in his hand.

He was standing very still, his back to the wall, watching
Goldberg with a bright-eyed smugness that made Goldberg
want to paste his face across the wallpaper. But the gun was
cocked. Bridie was watching, narrow-eyed, waiting for a chance
to get close enough. The man on the floor stirred; Goldberg
took a step closer to the umbrella stand and casually kicked
him.

"Oh, Mr. Goldberg," said Parrish. "What a way to carry
on. This won't do you any good with the extradition, I suppose you realize—"

Then there was a scream from upstairs—a child's cry of
terror—and a light came into Goldberg's eyes, and he snatched
a coat from the hook beside him and flung it over the gun

before springing for Parrish like a tiger. Bridie leaped for him too, but the man on the floor grabbed at her skirt, and she came down in a tangle of wet cloth and fists.

There were shouts from upstairs—doors banging—and then an explosion from the gun. And everything stopped.

In the silence, Goldberg found himself on the floor, and he knew at once he'd been hit. *Just like the time before—don't know where it's got me—hope I can stand—*

His senses reassembled themselves shakily, and then he knew it had all gone wrong, the raid hadn't worked, because there was Liam coming down the stairs, and there was Bill behind him, and behind them was a man holding Harriet, and at her throat there was the point of a knife.

Bridie slowly got to her feet beside him. Parrish was covering them with his pistol, and the man on the floor was struggling up too. The noise from the back door had stopped. Goldberg tried to get up, and as he put his weight on his arm, he found out where he'd been hit, for his left shoulder screamed at him.

Not fatal. All right. Think. Move to the right a little way—give him room to come down — flick your eyes to the door — good, Bill's understood—so's Liam—now for the shiv.

He knew that there was only one chance: he had to disable the man's arm before it could jab upward. Bridie was standing behind him, concealed from Parrish in the narrow hall. Pretending to look fainter than he felt, which wasn't hard, Goldberg put his good hand behind him and found Bridie's, with the shiv in it. She let him take it. The man holding Harriet came to the bottom step.

She was perfectly still in his arm, her tear-filled eyes wide with the understanding that something horrible was happening. Goldberg readied himself, but he was weakened by the shock, and his shoulder was beginning to throb with agony.

Careful—let him turn—now!

His right hand slashed down into the crook of the man's arm. At the same instant Bill on the other side snatched

Harriet and threw her to Liam, who caught her and ran. Bridie swung her fist wildly at Parrish, but missed, because at that very second something hard and white and porcelain hurtled down from the landing and smashed into a thousand pieces on Parrish's head. He went down, to a whoop of glee from upstairs, and then the others came pelting down, kicking aside the man who'd been holding Harriet. He lay moaning in disbelief and trying to stanch the astonishing amount of blood coming out of his arm.

They dragged Bridie away and out the door, and Goldberg followed in time to see a carriage careering along the quiet road with two whooping little boys on the box. It drew up in a squeal of brakes and a clatter of hooves, the horse whinnying with excitement as Bill raced for the door and tore it open.

Liam was first inside, with Harriet yelling in his arms, and then the others piled in after him—

But the pistol crashed again from behind them, and Bridie fell to the ground and lay still. Liam and another boy sprang out of the carriage at once and lifted her bodily inside. Goldberg felt his legs crumple under him as someone tackled him. He saw Bill hesitate, and yelled, "Go! Stay with the child! Move!"

The boy on the box cracked his whip, Bill leaped up beside him, and the carriage rolled away. Parrish's men ran out into the road, but they were too late to do more than watch the swaying four-wheeler disappearing around the corner.

Well, that's something anyway, thought Goldberg as he fainted.

INSIDE THE crowded, swaying carriage, some of the boys were joshing and laughing and crowing over the fight, and already embroidering it with more details than there'd have been time for. Liam and another boy bent over Bridie.

"Here it is," said Liam. He lifted the thick, wet hair to show a deep gash in Bridie's scalp. "If that's all it is, she'll be better in the morning. She's breathing like a trumpeter. There's nothing to worry about."

He lifted her up to make a little more room and brushed the hair tenderly back from her still face. Harriet watched it all, sucking her thumb. These people were laughing and singing. They were happy, and she liked happy people. They were very noisy. But it was a nice noise, and then one of them pushed another and he fell on the floor. Harriet thought he would be hurt, but he laughed. They all laughed a lot, and then she saw how funny it was and laughed too. She had to take her thumb out of her mouth to laugh properly. Then they saw that and laughed even more.

There was a banging on the front.

"What's the matter?" said someone. "That's Dermot."

One of the boys peered out. "There's a copper up ahead," he said. "Hush the noise, stow it away now, boys. . . ."

They all crouched down low, whispering and giggling and shoving, until the policeman had been passed and they could sit up again. But the laughter was over. They looked at Harriet.

"What are we going to do with her?"

"She's Bill's problem. This is his game."

"What about the gaffer back there?"

"He might have got away. . . ."

"I saw him fall."

"Dead, eh? Be Jasus . . ."

"Bridie'll know what to do about the kid."

"Bridie?"

"She's a girl, ain't she? She's bound to know."

"But Bridie . . ."

"*We* can't look after her, and that's a fact."

"Who is she, anyway? Who's she belong to?"

"Damned if I know, Sean. She's a grand little girl though, isn't she?"

"Look at her sitting there like a lady. . . ."

"She's wet herself."

"Devil, and don't all kids wet their bloody selves? There's you not out of diapers yerself more than a year—"

"What if Bridie doesn't wake up?"

Silence. They looked at her. She lay very still in the corner of the carriage.

"Is she done for?"

"Her that walloped the giblets out of Johnny Rodriguez the half-caste?" said Liam scornfully. "Done for? Never."

"But he shot her. . . ."

"And didn't we crack him on the napper with a jordan, the dirty little devil!"

"If there'd been time, we'd have filled it first. . . ."

"What are we going to do with the kid, though?"

A longer silence. Harriet watched them all, fascinated.

"The orphanage?" said one, uncertainly.

They turned on him.

"You bloody fool, Johnny Coughlan! We spring her out of one jail and pack her off to another?"

"The nuns, then . . ."

"Talk with yer head, not yer backside."

"But *we* can't look after her. . . ."

"And why not?"

"Well . . . they need food. . . ."

"She's past the sucking stage; you won't have to offer *your* skinny chest, Sean Macarthy."

"Ah, shut yer foolishness!"

"So she can eat what we eat. Mashed potatoes, meat pie, jellied eels. A drop of stout won't do her any harm, neither."

"But her clothes and stuff . . ."

"And stuff? What stuff? When did *you* last change yer clothes? The year before last, by the hum coming off yer. She's got a fine set of duds; they'll do for now. Begob, ye're a fine bunch of pessimistical bastards, ain't ye, though? Come here, princess."

And Liam lifted Harriet onto his lap and sat there glaring at his companions as the carriage rolled on toward Lambeth. Harriet just went on gazing at them all, thumb in mouth. Then she yawned, and with the air of a duchess conferring a favor on a footman, she laid her head on Liam's shoulder and went to sleep at once.

GOLDBERG LAY on the kitchen floor, listening carefully. Although his shoulder hurt like the devil, the rest of him was unharmed, and his head was clear.

They were talking in the front room. He heard Parrish's voice: " . . . Solomons's Bakery in Holywell Street. At the corner there—Brick Lane end. That's it, yes. Burn the bloody place down. There's a painter and decorator's store just behind it—full of kerosene. Get the mob out there—stir 'em up. I want the whole bloody street on fire, get it? Early, before they wake up. Now *go*, go on, move. The rest of you get packing. Charlie, run and fetch a cab from the jobmaster's. Wake him up. Yes, we're moving out, soon as the coppers take that Yid away. Is he safe in there?"

Another voice said something inaudible, and someone laughed. Parrish snapped; being laid low with a chamber pot had done nothing for his authority. Goldberg looked around. He could see chair legs and table legs and a coal scuttle, but nothing that could serve as a weapon. Could he get to his feet? Find a knife, perhaps? Or even a broomstick?

He moved and nearly groaned aloud. But then there came a thunderous knocking at the front door, and a man ran to open it, and there were the police.

Goldberg pulled himself upright before they did it for him. A sergeant, two constables, and a police carriage—lanterns—billy clubs—explanations, accusations—handcuffs.

Here he shook his head.

"I'm bound to come quietly," he said to the sergeant. "But I'd be obliged if you'd leave off the handcuffs; I'm wounded."

He held up his bloodied left hand with his right in a way that suggested it was the wrist that was injured, and the sergeant nodded.

"All right," he said to the constable with the handcuffs. "He won't make any trouble. Put him in the van."

"Excuse me, Sergeant," said Parrish. "This man is extremely dangerous. I've already told you he's wanted for a political offense. He's escaped from prisons in Russia and Germany—"

"There aren't any political offenses in this country, as far as I know, sir," said the sergeant. "Did he cause that lump on your head?"

"Not directly—"

"And who shot him?"

"I did. As I'm entitled to do in order to protect—"

"No doubt, sir. I'll stay behind and take full statements from you and the other gentlemen. Take this man to the station, Constable."

A fair man, anyway, thought Goldberg as he climbed stiffly into the police van. *And at least I haven't got handcuffs to think about.* . . .

The driver shook the reins.

And as the van began to move away, two bedraggled figures scuttled out from the shadows and clung to the back of it. There was a step there for policemen to stand on when they were being brought in to control crowds, and it made a fine platform for two twelve-year-old boys, especially the two who'd been hammering at the back door of the house, frantic with impatience, during the fight.

"Ye all right, Tony?" whispered one.

"I'm with ye, Con," the other whispered back. "We'll have a bit of a fight yet. Hold tight now. Don't fall off. . . ."

MOISHE LIPMAN rubbed his heavy jaw. He was sitting in a four-wheeled cab at the corner of Fournier Square with three of his men. There was a lot of activity going on in the house—lights being carried here and there, curtains being carefully drawn shut—but no sign of a child. One of the men had slipped across the road and listened outside the kitchen door, but had heard nothing, and another three had been around the back, where the tall old houses of the square looked out on a churchyard, but had come back without any sign of the child they'd been sent there to look for.

"What d'you reckon, boss?" said one of the men in the cab.

Lipman said nothing. He wasn't a thinker, and he couldn't

see through bricks, but he knew about fighting. Stay canny for a bit; hang back, let the other man commit himself. If you rush in like a headstrong kid, you'll get a bang that'll lay you out.

The problem was, he also knew the value of a surprise attack. Whoever was in the house didn't know they were being watched, and if Moishe flung all his men in at once they could take the place in less than a minute. But less than a minute would still be plenty of time to point a gun to a child's head. . . .

"I reckon we sit tight," he said.

He gazed stonily through the rain. Such rain. . . . You could hardly see the difference between the pavement and the road, there was such a torrent sloshing along the gutter. It was clogged by a bit of rubbish, a dead dog or something, and the water swirled around it like the rapids on the Pecos River in the Deadwood Dick story Moishe had one of his boys read to him in the evenings. Bits of scum and foam and papers and scraps of anonymous filth were borne along like Deadwood Dick's raft. . . .

The front door opened. Moishe blinked and tapped the man opposite on the knee.

"Wake up," he said. "Look."

The other man started and leaned forward. Out of the narrow cab window they saw two figures in the doorway—one in a raincoat and a hat, the other in what looked like a dressing gown.

Raincoat set off, Dressing Gown called him back and spoke briefly. Raincoat set off again, holding the collar high around his neck; Dressing Gown shut the door.

Moishe said, "Get him."

The three men in the cab jumped out at once. Raincoat didn't look back, but hurried on, head down against the lashing rain, and the sound of it on his oilskin hat prevented him from hearing footsteps behind him; so it wasn't long before they caught up with him.

Lipman had ordered the cab to follow at walking pace, and within a minute of leaving the house, Raincoat was bundled inside, struggling. When they pulled his sou'wester back, Sally would have recognized him: it was the secretary, Winterhalter.

"Who are you? What do you want?" he said.

"Never mind that," said Lipman. "What's going on in there?"

Winterhalter stared in astonishment. "How dare you? What do you want with me?"

"Answer the question," said Lipman. "What's going on in that house?"

"How can I answer a question like that? You must be an exceptionally stupid man. Let me go at once."

He struggled to get up. Lipman shoved him back.

"Is the child in there?" he said.

Winterhalter fell still, and a complicated understanding came into his eyes.

"I see. That makes it clear," he said. Lipman watched him narrowly. "I think the best thing would be for you to talk to my employer directly. You understand, I am only his private secretary. I am sure that—"

"Cut it," said Lipman. "What are *you* doing, then? Where are you going?"

"For a doctor," said Winterhalter smoothly. "One of the servants has been injured in a domestic accident."

"Why not send out another servant? Why's it *you* going out in the rain?"

"Because I happened to be still up and dressed. Now let me do two things: First, go and communicate your concern to my employer. He will be pleased to give you any information you wish about a child. And second, complete my errand to the doctor. It is not a matter of life and death, but it could have serious consequences for the poor man's sight. I am sure you would not wish that on your conscience."

And now Moishe Lipman was troubled. He'd done something wrong, but he wasn't sure what, and he wasn't sure how he could undo it, either. He knew what he should have done: have the man followed, not catch him. Too late now.

Still, if he let the man do what he suggested, he could get into the house without a fight. And that would give his boys the chance to look around. . . . Not even Kid Mendel would have managed that. That would be really clever.

"All right," he said. "You go and tell your employer we'll come in and talk. Then you can go and fetch the doctor."

Winterhalter nodded and pulled his sou'wester back on.

"You understand it will take my master a few minutes to dress and get ready. The butler will come out to tell you when he will be able to receive you."

"All right," said Lipman. "No tricks, mind."

"No, no, no," said Winterhalter. "Of course not."

He left the cab and ran back to the house.

When he'd gone in and shut the door, one of Moishe's men said timidly, "Boss? You don't suppose he's going to call the rozzers, do you?"

"How?" said Lipman. "Carrier pigeon?"

They laughed dutifully, and he said it again, in case they hadn't caught the full richness of the joke; but nobody laughed five minutes later, when the police did come.

"So Parrish has got the child," said the Tzaddik to Winterhalter. "Of course. And these foolish men were watching the house in case he'd brought it here . . . which means that although they know he's got it, they don't know where he's gone. If they were as foolish as you say, though, how did they know this address? They must be connected with the Lockhart girl."

"They didn't mention her," said Winterhalter. "There might be someone else organizing them."

"Goldberg, perhaps . . ."

"They were Jewish."

"In that case, certainly Goldberg. Well, this alters things, Winterhalter. Parrish has got the child, and he has not brought it here; so he is going to bargain. There is no point in your going to see him, then. We shall save you a wet journey and let him come to me. Have the police come yet?"

Winterhalter looked out the window.

"They are taking them away now, Mr. Lee," he said.

"Excellent. What a fine thing it is to pay one's rates and taxes and have the protection of the police. Well, if Parrish has the child, I have the mother. I want to go down and interrogate her. Send Michelet in to me, please."

"Dr. Strauss said he was to rest his eye, sir. . . ."

"Send him! I need him!"

Winterhalter went into the valet's room. Michelet groaned and sat up.

"I heard. . . . Very well, I shall come. What is the time, Herr Winterhalter? I cannot see my watch. . . ."

"Two o'clock in the morning. I have every sympathy with you, Michelet, but Dr. Strauss has done all that is necessary, and now Mr. Lee needs your help."

Michelet pulled on his dressing gown, shivering pitiably.

"I cannot do it on my own. I need the other manservant. . . ."

"I shall help you. Mr. Lee wants to go down to the cellar. I have no doubt he will need you to go with him."

Michelet's good eye, bloodshot, peered curiously under the swathe of white bandage at the secretary, whose face remained closed. The valet licked his lips and went through to his master.

"Yes, Mr. Lee? You wish to dress fully, sir? Shall I shave you first? It is very early, but no doubt you will feel the better for it. . . ."

"Show me your hands."

The valet held them out. They were shaking badly.

"No. Shave me later. Wash me and dress me now."

"Very good, sir," said Michelet. He sighed heavily, the picture of dutiful misery, and pulled back the covers.

Running from side to side under the lower sheet were three wide leather slings, the ropes at each end of them terminat-

ing in hooks and tucked out of sight behind the valance of
the bed. Michelet brought them out and hooked the ends of
the top sling to a block and tackle on the iron frame, and
began to wind a handle near the head of the bed. The rope
tightened, and little by little the top half of the Tzaddik's
body was lifted off the bed.

Michelet made the tackle secure and removed the man's
nightshirt. Then he fitted the other two slings to similar blocks
and wound them up until the Tzaddik's body was completely clear of the bed, and laid a mackintosh sheet over
the linen one before running some hot water into the basin.

As Michelet was about to lower the Tzaddik onto the bed
again, his employer spoke.

"Winterhalter—a marron glacé."

The secretary found the box beside the bed and put one
of the sticky sweets into Ah Ling's mouth with a pair of little
silver tongs. The Tzaddik chewed it slowly as Michelet
washed him from head to toe, turning him over by manipulating the slings halfway through so as to clean him behind
and dress the sores on his thighs and buttocks. He took off
the plasters, washed them gently, dried them and applied a
mineral lotion before putting fresh plasters on. Winterhalter
had never seen this process; he was appalled at the extent of
these sores, new ones eating into old ones, crusts and scabs
and pus on the places which bore the man's vast weight all
day long.

When the dressings were changed, Michelet dusted the
great body all over with talc.

"Leave the room please, Winterhalter," said the Tzaddik.
"I want to empty my bladder."

When Winterhalter came back, Michelet was putting silk
underclothes on his master, easing them gently over his heavy
feet and little by little upward. By manipulating the slings
and the pulleys, making little adjustments here and there,
Michelet dealt with the man's great, still weight as easily as
a nurse deals with a baby, and he had the same close and
fond and tender control, teasing and even grotesquely seem-

ing to flirt a little. One damaged man tending another more damaged one: how much they needed each other, Winterhalter thought, like crocodiles and those little birds who pick their food out from between the reptiles' teeth. The Tzaddik was all dignity, and even at the most undignified moments his impassivity and cold command never left him; whereas Michelet was all servility.

Winterhalter wondered again, as he had done many times, what would happen to the child. It was difficult. Clearly his employer needed someone to perform these degrading duties, and clearly they would be beyond the powers of the child for some years; but there would come a time when the child was fully competent, and as necessary as the monkey. Whoever controlled the child then would have the key to everything. No, he couldn't afford to let Michelet have charge of her. There was an unhealthiness about the man. It would be better without him. The secretary made a mental note to find a nursing agency.

He wheeled the chair beside the bed to the spot Michelet indicated, and the two of them lifted the Tzaddik, with the help of the slings and the gantry, and set him down in the seat.

Finally Michelet took a jar of pomade from the dressing table, spread some on his palms, and smoothed it over the Tzaddik's hair before brushing it down flat and glistening.

He wiped his hands, adjusted his master's tie, and settled a rug over his knees. Then he whimpered with pain and put his hand to the enveloping white bandage over half his head.

"Please, sir, may I lie down?" he said. "My eye is so painful. . . ."

"Later. I want you to take me down to the cellar. Thank you, Winterhalter. I shall not be needing you again tonight."

The secretary bowed stiffly and withdrew.

Michelet opened the double doors and wheeled the chair out onto the landing before opening the doors of the lift. The house was silent around them as they sank smoothly down into the cellar where Sally was lying in the dark.

THE POLICE VAN slowed. Tony, the elder of the two boys clinging to the back, said, "Watch out, now. Here we go."

As it came to a halt they dropped off the back and crouched behind it, Tony watching around the side for the chance they'd planned for.

Above them the blue POLICE light glowed over the steps leading up to the station entrance. As long as the desk sergeant didn't come and have a look. . . . No, it was too wet; he was in by the stove with a cup of cocoa.

The van door opened. Con clutched the dripping, gritty edge of the wheel, ready to swing himself around. Another second or two and—

"Go!" said Tony, and the two of them darted out like greyhounds and sprang for the legs of the startled policemen, who fell in a crashing, cursing tangle to the pavement, leaving Goldberg upright and free.

"Run, you bugger!" yelled Con, before a heavy official hand grabbed his hair and the other reached for the nearest limb.

But Tony was equal to that; he sank his teeth into the hand, and the policeman let go with a yell.

Both boys were up in a moment, and together with Goldberg they reached the corner of the street and were away before the two policemen, bruised by their fall and soaked with the water they were sitting in, could do anything to stop them.

Even the driver was helpless; jumping down to try and grab them, he'd caught his oilskin in the shafts and was twisting around trying to free himself.

The desk sergeant had heard all the commotion and stood at the top of the steps, cocoa in one hand and bread and butter in the other, grinning all over his face at the sight of three large men tangled helplessly in the downpour.

"Well, at least you've drawn your billy clubs," he called down. "Why don't you hit each other and finish it off?"

They told him what to do with his cocoa.

And two streets away, ashen with pain, Goldberg hurried along in the dark, his two crowing rescuers capering like imps beside him.

26

Blackbourne Water

ARTHUR PARRISH HAD FOUND THE POLICE SERGEANT ABOMinably persistent and confoundedly curious. The way he'd raised his eyebrows when he saw the room the child had been in wasn't pleasant, either.

"Forgive me for asking again, Mr. Parrish—this is your daughter we're talking about?" he'd said, his eyes taking in the bare boards, the rusty bedstead, the soaking mattress, the absence of sheets and blankets.

Parrish forced himself to be patient. The law was with him, after all, even if this minion wasn't.

When the sergeant finally left, Parrish called his men together. His head was throbbing, but there was nothing he could do about that now.

"They're asking for trouble," he said. "Well, they're certainly going to get it. You, Harvey, go down to Whitechapel after Gorman. Make sure he whips 'em up well. Cropper, you stay on here till the police come back with the kid."

"Think they will, Mr. Parrish?"

"I know they will. Take no notice of that sergeant; I've got an assistant commissioner in my pocket. Like I said, stay here till they fetch the kid back, then tell 'em to bring it on to me in Twickenham. That's where I'm going now."

He threw some things into a carpetbag. The man seemed unconvinced.

"But what about Mr. Lee?" he said.

"What about him?" said Mr. Parrish, looking up. This ordinary, dapper, clerklike little man had a ferocity in him which he seldom unleashed. When he did, as now, hardened criminals, graduates of Pentonville and Dartmoor, quailed. "He's put himself out on a limb, Mr. Lee has, trusting me," Parrish went on. "I'm going to make the most of it—and there's not a bloody thing in the world he can do about it, because the kid's legally mine and always will be. Come on, hurry up, move."

DANIEL GOLDBERG winced. The doctor prodded deeper and said, "What's the matter? Drink the medicine."

"It's the wrong kind of medicine."

"It's the best. Scotch medicine. Here we are."

There was a clink as something dropped into a metal bowl. Goldberg let out his breath in a low whistle.

"Tell you what, I'll have a cigar instead," he said.

"No cigars. You can't smoke medicine. Keep still."

The doctor dabbed on something that stung.

"Can I have this, mister?" said Tony, picking up the bloody, distorted bullet.

"Help yourself," said the doctor. "No use to me. Wasn't much use to Mr. Goldberg, either."

They were in a small doctor's office in Soho. The doctor was the man Goldberg had summoned to attend Jacob Liebermann, a friend and a socialist, and when Goldberg and the boys had banged on his door he'd merely sighed before letting them in and setting to work.

As he strapped a bandage around Goldberg's shoulder he said, "Of course, I'm a citizen as well as a medical man, you know."

"What's that mean?"

"It means I ought to tell the police when people come here with bullet holes in them. What's going on, Goldberg?"

Goldberg sipped the whiskey and made a face. "White slavery, fraud, kidnapping . . . it's too complicated to explain now. I will when it's over. Now, listen, boys. Liam and Bill and Bridie and the others—where will they be?"

"Couldn't say, mister," said Con. "There's half a dozen kips they might be using."

"Is he all right?" said Tony suspiciously, jerking his thumb at the doctor.

"Are you all right?" said Goldberg.

"I'm not even here," said the doctor, putting his instruments into a bowl of disinfectant. "I'm a hallucination, and I'm going back to bed. Don't put any strain on that arm. Let yourselves out, and throw the key back in through the broken fanlight."

Con and Tony were shocked.

"Hey, mister," said Tony. "Doctor, I mean. You shouldn't do tricks like that with yer key—it's as good as an open door. Me and Con here'll come back tomorrow and show ye how to make the place safe. There's all kinds of villains about."

"Well, that's a fair offer," said the doctor. "And if anyone plants a bullet in you, young man, you know where to come to get it plucked out. Now be off with the lot of you—it's three in the morning."

Outside in the street Goldberg said, "The kip. You were telling me where the others might be."

"Oh, aye," said Con. "Ye see, mister, there's half a dozen different places they might have took her to. They'll move around, like. D'ye want to go and look?"

"I've got something else to do, and straightaway, what's more. You get back to Lambeth, the pair of you. When you find out where they've gone, get a message to me at twenty-seven, Dean Street, Soho."

"Twenty-seven, Dean Street. Hey, mister—what's it all about, this hooley? Eh?"

"It's about the Jews in the East End."

"Is there going to be a fight?"

"Probably. But—"

Con slapped his thigh and crowed.

"And won't the bloody sheenies get a pasting!" he said. "Begob, I'd love to—"

He stopped. Goldberg was looking at him steadily, and Tony was mortified.

"Ye crack-headed fool," he hissed. "Can't ye see yer man's a Jew?"

Con gaped. And then he blushed. It was a new sensation; the others couldn't see it in the rain and the murky lamplight, but he felt it most acutely.

"Arrah," he moaned. "Man, I beg yer pardon. If I'd known ye was Jewish, I'd . . . I'd . . . I'd bloody fight for them."

"He'd still have rescued ye," said Tony to Goldberg. "I'll go bail for that."

Con held out his hand, and Goldberg shook it.

"I believe you," he said. "But don't you talk like that again, or I'll make you wish you hadn't. Here . . ." He fished three cigars out of his pocket. "Three left. That's one each. Remember—get that message to me, and if I'm not there get someone to make a telephone call to—"

"I can make telephone calls," said Tony. "What's the number?"

"Four-two-one-four. You heard of Kid Mendel?"

They nodded, wide-eyed.

"Well, that's his number. There'll be a man on the line who'll take a message."

"Where are ye going, mister?" said Con. "Is there a chance of a fight?"

Goldberg looked down at the dripping little savage and shook his head.

"Another time. Go and find the kid."

The boys lit their cigars, and Goldberg's, and strolled off philosophically. He turned to the east, through the narrow streets around Covent Garden, packed already with carts and wagons of produce for the morning market. Porters lifted boxes of oranges, sacks of nuts, crates of cabbages; the air was full of shouts and the trundle of heavy wheels, and the warm interior of the pubs steamed invitingly. In the early hours of the morning, this was the busiest part of London.

But they were busy in Whitechapel, too. The baker in Holywell Street would be building his fire; Parrish's thugs would be gathering in the darkness. Goldberg quickened his steps and hoped he'd be in time.

SALLY HEARD the hum of the hydraulics and sat up. It wasn't quite dark; a little light came down the lift shaft, and she saw a faint shadow move on the floor, which told her the lift was coming.

The first thing she'd done when they'd thrown her down there in the dark had been to feel her way around the walls. The room was empty; the table and chair she remembered from her previous visit had been removed. There was nothing there but the lift shaft, the door to the stairs, and the door into the other room, both of which were locked.

She felt her stocking. The paper was still there. She smoothed her cloak down over her lap and sat up as straight as she could.

The lift reached the bottom, light spilling out of the iron grille. It sank into stillness with a whisper, and then the door clattered open. She watched as Michelet pushed the great chair out of the lift and onto the parquet floor.

Ah Ling looked around.

"This is the first time I have been down in my cellar," he remarked. "What is that noise?"

Michelet cocked his head on one side. It was the sound Sally had heard before, the subterranean rushing of water, much clearer now, much closer and louder.

"I could not say, sir," said Michelet.

In the wavering light of the lamp he held, the valet's face was ghastly pale. The dressing gown and the bandage over his eye made him look like some shrouded corpse, and Sally seemed to see for a moment a procession of figures like his, all the dead of Spitalfields, all the unknown silent ones from centuries past—under the ground as they were too.

She met the eyes of Ah Ling, Henry Lee, the Tzaddik.

"I have had time to think," he said. "Of course, I have

been thinking of this moment for several years, but another hour or so's thought is never wasted. You are a very clever and resourceful woman, Miss Lockhart."

"I wish there was a better witness than this man to hear you say that," she said.

"Why?"

"Because you have twice called me Miss Lockhart and not Mrs. Parrish. I'd like to summon you as a witness against him in court."

He smiled. "Oh, Parrish," he said. "He's disposable. We shall find a way to get rid of him."

"You haven't found a way to get rid of me yet. Or is that what you came down here to do?"

"No. As I said, I've had an hour or so to think in. How did you find out my address?"

"From a girl who followed you from Moscow."

"I see. And what were you intending to do in my bedroom an hour ago?"

"Simply to find out if you were the man I thought you were."

"And if you'd seen no scar, no bullet mark?"

She was silent. And she realized how long she'd known, how long she'd kept it from herself.

"Well," he said, "I want to ask you some questions, Miss Lockhart. To begin with—"

"I've got some questions for you. Why are you persecuting the Jews?"

"Someone has to."

"What a stupid answer."

"It was a stupid question."

"It was a good question. Why are you doing it?"

"Because they are there. Because they are an easy target. Because no one else objects if I do. I'm trying to recall what your maidservant character—Kemp, was it?—can have overheard. . . ."

"I've overheard enough to judge when you're telling me the truth."

"You are in no position to judge anything."

"I'm in the best position of all. I assume I'm about to die; there's nothing to be afraid of. I can see you very clearly now, Mr. Lee, Ah Ling, Hendrik Van Eeden, Mr. Eliot, Mr. Todd, however many names you have. You remember those last two? You used them when you killed Mr. Bedwell the sailor and Mr. Selby, my father's ex-partner. In no position to judge?" She found herself getting up—found herself on her feet almost without realizing she intended to stand. "By God, I was born to be your judge! So now you can listen to my judgment."

She was facing him, balanced lightly, her short hair disordered, her cloak adrift from her shoulder. Michelet stood by, like a corpse holding a corpse light, and Ah Ling sat stolidly with his eyes blazing black.

"You've been buried inside my life like some filthy worm. You know everything about me. So you know about Frederick Garland, my lover, and Jim Taylor and Webster Garland, my friends; you know about my daughter and my house and my servants, and you know about my business and my partner. . . . You know everything I've done. So you'll know about Axel Bellmann, the man who killed Frederick. The man who made the Steam Gun. I was reminded of him just now, but only for a second. I was in his power then as I am in yours now, but really it was no contest, Ah Ling. You see he was a genius, of a kind, and you're not. He had a vision, of a kind, and you haven't. He was serving something greater than he thought he was, even though it was evil. But you— you're just greedy. Your mind is coarse and your appetite is coarse and you haven't a shred of wit or imagination or grace in your entire soul. There are only two things that keep you going: one is making money, and the other is hating me. So when I ask why you're persecuting the Jews, you don't have the strength or the boldness to say 'because I'm greedy' or 'because I'm cruel'; you just make some cheap little gibe. It was the same all those years ago, with your opium smuggling. Nothing behind it but greed. A little fat boy cramming sweets into his mouth, forever and ever . . ."

He opened his mouth to speak. But she took a step forward, ferocious now, and Michelet flinched and drew back, making the lamp flicker. Ah Ling's eyes were flaring, poisonous, corrosive, but Sally didn't care. She went on. "You see, another thing I've learned, and I suppose I ought to be grateful to you, is what evil looks like. It doesn't look like a sinister fat man in a wheelchair; it doesn't look Chinese or Russian or exotic or foreign. Or strange. Those things aren't evil. You're not evil. You're too bloody picturesque to be evil, with your monkey and your schemes for training my daughter to do your bidding and wipe your fat mouth—"

"How do you know that?" he cried.

"Because I came down here one night and heard that man behind you trying to bargain with the secretary to let him train her!"

"It's not true, monsieur!" Michelet cried.

"It is true, and he knows it because he caught me on the stairs afterward. I heard everything—"

Michelet put the lamp on the floor and sprang at her like a furious dog. And because she saw him coming, and because for this one moment she was not afraid of anything, she didn't give an inch. She met his fists with her hands, her nails, her teeth; she clawed at his face, his hair, his arms— and the bandage came loose from his head, and he pulled away in terror, and she pushed him, whimpering, to the floor.

"Michelet, put the lamp on that bracket," said Ah Ling, his voice heavy with contempt.

Sally stooped and did it for him. The valet was clutching his head and moaning—but then Sally saw the handle of her pistol in his pocket. If he remembered that, he could kill her in a second. And she hadn't finished yet.

She turned back to the man in the wheelchair.

"I was telling you about evil," she said, "now that I know what it is. It's what makes a man get drunk and press a red-hot poker on his child's back. It's what makes men have to queue for hours at the dock gates for the chance of a job when there are only a dozen jobs for a hundred men, so they fight each other to get them, and the foremen laugh and egg them on. That's evil. It's what takes an old couple who've got nothing left but each other and splits them up to go in the workhouse so they each die alone. It's what takes rent out of tenements and slums and refuses the responsibility of mending the drains, so that children have to wade knee-deep through filth to get into their houses. . . . Don't interrupt. Don't open your mouth. Listen to me and learn. Evil . . . it's what makes a family starve—the family I heard about the other day, five of them, father and mother and three children all dead, with nothing in their little room, *nothing*, because they'd pawned every spoon and every blanket and every chair, and there was no work, and they starved to death. And I've never gone without a meal in my life. My city. The same city that I live in—this happens. That's evil. And you know what's at the heart of it all? Eh? The gnawing poison cancer destroying and eating and laying waste at the heart of it all? It's not only you, you poor pitiful man; it's *me*, too. Me and ten thousand others. Because we have shares in the company that owns those buildings and doesn't repair the drains, and we make money out of the docks that prosper by denying men work, and because we've never *looked*. All this time, all the money we've made so cleverly by buying and selling and buying again—we never knew what it meant. Didn't know what a pound meant. Didn't know what a shilling meant.

"Well, I know now. Thanks to Daniel Goldberg, and Miss Robbins of the Spitalfields Social Mission, and people like them, I know better. And thanks to you, too, you poor, ignorant, helpless man. I didn't know about the consequences of things, the way everything's joined up, till I saw that wound in your chest. All those poor opium addicts you killed, and my father, and all the Jews you've swindled, and me. . . . We're all connected. Goldberg's right."

She brushed aside the tears. They kept on flowing, irrelevantly.

"And in the carriage, that night . . ." she said. "What were you intending to do? Kill me? Among other things?"

His face was still.

"Possibly," he said.

"Then I should have killed you. I tried to, didn't I?"

No answer.

"Yes, I tried. And look what I did instead. Condemning you to this. . . . No, I never intended this, Ah Ling. You didn't deserve this. But I did it. Just as I made that family starve and I put those men out of work and I drove that man mad with misery and despair so that he tortured his child with a red-hot poker. I did it, without knowing it. So I'm guilty, me and all the other shareholders and speculators and capitalists. You know where *evil* is? It's not just in you. It's in . . . pretending not to know things when once you've seen them. Seeing something bad and shutting your eyes, turning away. All right, I didn't know. But there's no excuse now that I do. So I'm going to—"

She stopped, the passion shaking her voice into silence, clutching her chest. And through the tears which flowed helplessly from her eyes she saw him sitting there, bored.

There was no mistaking it. He just couldn't understand her. And she saw how right she'd been: he was a coarse, brutal, limited man whose manners and graces and fine connoisseurship were no more than perfume sprinkled over garbage. She'd confessed to him. She'd opened herself to him, in acknowledgment of the hurt she'd done him. She'd offered him that—and he was bored.

But what had she been going to say, anyway? *I'm going to join Goldberg and work with him.* . . . She wasn't going to do anything of the sort. She was going to die. She felt cold. In a minute he'd tell Michelet to shoot her, and that would be that. Well, at least Harriet was safe. If Jim came back, if Margaret traced her, then she'd be looked after. If they didn't, then she couldn't imagine a kinder, safer place than the

Katzes' household. Goldberg would make sure. . . . Oh, if he was free still, if they hadn't caught him. . . .

"By the way," said Ah Ling. "You will not have heard. Parrish has found your daughter."

Was he joking? The flat, heavy face was sly and triumphant.

"Where—? How do you know—?"

"Winterhalter spotted some men hanging about outside. Jews. They were looking for the child, because it was missing, and when the police questioned them, they admitted it was Parrish who'd taken her."

"No!"

"True. She is in Parrish's hands, and very soon she will be in mine."

"I don't believe you—"

"Well, let me convince you. She had been held illegally in the household of a man called Katz. Do you believe me now? You have got nothing left, Miss Lockhart. After all this time, I've won."

She sank to the floor. There was a roaring in her ears—but it wasn't in her ears; and her arms and legs were shaking—but, no, it wasn't she, it was the floor and the walls—

And then the wheelchair began to move, rolling slowly toward her, although Michelet was still lying on the floor.

Ah Ling's expression was wild with alarm. Sally, numb and astonished, scrambled out of the way just in time, as the heavy chair struck the wall and Ah Ling slumped forward.

"Michelet!" he cried as he fell.

But Michelet couldn't move. Couldn't even cry out; he was dumb with amazement, for the floor was not there under him anymore: he stood waist-deep in swirling water.

It had happened too quickly for him to do more than gasp. The bandage trailed over his shoulder; his wounded eye, bloody and inflamed, glared like that of a Cyclops as the shaking lamplight shone on him; and then he cried out in fear and lost his footing on whatever was below, and in an instant he was sucked under the water and away.

Sally hadn't moved. She couldn't. The floor was cracking and splintering; huge fragments of stone and concrete were falling into this swirling, surging torrent which had suddenly thrust itself into the room. She was lying against the wall next to the wheelchair, and her cloak was caught under its wheel, holding her down as she struggled to get up. The floor had tilted back at first, making the chair roll toward the wall and tipping her with it, but now as she tore loose the buttons at the neck of her cloak and struggled up free of it, something far below gave way, and the water responded with a surge. The floor tipped sickeningly forward—toward the hole where Michelet had disappeared.

And the wheelchair began to roll backward.

"The brake!" Ah Ling gasped. "The brake!"

Sally flung herself at the chair, trying to hold its weight back while she fumbled for the brake. It was so heavy . . . it rolled so smoothly; where was the handle, for God's sake? Here, under her hand—

She snapped it down and the chair stopped, inches from the edge.

Ah Ling was still slumped forward across his knees. Little by little she heaved him upright again. His face was dark with the effort to breathe, his eyes protruding, but as soon as he was upright he took a breath and looked around commandingly. Sally, breathless, leaned on the chair and looked as well.

The entire center of the room was gone. In its place was a pit with jagged edges, opening onto a dark, surging waste of water—the surface of a torrent that swirled from right to left, whirling, gushing, and splashing the whole room with mud and filth. It stank, and it gave off cold as a fire gives off heat.

As she clung to the chair and watched, another great chunk of masonry fell from the floor on the other side of the pit, and then another, and then there was no way across. The door to the stairs hung over nothing.

The walls were shuddering; the whole house must be

shaking. The oil lamp still burned in its bracket, where she'd placed it only minutes before, but it was shaking so much she feared it would go out altogether and leave them in the dark.

"Turn me around," said Ah Ling. "Release the brake a little at a time. Brace yourself first to take the weight."

The wooden floor was so slippery that it was hard for Sally to get a grip on it. But just within reach on the other side of the chair was the iron grille of the lift, and if she could reach it . . .

The lift! They could go up in that!

But even as she turned to measure the distance and work out how to get him there, a deep series of shocks, like subterranean bombs, shook the ground and the walls. Sally clung to the arm of the wheelchair for balance, and then found herself knocked off her feet and sent sprawling by a jet of water which hit her between the shoulder blades. She landed half on Ah Ling's lap and clutched his sleeve for safety. Something was drenching both of them—the spray filled the room—and then as it cleared she saw that there was no safety at all, for the hydraulic pipes that powered the lift had sheared. Water was gushing out of them to add to the filthy torrent splashing from below. Already the level part of the floor was awash.

The lift shaft with its iron frame hung crazily above them, and the lift itself was immovably wedged under the twisted iron of the pipes; but it was hanging securely from the cable, and if she could haul him onto the floor . . . It was level with his chest, though. How in the world was she . . . ? *Never mind. Get on and do it.*

She scrambled up onto it herself, and then, sitting on the edge, reached forward and gripped the lapels of his coat. She heaved as hard as she could and lifted him perhaps an inch.

Her position was wrong; she had no leverage. She jumped out, dragged the chair closer, and lifted his arms over the edge of the chair (and they were each so heavy) so that she could put her arms around his chest from behind.

Her hands didn't meet. She tried to lift anyway, but the chair was in the way. She could hardly shift him at all.

"I'm going to have to pull you up with the rug," she said.

She dragged the sopping rug off his lap and fastened the right-hand end first to the stanchion at the corner to give herself more room to work with the other. Then she passed the rest of it under his arms, climbed up onto the floor of the lift, knelt at the edge, and pulled with all her might.

It worked. At first his body slumped forward against the edge of the floor, and she thought he'd slip down and into the water, but by hauling and shoving and bracing him while she rested to take a breath, she managed to get most of his upper body onto the floor, and then the rest was easier. Dripping, sodden, immense, like a huge, dead water slug, he lay at last on the edge of the lift floor, and Sally clung, exhausted, to the stanchion, waist-deep in water.

She hardly had the strength to pull herself up after him, but she managed to scramble up, and lay panting, frozen, trembling, on the floor beside him.

After a few seconds' rest she pushed herself up and made sure he could breathe, rolling him over onto his back and loosening the tie and shirt collar. He looked up at her. His expression was impossible to read; but so was hers.

"They must have heard upstairs," she whispered. She'd intended to speak normally, but there was no voice there.

"Look," he said.

His eyes indicated the staircase on the other side of the room. The door had vanished; the doorframe and a section of the wall had slid into the water, and the stairs themselves were visible. Lights were flickering down; shadows wavered; there were voices, shouts of alarm over the noise of the torrent.

But something deep had rotted, and the scouring of the Blackbourne had weakened the very roots of the foundations; and the rescuers—Sally couldn't see, but she thought her footman Alfred was one, and the butler was another—

had no sooner reached the foot of the steps than the whole of that side of the cellar collapsed into the torrent with a rending, splitting roar. Lamps, doorway, stairs, arms, and heads—a confused and terrible slide, and they all vanished in the slimy, surging water . . .

And then the flickering lamp fell off its bracket as a great crack split the wall from side to side, and darkness fell over everything.

Bricks, beams, stones were falling all around; the frame of the lift shaft was groaning and buckling, and the lift itself shook as something huge and heavy crashed down onto its roof.

Sally clung to the stanchion and knelt by Ah Ling in the darkness.

GOLDBERG SAW THEM before he reached the corner of Fashion Street: a little knot of men coming out of a court near St. Botolph's Church. There was no mistaking their manner, that look of furtive lust for blood which he'd seen in crowds in Russia and Germany, but never in London, never yet. They were carrying sticks. One of them was swinging a heavy belt.

They saw him and stopped. Even across the street and through the rain he could feel the pulse of their excitement.

"There's one! There's a Yid!" one of them yelled.

There were half a dozen of them, and for a moment Goldberg thought he'd have to take them on, stiff with pain as he was; but the leader growled something at the man who'd shouted, and with a final jeer they slouched off.

They were going in the same direction as he was, and moving quickly. Goldberg took a deep breath. His whole arm was throbbing abominably. Nothing to be done. Move.

He forced himself onward. Running, even if he hadn't already walked halfway across London, was out of the question. He wished he'd taken more of that damn whiskey.

Left into Commercial Street, right down North Street, left

up Brough Street. . . . Careful now. This led into Holywell Street. He went to the corner and looked around.

No, they weren't there yet. He ran to the nearest door and banged on it. Never mind who; they were all Jewish. Then to the next, and the next, and the next.

Windows flew up. Heads looked out—angry, frightened, men's and women's, sleepy-eyed, ringleted, bald, bearded, young, old.

"Wake up!" Goldberg shouted to them all. He stood in the middle of the road as the sky lightened and the rain teemed down endlessly. He looked around at the faces in the windows and shouted again, "Wake up! Come and defend yourselves! Every man who can fight, come out now and help me! Wake up! Wake up!"

And peering through the rain in the thin dawn light, one after another of them recognized him.

"It's Goldberg—"

"It's Dan Goldberg! It's him—"

And again he shouted, so the whole street heard: "Wake up! Come and follow me! To Solomons's Bakery—come on!"

And he ran on, down Wilson's Place and Lower Heath Street and Keats Court and then through the little alley behind the Jews' Soup Kitchen at the end of Flower and Dean Street, and then to the houses by the synagogue in New Court; and very soon one man came out of his house, and then two more, armed with sticks, thrusting their arms into their coats, shivering as the chilly rain hit their sleep-warmed faces; and then there were a dozen, and then a dozen more, and then someone cried, "Look! There they are—by the bakery—"

And sure enough, there was a mob of men surging up from Brick Lane, shouting, yelling . . .

And then the first stone crashed through the air, and the first window shattered.

THE LIFT SHOOK; the cable groaned. Only the roof of the lift saved them from the weight of masonry which had fallen

down the shaft—and only the cable stopped the lift itself
from plunging into the water.

There was nothing she could do. He lay on his back beside her, and the water was already lapping at the edge of
the floor.

27

The Tiger in the Well

THE AIR WAS THICK WITH MOISTURE: SILVER GRAY, FOG
yellow, ash white. Somewhere high above and inconceivably
far away, over Venice, perhaps, or Mont Blanc, the sun was
shining. Some of the sun's brightness filtered down through
layer after layer of smoke and steam and dust and swagging,
heavy mist, looped and festooned like curtains, through the
trailing clouds that dragged their swollen bellies over roof-
tops and chimneys, in among the sodden bricks, the glistening tiles, the dripping eaves, the cluttered gutters.

After the long night, you could see from one end of
Holywell Street to the other.

Behind Goldberg stood eighteen men and boys. They were
small traders, craftsmen, scholars, one or two of them; the
oldest was sixty-six, the youngest thirteen. Some of them
had seen violence before. One walked with a limp from when
a Cossack's horse had crushed his leg; another had a scar
under his skullcap from a saber cut. The boys were used to
scrapping in the street or the dingy schoolyard, but this was
different; this was worse. There was poison in the air. The
most nervous of them all was the one who had least need to
be. He worked as a professional strong man, lifting dumb-
bells in a music hall, clad in a leopard skin, but he was the
mildest of souls, and he'd never had a fight in his life. One
of the scholars, a round-shouldered middle-aged man, could
hardly see a thing, for he'd come out without his spectacles.
He gripped his stick tight in his shaking hands and whis-

pered to his neighbor, "Point me in the right direction, Mr. Mandelbaum. Tell me when to strike. . . ."

Goldberg looked back at them. They were a feeble, timorous, uncertain bunch, but he was proud of them. Then he looked along the street at the enemy.

Forty? Fifty of them? Couldn't be sure. Big men with hard fists and muscles; tough, lean boys like the Lambeth gang, with hard, narrow faces, and here and there the glint of brass at their knuckles.

They were still, watching. The sound of the brick shattering a window a second or so before still hung in the air like a false note, an embarrassment. The stillness was entirely due, Goldberg realized, to the sudden appearance of his ragged, sleepy army. It was so unexpected that the mob had been shocked out of itself, and just for a second or so they weren't a crowd; they were individuals. He could see their faces.

So he had just a moment to act, before that craziness flowed back and made them into a hundred-handed, howling monster without a soul.

"Stay here," he said to his men, and then he walked along Holywell Street toward the mob, in the narrow, brick red canyon between the houses.

A crepitation of astonishment whispered through the gang by the bakery. One or two of them took a step forward, but they were human still, not yet monstrous, and to be human is to be curious: they only wanted to see better.

And Goldberg felt a moment of pure, clearheaded elation. It was a kind of religious glee: holy mischief. He was weak with loss of blood, he was exhausted, his arm throbbed with an abominable pain, and there was a crowd in front of him that the slightest miscalculation would send mad. He thought, *Is there anywhere else I'd rather be? Anything else I'd rather be doing now than this?*

What a lucky bugger I am, he said to himself. *Talk for your life, Danny boy. Tell 'em a story.*

"I need a chair," he said loudly. "The man over there by

the door—knock on it, will you? Ask the lady for a chair. She's just inside. That's it. Fetch it over here, don't be shy." They didn't know what to make of it, but in the face of his brazen confidence they felt their anger tremble a little, uncertainly. The weight of their suspicion, the undischarged burden of their hatred, still hung in the air like electricity; but as he climbed up to stand on the chair, Goldberg saw a young boy on the fringe of the crowd look away from him, and then up uncertainly at the man beside him, whose features were similar; a father, or a brother. And then he knew how to begin.

"Brothers," he said. "Yes, I'm not ashamed of you, I'm not ashamed to call you brothers, though I'm a Jew and you're Gentiles. Brothers, d'you know what brings you here? D'you know why this man, Harry Solomons the baker, d'you know why the good Lord picked on *him* this morning to have his business threatened and his wife and children terrified? Is it because he doesn't make good bread? No, it can't be that. Smell it, brothers. Put your noses up and sniff that good smell. Harry Solomons is a fine baker. If this place burned down, there wouldn't be more good bread in the world— there'd be less.

"So there's a puzzle. There's a mystery. We all want more bread, but we're going to burn down Harry Solomons's bakery where he makes the stuff.

"But I can see a man down there, one of my brothers, one of you, who can explain. I won't tell you his name, but I know a lot about him. He's got a wife called Florrie. He's got three kids living and two that died before they were a year old, poor little scraps. He's a docker. Now the other day he goes down to the dock gate as usual. To the cage. He hasn't had work for two days. He's hungry, he's not in his full strength, and there's six hundred men crammed in there down Nightingale Lane, all of 'em desperate.

"And the foreman there—you seen him? Big belly on him as if he's got a bun in the oven? You know what—he felt the pangs of birth coming on the other day. Lay down and bellowed like a pig. 'Help me!' he roars. 'I'm giving birth! I'm having a baby!' They all come running—sent for the doctor—carried him in the office—bent over him to see what came out—and you know what it was? Wind. A whole bellyful of wind. They heard it down in Gravesend—thought it was a steamship."

And they laughed. There was a murmuring, like the pull of the tide on a shingle beach, but over and above that there was a shushing, an impatient shaking of heads. They wanted to hear more. *Tell 'em a rude joke, make 'em want more; now get on with the story, wind 'em in.*

"Anyway, Fartbelly the foreman, the other day that I was telling you about, he was rolling up and down with the tickets in his hand. Twenty jobs, six hundred men. You know the scene—howling, yelling, shouting men, pressed up against the bars, hands held out. 'Me! Me! Give it to me! Gimme a job!'

"And then he flips a ticket up, old Fartbelly, and he watches 'em scramble for it—kicking, shrieking, desperate men. One of 'em gets it, and they let him through. There's one man with food in the house tonight.

"Then up comes the second ticket. Little brass thing flipping through the air, and another scramble, another fight, another torn ear, another broken finger. Twenty times it happens; twenty men are safe in the docks with a day's work to do and three or four bob at the end of it.

"But not our friend. Not the man in the crowd down there—he knows who he is. No job for him. Old Fartbelly's got his favorites; days when he doesn't want a scramble, or when the boss is looking, old Fartbelly calls out the names he knows won't be any trouble to him, doesn't he—hungry men, men with injuries, men who've lost the will to fight, men who won't complain if he gets a day's work out of them and sends 'em home with a shilling short. But our friend—he's not one of them, not one of Fartbelly's favorites."

They were still now. Goldberg knew that people are hungry to have their own experience voiced; he was saying all this for them. They wanted to hear more.

"So there's no job. Nothing in his pocket. Nothing in the cupboard at home; nothing in his belly; nothing for the kids. So he puts his hands in his pockets—yes, I can see him now, I know who he is—and he sets off home.

"And on the way he goes past the workhouse. On a sunny day, the shadow of the workhouse never leaves the street, does it? They never see the sun down Old Gravel Lane; the workhouse shuts out half the sky. And he wonders—didn't you, mate?—he wonders how long it'll be before he's drawn into that great dark shadow, him and Florrie, and the three little kids; how long it'll be before they're split up and taken away, and he has to look at 'em one last time with shame in his heart. . . .

"It's enough to send a man mad. It's enough to make him cry out to God and beat his head against the walls; enough to make him fling himself in the river with despair. He knows that feeling. *You* know that feeling."

The street was silent. The Jews had crept closer to hear, and behind the shutters of the bakery, the baker and his wife and children were pressed to the window, listening. Every man in the crowd stood still, and he looked into their eyes, and he drank in all their attention and focused it back through the story.

"And then he sees a mate of his outside a pub, and his mate beckons him over. 'Come over here,' he says. 'There's a bloke in here buying drinks.' And he follows his mate into the pub, and sure enough there's a fellow sitting at a table, an agreeable-looking bloke, smartly dressed, soft hands; he's not a docker. You'd put him down for a clerk of some kind.

"And, yes, he's buying drinks. Pint of bitter? By all means, mate, sit down, have a bit of baccy for your pipe.

"And then a strange thing happens; Soft Hands starts dripping poison. Not the sort you can see. This is invisible poison; it's lies. 'D'you know what's behind all this?' he says.

'D'you know why good men like you are thrown on the scrap heap while others prosper? It's the Jews. . . .' Then he puts his soft lips 'round his little cigarette, and he blows out a stream of smoke, and you can see his little eyes calculating, watching how the poison's going down."

They were all quiet, all listening. After a moment's pause, Goldberg went on. "Now, our friend down there, he knows a couple of Jews. He knows Solly Moskowitz the tailor; he knows Sam Daniels the boxer. He's proud to know Sam Daniels. He's won a few bob on him in the past; he bought him a drink once, and Sam Daniels remembered him after that and called him by his name whenever he saw him.

"But Solly Moskowitz and Sam Daniels—they're not rich and powerful. They're men like he is, men of the East End. He can't see how they came to have such power in the world that they can deny a job to six hundred dockers every day. And he can't work out why old Solly Moskowitz is as poor as he is, if he's so almighty powerful.

"And he thinks: old Fartbelly—is *he* Jewish, with the power that he's got? And the men who own the docks, sitting up there in the West End, with their cigars and fancy wines and pretty women—*they're* all Jewish, are they? The members of Parliament and the lords and the lawyers and the judges— Jewish? No, course not. There's something wrong with what Soft Hands is saying, but our friend can't see his way through it.

"And here comes another pint, and another, and here's some more poison with it: Burn down a Jewish house or two. Show them who's master in this country.

"But our friend down there—he's no master. What's happened down in Nightingale Lane by the docks has proved that, if anything will. Who's master? Even old Fartbelly's not master. The real masters are the men you never see except when they sweep past in their carriages and splash you with mud; they're masters, and we're not. Smashing windows and burning houses won't turn you into a master. Only a desperate man would think it could.

"So our friend's still not sure. But it's warm in the pub, and here's another pint, and—'Come a bit closer,' says Soft Hands. 'I'll tell you something that's not for everyone's ears.' "

Goldberg paused. They were caught now; they were his. When he dropped his voice and said *Come a bit closer*, they'd all moved in a step, rapt, held.

And he saw that a policeman had appeared—two, four, five of them. Out of the corner of his eye he saw one of the Jews urgently explaining something, saw the policeman look along to him. . . . Could he slip out through Solomons's place? *Finish this first.* . . .

It all took less than a second. Back to the audience, back to the story.

"So our friend moves in close, brings his chair right up to the table. And Soft Hands leans across, looks over his shoulders, licks his lips.

" 'There's talk of murder,' he says. 'Human sacrifice. You know what these Jews do? They kill Christian children. They mix their blood in the bread. It's been proved.'. . .

"And that's too much for our friend. Because if it's true, it's the most horrible, filthy thing anyone could do. People who did that would deserve all they got. So that eases his mind a bit; he doesn't mind attacking Jews if that's what they get up to; it makes sense of it.

"So that's why he's here today. That's how *he* came to be standing out on a wet morning with a stick in his hand, about to smash down a baker's shop and ruin a man's business.

"Because everyone needs a reason to do wrong things. No one'd do 'em if they thought they were wrong. They think they're right, that's why they do 'em, isn't it?

"So our friend down there—I can see him, he knows I'm right—he's on the right line. But he's going in the wrong direction. Of course it's right to fight against people who sacrifice children. Of course it's right. But ask yourself this: Who sacrificed *your* children, my friend? Who made sure you couldn't buy any medicine for your little daughter? Who refused to pass the law that would have made the landlord keep the drains in good repair, so your little boy had to catch typhoid and die?

"I'll tell you who did it. Every one of those rich men—the landlords, the factory owners, the members of Parliament, the judges, Lord This and the Earl of That and the Duke of Something Else. They're the ones who go in for human sacrifice. They're the real murderers. You can see their victims every day along Nightingale Lane and Cable Street—"

There was a growl from the crowd. Goldberg knew he had them, but something had interrupted, something was shoving the crowd aside. The policemen—

"All right, all right, break it up," came a loud, commanding voice. "Move along there. That man—Goldberg—hold him. He's a wanted man. Goldberg! You're under arrest."

Not yet, thought Goldberg.

He jumped down from the chair, and before the crowd had parted he slipped through the door and into the bakery.

Harry Solomons slid the bolt home against the tumult outside.

"God bless you, Mr. Goldberg," he said. "Look, there's a man here—from Moishe Lipman. He says—"

In the warm, clean little front shop, fragrant with the smell of new bread, Goldberg looked around to see Mrs. Solomons and several children, all gazing at him with wide eyes, and a small man anxiously twisting his cap.

The clamor outside got louder as the police forced their way to the door. Moishe Lipman's man spoke quickly: "Moishe and the other boys was arrested, Mr. Goldberg. Someone spotted 'em. I don't know how it happened. But the house . . ." He clutched his head. "God, I can't describe it, Mr. Goldberg—"

"What? What?"

"The whole house—it's collapsed. The one we was watching—it just fell into rubble in front of my eyes. . . . It's just not there anymore! Like as if a bloody bomb'd hit it."

Goldberg was dazed. He shook his head to clear it. *How could Sally have . . . Never mind that. Move. Get out.*

"Come on," he said to the man. "Give me a hand."

"But, Mr. Goldberg—"

It was Mrs. Solomons. The whole family was pressing around him, trying to thank him, blessing him, kissing him, and he wanted to sweep them out of the way and run with the last of his strength and find Sally, tell her Harriet was safe, tell her—

There was a hammering at the door.

"Open up! You've got a wanted man in there! Open this door or we'll smash it down!"

Solomons took Goldberg's good arm and tugged him through into the back of the shop while Mrs. Solomons pretended to fumble at the bolt.

"All right, all right—hold on. I'll just find the key—"

"There's a gate in the wall," the baker told him hastily. "Here's the key; it leads into Cropper's Alley. You can duck through the yard of the Queen's Head and out into Brick Lane—"

But it was too late. A policeman stood framed in the back doorway as Solomons opened it.

"Gotcher," he said.

Goldberg turned to Moishe Lipman's man and said in Yiddish, "Telephone Kid Mendel. Four-two-one-four. Tell the man what's happened." And in English to the policeman, "All right, Constable, I'll come. I'm too tired to run. Don't pull my arm, please; it's had a bullet in it."

The baker picked up a couple of hot rolls and thrust them into Goldberg's pocket.

"That's all I can do, Mr. Goldberg," he said. "God bless you."

The bolt of the front door slid back; the other policemen shoved their way in. Moishe Lipman's man watched as they led Goldberg out, and then heard a strange sound resounding down Holywell Street, a sound no one would have guessed at half an hour before: a hoarse and ragged cheer from the crowd, Jews and Gentiles alike, all united now in their sympathy for the outlaw captured.

He watched as the hero was led away and the crowd was dispersed by the other policemen, and went in search of a telephone.

SALLY HAD no way of telling how much of the house had fallen. The lift, which was holding them above the water, had kept some of the rubble off them too, but it was totally dark, and her only sensations were cold, and noise, and smell. The stench from the ancient sewers that emptied into the Blackbourne was foul and getting worse.

The water was rising too. Already it was an inch or so deep on the floor of the lift. Sally crouched beside Ah Ling's head, trying to describe what was happening.

"Is there any light?" he said.

"No. Not a bit. Are you cold?"

"Yes. How many men came down the stairs?"

"A footman. The butler, I think. But they were only there a moment before they fell in and then the light went out. I think the whole wall collapsed."

"It should have blocked the stream."

"It must be very deep. All that rain—"

Something crashed into the lift from above, shaking both of them. Sally grabbed him for balance, and then heard a straining, creaking sound as the lift slowly tilted sideways. *The cable!* Sally thought—and then there was a bang as loud as a gunshot, and the floor plunged downward.

It was only a foot or so, but it sent her sprawling, and then the water surging in knocked her off balance again as she tried to struggle up, and then she gave a little cry, for Ah Ling was under the water and couldn't move.

She found his shoulders, his head, and lifted him in a burst of strength, hauling his head out of the water, gasping, retching, choking. She cradled it on her knee.

When he'd recovered his breath and she'd wiped his face

and eyes with her hand, she said, "I'm going to try and help you sit up. Otherwise you'll die."

Taking care not to let go and drop his head under the water, she maneuvered herself into a kneeling position behind him and tried to push upward. Everything was against her. His clothes were waterlogged; the floor was angled the wrong way so that his head was lower than his feet; her own arms were shaking so much with cold and effort that she could scarcely hold him. She got his shoulders up, but his head lolled sideways, and in trying to hold that she lost her grip on his shoulders. She tried again, but she pushed his head too sharply forward and felt his neck jerk desperately; he couldn't breathe. She rested, cradling his head once more on her lap, holding it tenderly, like a mother.

The water was up to his chin. And it seemed to be coming in faster.

"Is the lift on solid ground?" he said. "Not still suspended?"

"The cable's broken. It must be resting on something, but I don't know how solid it is. I'd have to let you go to find out."

"It's getting deeper."

"I'm resting my arms. In a minute I'll try to lift you again."

She felt him sigh. He was utterly still; she supposed he couldn't even shiver.

"In the village in China where my grandfather was born," he said, "they used to fetch water from a well. It was a little outside the village, down a path through the bamboo. It wasn't the only water, because there was a stream as well, but the stream water was no good because of the paper works above the village. So every day the people would be going up and down the path bringing buckets of water to their homes.

"One day a little boy ran up to the village screaming. 'There's a tiger in the well!' he said. All the village people came running with sticks, ropes, anything that came to hand. They crowded around the top of the well to look, and sure enough, there was a tiger. It was a large well, with a little

stone platform partway down, and the tiger was crouched on
that, and it couldn't get up.

"They didn't know what to do. While it was there they
couldn't get any water, because the tiger was angered by the
buckets and smashed them down off their ropes. And if they
killed it, it would fall into the well and pollute the water;
and, in any case, they had no means of killing it. And they
certainly couldn't get it out alive."

He paused. Sally lifted his head a little higher.

"What did they do?" she said.

"They prayed to the gods, of course. The gods sent rain—
lots of rain. The well filled up, and the tiger was drowned.
Then they could pull its body out, and the well was safe
again."

"I see."

"I was reminded of the story by our present circumstances."

"Which of us is the tiger?"

He didn't answer.

She sat there, shivering, wondering if she had the strength
to lift him again. If she managed to prop him against the
side of the lift, the upper part of his body would be clear of
the water. She'd have to do something.

"Take a deep breath," she said. "I'm going to make another effort. I'll have to let your face go under for a moment
and get a grip."

He nodded, breathed in, nodded again. She found her
balance, let his collar go, got a grip on the shoulders of his
coat, and heaved upward. It might have been his buoyancy
in the water, but he was easier to lift this time; one heave
and he was upright.

But then something happened inside him. His great frame
convulsed as if someone had caught him in a mighty fist and
squeezed, and then he retched and gasped. A hideous, deep
sound halfway between a groan and a sob came from him.
His head fell sideways.

She held him there propped up partway, off balance, her

heart thumping. She felt around for his face. Her fingers touched his open eyes, and he didn't blink.

She snatched her hand away with horror. An instant later she controlled herself. He was dead; so . . . She found his face again and closed his eyes. Then she tried to lower him gently into the water, but he slipped from her grasp and fell in with a clumsy splash.

She shook the water off her hands and brushed them together automatically, and then sighed so deeply that it turned into a yawn which felt as if it would never stop.

She put out her hand to feel for the side of the lift, and it met the iron grille of the door, twisted and crumpled but firm enough to hold on to. She stood up.

The floor of the lift was tilted toward the gap in the floor where the water was coming in. The weight of the rubble falling down the shaft, which had caused the cable to snap, had driven it down onto solid ground; at least it felt solid, and it didn't rock when Sally moved about, clinging to the wall, trying to avoid treading on the body.

At the shallowest part—the back—the water was already up to her knees. At the open front it was near the top of her thighs. She clung to the door and felt around outside, trying to find a solid spot, but as she leaned out the lift creaked and swayed forward, and rubble fell heavily somewhere above and behind her.

She froze. The lift held. If it fell forward, she thought, she'd be trapped under it for good.

Gingerly, delicately, she shifted her weight backward and into the lift again. She'd felt nothing underfoot but the swift-flowing water—and now the lift was at an even steeper angle.

Center of gravity, she thought. *Get it down so you don't pull the lift even farther out.* She lowered herself to a crouching position, up to her breast in the water, and once again felt around for a foothold outside.

Then something soft and massive began to press against her from behind. . . .

Ah Ling's body, sliding down on her.

She screamed.

The terror caught her off balance, and the extra weight was too much for her strength. Her hand slipped off the grille and she fell, scrabbling for the edge of the floor, finding it, and being swept off like a fly as Ah Ling's body slid down, down, and down, and then fell with her into the flood.

IN A DUSTY ROOM over a stable in Lambeth, Harriet sat chewing a crust of bread while her guardians toasted some kippers over a smoky fire. They'd ditched the carriage and the horse somewhere in Vauxhall. Liam was bitter about letting them go, but he saw the force of Bill's argument.

"We gotta look after the kid first. That's what we done it all for. All right, we might get a quid or two for the nag, but so what? We can always get a nag—there's thousands. If we lose the kid, though, that's it, innit?"

So they'd come to one of the many squalid dens they used (one step ahead of the law or the landlord each time) and laid Bridie, still unconscious, on a heap of sacking in the corner, planted Harriet beside her with some bread one of the boys had found in his pocket, and set about cooking the kippers that had been hidden there since their last visit three days before.

Two things were concerning the gang. The first was finding a safer place than a succession of kips and hideouts for Harriet to stay in, and the second was Bridie. It was a long time for her to be unconscious, tough as she was. There'd come a time soon when they'd have to find help for her. Maybe they should have done so already. Maybe she'd die.

Harriet sat stolidly beside her and stared with interest. This lady was asleep, but the men weren't. They were making some breakfast. There was a nice horsy smell in the sacks, like the stable at home. And the breakfast smelled like Mrs. Perkins's breakfast sometimes did.

Then she noticed that the lady's eyes were open and gaz-

ing at her. She'd woken up. Politely Harriet held out her
crust for the lady to share. The lady didn't take it, but a
slow awakening smile filled her eyes from inside, and she
reached out to stroke Harriet's tangled hair.

"She's awake!" said someone.

They were around her in a moment.

"Devil, Bridie, but you scared us," said Liam. "We thought
you was about to stick your spoon in the wall."

"Not bloody likely," said Bridie.

"Buddy likely," said Harriet, agreeing. She liked this lady.
She especially admired the way she spoke: a warm growl like
a big cat. She tried it again. "Bloody likely."

"It's *not* bloody likely, colleen. Hush—what's that?"

A shouting below, and then a thunderous banging on the
trap door.

"Get out of it! Go on, scram, you vermin! I'll set the dog
on yer!"

Terrifying growls accompanied the voice. Groaning, the
gang collected its half-cooked kippers, helped Bridie to stand,
hoisted Harriet into someone's arms, and opened the trap
door.

"All right, mister," Liam called down. "We'll go. Hold
the dog back."

"Hurry up then," said the owner.

They scrambled down the ladder and out through the
stables into the dawn light, Bridie staggering a little, Liam
chewing a kipper.

The owner of the stables watched them go with narrowed
eyes. Was that a child they were carting about? Yes, it was.

"Here—" he called, starting after them, but they heard
him, saw the dog, and fled.

Bloody nuisance, he thought. For he had a conscience,
and he'd heard of baby stealing. Some poor woman would
wake up this morning to find her baby missing. Couldn't
have that. He locked the gate and set off with the dog to
find a policeman.

So when Con and Tony arrived two minutes later, having done the rounds of half a dozen kips already, there was no one there.

"Man, I'm done," said Tony, as they climbed the ladder. "It won't matter if we take a wee nap, now will it? We'll find 'em soon enough."

"We promised the man," said Con. "We have to make the telephone call."

"As soon as we find her," said Tony. "She'll be safe, and we'll find her soon enough. I'm going to have forty winks."

"Hey, they've been here! Look! The fire's still—"

A dog growled below them. They looked at each other.

"There's some of 'em still there!" said a man's voice.

"All right, come on down," said another voice, an official voice, a police voice. "Else I'll come up and get yer, and yer won't like that. I'm not having baby stealing on my beat. You're nabbed, that's what you are. I've gotcher."

FOR DAYS NOW, Sarah-Jane Russell had stood outside Orchard House. That odious man Parrish had paid her off, her and Ellie and Mrs. Perkins, and told her to be about her business, find another job—the position of nurse was filled.

And no one knew where Miss Lockhart was; no one knew whether Harriet was safe; no one could help at all. Sarah-Jane didn't know what to do. Ellie was staying in the town, and Mrs. Perkins had gone to stay with her cousin in Reading. Sarah-Jane was staying with her married sister, but there wasn't really room. . . .

There was no law against her standing outside the gate, though. Watching them cart away all the family's possessions. Watching them bring in vanloads of property from somewhere else. Watching new servants appear, take down curtains, change locks, repaint the woodwork a vile shade of red. Sarah-Jane stood there for days, watching, noting, weeping.

Parrish saw her eventually and sent for a policeman to tell her to move away. She knew the policeman: he was Ellie's sister-in-law's cousin. Both of them were embarrassed. She went away then, but came back later and kept out of sight in the bushes.

She didn't know what she was going to do. But someone had to stay there. Someone had to keep watch. She had vague thoughts of waiting till they brought Harriet there (she had no doubt that they would, in the end; they seemed to be able to do everything they wanted) and kidnapping her, snatching her away, running off somewhere. But she knew she probably wouldn't. She wasn't brave enough, not on her own. That sort of thing only happened in Jim's stories. Oh, if only they'd never gone away. . . .

She arrived outside the house that morning to find that something had changed. There was smoke coming out of the chimney, and a carriage in the drive. Servants were moving about in the dining room.

As she crouched down in the bushes outside the gate and peered through, the front door opened and Parrish came out.

He stood in the doorway, stretching, yawning, scratching himself. He looked as if he owned the place, and he didn't care who knew it. She longed to throw something at him. She longed to run out there and shout at him, attack him, beat him down. She even felt for a stone; but then a woman came out, in an apron like that of a nurse, and said something to him. He nodded and went back inside, closing the door.

Did that mean Harriet was there? Had they got her after all?

Sarah-Jane felt tears come to her eyes. That something like this could happen in England, that the law actually helped it on its way . . . She gulped and swallowed hard. Her head sank down into her hands. It was too much.

"Sarah-Jane?"

Her heart thumped against her throat, and she spun around. Then her mouth fell open, she felt suddenly dizzy, and she put a hand on the wall to steady herself.

For standing in the road, a knapsack over his shoulder and

a straw hat on his head, was a slim young man with bleached hair and a sun-darkened face and clear green eyes.

"What the bloody hell's going on?" he said.

"Jim! Oh *Jim—*"

And she flung herself at him and clung, trembling and sobbing and laughing. He'd never been so surprised in his life.

28

India Ink

IT WAS ALMOST A MINUTE BEFORE SHE COULD SPEAK. SHE kept laughing, crying, clinging to him—and glancing back at the house, so that he knew without asking that something was wrong in there. He pulled her out of sight, back into the bushes, and made her let go of him and sit on a stone.

"We got back to Southampton last night," he said. "Mr. Webster's still there supervising the luggage; I came back early with Charlie Bertram. I was going to give you all a surprise. But didn't you get our letters? What's going on?"

"We haven't seen any letters for weeks—they must have thrown them away. Jim, they've taken everything—"

"Calm down. Stop gabbling. You're not making any sense at all. Tell me the whole thing, and start at the beginning."

She took a deep breath.

"Yes. Sorry. Of course. Oh, Lord, I don't know where she is even—"

"Get on with it," he snarled.

"Yes. I will. It began . . . oh, it was the man with the divorce papers. He came one morning. . . ."

As she told it all, stumbling and forgetting and going back to fill in details but trying to get it clear and tell it plainly, he found himself at first incredulous, then outraged, then chilled—and finally murderous.

"You mean that bastard's in there now?"

"Yes. He must have come last night. There's a whole lot of them in there. He's got new servants; all our furniture's gone, every stick of it—it's all his stuff—"

"Has he got Harriet?"

"I don't know. There's a woman there like a nurse, so perhaps he has. What are you going to do?"

"Throw him out."

He took a clasp knife from his knapsack and hacked a stout stick from the nearest tree.

"But, Jim, there are lots of them in there. He's got a gang—"

"Just watch," he said.

He swung the knapsack over his shoulder and stepped out into the road. She'd never seen him like this; every atom in him seemed to be crackling and blazing with fury. It frightened her. She stumbled after him—and then stopped suddenly.

A man stood in the road in front of them. Not Parrish; a man she'd never seen before—elegant, dark, and somehow dangerous-looking. He was looking at Jim with a speculative expression, but he didn't move out of the way.

"Who the hell are you?" said Jim.

"My name's Mendel. Jonathan Mendel."

Sarah-Jane saw Jim's head lift as if he recognized the name. He was still electric with anger, but now he was puzzled, too.

"Kid Mendel?" he said. "From Soho?"

The man nodded.

"Are you mixed up with this?"

"Yes. Wait a minute," he said, coldly and firmly, as Jim took a step toward him. "I don't know who you are, but you look as if you're about to go and do some damage to that man Parrish. I had the same idea. But I'd remind you that we're both in sight of the house, and till we understand each other's position, I suggest we move aside."

Jim took a breath and nodded. Mendel lifted his hat to Sarah-Jane. He looked like a scholar of some kind, with his balding head, his intelligent eyes; but a tough, worldly one. She couldn't place him at all. They moved out of sight of the house, behind the wall again.

"Well?" said Jim.

"If you give me a couple of minutes, I'll tell you everything I know about this business," said Mendel. "Then you can tell me who you are, or not, as you please. And you can decide whether or not you'd like some help. I've got half a dozen men around this house, and if you know who I am, you'll know what sort of men they are."

Jim whistled quietly. "All right," he said. "Let's hear it."

Sarah-Jane was completely nonplussed. Despite the man's suave expression, the elegant overcoat, the beautiful hat, there was something definitely frightening about him.

He began to speak. It took nearly five minutes. He explained about Goldberg, about the Tzaddik, about what he'd heard that Sally was doing, about Harriet, about Rebecca and the Katz family, about Parrish's stealing Harriet. Sarah-Jane gasped then and caught Jim's hand.

"Miss Russell here's the child's nurse," said Jim. "Carry on."

"We were waiting here, watching, as Mr. Goldberg instructed. We saw Parrish arrive, but we didn't see the child. It might have been that it was too dark, or it might have been that they've left her somewhere else. That's why I haven't given the order to go in yet; we just don't know. As soon as it's possible, I'll send a man to telephone and see if there's any news from the other parties."

"I see. Who's this Goldberg?"

"Many things. A refugee. A journalist, a politician. Even a kind of bandit. I respect him greatly."

Jim digested this. Then he put out his hand.

"Jim Taylor," he said. "Where I come in is this. I live here; I'm Miss Lockhart's oldest pal, and I'm the child's godfather. I've been away in South America and I've just got back, and this is what I find. Yes, you're right—I was going to do some damage. Was that an offer of help?"

"It certainly was."

"Then I'm greatly obliged. How many blokes have you got?"

"Six."

"Then what we'll do is this. There's going to be no question of breaking and entering. I don't believe in going outside the law, do you?"

"No, no," said Mendel. There was some complicated kind of understanding between them that Sarah-Jane couldn't fathom, but both of them seemed to be smiling somewhere, even though it didn't show.

"Out of the question," Jim went on. "So I invite you and your associates to join me for a spot of breakfast, since it's such a miserable bloody morning, and since I can ask who I like into my own home. Only we're feeling like a bit of a lark, so we don't go in the front door, we go over the back wall and up the side and in through a first-floor window. Then, my goodness, we find some strange furniture on the premises. How shocking. We better sling it out the window. Then we find some bloody stranger galloping up the stairs to see what's going on. If he has the nerve to offer us violence, provoking most justly our wrath and indignation against him, he can have a bucketful."

While Mendel called up his men, Jim trimmed his stick and swung it once or twice, testing the balance.

"I usually carry a knuckle-duster in a fight," he told the gangster. "But they're no use against thirty-foot snakes or poison frogs, so I left it behind. This'll do."

Sarah-Jane looked around the little group of Soho criminals. Hardened, scarred, they looked as if they'd been pickled in sin for years; and Jim, with his suntanned skin and the wicked glitter in his eyes, looked like a pirate captain.

"Right, gentlemen," he said. "It gives me great pleasure to invite you to breakfast. Sarah-Jane, as soon as we get in, you go and look for Harriet. You never know. If she's there, stay with her till it's safe to come out."

Her heart was thumping; she didn't know whether it was fear, or excitement, or both. She walked with Jim, Mr. Mendel, and the others along the wall, down the brick-walled lane, and through the wicket gate into the thick shrubbery at the bottom of the garden.

Jim pointed to the glass and iron structure by the garden wall to their right.

"If we get on top of that wall, it's no more than a stroll along to the bathroom window up there—see it? By the ivy? Course, if he's in the bath, we'll have to close our eyes when we climb in. All right, Sarah-Jane?"

She nodded. She wasn't sure about heights, but it wasn't very high after all: ten feet or so. And it was out of sight of the kitchen and the dining room, which was where they all seemed to be.

Jim found the old wooden ladder in the grass and propped it up.

"Here we go, then," he said.

SALLY'S HEAD struck a lump of masonry and then she was underwater and the nightdress was clinging around her and she couldn't get free, struggling, struggling—then her face broke surface and somewhere there was solid ground underfoot.

She flung her arm up and grabbed for whatever was there—nothing—then there was: something hard. She got her fingers on it and clung, in the roaring, crashing swirl of water.

Something to stand on, something to cling to.

"I'm not going to die!" she shouted. "I'm not going to! I bloody won't!"

Then because the foothold was slipping and because she found a better place for her hand a few inches along, she kicked off and tried to haul herself up.

If only she could see; for all she knew there was safety a foot away on one side and certain death just as close on the other. If you thought like that, though, you'd be paralyzed. So she clung to her handhold (an iron bar, wedged in somewhere among the rubble) and little by little, gritting her teeth, ignoring the shaking in her muscles, she pulled herself up and half out of the water.

She felt about in front of her and found space. Behind the iron bar was a mass of bricks, mortar, rubble, and plaster, but there was room above it.

One more effort and she was clear, bruised and grazed and numb with cold; she lay panting on the gritty, rocky surface and regained her breath.

She rolled over onto her back. Stones, the sharp ends of bricks, pressed into her ribs—but there was light above her. Real, too.

It didn't go away when she opened her eyes: a little gray patch of daylight far above. . . .

She sat up, craning to see, and cracked her head on something, starting off a fall of stones. She cried out with the pain and swayed, nearly losing her balance and falling back into the water.

She put her hands up, sheltering her head, and looked again. No doubt about it: this was the lift shaft, and up there was the sky.

"Help!" she shouted, and again, "Help! Help!"

Though if the whole house had collapsed, there might be no one there to answer.

"All right," she said aloud. "I'll get out. You're not killing me down here like a rat."

Her voice sounded muffled and enclosed, and drowned in any case by the water, but it felt good to speak.

"Stand up," she told herself. "Go on. If you can see a light, you can climb up there. *Move*, you lazy baggage. If you're too fat to get through, hang there and yell. Now *go*."

Feeling her way, trying not to bang her head, she carefully stood upright on the crumbling, precarious rubble and looked up. She could smell fresh air; it was wonderful. She began to climb.

PARRISH WASN'T in the bath. There wasn't anyone upstairs at all, as Jim found out within a minute, while the others were climbing in. They were good, he thought: quiet, practiced . . . Well, they're professionals, they should be.

"There isn't even a nursery prepared," he told them in a whisper. "Her bed's gone, her toys aren't here. . . . I don't think he's going to bring her here at all. Sarah-Jane, stay upstairs anyway. Look after me knapsack, will you? Don't drop it—there's a shrunken head in there for Ellie."

She took it doubtfully while he conferred with Mendel. Sarah-Jane had been right about the furniture: all the stuff here was new, he said. So they'd throw it out. They'd start with a great, heavy, ugly wardrobe in the main bedroom. It should land on the drive outside the dining room.

"I'd love to see 'em jump," Jim said longingly. "I'd pay a quid to see that. . . . Come on. We'll start with the wardrobe and carry on from there."

They tiptoed along the landing and into the room. Sarah-Jane watched from the landing. She had a good view of the hall and of the front garden, too, through the landing window. She could hear laughter from the dining room, and the smell of frying bacon came up from the kitchen as a maid-servant carried a tray along the hall. She felt alight with excitement.

There was the creak of floorboards; would they hear it? Then a scraping sound . . .

And then a mighty crash from outside.

And a ringing silence all through the house; and after a second or two, a shout of surprise from the dining room. And then more objects began to fall from the windows, and as Sarah-Jane looked out it seemed to be raining furniture: a bed, two chairs, a dressing table, half a dozen drawers, one after the other, and then the chest they came from, with their contents—ties, shirts, underwear—fluttering down over the lawn like dead birds.

And more furniture flew out: a bedside table, a bureau, another bed, a linen press, another chest of drawers, a bamboo chair—and then the dining room door flew open.

"What the hell's going on?" shouted Parrish, and stopped as he saw Sarah-Jane at the top of the stairs.

Three or four men rushing out behind him bumped him

forward a step or two, and then stopped themselves. He had a napkin in his hand. Without taking his eyes off Sarah-Jane, he wiped his mouth carefully.

"Right," he said.

The glare in his eyes—greed and triumph and anger—frightened her, and she looked back along the landing. Then there was a huge crash as something heavy struck the drive outside, and all the men jumped.

"There's someone else up there," said one of them.

Parrish flung his napkin down and leaped for the stairs. Sarah-Jane stepped back nervously and found Jim beside her.

"Who's this, Sarah-Jane?" he said.

Parrish stopped, halfway up the stairs, and looked up.

"It's Mr. Parrish," Sarah-Jane said. Her voice was hardly audible. She stood back out of the way as Mr. Mendel and the others came to the top of the stairs. She'd never seen men fighting before, but she knew she was going to now.

Jim set off down. Sarah-Jane realized why he'd made them come in through the window: it gave him the position of the rightful occupant and made Parrish look like the intruder; it showed the truth of things. He stopped a couple of steps above Parrish.

"Who are you?" said Parrish.

"You don't come into someone's house and then demand to know who they are," said Jim. "I live here. You don't. I'll give you five minutes to get all your men and all your staff off the premises. Then we throw you out. That's a handsome clock you've got standing down there. Five minutes, by that. Move."

A maidservant came out of the kitchen, apprehensive, and stopped with her hand to her mouth. Sarah-Jane saw her from above, saw her glance back, saw a man's head appear there in the shadow behind her, look past her, and then retreat silently.

She wondered if she should tell Jim. Parrish was going downstairs now, slowly, backward. When he reached the hall floor he went to join his men at the door of the dining room, and all of them watched as Jim and Mendel and the others came down after them.

She saw Jim standing easily at the foot of the stairs, holding his stick, waiting; she saw Mendel standing next to him, arms folded, with the air of a gentleman inspecting a painting at the Royal Academy; she saw his men ranged behind him, brutal and frightening and intense; she saw someone behind Parrish slip an object into his hand. . . .

And then he was holding a pistol. In a moment, all the power had swung the other way.

"Put up your hands," he said. "All of you. Back against the wall, go on."

Jim took a step forward. Parrish fired into the floor at his feet, and Jim stopped.

Sarah-Jane felt as if she were dreaming. She could see little things very clearly, like the bullet hole in the carpet, like a piece of sticking plaster on top of Parrish's head. . . . She was looking right down from above, and her mind whirled, and she looked around hastily. Yes. There was something on the floor outside the nearest bedroom door. She picked it up, tiptoed back, leaned over, took aim, dropped it . . .

The white china burst into fragments, and Parrish went down at once. The gun fell from his hand. Jim was on him in a moment, and Mendel seized the gun, but one of Parrish's men charged him and sent him flying into the umbrella stand. Then the fight began, and in a moment the hall was a melee. Sarah-Jane shrank back; the ferocity of it . . . One man was kicking another in the head . . . Someone had a *razor* . . . The *sounds* they were making, the grunting, the sickening crunching noises, and without a word spoken, going about this violence as if it were a difficult trade they had to concentrate on, like hewing rock or stoking a boiler. . . .

She turned away, shivering, and looked out the window. A man was running along the drive toward the gate; it was the servant whose head she'd seen looking out of the kitchen. Should she shout and stop him? Tell Jim? What?

By the time she'd seen him, the fight was over. Someone

downstairs let out his breath in a long whistling sigh, and then there was the sound of hands brushing together. And the front door opening, and stumbling feet.

She looked over the banister again. The last of Parrish's men was crawling out on his hands and knees. Mendel was bending over one of his men, another was sitting on the stairs mopping his cheek with a dirty handkerchief, another was combing his hair in the hall mirror.

Jim was standing over Parrish, who was stretched senseless on the floor.

Sarah-Jane, trembling in every limb, crept down the stairs. She'd killed him. She'd be hanged. It was almost the worst thing she'd ever known.

Jim looked up. "What'd you drop on him?"

"A chamber pot," she whispered. "Is he dead?"

Jim chortled. "Dead? He's snoring like a baby. I bet he's never been laid out by one of them before. . . ."

Mendel handed him a vase of flowers which had escaped the destruction, and Jim tipped the lot over Parrish's head. As Parrish spluttered awake, Jim bent down and pulled him up by his lapels.

"Where is she?" he said. "Where's the child?"

Parrish said nothing. Even dazed and soaked and beaten, he had a formidable coldness in his eyes, and he merely glared up at Jim with hatred and said nothing.

"Not going to talk, eh," said Jim, and dropped him.

"It's nine o'clock, Mr. Taylor," said Mendel. "The telephone exchange will be open. I'm going to send a man down to the hotel to make a call. I think you said something about breakfast."

"So I did," said Jim. "Have his servants made a run for it? Yes? Well, we can fry some eggs and bacon, make a bit of toast. Oh—not bacon in your case, I beg your pardon. Let's tie up this bugger, and then we can go and see what there is."

He spoke lightly, but Sarah-Jane could see that he was worried about Harriet. He and Mendel tied Parrish to the newel post by his thumbs and then went through with the rest of the men to the kitchen. Sarah-Jane looked back at Parrish, and then away hurriedly, for the hatred in his eyes chilled her.

"Tell me about this man Lee," said Jim a few minutes later in the kitchen. "The whatchacallem—the Tzaddik. What's that mean, by the way?"

"It's a Yiddish word," said Mendel. "It means a righteous man, a holy man, a saint, something like that. Unless it means precisely the opposite, which it does here. He's Parrish's principal; he set him up in business. He's involved in a complicated fraud on Jewish immigrants, which Mr. Goldberg has been investigating. But he comes into this because it seems to be him rather than the little man out there who wants Miss Lockhart's child. He's her real enemy; Parrish is only an agent. I imagine he was allowed to have this place as a kind of payment. Might I trouble you for the marmalade, Miss Russell?"

Sarah-Jane was becoming impressed by this elegant, worldly man; he seemed to breathe an air of power and wealth and authority, and to have more time and space around him than other people, so that he could move through it like a prince. And yet he was a Soho criminal! And here he was in the kitchen at Orchard House listening respectfully to Jim, treating him like an equal. . . . She didn't know whether to admire, or deplore, or join in.

She heard a noise from the hall: a voice—and suddenly remembered what she'd seen from the upstairs window.

"Oh, Jim!" she said. "I'm sorry, I forgot! While you were fighting there was a man running out the gate—one of the servants—"

She looked toward the hall door. Jim heard the voice too and got up at once.

Sarah-Jane was behind him. Parrish was standing next to the stairs, rubbing his thumbs. Beside him was a policeman. Sarah-Jane could see two more policemen through the open front door, looking at the scattered furniture.

"This is the girl I dismissed, Constable," said Parrish. "She must have let them in."

Jim stepped forward. "Morning, Constable Andrews," he said. "Glad to see you."

The policeman looked uncomfortable.

"Look, Mr. Taylor," he said, "I know you've just got back—you won't have heard, I expect. But we can't have this kind of thing going on. I'm sorry, Mr. Taylor, but I'm afraid I'm going to have to take you down to the station."

"Me? What for?"

"Breaking and entering. Affray. That'll do for a start. I daresay Mr. Parrish will want to sue you for trespassing, but that's up to him. Now, let's not have any trouble—"

"You're joking!" said Jim. "You know I live here, you dozy clod! You've had a glass of beer in the kitchen dozens of times. It's that man you ought to arrest."

The policeman shifted his feet, looked at Parrish, looked at the floor.

"I'm sorry, Mr. Taylor. The law's on his side, not yours. If you won't come quietly, I'll have to arrest—"

"You don't suppose this little louse would have been able to get away with it if Mr. Garland and I'd been here, do you? He hasn't got a leg to stand on, and you know it!"

"I have to deal with the situation as I find it, Mr. Taylor."

"Boss!" a man came running in at the front door and stopped on seeing the confrontation. It was the man who'd gone to telephone.

"Yes, Al?" said Mendel from the kitchen doorway.

"That's Mendel!" said Parrish at once. "The Soho gang leader! There's bound to be a reward—"

The policeman was bewildered. Mendel came forward, and Parrish fell silent.

"Well?" he said to the man in the doorway. "What's the news?"

"One of Moishe Lipman's blokes telephoned in just a few minutes ago. He says the house in Fournier Square—you know, the one they was watching—it's collapsed. Just fallen in!"

"That the one where Miss Lockhart was?" said Jim to Mendel. "In Spitalfields?"

Mendel nodded. The policeman was looking from one to the other, uncertain what to do; so he was unable to stop Jim, who slipped past him out the front door and away.

"Stop him!" the constable yelled to the other policemen outside, but Jim evaded them easily. Sarah-Jane knew he'd go straight to Spitalfields—and she knew, too, that the responsibility for coping with this was suddenly hers, because Mendel was a guest and had no authority in the house.

So in the little silence that followed, she cleared her throat and said, "Well, Constable. I suggest we go and sit down and try to get to the bottom of this. There's obviously some confusion in Mr. Parrish's mind; you can see he's been hit on the head. Shall I make us all a cup of tea?"

THERE'D NEVER BEEN such a crowd in Fournier Square. The rain had lifted, and the two hundred or so onlookers jostling for position in the road gazed through the misty air at the ruined house, gaping in wonder.

The fire brigade had pulled half a dozen men and women out of the rubble so far, but it was a big house, and the rumors going around the crowd spoke of a large household—mysterious owner—crippled—strange machinery—secret rooms—screams in the middle of the night. . . .

It got better and better.

By midmorning, the occupants of the houses on either side, who'd been evacuated, were allowed to go back in and get dressed while the firemen inspected the structure. Reporters from the major papers had interviewed the chief officer, the neighbors, the passers-by; artists stood there sketching assiduously for the engravers who'd turn their drawings into plates to be printed in the illustrated weeklies; sellers of meat pies set up their barrows; a mobile coffee stall pulled by an arthritic horse was soon open and doing a flourishing trade.

And all the morning the rescue continued. One after another the staff from the house were helped, or dragged, or carried out. Three of them were dead, another six injured, and from what the survivors said, another five were missing: a valet, a footman, a maidservant, the butler, and the master himself, a Mr. Lee.

The secretary, Herr Winterhalter, had broken a collarbone, but otherwise he was unhurt, and he stood beside a police officer identifying the servants who were being brought out and describing the layout of the house so that the rescuers knew where to look.

At the edge of the crowd, Margaret Haddow was standing. Next to her were Rebecca Meyer, her arm in a sling, and James Wentworth, the lawyer. Each time a shout went up from the firemen clambering over the rubble they took a step closer, tried to peer over the heads of the crowd, held their breath; and then sighed. They didn't say much.

Margaret felt a tap on her shoulder.

She turned, and saw Jim—sunburned, disheveled, travel-stained, grim-faced. She gasped with surprise and seized his hand. They'd been on first-name terms for as long as she and Sally had; she felt like embracing him.

"Do *you* know what's happening?" she said after they'd shaken hands. "Oh, sorry, this is Miss Meyer, who looked after Harriet. And Mr. Wentworth, the firm's solicitor. But when did you get back?"

He explained what had happened at Orchard House.

"Parrish was still there when I left," he said. "Sarah-Jane's coping with it. Mr. Wentworth, I'm going to need a lawyer myself: that little weasel had the police at his beck and call. How the hell—excuse me—did all this *happen?*"

Rebecca said something in German. Mr. Wentworth translated: "There was no sign of the child at Twickenham, Mr. Taylor? Miss Meyer is very concerned. She blames herself for letting it happen."

"Well, tell her she's not to. According to Kid Mendel, this Mr. Goldberg sent off three parties to find Harriet. One came here to watch this place, Mr. Mendel went to Twickenham, and Mr. Goldberg himself went to Clapham. If she's not here and she wasn't at Orchard House, then she must be—"

Rebecca was speaking again, urgently. Jim heard the name Goldberg and watched the lawyer, intrigued by this shabby-looking man with his shrewd, ugly face and his flaming red hair.

"Apparently," said Mr. Wentworth, "Mr. Goldberg single-handedly stopped a riot this morning. There was a mob about to attack a bakery in Whitechapel—so Miss Meyer has heard—and Goldberg roused the local people, called for a chair, stood up and began to tell a story, of all things—and they stopped to listen! It's gone all 'round the East End— he's a figure of some fame in this community, Mr. Taylor. But then he was arrested, so Miss Meyer says."

"Arrested? Him as well? But hang on: if he was in Whitechapel, he can't have been in Clapham. So maybe—"

Margaret gave a cry and seized the lawyer's arm, pointing up at the house.

One of the firemen was waving. He bent to lift some bricks out of the way, and then there was a head, a shoulder, an arm—

"That's not Sally," said Jim, disappointed.

But Rebecca was nodding, her face animated, and she spoke rapidly.

"It is!" said Mr. Wentworth. "Miss Meyer says she dyed her hair and cut it short—"

Jim didn't wait. Dodging through the crowd, he snatched a blanket and scrambled up over the rubble, shoving the firemen aside—and then she was clear, lying exhausted and bruised and torn on the broken bricks, and then she saw him, and they were only a few feet apart.

He stopped, looking down at her.

"What do you think you look like?" he said softly. "You ought to be ashamed, clambering about in your underwear. Sling this 'round you, go on. . . ."

Then she was trembling against him, huddled up in the

blanket, and he began to help her down toward the pavement.

"Where's Harriet?" she muttered.

"We're still looking."

Helping her clamber over the bricks and stones, her torn stockings, her bloodied feet—and hands coming up to help, Margaret close by, and the little Russian girl, and a policeman.

And a man with his arm in a sling, and a German voice: "Yes, this is the one."

Her other arm was already held by the policeman. He said, "Miss Lockhart?"

They were on the pavement, only six feet from the barrier holding back the crowd. Margaret was reaching out—but they'd stopped, too far to touch.

"Yes?" Sally said, shivering, hoarse.

"Miss Lockhart, it's my duty to arrest you on the charge of attempted murder. Anything you say will—"

There was a surge of excitement in the crowd; the three nearest reporters lunged forward at once, clamoring for details; James Wentworth tried to restrain Jim, who seemed to be about to hit the policeman; the secretary stood by, stern, biting his lip; Margaret and Rebecca darted through the barrier to help Sally, who had fallen to the ground.

Except that she hadn't fallen. She pulled free of their hands, impatiently, and sat up to tug down her torn, wet stocking, taking out a folded piece of paper, handing it with shaking fingers to Margaret. "Open it! Unfold it, *carefully*. . . ."

All the urgency of the crowd, the moment, seemed to have swirled in a curious vortex around this still point: a bare patch of wet pavement surrounded by a thousand eyes. Margaret, sensing the importance of the paper, desperate not to tear it, went slowly and methodically along one edge and peeled it open before trying the next. Sally had folded the paper into four. If the ink had run . . .

Margaret carefully separated the two corners and gently peeled it back. Winterhalter was a thorough man: his records were meant to be permanent. He'd used India ink, and there it still was, that column of payments labeled *P* for Parrish.

"There!" said Sally, looking up at them all, pale in the triumph no one could understand. "I've done it. Now *where's my child?*"

29

Rabbits

THE ONE PERSON IN THE CROWD WHO KNEW WHAT THAT paper meant was the secretary; and as he slipped away Jim saw him and shouted, "Hold him!"

Hands reached out to seize him. He struggled, glaring at the sergeant who'd tried to arrest Sally. The policeman looked back, bewildered, and then Mr. Wentworth spoke.

"Sergeant, whatever claim you have on Miss Lockhart, as her lawyer I must insist that she first has medical attention. Once we've heard what she's got to say about this obviously very important paper, you'll be able to decide whether or not to go ahead and arrest her."

The sergeant was confused. There was just too much going on; and he was conscious that he'd overstepped his powers in trying to arrest Sally in any case, since he didn't know for certain who she was, and was only going on the word of the secretary and a vaguely remembered circular about a kidnapping, or something—a child involved—and yet she was asking where the child was, so *she* couldn't have stolen it. Damn it, he couldn't sort out this confounded betanglement. . . .

"Move along there," he said sternly to no one in particular.

Winterhalter was loudly demanding to be set free, to see his lawyer, and no one was taking any notice, because Sally had fainted. Jim was holding her, and Mr. Wentworth and Margaret were clearing a path through the crowd.

"Oy," said the sergeant uncertainly. "Constable Willis,

follow the cab. Don't let her out of your sight. And as for the rest of yer: move along! Clear the road! Move along there!"

"Don't lose the paper," Sally said, half-conscious. "Jim, is that really you? Jim, you know who that was? The man in there?"

"The Tzaddik," said Jim. "That's what I heard."

"He was Ah Ling! He was Hendrik Van Eeden! You remember—back at the beginning—he killed my father—opium—"

Jim nearly dropped her.

"But—but you shot him!"

"And paralyzed him. Didn't kill him. Someone got him away that night. And ever since then—"

She had to stop then, as they helped her into a cab.

"Ever since then," she whispered, "he's been dying for revenge. Dying. He's dead now. Dead of revenge. But in the cellar, Jim, I tried to save him. I did. I pulled him out of the water, I kept him alive. . . ."

She fainted again. Jim looked at the others; he was dumbfounded.

"Did you hear what she said? The bloke at the back of this was . . . So *that's* what it was all about!"

"As I understand it," said Mr. Wentworth, "Miss Lockhart could defend herself against the charge of attempting to murder that man yesterday by claiming that in fact she tried to murder him eight years ago. Or have I got it wrong?"

Jim, holding Sally in his arms, looked at the lawyer sharply to see if he was being ironical, and decided he wasn't.

"That's about it," he said.

Margaret was still holding the paper. She looked at it, trying to make sense of the columns of figures.

"This is a record of payments—of money received," she said. "But which column is the important one, or whether they all are, I couldn't say."

"Better let me dry it out," said the lawyer, opening his shabby Gladstone bag and taking out a folded sheet of blotting paper. He put the paper inside it.

"Goldberg," said Sally, waking dimly again. "He's got a pocket book . . . belonged to Parrish . . ."

"Ah!" said Mr. Wentworth. "I begin to see."

His ugly face was brimming with a kind of wicked delight. Jim couldn't help smiling in response. Then he said, "I'll have to get back to Twickenham smartish. Sarah-Jane Russell's coping with Parrish and a policeman, and what with one thing and another, she's feeling a bit shaken."

He told them what had happened at the house, dwelling with pleasure on the crash the chamber pot had made.

"She thought she'd killed him," he said. "She thought she was going to be taken away and hanged; you could see it in her face. . . ."

"I expect she was alarmed by the shot and dropped it accidentally," said Mr. Wentworth. "I daresay you'll be able to remind her of that. But it doesn't sound as though he's been harmed by it."

He looked out the window and banged on the cab roof.

"Cabbie!" he called. "Turn up here, if you will. I'll walk up to Clerkenwell—it's only a step from here to the tench."

"The tench?" said Margaret, as the birdlike little man got up.

"Clerkenwell Detention Center," said Jim. "Goldberg?"

The lawyer nodded. "Take them on to the hospital," he said to the driver as he got out, and then to the others, "I'll join you there as soon as I can."

And he was off. Jim watched him limping briskly up the road and turned to Margaret.

"He's a decent feller," he said. "Where'd you find him?"

"Around the corner from the office," she said. "He was there all the time, while that other helpless, cringing weakling of a solicitor allowed them to take everything away from her. . . . If only she'd had Mr. Wentworth from the beginning!"

"What a hell of a mess," said Jim. "I feel I ought to be in six different places doing things. There's this crazy charge hanging over Sal, there's Harriet still missing. . . ."

"There's the firm nearly bankrupt," said Margaret bleakly. "Parrish has taken out as much as he could grab, and it was all perfectly legal."

Jim looked out the window. The cab was turning in through the gateway of St. Bartholomew's Hospital in Smithfield.

"Here we are," he said, and looked at his watch. "Can you stay with her?"

"Of course. There's nothing to do at the office; there's nothing much left in it."

"I'm going to find a telephone. There's a number where there might be some news."

He looked at Sally for a moment, stroked her short hair with a rough tenderness, and swung himself out and away.

A LITTLE EARLIER, in a police station in Lambeth, Con and Tony had been arguing with the sergeant. They'd been dragged there by the constable who'd found them in the stables, and both of them were pouring scorn on his reason for pulling them in.

"Babies?" spat Con. "Is he touched in his head, that copper?"

"I'll touch you in yours—" began the policeman, but Con ducked out of the way.

"Here, look," said the sergeant. "Constable, what's the complaint?"

"His complaint is he's blind," said Tony. "Blind or touched."

"Quiet!" roared the sergeant.

"They was seen," said the constable with dignity, "in the charge of a baby or young child, what the landlord or proprietor of the stables, Mr. Hackett, thought was likely to be stolen—"

Jeers from Con and Tony. Bang of the sergeant's fist on the desk.

"—so I apprehended 'em," finished the constable lamely.

"And where's the baby?"

"Ah. Well, that was with the other lot."

"What other lot?"

"The first lot, what he kicked out."

"He *what?* He sees one lot with a kid, kicks 'em out, and you go and pinch another lot to make up for it?"

"Well . . ."

"Constable, I congratulate you. You've invented a whole new theory of policing. We don't look for the ones as did the crime; we pick up the next lot that comes along. What a saving in boot leather! What an astounding advance in criminal jurisprudence! What a—"

"Can we go, then?" said Tony.

"No!" shouted both sergeant and constable together.

"But, Sergeant—" said Con, and Tony said, "Oh, go on, we ain't done nothing," and Con said, "We'll be a nuisance, man! Ye'll have to charge us with something!" and the sergeant said, "I'll charge you with a bloody regiment of cavalry—" and Tony said, "I'll send for me lawyer," and the constable said, "I'd like to see you try," and Con said, "Where's this baby, then?" and Tony said, "Ye can turn me pockets out and hang me upside down, but ye won't find no baby on me," and the sergeant said, "That's enough of that," and Con said, "Who wants a baby anyway?" and the constable said, "They *did*, Sarge—he *swears* it—" and Tony said, "He doesn't know what he's talking about," and Con said, "I know the law! Habeas corpulus! You got to produce the corpse! So where is it, eh?" and Tony said, "Begob! Where's the body?" and the sergeant said, *"Get out!"*

Five seconds later they were out of the building and around the corner. Con shook his head with pity and contempt.

"Can you believe the helplessness of them?" he said. "Now let's find the others. I bet Ravelli's."

"I bet the Dog and Duck."

Ravelli's was their shorthand for The South London Imported Italian Goods Warehouse, Antonio Ravelli e Figli, Props. Italian goods were pasta, dried fruits, olive oil, and the like, and Antonio Ravelli and the Figli stored them in an unsupervised shed behind an engineering works off Duke Street. The gang had found a way in a month before and discovered a sheltered little yard behind the main building; they had loosened a plank in the fence to make an easy exit. Con and Tony went there first and struck lucky.

They were lucky enough, in fact, to find Bill and Liam having a fight in the yard, with most of the gang enthusiastically watching and placing bets.

"What's got into them?" said Con to the nearest spectator, as he eased himself through the hole in the fence.

"Bridie," said the boy. "They's each of 'em jealous of the other."

"Oh," said Tony, disappointed. If they had nothing better than a girl to fight about, they must be getting soft, he thought. The scrap was furious, though: fists and feet and heads and knees and elbows were all fair weapons between rivals, though belts and knives and knuckle-dusters were barred.

"Is the kid here?" said Con, but the fight was getting exciting, and no one answered. He looked in through the window and saw Bridie and the child both sitting on a heap of straw with a bag of macaroni between them. Bridie was showing the little creature how to blow a feather in the air through a tube of macaroni.

"Well, that's all right," said Con. "D'ye think they've got a telephone in the warehouse?"

Tony looked at the roof, nodded absently, and turned back to the fight. Sighing responsibly, Con began to pick the lock.

So it was that when Jim asked the operator to connect him with number 4214 and spoke to the man in Soho, he was told to go to Duke Street, Lambeth, and there he'd find the child.

"Let me come," said Sally five minutes later, trying to sit up. "I must—"

"Stay there!" said Jim sharply. "You're not moving till you've had all those cuts and grazes cleaned and stitched and stuck together. Gawd knows what horrible diseases you picked up paddling around in that sewer. Isn't that right, Doctor?"

The doctor nodded. "I haven't finished examining you, Miss Lockhart. I can't take any responsibility if you leave."

"Sit on her, Margaret," said Jim.

"But what *happened?* Where *is* she?"

"Apparently your man Goldberg managed to get her out of Parrish's place in Clapham. She's with some friends of his now, down in Lambeth. If you let me have my hand back, I'll nip across the river and fetch her."

Sally released his hand. "Goldberg?" she said, and then the tension and the relief were too much for her, and she began to cry helplessly. Jim left.

A crawling cab ride over Blackfriars Bridge, a furious exchange with a dirty and suspicious Irish boy through a broken fence, a muddy scramble through a gap, and he was in the yard of the Italian goods warehouse. A gang of—what were they? Leprechauns? Street goblins?—were squatting in the open, pitching coins, and the boy who'd let him in pointed to the door.

"He's reading to her," he said proudly. "From a book."

The fight was over. Bill and Liam had decided that any girl tame enough to let herself be fought over wasn't worth the bother, though it had been a good scrap, and they were lolling at their ease on the straw while Bill read his book aloud to Harriet.

"See the rabbits?" he said. "Listen to this, now. This is good. 'How very pretty the young ones look by the side of their mother; they all seem so happy.' "

"Bloody miserable-looking bunch," said Liam. "I wouldn't give ye three ha'pence for 'em."

"Bloody misable," agreed Harriet.

"No, listen, listen. 'All brothers and sisters should love

one another, and then they would be happy too. We should never let the dumb animals ex—ex—excel us in affection.' "

"Is that the best ye've got?" said Liam, but Harriet was pointing at the door, and the boys looked up, and there was Jim.

They sat up slowly, and each of them moved in closer to Harriet. Their expressions had changed in a moment: they were tense and dangerous, ready to fight. Jim was impressed.

He put down his knapsack slowly and crouched, holding out his arms, letting Harriet come to him.

"Look," she said, not letting him hold her, impatient. "Uncle Jim, look!"

She had a broken piece of macaroni in her hand, sticky and begrimed. She put it in her mouth and blew a feather off the palm of her filthy hand.

"Good game," said Jim. "That's a blowpipe. They have them in the jungle, where I've just come from. You going to come home now? See Mama?"

She looked doubtful.

"There's Uncle Webster at home now, as well," Jim went on. "And Sarah-Jane. And I bet Mrs. Perkins has got some macaroni in the kitchen to play blowpipes with."

"Here," said the most beautiful voice Jim had ever heard. He looked up, astonished, to see a girl of fifteen or so, as wild as the rest of them, narrow-eyed, slender, dirty, but with a voice that you might hear in a dream and never forget. She was holding out a brown paper bag to Harriet. "Take 'em home with ye, for yer dinner."

Harriet took something out of the bag and chewed it stolidly.

"Dried figs," the girl explained. "I found 'em in a sack. There's plenty more."

Jim stood up. The two boys were still looking wary, but the tension had eased.

"What happened?" Jim said. "Was she in Clapham, then?"

"Yeah," said the boy with the black eye. "Mr. Goldberg led the raid. We got her out."

"We dropped a jordan on the wee man's nut!" said a boy at the door.

Jim blinked. *Twice in one night!* he thought. *I was wrong.* . . . "Good for you," he said. "You like reading?"

"Yeah," said the boy with the split lip. "I can read anything."

"I'll send you a pile of penny dreadfuls. I reckon you must've had some expenses, looking after this young lady. Here's five pounds for you. You've done a good job, the lot of yer."

The money was received with shrewd nods. What they were approving was Jim's sensibility and perception in putting a realistic price on their efforts.

"Them penny dreadfuls," said the boy. "Don't send 'em here. This is just a kip. Send 'em to Mr. Goldberg's, in Soho."

"You're a pal of his, are yer?"

The boy nodded.

"He's in jail, they tell me. In the tench."

"'S nothing," the boy scoffed. "He'll be out. They can't hold him. They couldn't hold him in Russia, they couldn't hold him in Hungary. He escaped from this castle with a big round tower—place called Kufstein. He climbed down the outside. If they think they can hold him in the tench, they don't know nothing."

Jim had been to Kufstein; he'd seen that castle. "So he's all right, is he, this Mr. Goldberg?"

Nods all around, particularly vigorous from Con and Tony.

"He shared his last cigars with us!" said Con. "There's no bloody side on him, mister."

"Right," said Jim, hoisting Harriet up and discovering too late that she'd wet herself thoroughly. "Let's go home, then, princess."

Harriet, mouth full of fig, waved good-bye regally with the brown paper bag as they set off along the busy street, which was beginning to steam in the watery sunshine.

THE MOST NOBLE AND SACRED ORDER
OF THE EMANATION OF THE BLESSED AND HOLY
SANCTISSIMA SOPHIA

To whom it may concern:

I am writing this in order to correct a faulty entry in the Register of Marriages for the parish of St. Thomas's Church in Portsmouth, where I was rector from 1870 to 1880. The entry refers to a marriage solemnized on January the 3rd, 1879, between Arthur James Parrish and Veronica Beatrice Lockhart.

No such marriage took place. I myself falsely made the entry in the register, being at the time under personal and medical pressures of an intolerable order. I now regret my action profoundly and apologize humbly for the distress it has caused to innocent parties.

I beg that I may be excused any further involvement in this unhappy matter. I consider that I have discharged my responsibility to earthly truth, and intend to devote the remainder of my days to matters of far higher importance, namely the Salvation of my Soul and the contemplation of the Divine Mysteries.

G. Davidson Beech.

Margaret put down the letter and looked across her desk at James Wentworth.

"How did you do it?"

"I told him that if he didn't do it like this, he'd have to come to court and do it, but do it he would. Oh, he whined and twisted, but there was no way out. He's a contemptible piece of work."

"And what happened in court?"

"We won, of course," he said—a little smugly, she thought. "Together with Mr. Goldberg's notebook and Miss Lockhart's paper, it did the trick in five minutes flat. Everything's going to be restored. And I think you'll find that there's not much missing: he was a careful businessman. Very efficient. There'll be a claim against him for any losses, and they'll be paid in full. All the paperwork will be done as soon as possible—"

"How soon is that?" she said. "I know lawyers."

"You don't know this one. It won't take long. Parrish has had the cheek to enter a claim for damages to his furniture, but that won't stand up. They're preparing the prosecution case against him at the moment, but it's taking longer than they thought; more and more stuff keeps coming to light."

"And what about Mr. Goldberg?" said Margaret.

"That was more difficult. There's no doubt that the offense he's accused of, if it is an offense, is political, so extradition wouldn't be applicable, but they could still deport him if they had a mind to. And they *did* have a mind to—at least, the assistant commissioner in Lee's pocket did. So I showed him the affidavit sworn by the woman who ran one of the houses Parrish was taking money from, testifying to all the visits he'd made."

Margaret made a noncommittal sound; she wasn't sure how to talk about brothels without blushing. He went on. "The scandal would be appalling. He saw that, and so Goldberg's safe. He's going to be released this afternoon, as soon as all the formalities are completed. Miss Lockhart's coming with me to meet him; so's Mr. Taylor."

"Jim's desperately curious," said Margaret. "He's Sally's oldest friend, you know. They're like brother and sister. He feels angry with himself that all this happened when he was away. And now he's heard so much about Daniel Goldberg— and he was such a close friend of Harriet's father. . . . Well. I think he's intrigued."

NEXT MORNING, behind Orchard House, Jim was repairing the glass-roofed structure by the garden wall with a lean, tough-looking man in his sixties, with a gray beard and short gray hair, who was even more sunburned than Jim.

As they carefully lowered another pane into position and trimmed away the putty, the older man said, "Tell me about this Goldberg, then."

Jim squinted up at the sun and brushed the hair out of his eyes.

"Well," he said, "he's . . . I'll tell you what happened. There's me and Sal and the lawyer all in this stuffy little room in the prison lodge, and making polite conversation— what a relief the rain's stopped, do they really need so many keys, and so on; and Sal was twitching like a flea. Finally we gave up talking and stared out the window. Then there was another jingle of keys, and the door opened, and in he came with a warder.

"He's a strong-looking feller; big shoulders, big hands. Dark—black hair, big nose, powerful eyes. And Sally's up on her feet as soon as the key turns in the lock, and he didn't seem to move and she didn't seem to move, but there they were, arms around each other, kissing as if they'd just invented it."

"Kissing, eh?" said the old man, amused.

"Words fail me, Mr. Webster."

"No, they don't," said Webster Garland. "You might fail to find them, but that's a different matter. No wonder she was all misty-eyed last night."

"I didn't know where to put me eyes. Nor did the lawyer. So we did the decent thing and left 'em to it. Anyway, they came out after another minute or two, or ten, and we were introduced properly."

"And?"

"Oh, yes. Yes, I could tell at once. He's a good 'un. He's afraid of nothing, like Fred was. Just think: He rescues Harriet in Clapham, gets shot in the shoulder, marches all the way to Whitechapel, faces a howling mob—and tells 'em a story to keep 'em quiet till the police come. Oh, yes, there's no doubt about it. He's a tough one."

Webster Garland nodded. "Good," he said. "That's all right then." He looked along at the house, where Ellie and Sarah-Jane were hanging curtains in the breakfast room. "Good," he said again. "Come on, boy. Give me that putty. We've got all this to do before lunch."

ON THE Victoria Embankment, just below the Temple
Gardens, Sally was walking slowly along. Harriet was holding
her hand, watching everything solemnly.

They stopped near the Temple Pier, and Sally lifted Harriet
onto the wall to look at the boats. Steam launches, barges,
skiffs, lighters laden with coal or grain or bales of wool, all
moving busily on the gray-green water; and the trundle of
traffic behind them, and the distant movement of vehicles
and pedestrians on Blackfriars Bridge to the left and Waterloo
Bridge to the right. . . . It all seemed innocent now, harm-
less. There was no threat lurking in them; she could walk
with her child without having to hide, she had money in her
pocket, she had a home to go to.

The city was a safe place. But not a good place, not yet.
She and Harriet had just come from the mission in Whitechapel, where they'd been to say thank you, and they'd found
Angela Turner dealing with a woman so badly beaten by her
husband that the doctor wasn't sure if she'd live. And she
couldn't give all her attention to that because of an outbreak
of typhoid in the houses down the street, and women were
besieging the mission, begging for medicine.

So it went on. They'd visited Rebecca, too, at the Katzes',
and heard of a number of Jews who'd been put ashore at
Hull by a courier whom they'd paid to take them to America.
He'd told them that they were in New York, then vanished
with all their money. There was no end to it. The Tzaddik's
empire had collapsed, but nothing had changed. There were
plenty willing to fill the gap.

And there was so much for her to do. Not single-handedly:
she'd learned that lesson. Things got done in the world when
you worked with other people. There were movements to
join, things to learn, groups to organize, speeches to make.
How strange it was; during that hour in the cellar with Ah
Ling, her ancient enemy, she'd seen at last the work she was
born to do. She felt absurdly lucky. To have real, important
work to do, and to know it!

And there was Goldberg. That moment in the prison lodge

had caught them both unawares, and they'd been very formal afterward, very polite. But she was going to marry him. She'd decided that in the cellar too. He didn't know yet. She wondered when she'd tell him. It would be—oh, risky, challenging, stormy, even dangerous, because despite his respectable intentions—applying for British citizenship, starting his journal, eventually standing for Parliament—he had an instinct for trouble as unerring as Jim's. And there were those appalling cigars.

But he was the only man. The only man in the world who . . . who what? Who measured up.

Born for it . . .

A gust of wind plucked the bonnet from her head, and she caught it just in time before it floated down to the river. Harriet laughed and said, "Again!"

"No," she said. "Once is enough. Let's go, Hattie. We're going to be late."

"See Dan," said Hattie, as her mother lifted her down.

"That's right. We'll go to Soho and see Dan. And I'm going to tell him something. And then . . . we'll go home and have some tea."

She hailed a cab and gave the address in Soho. As they settled down, Sally in the corner with Harriet on her lap looking out over the horse's back, with the reins coming down from above and the harness jingling, she said, "And we won't let anyone be bad to us again, will we?"

"Not bloody likely," said Harriet.

Philip Pullman

graduated from Oxford University with a degree in English. The author of *The Ruby in the Smoke* and *The Shadow in the North*, he is also the author of a novel for adults and a Gothic comedy for children. *Spring-Heeled Jack*, a comic thriller based on the Victorian "penny dreadfuls," will be published by Knopf in 1991.

He lives with his family in Oxford, England.